What We Leave Behind

A Novel

by

Rochelle B. Weinstein

ISBN: 1466236310
ISBN-13: 9781466236318

For Steven,
Jordan, and Brandon

You have taught me the meaning of true love.

BOOK I
1972–1988

∽

The heart that truly loves never forgets.
Proverb

And the good-bye makes the journey harder still.
Cat Stevens "O Very Young"

Chapter 1

I always thought if I loved Jonas enough, it would be impossible for him to leave. And if he tried to leave, I was sure he'd feel the beating of my heart against his back when he turned from me, and the thundering sound would make him stop. You think loving someone so completely means you have control over him, but it doesn't; and it wasn't that way with Jonas either. On the day he said good-bye, he didn't just walk. It was a deliberate yank that ripped him from my grasp and sent him sprinting, all the magic surrounding him fading into nothingness. I was wrong about the other stuff too. Jonas didn't notice a thing. Not the deafening sound of a quickening heart, not the wince fastened across my face, nor the struggle that ensued when my hands reached for him to stay. Instead, I was left in silence, the kind that echoes with emptiness, reeks of abandonment.

I speak of love and loss, though you might think since I'm only sixteen, I'm too young to know much. The wisdom I boast of was learned early on, and for this, I have my father to thank. Jonas may have been the *one*, but according to my mother, Dad was the originator of my *crushed childhood fantasy* when he died on my fourth birthday and left me questioning what *being there* means. I remember my mother telling someone on the phone, "She's four, old enough to know him and sense there's an absence in her life, but too young to understand the magnitude of the loss." She said, "If the one man who was supposed to love her first and best couldn't stick around, what do you think that tells her about love? What do you think that tells her about trust?" Had I understood what my mother was saying at the time, I might have put an end to the events that have unfolded this summer, but I didn't. I was four, and my father's early absence had already laid the groundwork for the issues that would later plague me.

Two weeks have passed since Jonas said good-bye. I get into bed hoping tonight is the night it won't hurt anymore, that tonight the pain will stop. The ache he has left in me runs raw and deep, a throbbing so profound, it has taken over my soul and devastated my spirit. Jonas wasn't supposed to leave. Our kind of love was meant to live on, to conquer the obstacles that have divided us. His departure tore me to pieces; I know of no other sadness. As the blankets warm me and my head hits the pillow, I feel convinced that when someone enters your life as dramatically as Jonas entered mine, he can't vanish quietly into thin air as though he never happened, but owes his audience an encore performance, an ending worthy of a standing ovation.

The phone sits by my bedside, and I will it to ring. The silence is an imposter that I'm not quite ready to deal with. I could just as easily pick up the receiver and dial his number, but I have prevailed in my resistance, suppressing the urge to hear his voice. Although Jonas's leaving left most everything inside of me broken, my defiance remains whole. This lingering stubbornness is the one attribute that has trumped my burgeoning sorrow. I have always been hardheaded, opinionated, stubborn. That is probably what first attracted Jonas to me.

Let me go back to the beginning.

"We need to talk about him, Jessie," said the child psychologist I was sent to when I was in grade school.

God, I despised when she called me that and not Jessica. Those closest to me called me Jessie. Dr. Norton was not one I considered close.

"Who?" I'd say, unwilling to share.

"Your father."

"There's nothing to talk about," I'd tell her, sometimes spelling it out for her, "N-O-T-H-I-N-G." That would really piss her off, and I loved watching her shift her glasses from her nose to the top of her forehead as if through this intentional motion came the heightened ability to decipher what I was subtly trying to say. What she should have done, what anyone else in her right mind might had done, was to have thrown me out of the office.

"Dr. Norton," I was told by my mother, "is here to help you feel better." My mother believed that my behavior was problematic. The school had already disciplined me to the fullest extent and the next step would be expulsion.

I didn't know this at the time, not until sweet little Dr. Norton pointed it out to me, but I was apparently "acting out." "Acting out?" I asked her. "I'm ten years old. Isn't that what I'm supposed to do?"

"There are many ways we show the outside world what we are feeling inside," she said. "Why don't we talk about the bug you put in Miss Brown's coffee at the playground?"

"That was no big deal," I said.

"To Miss Brown it was. Why do you think you did that?"

I shrugged. It was funny at the time.

"And what about the bathroom incident? You know you can't enlist other children to hide out in there with you all day. It's disruptive and against the rules. Why do you think you do that? What do you think you're hiding from?"

I didn't answer. I never did.

She'd tell my mother I was too smart for my own good, that I was difficult to reach, the therapy wasn't going, what did she call it, *favorably.* I know this because Dr. Norton would call our house every Friday night after our sessions to give my mom as much of a recap as she was allowed, and of course I would be listening in on the line downstairs. Not that I ever told her anything private or personal. Sometimes I would just make up stuff from television or from one of my Judy Blume books. She never seemed to notice except for that one time when she asked my mom if I was menstruating at such a young age. Guess she didn't believe I had the capabilities of one of Blume's mature heroines, Margaret.

In the meantime, despite my antics within the classroom that caused me to be sent to Principal Martin's office on a regular basis, I was a straight A student. This baffled them all because usually the two behaviors worked in opposition of one another. With delinquent behavior, one might expect plunging grades, but not for me. It was very important for me to be very good at the things I was good at; school and misbehavior just happened to be two of those things.

Then one afternoon she brought him up again. I hated talking about him as much as—and I'd never tell her this—I hated him at times. Somehow, I knew if I told her this deep, dark secret, she'd use it against me with her skillful psychobabble.

"Jessica, do you remember anything about your father?"

I stared blankly at her. It was a game for me to see how long our silences would last. One time we stared at each other for the full forty-five minutes without saying a word. Then she looked at her watch and said, "I'll see you next Friday."

"We're finished so soon?" I'd asked her. "I was just getting warmed up."

And she'd snort in this way that totally grossed me out.

This time, she repeated herself, which was something she rarely did, and I was, quite obviously, intrigued. "Jessica," she said, with a vigor that I hadn't heard before, "do you remember anything about your father?"

And there it was, a flicker of recognition. I didn't know if it was real or something I'd seen in a picture, but this feeling just rushed through my body as if he was there, close by. It was frightening, really. The need to protect myself was taking over. Dr. Norton moved in closer. I guess with all her fancy degrees, she saw the look that passed across my face. She didn't say anything, though; she just watched me watching her. I really wasn't in the mood for another staring contest.

It was difficult for me in that precise moment to separate myself from what was going on inside my brain and from the power of Dr. Norton's relentless glare. Then she asked, "Do you miss him, Jessica? Do you ever miss your father?"

My eyes met hers and I loathed her for asking a question that left me feeling dangerously close to exposed and vulnerable. It was a *trigger* question, the type that, no matter how hard you try to ignore it, sends a sensory message to your brain that causes a catastrophic spilling over of feelings.

I would *never*, not *ever*, let Dr. Norton see me cry. My mother never saw me cry, my best friend Beth never saw me cry. Instead, I drew a deep breath, conjured up my most convincing smile, and said, "How could I miss something I never even had?"

My mother always told me I looked exactly like my father. I was tall like him, fair-skinned, hazel eyes, dirty-blonde hair. She said I acted like him too: smart, smartass, daring, confident. I wanted to remember him, but as our time was limited to a brief passage from infancy to preschool, my undeveloped memory capacity couldn't process it. She'd tell me stories that felt familiar, but they tricked my mind into thinking the memories were mine. And I knew they weren't. Without owning the memories, they seemed ultimately meaningless.

She hung only one picture of him in our house. It was their wedding day. It wouldn't have helped Mom with her successive boyfriends to have a variety of her dead husband's photos prominently displayed. It was the picture I thought about that afternoon in Dr. Norton's office, and how Mom looked so happy and beautiful. Her blonde hair was pulled back high on her head, the olive skin was clear and glowing, and her blue eyes sparkled against the fancy lace dress. He was as good-looking as any man I'd seen in the movies, and sometimes I'd pretend he wasn't really dead, but somewhere posing as a famous actor. When I'd go to the movies, I'd pick out the most handsome man on the screen, the one that closely resembled what he might look like seven years later. At the end, I was always the last to leave the theater—which undoubtedly irritated whoever I was with at the time—because I was busy searching for his name in the credits. The leading man would pass, then the supporting actor, and by the time the key grip was mentioned, the songs that played in the film, and the thank you to whatever city was featured, I'd feel the let-down creep into my heart.

But back to the photo. They were standing next to each other, close in so many ways, her shoulder tucked into his side, hip touching leg, dress touching jacket. Their individual parts fit together perfectly. They were holding the cake knife, his hand pressed against hers. I bet they were laughing at something, a private joke maybe, because there was a twinkle in her bright blue eyes as she looked up at him, a blush across her face; and the photo became for me the image of ideal, a union that no one could penetrate.

I closed my eyes and breathed it all in. At the time, I was sitting on Dr. Norton's worn-out couch, but I was somewhere else. I could see them so clearly in my head, their loving faces, the flowers around them, the room. The picture was theirs, a moment captured now long since passed, but I knew, I just knew, I was conceived in love, even when the memory belonged to them, and its impact would swell around all of us for years.

That's not what got to me in Dr. Norton's office, though. No, not entirely. What passed through my mind while sitting on her frumpy couch started with that picture, but turned into something like this.

Every time I passed their wedding picture in the hall, I would recognize the startling truths: I would never be held like that, I would never feel as safe and protected as my mother looked that night, I would never hear my father call me beautiful as he must have exclaimed when he saw his bride-to-be in that dress. And even though I was his daughter, and he my father, we would always be connected, and yet very, very separate.

I never understood why Dr. Norton stayed with me as long as she did. I was comfortable within the shell I had built around myself and refused to come out. Weeks slipped into months, months into years, and not once did I disclose the truths that flooded my insides.

"We're not making sufficient progress," she told my mother after our two-year anniversary. "She's bright, articulate, witty, but she won't let me in. Maybe it's time to think about a different therapist."

I was furious at her for giving up on me just as I was starting to enjoy our afternoons, mostly because I knew I had the key to what she wanted. The more I held onto it, the more amusing our discussions became. So instead of letting her know on our last day together that I was upset she was saying good-bye, I smiled, politely thanked her for her time, and walked out of her office.

Stopping at the drugstore on the way home that afternoon, I added petty theft to my resume of misdemeanors by stealing my first cassette tape. It was the soundtrack to *Grease*. I also stole a pack of cigarettes, not that I smoked.

Beth, my best friend, slept over that night. She never asked me about my therapy sessions, and I didn't offer up any information. It's not that I thought it was weird. I happened to understand the whole Freudian thing more than most twelve-year-olds, and having an *analyst* gave me an added sophistication.

Beth was the most beautiful girl in our school and probably the most popular. Her hair was a deep shade of brown and fell straight down her back. Her blue eyes were so clear and wide, they gave the impression she was perpetually surprised. High cheekbones, flawless skin, and what many called a button nose were a sharp contrast to my "strong nose," sprinkling of freckles, and the inches that separated us in height—four, to be exact. I think she became my best friend because she secretly longed to depart from the hullabaloo of the popular circles and join me on my expedition to madness. Unfortunately, she was never good at madness. She was nervous and uptight about getting into *trouble*, and worried incessantly about upsetting her parents. "Are you sure we should be doing this?" she would ask, and I would roll my eyes at her while toilet papering the neighbor's tree. She kept watch, trying not to laugh, living vicariously through me, as I would do the same with her—imagining what it would be like to be so sought after and adored by every boy and girl in Tremont Middle.

We were sitting in my family room watching our usual round of movies that night, music blaring in the background, munching on popcorn, when she came across the items from the drugstore.

"Whatcha got in the bag?" she asked, remnants of popcorn falling out the sides of her pouty lips.

"Nothing," I answered, shielding my valuable stash.

"It's not nothing," she said, imploring in such a way that I almost wanted to tell her.

"Just some stuff."

"You're lying, Jessie Parker. You know I can tell when you're lying."

I said, "It's stuff, private stuff, has to do with my analyst." Besides, it wasn't so untrue. That I was pissed at her for dumping me was of no business to Beth.

"Really?" she asked, engrossed by this discovery. "Can I see it?"

"No, you can't see it. It's private." But I liked that she was excited about it.

"I thought we shared everything with each other."

"Well, not this," I answered.

"Come on, Jess. That has nothing to do with your therapy sessions. Just show me."

I was planning on it anyway, but sometimes with Beth you had to build the momentum.

She took the cassette tape in her hand and asked, "What's the big deal? It's a cassette tape."

"I stole it."

"You did not."

"Did too."

"That's so cool," she said, but I could tell she didn't mean it.

"You think?" I asked.

She nodded, if a slightly undecided tilt of the head can be called a nod.

"Then check this out," I said, pulling the pack of Benson & Hedges out of the bag.

"Why'd you get those?" she asked. "You know how I feel about those things."

Everyone knew how Beth *felt* about things. She was a walking commercial for Hallmark.

"You're crazy, Jessie."

What I didn't tell her was that they were the last pack on the shelf and I didn't want some poor soul to grab them and get lung cancer or contribute to the already toxic levels of pollutants in the air. She wouldn't have believed my altruism because it clearly might have rivaled her own.

"Did you finish it yet?" she asked me, changing the subject completely.

"Finish what?"

"Come on, Jess, you know."

I held off on the enthusiasm. "Yeah, it was good."

"You didn't love it? I loved it."

"It was good," I said.

We were referring to *Forever*, Judy Blume's latest book. Beth and I were obsessed with Judy Blume. We had plodded through *Blubber*, *Tales of A Fourth Grade Nothing*, *Deenie*, and *Are You There God? It's Me, Margaret* in record-breaking speed, with *Margaret* being the pinnacle, the literary work we judged all other books against, until *Forever*. With *Margaret*, we witnessed our chests blossom from flat boards to mosquito bites, culminating in the extremely delicate and life-changing ritual of menstruation. We celebrated with Margaret and hoped for the same surge of hormones in our own bodies by the book's end, but much to our frustration, that didn't happen, no, not until we got to reading *Forever*. There began the hormone surge.

Forever was not the same identifiable literature that had answered most of the questions and concerns I had about the awkward, teenage years. This particular book stumped me.

"Didn't you just love Michael and Katherine together?" she asked.

"Yeah," I said.

"And what'd you think of her with Theo?"

I hadn't thought much about it. I was still harping on other things. She hadn't noticed my silence when she said, "Ralph. Isn't that the funniest thing you ever heard?"

She was referring to Michael's penis. That was the name he had given it. I laughed, not wanting to hurt her feelings.

"I can't wait to be in love," she said, "just like Michael and Katherine."

"And look where it got them," I sadly stated, disillusioned that their great love was compromised by a boy named Theo.

I didn't tell Beth this, but I read *Forever* four or five times that week, or at least parts of it. I earmarked page eighty-five until the pages were folded and worn. You could set the book down and it would flop over, opening itself to the page of discovery, and what I now think of as the awakening of my own libido. The particular passage caused these sensations in my legs and down *there* that I didn't quite understand. I would go to the bathroom after reading it and wipe myself, feeling the dampness upon the soft paper. What was happening to me? Was I peeing in my pants? It didn't smell like pee.

At first I liked what I read, the feelings between Michael and Katherine, the tenderness, but then it got confusing. *He rolled over on top of me and we moved together again and again and it felt so good I didn't ever want to stop—until I came.*

Came where? I didn't understand. If she was there with him, how could she just be entering the scene? Had Ms. Blume made a mistake? My knowledge of sexuality was clearly limited at the time. I grasped the car in the garage concept, but no one had ever explained to me what happened when the battery in the car overheated, or that the car could overheat when it wasn't even in a garage.

I didn't ever want to stop—until I came.

I repeated it in my mind over a thousand times until it became a mantra, and not because it perplexed me, but it brought the tenderness to an end. Something was amiss, I knew that, and I didn't have the courage to ask Beth when a glance in her direction told me she very much understood the things I didn't.

"Do you think you'll name your boyfriend's penis?" she asked.

"I don't know."

"What would you name it?" she asked.

"I don't know. I told you, I never really thought about it."

Beth's emotional radar was on high alert. "You don't have to be so dismissive," she said. "I'd name it Richard, in case you were wondering."

Yeah, that was exactly what I was wondering.

"'Cause then I can call him Dick for short." Now that actually got a laugh out of me.

We lived in a quiet neighborhood in the valley. It wasn't glamour, it wasn't squalor, just the life my mother and I shared—the in-between. My mother was a good woman, and though we didn't have a lot of money, and my father left us with even less, she never passed along the brunt of her worries, never extended her gripes and grievances my way.

My mother liked to flitter. What I mean is, she would flit around the room like Tinkerbelle. I think a nervous energy took over her body after my father's death, a need to be at all places at all times. She'd sidle up to you before you even knew she was in the room and like a trained flitterer, satisfy all your whims with one little swoop of her wand before she'd flutter off to the next recipient. This was my mother's way of dealing with her pain; keeping busy, fixing, helping and caring, drew people to her and served her well in her job as a nurse at the local hospital. In fact, the years after my father's death were my mother's most productive work wise. She was promoted to head nurse in emergency. My mother, when she would stop her flitting, was quick as a whip. She was smart and industrious.

Mom wanted to get married again, and she desperately wanted to have more children. She was always saying, "Jessie, you can't use filthy words like that. You have to be a role model one day. Who knows? You might be a big sister." Procreation was living proof that she was young enough and lovable enough to be a woman, and not what the ladies around town called a *widow*.

"Widow sounds so wretched," she would say to me when I sat in her bathroom with her and watched her apply makeup.

The men would come in droves. I told you, my mother was an attractive woman, and because of her combined Mary Poppins and fairy godmother skills, men were always parading around the house. When they'd pull up in the driveway, I'd run to the kitchen for a white paper plate and a marker, the supplies needed for my little game. She would be putting on perfume, flittering around, snapping on a last earring, and I'd be peeking through the curtains. "Don't do it," she would say, and I'd reply, "I'm not," and she would say again, "Jessica, don't do it," and I'd say, "But Mom, I can't help myself," and she'd relent, finally asking, "Okay, what is it?" and I would scribble on the paper plate and just before the doorbell rang, I'd hold it up.

This careful assessment of her date on a scale from one to ten usually determined the amount of perfume she would throw on herself as well as the outcome of the evening. My mother had grown to trust and rely upon my filtering process. The displeasure on her face when a man scored below five was unbearable. "A two," she asked me one night, "just a two?" I nodded, sorry for her, thinking she might not want to answer the door, but she always did. She went on every single one of those dates, even the twos and threes.

I enjoyed visiting my mother at work after school. Now that Mom was high on the ranks there, I'd ride my bicycle over and wander around the floors and halls. Every Friday, I'd put on my best jeans and blouse, pull my hair back into a ponytail, and scope the floors in search of *him*, the nice doctor to introduce to my mother. The criteria were simple: he had to be tall, he had to have straight, white teeth, his hair had to be blonde, eyes of brown, and well-kept hands. That meant no dirt, no grime, no hangnails. I despised dirty fingers.

A few came pretty close to fitting the bill, but there was always something that ended up bothering me about them. Either they had hair in places where hair normally didn't grow, or their personalities were void of just that: personality. If they didn't laugh at my jokes, they were nixed from the list, and pediatricians weren't allowed in the running, since we all knew that they are the last ones to conceivably want to be around more children.

I was fifteen that year when summer began and progressing rather nicely from the prepubescent pain in the butt my mother liked to call me. The hospital had become my sanctuary, and the insulated world of doctors, nurses, and patients had beckoned me. The building was like a hotel—people checking in, people checking out. I knew the inner workings, the hierarchy, and the inroads like the back of my hand; still, I remained happily anonymous, which didn't explain how I ended up on the fifth floor. I knew right away that I must have hit the wrong number button when the elevator doors opened. It was a floor I had never visited before—in fact, one that I tried to avoid. But there he was, the handsome doctor, and, at first glance, the only one to boast of all the attributes on my checklist. The fifth floor housed the *really* sick patients, not contagious sick, but terminally sick. I watched him talking to some other doctors, smiling at the appropriate times, laughing at what sounded like a joke told by one of the nurses behind the desk. He garnered double points for owning a sense of humor on an otherwise humorless floor.

When he went through the doorway to visit with his next patient, I followed close behind; and when I was absolutely sure he could not see me, I pressed my nose to the windowpane. They were huddled around the bed. Tubes, lights, monitors abounded. A woman was crying in the corner. She didn't see me, but my heart sank from her tears. Nearby was a boy. He looked older than me and he was holding the man's hand, the man who lay weakly on the bed amidst the mass of lights and monitors. It didn't take a genius to know that the man was not doing well. I stepped back, ashamed that I was intruding on their private moment. I figured I could linger outside their door and maybe catch the doctor on the way out, but what I really should have done was taken the pain this family brought forth in me as an omen of some kind.

"Jessica Parker, what are you up to?"

The voice from behind startled me from my reverie. I turned to see my mother swiftly approaching. "You're at it again, aren't you?" she asked.

Instead of answering, I eyed the door that was now opening, expecting to witness Prince Charming make his way to his ladylove. My mother followed my eyes, both of us fixed on the figure that was passing through the opened door, but it wasn't him. This person was huddled over, clenching his stomach. My mother sprang into action, flitting across the hallway. I stepped back, not exactly sure of what to do. At first I thought the man inside the room might have died. There was a bustling, some raised voices. I watched while the boy before me, leaning now against my mother for support, proceeded to vomit all over the floor. And that's how I met Jonas. A chunk of his vomit fell neatly across my brand new, favorite shoes.

Jonas Levy, the one who taught me that the very things we wish for are the same things we should turn away from and run.

Chapter 2

My mom whisked him away to the nearest bathroom while the woman I assumed to be his mother stood in the doorway. She didn't seem to be registering any of what had just happened; her eyes were stuck in a deadened glaze. Propping the door open with her narrow shoulders, the woman was unsure about stepping out into the hospital corridor. She was so petite and pretty with wavy, dark hair; I thought the doorway might swallow her up, and before it did, I said, "My mom's a nurse, she'll take care of him." But my words didn't seem to make a dent. This was a woman who had already lost a lot of faith in her family's well-being.

I stood there in a similar swell of uncertainty, not sure if I should offer my help. The vomit was spilling off my shoe and onto the floor. I longed for something that would have lessened the discomfort I felt beside this woman, but I knew it served me right for searching for love on the terminal floor. Why would I think there would be hope in a place where none dwelled? The potential prince who had started all of this in the first place was nowhere to be found—a cad, I'd decided—having slipped out just as things got dicey. Thank God Mom never ended up with the likes of him.

Since nobody seemed to care that I was standing there dripping in humiliation, I decided to get a paper towel from the bathroom to wipe the boy's lunch off my shoe. On my way, I saw Jonas coming out of the men's room, my mother floating nearby with a cup of water.

"This is my daughter, Jessica," she said to him.

"I'm sorry," he said. "I'm sorry about your..." and he looked down, as if saying the word would embarrass him even further.

Now, I was pretty tall for my youthful age, already five feet seven inches, though this boy was *really tall*. He had to be well over six feet, so when he approached me, it wasn't his face in my line of vision, but his messed-up shirt. Nevertheless, his clean, manicured fingers were acceptable. I slowly started moving my gaze up his body.

He said it again. "I'm sorry." I know he tried to remember my name, but like most boys, he drew a blank.

"Jessica," I heard my mother say again.

I looked at her, wanting her to leave, to quit lingering and being so nice to this boy.

In the meantime, he was apologizing to me again.

"It's okay," I heard myself say, straining my neck upward to look at his face. I was beginning to get agitated by my mother's looming presence and this strange boy apologizing over and over again. I really just wanted to flee from the two of them, which I probably should have, but for reasons I'll never know, I didn't. I stayed and then noticed the two most beautiful eyes I'd ever seen in my life.

I think he was still apologizing, fumbling over his words, mortified, cheeks flustered, but I didn't hear a word. I couldn't take my eyes away from his. They were just stuck. It was like being in the planetarium when the universe moves around you and bits of movement and light flood your mind, but your eyes are fixed, staring at a single star. Forget that his were a shade of green I'd never known before or that they were shaped like almonds, a description I'd read in books, but had never observed myself. Delicate and kind, that's what they were, and deep and soulful. He was a boy who could win every staring contest because you had to avert your eyes from his. If you didn't, you'd be sucked in by their intensity. I did my best, I really did, having had forty-five quality minutes every Friday with Dr. Norton to perfect my technique, but I didn't stand a chance against this guy. I tore myself from his pull and searched the floor for something that wasn't there. When I raised my head, I was careful not to look him straight in the eye. "These were new shoes, you know."

"Jessica," I heard my mother say. I thought she had disappeared, but she hadn't. There she was, scooting down by my side with a paper towel, cleaning the mess off my shoes until they looked brand new again.

He said, "I told you I'm sorry. How many times do I have to apologize?"

"You can say it like you mean it," I answered, unimpressed with his lack of remorse.

"Jessica!" my mother snapped again. "Leave the boy alone. He said he was sorry."

"It's alright, Mrs…"

"Parker," my mother answered, annoying me again with her kindness.

"I can handle your daughter, Mrs. Parker. I have a little sister myself. She's about your age. Eleven? Twelve?"

I turned to him, catching the sarcasm of his tone, even if my mother hadn't.

"I'm fifteen, for your information, *almost sixteen*. And at least I can hold my lunch instead of losing it on public floors."

"Jessica Parker!" my mother yelled, furious. I think at this point she grabbed me by the hair and dragged me down the hospital corridor while Jonas stared at us as though we were some ridiculous circus act. I caught a glimpse of his bleak expression when we turned the corner. It occurred to me that maybe, just maybe, I had been a complete idiot.

I took my punishment like the mature adult that I was. "No hospital visits for two weeks," my mother told me.

"It's more your loss than mine," I said. I mean, really, *I* wasn't the one looking to find a husband. And when the two weeks were up, nothing gained, nothing learned, I returned to the hospital and resumed my position on the terminal floor, pacing outside the familiar door like a lion in search of its prey. When nobody was looking, I peeked through the window, curious about this boy and the man inside the room. The dad was still there, hooked up to the tubes. The queasy son was nowhere to be found.

I watched his dad, alone in the narrow bed, wondering what he might be thinking. Was he thinking about anything? Was he praying, or had he given up hope, merely succumbing to his illness? A sound from behind coaxed me from my stance. My eyes followed the noise to the boy, clutching his stomach, and making these grossly distorted sounds. I was amazed that a person could be such a complete moron.

I said to him, "It's quite astonishing how you ever grew to be so tall when your brain is evidently stunted."

"And which part of my brain might that be, Miss Know-it-all?"

"What, you think I don't know about the pituitary gland?"

"Kudos to Jessica Parker. She knows about the endocrine system. What else do they teach you in the seventh grade?"

"You mean almost eleventh, and they actually just taught us about the beauty and drama of the living world in biology, and I'm wondering where your vile bodily secretions fit into the scheme of things."

"For such a pretty girl," he said, "you have a lot of ugly things to say."

I ignored the compliment, sort of. This is what we girls do. We file them away for future reference, and when we're alone, we take them out and repeat them over and over in our minds.

"I guess I've witnessed a lot of ugly things in my life, namely the most recent nasty thing that was left on my shoe."

"You're fifteen," he said, "what ugly things have you had to endure?"

"That's for me to know and you to find out."

"You didn't just say that, did you? I used that line back in the fifth grade."

"I've seen fifth graders with way more self-control than you."

"Friends of yours?" he laughed. I wasn't used to cute boys keeping up with my quick wit. I studied his face; the green eyes were positioned perfectly across a smooth, olive complexion. A thick brush of unruly brown hair contradicted his chiseled appearance.

He said, "I'm twenty-two."

"What makes you think I care?"

"Next you're going to ask me when is my birthday."

I laughed to hide my astonishment.

"It's December seventh."

I said, "Looks like bombs weren't the only stupid things they dropped on Pearl Harbor Day."

"What exactly does that mean?" he asked, cocking his head to the side.

I hadn't a clue. I was busy rifling through my brain, *Aries, Aquarius, Sagittarius.*

"You're weird," he said.

"Thank you," I smiled.

"Jessie Parker," I watched his generous lips say. "One weird chick. Do you go to school around here?"

"You should know, you seem to have all the answers."

"I'm just playing with you. It's called friendly conversation. You should try it sometime."

We turned to the door to his father's room. The nurse was going in with what looked like an excess of medications. This distraction stopped me from my next thoughtless and facetious remark. I observed a tightness spread over his face. His eyes became sad, his mood morose. I could tell this by the way his eyebrows burrowed and his lips closed shut. Through the crack in the door, I saw his father lying there. He was still, calm as death, and it was probable that this boy knew the end was near. Empathy cast over me, an emotion I typically stayed away from. I didn't know where it was coming from, but it was there, and I wanted to take back all those ugly things I had said. I had to do something. The urge was overwhelming, but I didn't know what to do about it.

I think he might have said he was going to get some air. When I turned around, he was walking toward the elevator. Hesitating for a minute, I walked into his father's room, not having a clue what I was about to do. The nurse, Maria, recognized me and said, "He's only allowed to see family members," and then, winking her approval, she added, "but I won't tell anyone." I moved in closer to get a better look. She was administering his medication while I found his chart there beside the bed.

His name was Adam. Adam Levy. Diagnosis, idiopathic pulmonary fibrosis. It was his lungs. That much I knew. The rest was foreign and filled me with dread.

"We have the same birthday," I whispered, surprising myself both with that fact and that I said it out loud. The nurse continued with her dosages, drugs I knew by first name from times spent in the ER. She acknowledged my announcement with a friendly nod, while I calculated the years in my head. He'd be fifty next month.

I studied him closely. From what I could see, he was an impressive man, standing probably as tall, if not taller, than his son. That is, when he stood. He was the kind of man you could feel in the air around you. He once probably filled up a room, but now the broad shoulders were weakened bones protruding beneath layers of skin that had no life to cling on to. His hair was gray, capping his head, and his eyes were closed so I couldn't tell their color. They could have been the reason his son's eyes were such an astonishing shade.

If it were summer and he were tanned and if, well, if he were healthy, I'm sure he would have been handsome, with a rugged face and a jovial grin, but what I saw were dry, cracked lips, an inverted smile, life lines incising the exterior of his face. The monitors hummed around me, beeping with each breath he took.

The nurse left me alone in the room. I took the vacant seat beside him and watched.

I tried to imagine how it would feel if he were my dad.

I squeezed my eyes shut, willing myself to feel the feelings, wanting to form the connection, but I couldn't do it. I understood that if that boy were in this chair, or his mother, they would undeniably be able to feel. They would have memories and emotions and a bond with this man from sharing years of his life. There would be words for their pain and anguish. They would know what they were losing because they were experiencing a life with him.

I had never learned to feel these things. Even when I closed my eyes and pretended this man was my father, something inhibited me from making a deeper connection, the kind I never experienced that is formed through the bond of touch and the passage of years.

"Who are you?" he asked in a barely audible voice.

"I'm sorry," I answered, composing myself from the thickness of my thoughts and abruptly getting to my feet. "I shouldn't be in here."

"Why are you?" Each word was a struggle, I could tell, but was that a smile on his face? And yes, those eyes, he definitely passed them down to his son.

"I'm Jessica Parker." I hesitated. "My mom works in the hospital. Your son puked on my shoe." Where did *that* come from?

He responded with something that resembled a laugh.

"Have I gone?" he asked. "Is this heaven?"

"No, no," I said, repeating the word, stopping it from happening. "You're not dead yet. I mean, you're not dead. You're just in the hospital."

"I thought you were one of those beautiful little angels."

"Angel?" I responded with a laugh. "Hardly."

"Then what happened to Jonas?"

"Jonas? You mean your son?"

He nodded.

"Well, I think he doesn't take to hospitals very well."

"Like his father."

I figured some manners would suit me right about now. "I didn't mean to disturb you, sir. I don't really know why I came in here. Your son, I mean, Jonas, was out there talking with me, and I, I was just curious."

"Jessica Parker, can you get me some water, please?"

"Sure," I said, a little too excitedly. I took the pitcher from the tray beside him, filled one of the empty plastic cups, and handed it to him, but he didn't move.

"You'll have to help me."

I looked around, hoping he was talking to someone else in the room. When I saw that he wasn't, I shrugged a little, remembering yarmulke boy from school who was always talking about doing mitzvahs. I decided this was a mitzvah and helped a dying man drink a glass of water.

I held the cup up to his lips as he took a few sips. We were in close proximity to one another.

"Are you sure you're not an angel?" he asked.

I laughed. Then a thought crossed my mind. Maybe it was the drugs; he *was* a little loopy and out of sorts.

The laughter caused the cup I was holding to spill water down the front of his gown.

"I'm so sorry, sir, really," I said. "Here, I'll get a towel."

This was all too much for me. All this touching and being close to an older man who wasn't my father, or even an uncle or big brother, was weird, weird, weird. Maybe he was a pedophile, I thought, but that didn't even make me want to laugh. I knew that was impossible. I was torn. My body told me to walk out of the room, but my head told me to stay put. The inner battle didn't last long.

I said, "You have the same birthday as I do."

"Is that so?"

"Maybe it's some destiny, fate thing," I added.

"Serendipitous?"

"Yes, serendipitous."

"How old are you?" he asked. I wasn't sure if this was his way of implying I had childish notions or if it was something he wanted to know.

"Fifteen. Actually, I already feel sixteen. I've been practicing it for months."

"You have? You must be very good at it by now."

"Your son doesn't seem to agree."

"What does he know?" he laughed, while I shrugged my shoulders. "I remember fifteen," he said.

"You do?"

"Yes, I do, Jessie." I decided it was fine for him to call me Jessie.

"Fifteen was a good year," he continued, as I watched him speak, traveling back through his memories. "I shared my first real kiss with Rachel Kaplan."

"Who was she?"

"Only the most beautiful girl in the eleventh grade. I thought about her every day and every night, and the more I thought about her, the meaner I'd be to her."

"How'd you end up kissing her?" Spoken by a true novice, one that personified *sweet sixteen and never been kissed.*

"We took turns torturing each other for awhile and then we became really good friends. We were invited to all these, what do you call them, those boy-girl mixers."

"Kissing parties?" I interrupted.

"Yes, kissing parties, and we realized we were both pretty apprehensive about kissing for the first time, so we decided to help each other, be each other's first kiss, to practice, so to speak."

I visualized their practice session, wondering if there were any boys at Tremont I could bully into being my test model.

"Then it was all over for me. I was *smitten.* That kiss changed *everything.* When I next saw her, gone was the girl who tutored me in math. She was a woman now, and growing more beautiful with each passing day. I was the one being tortured, all nervous and tongue-tied around her, something I'd never experienced before. When I finally had the nerve to invite her to my senior prom, she'd already been asked by some tennis player, Rory Seligman. And then the worst happened. Her father got a job in Washington, DC, and they were moving east."

"And she moved? Just like that? Were you devastated?"

"I was very sad. Particularly because I never got to tell her I was madly in love with her." He had to stop and take a breath because I think all the talking had exhausted him. The lids of his eyes fell forward, his breathing following in a rapid succession of inhaling and exhaling. Shoot, I hoped I hadn't killed him, but the monitor was blipping, indicating his heart was in motion.

"Did you ever see her again?" I asked with anticipation. It didn't matter that Adam Levy looked spent and about to collapse before my eyes, I had to hear the rest. "What happened to her?"

A voice from behind me resounded, "He married her," and I turned to see Jonas Levy standing there in the doorway. I wasn't sure how long he had been there or how much of our conversation he had heard, but he brought his finger to his lips, telling me without words that his father was falling asleep.

"He married her?" I whispered, enjoying the intimacy of the tale, the peek into his family's history.

"Rachel Kaplan is my mother," he said, entering the room, closing the space between us. Then he asked, "Why are you in here?"

"I don't know. Friendly conversation, didn't you tell me I should try it sometime?"

When I saw that he didn't find that funny, we retreated into our individual corners and watched as his father fell into a comfortable snooze.

"My father loved her a lot. I mean, he still does. I don't know how she's going to live without him." His tone was hushed and sad, and I had to move in closer to hear his whispers.

"They must really be in love," I said aloud.

"Yeah, they are. It's pretty cool to see your parents like that."

I said, "Are you going to tell me what happened? If she moved back east, how did they end up together?"

Maybe it was the man on a train syndrome, how when you're sitting next to someone you don't know, you spill your truths in a safe, finite passage of time, knowing you will never see the person again. Whatever it was, it didn't take Jonas long to tell me what I wanted to hear.

"She left for DC and he was devastated. They wrote each other every week, and then one day the letters stopped. Dad became frantic and called her parents, and they assured him everything was okay, that Mom had met someone and was consumed by her new friend."

Dad was miserable and depressed, berating himself for never telling her how he felt and hating Mom for ignoring him, when a letter came. It was her handwriting, he knew. He said he could recognize that scrawl anywhere, but the letter this time was different. He said he was too afraid to read it, didn't want to hear about her latest love, so he stuck it in a drawer while he prepared himself."

I was riveted, caught up in the details, the strife, the heartache, and the impatience of uncertainty. "When he finally read it, he thought he was ready for what she had to say. Mom had written to tell him that she'd fallen in love with a boy with hair the color of night and eyes the color of the sea. She couldn't live without him; her life wasn't complete without him in it."

"You know this by heart," I interrupted. "Are we just a wee bit romantic?"

His eyes searched the ceiling in annoyance, tossing away that description of himself like one might a Frisbee. "Do you want me to finish?"

"I'm sorry," I said, knowing it was more my obsession than his.

"Dad's heart was broken, but at the same time, he didn't want to be angry when his best friend sounded so happy."

"That's a mensch, right?" I asked. "I've heard about people like that."

He was getting really annoyed.

"I'm sorry," I mumbled. "Finish."

"She said she wasn't sure when it happened. It felt as though she'd loved him her whole life, that he made her laugh and feel special when they were around each other. And one thing she realized in particular was how much she hated to be away from him, even for one night."

"My God, your dad must've blown a gasket," I interrupted again.

"He was pretty roughed up. I remember him telling this story at their anniversary party; the news of Mom's new boyfriend, how his heart hurt, how he could barely speak."

And as if to let us know he remembered also, Adam Levy shifted in the bed and a loud gasp escaped his chest.

"What else did the letter say?" I whispered.

"This is the best part. She said that she couldn't be without him anymore."

"I don't get it."

"See, you're not as smart as you think you are. She said she was coming back to California to see him, to see my dad, that it was no life without him in it, and he was the boy she'd always loved, always had. She was coming home for him."

"It was him all along?" I asked, images of the two of them swirling through my head. "There was never someone else in Washington?"

"Nope."

"Really?"

"You sound disappointed," he said. "Are you disappointed?"

I wasn't sure of my answer. "I'm just surprised. I guess I really thought she loved somebody else."

Maybe I was a little letdown by Rachel's pronouncement. I never thought love could be that simple.

I spent the next few days dutifully going to school and then sneaking off to the hospital. Beth kept asking to come along, but I told her she wasn't allowed. I'd watch her walk toward the direction of her house, knowing I was hurting her, but not willing to share Jonas and his father. Sometimes I wouldn't even tell Mom I was there.

When Jonas Levy asked me why I was there every day, I lied and said that it was part of the internship program at our school. I explained how the gifted students were required to do internships in their field of interest. "I'm studying to be a doctor," I told him.

"Really? That's funny. So am I. I just finished my second year at Harvard," he added.

I didn't let the prestigious name throw me or the shameless lie I'd constructed. "How are you going to stomach being a doctor with your track record and all?"

"You're never going to let me live that down, are you?"

"Not likely."

"Then maybe you should know that I only got sick because I looked through the door and saw you standing there, such a ghastly sight I couldn't contain myself."

Instead of cringing at those words, I smiled. Maybe Adam Levy had something there with that "being mean" theory.

And speaking of Adam Levy, the man was not doing particularly well. Although he was alert and talking to his family, the life inside of him had begun to deteriorate. By then I was schooled on idiopathic pulmonary fibrosis, and it was, quite frankly, a big fart of a disease. Jonas, who was a lot more advanced in his pre-med studies than I was, explained that "pulmonary fibrosis is a disease of the lower respiratory tract that damages the air sacs in the lungs, prohibiting the proper transfer of oxygen to the blood. Idiopathic," he added, "means no cause can be found."

I loved when Jonas talked like that. He sounded so smart. He was probably the smartest person I ever engaged in verbal banter with, precluding myself. Every afternoon, when the doctor visited Mr. Levy's room—Dr. Missed Opportunity, I now liked to call him—Jonas would request a debriefing, asking only the most important questions and expecting the most detailed responses. You could see on Jonas's face how important it was to be included in the updates. When his father's breathing became more erratic—"Velcro-like" he'd call it—I'd find him knee-deep in his textbooks on the couches in the waiting area. When cyanosis occurred, the blueness around his mouth and fingernails that marked a diminished oxygen supply, Jonas urged the doctors to attempt a more aggressive form of treatment, but the doctors felt that Adam's health was too fragile to bear it. Obviously, this was difficult for Jonas to hear. Still, he managed to use his keen understanding of medicine to face a devastating prognosis with learned optimism. Jonas would make an excellent physician. I knew that for sure.

Observing him reminded me of Mrs. Danziger, our English teacher. She was bright, sophisticated, degreed, and had a vocabulary that had us flipping through the dictionary regularly to keep up. Then there was Mr. Lipton, our history teacher. Average in intelligence—no use for Webster's when he spoke—Mr. Lipton knew how to *teach*, which embodied a lot more than spoon-feeding us the War of 1812. That element that differentiates the good teachers from the great teachers is the same that separates the good doctors from the great doctors. In hospitals and doctors' offices, they call it good bedside manner, and I suppose it can be indicative of teachers' strengths as well. Jonas had those added ingredients: the patient, selfless manner, the caring look in his eye, the understanding to be a fantastic doctor. Jonas had great bedside manner. How did I know this for sure? I knew. I watched this guy more closely than I inspected myself in the mirror every morning.

Chapter 3

School was out, and by then I had cajoled my mother into getting me a job as one of those cheery candy stripers. I would have much preferred a job at the local music store or even the video store so I could get discounts on my favorite items (not the five-fingered kind), but I astounded myself with my enthusiasm toward my new line of work.

I was pretty much there every day, all day, from the time I finished my shifts, up until dinner. He was there too, and on the days he wasn't, I felt incomplete. I'd watch for his white Jeep Cherokee every afternoon and hide my disappointment if he didn't show up.

Jonas was unlike any other boy I'd ever met, and I probably shouldn't be calling him a *boy* when he was clearly seven ever-present years older than I. Over the course of our meetings, I summarized the few things I had learned about him: His family lived in Malibu in what was presumably a large house. It had a name, so I couldn't be wrong. His little sister, Amy, was the light in his life. He and his dad played a fierce game of tennis back in the day, although he hadn't picked up a racquet since the diagnosis. His mother, Rachel, was a bright, strong woman, and when he spoke of her, there was no mistaking the pride in his voice. Like most boys his age, Jonas was self-assured and charming. Unlike most boys his age, he possessed a depth about himself that made him appear older than his years.

I was convinced early on that I had something to do with the latter side of his personality.

Jonas's life outside the hospital was foreign to me. There were limits to him, boundaries I constantly tried to push through. I couldn't tell you his favorite anything, not movie, not book, or song on the radio, so I took pride in the things I did know, the other, more important things. Like, I knew when he was happy to see me. I knew the way he'd try not to smile when he saw me open the door to his father's room. And I knew when he was amazed at something I'd say or do, which was quite often. I also knew how scared he was to lose his father, how he'd go off into one of the waiting areas, closing the door behind him so that he could think and sulk in private. When he was really angry or upset, I'd catch him smoking a cigarette outside, even when we both knew how oddly ironic it was for him to choose something that might destroy his own lungs.

"You're joking me," I'd said the first time I caught him with one dangling out of his mouth. "The wise doctor-to-be smokes? Don't you know it's slow-motion suicide?"

He puffed away, as though if he puffed hard enough, I'd go away.

I continued. "It's disgusting. It fills your lungs with tar and gives you stinky breath."

"Don't worry, you're not kissing me," he answered, throwing the butt into the waiting basket and positioning himself before me.

Whenever he looked at me with those eyes, I could feel the air catch in my throat. I almost forgot what I was about to say.

"My friend Beth went to London last summer…"

"Is there going to be a point to this story?" he interrupted.

"And she saw this advertisement on the telly—you know that's what they call television over there, right?" Again, he rolled his eyes at me. "Well, it showed a picture of this woman's face, and all of a sudden her lips and eyes and nose turned into hot molten lava, and her skin was curdling from the heat, and she turned into this black smoldering creature, features dripping off her face like a volcano. Then the announcer came on and said, 'Imagine if what happened on the inside, happened on the outside.' Totally freaked Beth out. She swears she'll never even look at a cigarette again."

"That's a great story, Jessie."

I also knew when Jonas wanted silence and when I should back off.

One afternoon, Jonas motioned for me outside his father's room. I was pushing a cart back to the nurse's station, having finished my shift.

"Are you hungry?" he asked.

"No."

"I'm going to the cafeteria. Want to sit with me?"

"No."

"Okay," he said, "I'll see you tomorrow," turning his back to me and walking toward the elevator. Then he called out, "Hey, Parker, don't go bugging my dad anymore today."

I took offense, leaving the cart behind and catching the elevator door just as it was about to close. "What do you mean, 'bugging him?'"

"Exactly what I said, now let go of the door."

"I'm not bugging him. He loves my company."

"Okay, that's great, but let go of the door."

"No," I said. "Not until you explain yourself."

"There's nothing to explain, alright. Forget about it, just move out of the way, okay?"

It dawned on me that there were three sets of eyes waiting for me to let go of the door. Their impatient stares were almost as bad as Jonas's vain attempts to get under my skin. My hands dropped, and I stepped into the unwelcome space. Nobody said a word. When the doors opened on the first floor, there was no question I'd follow Jonas into the crowded cafeteria.

"You could have just said yes instead of pretending you meant no."

"You can be such a jerk sometimes," I said.

He ignored me, and when he walked through the lunchtime crowd in the cafeteria, he turned to me and said, "Why don't you go grab us a table?" And because I did whatever he asked, I started to walk away in search of an open seat when I heard him call out from behind me, "What can I get you?"

Walking the few awkward steps in his direction, I stopped right in front of him, close enough to touch, looked him in the eyes, and deadpanned, "Is this a date?"

When I laughed, and he proceeded to stare at me, it was clear he just wasn't getting my sense of humor. I was pretty hungry. I might have allowed myself to eat something, if not for the small fact that my stomach was tied in knots and my throat felt dry and tight, and I wasn't sure anything would go down because this would be our first meal together.

That's when "chocolate milk" popped out.

"Chocolate milk?" he asked.

It surprised me too, but it had always been a comfort food.

"Whatever you say," he said, rolling his eyes. "You do look kind of cute in that outfit." I looked down at my clothes and was reminded that I was wearing the shapeless candy striper uniform. In one powerful yank, I freed myself from the red and white fabric and crumpled it into a ball.

Jonas was watching me, and I wanted to smack the arrogant smirk right off his face. Turning, I stomped off in the other direction to a table in the back, where I threw the apron over the chair, took a seat, and surveyed the room. *This* is where I was at my best, in a crowded room of strangers.

I had oftentimes contemplated a career with the CIA or FBI, in large part due to this game I would play called detective. Beth and I played it all the time, whenever we went to a restaurant with her family. It was easy; you simply had to call a table. Upon entering a dining establishment, search the room, hone in on a specific table, and come up with the most accurate depiction of its inhabitants. That meant, by the end of the night, we would have to know how the people were connected and the various elements of that connection—love, hate, friendship, family, turmoil, or strife. I was not the easiest opponent to play this game with because I never believed I was wrong. Even if Beth was certain, even if she swore she knew the people, after she heard my argument and supporting evidence, she always changed her mind and ended up agreeing with me anyway.

Take the time we watched a couple kissing throughout the entire meal. Beth thought they were a happily married couple. She said, "They're madly in love after twenty years, three kids, a dog, and a house with a big yard."

Beth didn't stand a chance.

"Come on, Jessie, look how happy they are."

"First of all, married couples usually aren't that happy. Statistically, the only people that are that happy are the ones that are having affairs, and to prove my point, he's wearing a wedding band. Take a look, she's not."

Beth's face moved through varying emotions before settling on disbelief. "She's the girlfriend," I said. "The wife you're talking about, well, she's at home, probably watching those three kids, and walking the dumb dog."

Beth was dumbstruck. I said, "Didn't we just watch *Falling in Love* together? DeNiro and Streep had the same look in their eyes and they weren't married."

Jonas sat down with a tray of food just as I was about to call the table beside us. There were two of them, a man, probably around forty, a girl maybe Jonas's age. This one was tricky. She could have been his daughter; she could have been his girlfriend. He was good-looking enough to get away with such a pretty, young girl by his side. I just wasn't a hundred percent sure of the body language between them. She seemed sad, and he was doing his best to console her. We were in a hospital, though, and there was a lot of that going on.

"What are you doing?" Jonas asked, a puzzled look on his face.

"Shhhh," I said. Obviously, he didn't know that the agent could not be interrupted or the *call* might be inaccurate. Thinking these things, I scared myself at times.

"What are you up to?" he asked again, impatiently starting with his hamburger. When I waved him off with the flick of my hand, he turned to his food. I couldn't believe the crap he put on it, mayonnaise, hot peppers, loads of ketchup, mustard. No wonder he had a queasy stomach.

The man at the next table drew a hand out toward the girl. Without hesitation, she took it in her own. I watched as he cupped it in his, feeling the tingly goose bumps travel down my spine. She wiped a tear from her eye, and I began to feel terrible for watching; but like a car wreck, I couldn't turn away. It was a hospital, I reminded myself, sad stuff was bound to happen. Still, I always shamed myself a little bit by watching. A very little bit. Maybe her mother was dying, maybe she was dying, or Grandma Bessie from Seattle. This one was hard to pin down so I left it, for the time being.

"Drink your milk. You're a growing girl," he said to me, as I focused both my eyes and ears on him.

"Do I look like I need more growing?" I asked.

When I saw his eyes move from my face downward, I decided it was okay that he didn't answer.

"You're always trying to act all cool and macho, Jonas, but I know beneath all that med school arrogance, you like having me around."

"And you, Jessica Parker, you're always trying to act all cool and macho, but I know beneath all that grade school charm, you wanted to have lunch with me."

The music of Jefferson Starship was in the backdrop of our play, and I began to hum along to "You Can Count On Me" while Jonas pretended not to hear. Well, he wasn't wrong. I knew I was fascinated and sort of scared of him at the same time—a lethal combination when it came to matters close to the heart.

"What are you going to do for your dad's birthday?" I asked, suddenly at a loss for words. He didn't think to ask me how I managed to obtain knowledge of this kind.

"We'll probably just try to make it as normal a day for him as possible. Amy will be here. She's finishing this ballet camp thing in San Francisco. You'll finally get to meet her. And then some of Dad's friends from work mentioned visiting. The hospital might give clearance that day for more visitors, though I don't think he wants any of them to see him like this. I told him I'd sneak him in a bottle of his favorite wine."

You'll get to meet her, was all I heard, as if there was a progression in our friendship, an invitation into his family. The welcoming gesture poured out of him, and if he had wanted to filter it, he did not. To be part of a unit like the Levys was something I had been pining for my whole life.

"I'd like that," I said.

"I figured you would. You never leave this place. Why aren't you somewhere with Beth doing something fun?"

I thought about this. I knew what he was asking with those words. It was what lingered beneath them that bothered me. "You don't think I'm serious about becoming a doctor?"

"I believe you," he answered, shoveling a handful of greasy fries into his mouth. "You can be anything you want to be, anything you set your mind to. I just think you hang around this place too much. It's kind of unnatural."

"Unnatural? It's my job."

"You're a volunteer," he reminded me. "When your shift is up, you don't leave. When it's your day off, you come in. You can't possibly want to hang around sick people all day and all night?"

"I like it here. I like the way everybody knows each other, like an extended family."

"That's just it, they're not your family, they're not even your friends. What is it with you?"

I thought I heard Dr. Norton's voice reverberating in my mind.

"You're different, Jessie Parker," he said with a smile. "You're not like other fifteen-year-olds I've met."

"Do you comb the local high schools for friends?"

"And you're pretty sharp. That doesn't come from someone who's just plain ordinary."

"I never said I was ordinary, Jonas, you did."

I fingered the glass of chocolate milk, watching the smooth, clear line I painted across the frosty glass. I wanted to talk to Jonas. I wanted him to hear my voice, the collection of words that would tell my story, but I was frightened of the truth, frightened of what I'd hear, and frightened of what I'd learn about myself.

I turned to the couple beside me and all the while Jonas's eyes never shifted from my face. I couldn't look at him. Already I was convinced he could read my overflowing mind, and my vulnerability was a skin I never showed and never shed. That he saw me as nothing short of invincible was essential to our friendship.

"This couple here," I said, pointing discreetly to my left, "do you think that's his daughter?"

"You're changing the subject."

"Or do you think they're married? Or she's the girlfriend?"

"What's this about, Jessie?"

"Just answer me. What do you think?"

"I don't know. It's probably his daughter."

I turned to them again. He was still holding her hand. The girl no longer looked frightened. She looked at ease, safe. An exchange passed between them. There was admiration, possibly love.

I said, "I think it's his girlfriend."

"No way," he said, "definitely her dad."

"What makes you so sure?"

"Didn't you hear what he just said?"

It bothered me to admit, "No."

"He said, 'Don't worry, honey, it'll all be okay.'"

It seemed that maybe the young girl had heard us. She looked our way, catching Jonas's green eyes in her own, holding them there for a second. She seemed calmer, more relaxed.

"And that makes him her father?"

Jonas turned back to me. "Didn't you see her reaction?"

I was baffled how he had become super spy in a matter of moments. It took me years to perfect such skills. "That's all you could come up with?"

"Don't you remember being a kid…" and he stopped himself. When he saw that I didn't find the dig at my youthfulness remotely funny, he continued, "You know, when something bad was happening and everyone would try to tell you it would be okay, and you just refused to believe it, dragging the agony around with you because you knew no matter what they said, it would never get better?"

I half nodded, recollecting more than a few occasions where that was the case.

"It wasn't until someone like your dad told you it was going to be okay that you believed it." He stole another glance at them. "Look at her, look how she's listening to him, look how she believes him. Only fathers have that kind of influence over their little girls. It's definitely his daughter." Then he finished off his analysis with a triumphant bite out of his burger.

I was amazed, stunned into silence, something that happened to me infrequently. I found myself achingly sad for my mother, the woman who tried her best to give me the kind of reassurance and comfort that only a father was capable of giving. And now I sat before this boy who could express the words that my heart had felt for so long, but couldn't pronounce. I looked at Jonas, this time through different eyes. He was in front of me, and we were talking, and we were close; but there was something else connecting me to him, something deeper and greater.

I said, "Maybe you're right," but it sounded more like defeat.

"This is part of your problem, Parker. You spend way too much time nosing into everyone else's business."

"It's just a game, Jonas, consider the entertainment value."

"You keep telling yourself that."

"It is," I said.

"Right. Let's get out of here."

When we got up from the table, Jonas pushed the chair out of the way so I could get by. He kept turning to make sure I was following closely behind him, and I was, but all I could think about was how I'd been so wrong about my assessment.

That afternoon was the beginning of a friendship with the distinct trappings of something more. Romantic tension threaded its way through our conversations, capable of tying us up in invisible knots. We ignored it. We chose to talk about everything else in the world—his father's illness, our future plans, hopes, dreams, the trivial day-to-day nuances that quietly and patiently began to build our foundation.

I thrived on the days I'd see Jonas. The hospital became our little nucleus of a world, the one inhabited by just the two of us. In between tending to my patients and filling out medical forms and claims, stolen moments abounded, thick with deep innuendo, heavy debates about what if and what could have been, a world not bound by his being twenty-two and my being almost sixteen. There were silent moments and unspoken thoughts, times I knew we were relating on a level greater than that of any words we might have spoken aloud. Our conversations were deeply moving and intoxicating. When we weren't being sarcastic and sharp-tongued, I'd listen to Jonas speak about something with such enthusiasm, it pained me not to reach over and touch him, to emphasize that I understood how he felt. Then there were the occasions when he'd be talking about someone, and a wistfulness would cloud his face, and I'd think, maybe, just maybe he was talking about me. And when I learned he was not, I never allowed the disillusion to seep in, instead clinging to the intermittent connections that had my heart radiating like an antenna.

Maybe it was all in my imagination and I just reminded him of his little sister, or maybe he was a pervert who liked the attention of younger girls. I didn't know and he probably didn't either.

Chapter 4

The car lurched forward, and before I knew what was happening, Jonas grabbed the wheel and turned it sharply to the right. "Are you crazy, Jessie? You need to stay within those lines."

"I told you I suck at driving. I'm never doing it again."

The evolution of our friendship in the outside world had officially begun. Beyond the hospital doors, Jonas was giving me my first driving lesson.

"If you even went just a little farther to the left, you would have hit that old man on the bike."

"Do you want the wheel?" I asked.

"Don't be so pig-headed. You have to practice, but you also have to pay attention."

How could anyone concentrate on driving with Jonas Levy sitting beside her? And how could I maintain my cool when my palms were sticking to the steering wheel, and I felt more like an octopus with too many arms?

"I've told you ten times, you don't use both feet for driving. The right foot controls the brake *and* the gas." I pushed on the gas, hearing the car rumble to life.

"Good, now when you want to brake, move it over to the brake pedal. Put the car into drive and let's try it again."

"I don't know why we're doing this. I don't need to drive anywhere."

"Trust me, you'll be glad you learned. LA's a big place."

I switched into gear and maneuvered the car into the street. We weren't far from the hospital, a peaceful residential community about to be overrun by thrashing metal. How did he persuade me to venture out of our safe habitat and into this wild terrain anyway? I scanned the street before me. There were no little old men on bicycles to worry about, so I pressed on the gas a little harder.

"Good, ease into it," he said, as if he'd taught driver's ed his whole life. "You just might be driving by your sixteenth birthday. A little more practice and you'll ace the test."

We approached an intersection at the same time as another car. He said, "You know what to do right now, right, when two cars reach a four-way stop sign at the same time?"

I didn't answer. I vaguely remembered reading about the rules and regulations meant to keep us from hurting others on the road. Why wasn't there a manual like that for people?

"You did read the driver's ed guide, Jess, didn't you?"

"Uh, parts of it."

He was visibly irritated with me. "The person on the right has the right of way. That's you. Now go before this guy does and we hit him."

I pressed my foot gently on the pedal and began to move into the intersection.

"If you don't know the rules of the road, you're not going to pass the driving test. The written component is just as important."

"I told you, I don't even want the measly license."

"Watch out!" he cried out. "Brake!"

"What?" I answered, searching the road ahead of me, frantically trying to follow his direction. And there it was, a tiny little duck crossing my path. I hadn't even noticed him coming in our direction. With both my feet this time, I defied the rules, desperate for the extra push I'd need to stop the unwieldy beast I commanded. The car stopped short, and Jonas and I lurched forward. Without another word, we unbuckled our seatbelts and switched places.

"Fuck the right of way," I said, backing up against the seat and throwing my legs up onto the dashboard. "And while we're on the subject, what's the deal with neutral? I just don't get neutral. Why would anyone want to be in neutral? You're either moving forward or moving backwards. Seriously, this whole right of way and neutral business is too complicated."

"You're making it complicated, Jess. It's a driver's test. Don't get so bent out of shape."

But I couldn't help it. I was fixated on neutral, and where I wanted to be was moving forward, with Jonas, fast. Typical of him not to notice the deeper meaning in what I was saying.

Chapter 5

"How are you feeling, Mr. Levy?"

It was a Friday afternoon, the weekend was upon us, and I'd delayed going home. Visiting the Levy family gave me the fictitious belief that I was no longer alone.

"Old," he answered.

"You're not old," I said. "Mrs. Maxwell down the hall, now *she's really old*. She's fifty-five."

"Fifty-five?" he laughed, "I'll forgive you for that one, Jessie."

"I'm sorry. I didn't mean to say you're old."

"It's okay. Unfortunately I feel like a ninety-one-year-old. It's not good for business, that much I can tell you."

"What business is that?"

"It doesn't matter."

"It matters. What did you do before you got sick?"

"Guess," he said.

"I love guessing games. Banking?"

"No."

"Lawyer?"

"Do I come across that boring and stuffy?"

"Absolutely not," I said with conviction. "You're the furthest thing from boring and stuffy, especially with MTV playing in your room all day long."

"Why the uptight professions?"

"I see how the doctors and nurses take care of you, how they respect you. I guess I just see you in a position of power, like Blake Carrington on *Dynasty*."

"Now that's a person I've never been compared to."

"It's not a criticism. Blake Carrington's a pretty successful guy."

"Depends on how you define success. For some it's power and prestige. For others it's something different."

"What is it to you?"

"My family."

"That's nice," I gushed.

"You look very happy when you smile," he noted.

"I was thinking the same thing about you."

"Then let's do it more often."

"It's a deal," I said, kindly offering my hand to him, but he was having trouble reaching my fingers with the IV hooked up at an angle that made the stretch painful. His fingers had also turned that eerie shade of blue that Jonas was concerned about. I stretched my arm farther and slid my hand beneath his palm, giving it a friendly squeeze. "There, it's official. Now, tell me what you do. You're not some famous celebrity, are you?"

"You are persistent," he laughed, while a deep cough broke away from his chest. For a brief time, I had forgotten he was sick. "See that?" he said, nodding toward the television. It was MTV again. I was already thrown by his fixation on this new-borne phenomenon and wasn't sure if it had to do with the network or U2 singing on the screen. "That's what I do.

"And you see this radio over here?" he said, motioning to the boom box that had been brought in. "That's part of my job too."

I had noticed the stereo system, the piles of cassettes, the addiction to MTV, but I figured these were merely hobbies. It never occurred to me that they might make up a profession. Maybe there was hope for me to decide on a career after all.

"Have you heard of Mindy Samuels?"

"Of course."

"And Chuck Perry?"

"Hello. I'm a teenager in America. Who hasn't…"

"The Funk Brothers?"

"Oh, my God, I love them. They're one of my favorites."

"They're all part of my job." He then pointed to the *Los Angeles Times* that lay beside him. His coughing was getting worse.

"Guess you didn't read the paper this morning?" he asked.

"Only my horoscope, Dear Abby, and tonight's television lineup." *This*, I hadn't seen. There it was, a full-page article about the man in the bed.

"I'm too tired, Jessie. It tells you everything you need to know."

I held the crisp pages in my hand and began to read.

Adam Levy, the music world's most respected and talented executive, is facing the struggle of his life. Diagnosed early last year with idiopathic pulmonary fibrosis, a life-threatening degenerative disease of the lungs, Mr. Levy is residing in Randalls Hospital in the critical care unit while undergoing treatment for this condition.

Mr. Levy, 49, the reigning president and CEO of HiTide Records, one of the largest and most successful record labels in the business, has stunned the music world with the recent news of his hospitalization. Best known for such acts as the Grammy-award winning Funk Brothers and pop superstar Mindy Samuels, Adam Levy is personally responsible for the success and triumphs of...

I paused from the parade of celebrities to study the picture included in the article. "This is a nice picture of you." He was a handsome, virile man with a full head of hair, clean lines, and his son's eyes; only the picture was black and white, so the people of Los Angeles were cheated out of the spectacular color. I continued reading to myself, the words summing up Adam's Levy life, the beginning, the chances he took, the praise he received.

"It's unheard of, the type of success Adam Levy has achieved in this transient, ever-changing, fickle music community, but the statistics prove it," said his long-time rival Blake Friedman of Sony Music in New York. "I should despise the guy for his knack of finding number one acts, but he's just too decent and human of a guy. Anyone who meets the man can't say enough about him."

Doug Henry of Rolling Stone, recently wrote, "Adam Levy is one of the true talents of music media today. He can fine-tune an artist like one might an old piano. He plucks unknowns off the street, hands them over to the right personnel, and before you blink, they are an American Top 40. His gift is one that no other label executive has been able to procure."

When interviewed by the Times just last year, Adam Levy told reporter Ken Ronberg that the key to his professional success was, merely, "Doing something I love to do."

Mr. Levy is married to Rachel, his wife of 25 years, and they have two children, Jonas, 22, and Amy, 12.

"They make you sound dead already."

"They do, don't they?" he said, sullen and afraid.

"I'm sorry, I shouldn't have said that."

"No, it's okay. I've grown to appreciate your inability to filter your thoughts." The laughter that followed suppressed the idea of him dying and the fact that the man was practically a star.

"You should be very proud of yourself," I said, not knowing what more to say. There was a stirring within me as if Adam Levy was charting my destiny. "I can be doing my thing, going about my business, and then I hear a song, and it's like everything can change in an instant, everything I was thinking, feeling."

"I understand," he said, "more than you know. Music has taken me back to times in my life I thought I'd forgotten, places I never wanted to forget."

"Do regular people understand or is that just the gift of the music lover? Sometimes it feels like a curse."

"Why do you say that?"

I hesitated, choosing my words carefully. "Because just as a song can transport me back in time to a happy place, it can also take me back to a sad place."

"I'd say that most of the time it's been a gift. Have you ever just closed your eyes and breathed in a smell and you're back to that place, wherever it was?"

"Isn't that just nostalgia?" I interrupted, taken in by his sincerity, the depth at which he obviously experienced things. "You know, how you long for someone, something, or even someplace that made you feel good? But it's gone?"

He looked at me, saw my secret sadness. "Music does that to me," he said, kindly guiding us back to the present.

"Me too," I said. "And movies, they do that to me also, but now I'm not so sure if it's the movie or its music. Sometimes I fall in love with a movie more because of the soundtrack."

"That's because the movie has a good music supervisor."

My mind was racing with possibilities.

"You should pursue music or film if you love them so much. Trust me, if you do what you love to do, you'll never feel like it's work."

I looked at him, thankful that I had the chance to know such a nice person. Then came the imminence of his death, stealing the gratefulness away, replacing it with fear. I had hardly considered the actual death. To me, he was too real to succumb to the darkness that waited.

I was adamant about keeping my cool, but a thought flashed through my brain, a short-lived idea, rather. I had spent the better part of ten years avoiding such intense feelings, and here I sought out a man who made me feel the very same feelings I was avoiding. The realization overshadowed everything else.

"Jessica?" he asked.

I would have welcomed an intrusion by Jonas. This conversation was worse than ones I had with Dr. Norton, primarily because I'd never wanted to open up to her the way I wanted to share with Adam Levy and his unavoidable son.

Let's not forget just how astute I was, how years and years of practice had taught me to master the game of denial. The storms I'd weathered before this one, this slow drizzle, were far worse. Deep breath. Deep breath. Count to ten, clear the runway, and I was off.

"It's okay," I said, wiping the couple of tears that got away. "I'm okay. I'm just sorry that you're so sick. You've been so nice to me, you, your family, it's just sad to think…"

"You shouldn't be worrying…"

"Hmmm," I grimaced.

"This can't be easy for you, having lost your own dad."

I stiffened at this. "How did you know that?"

"Your mother."

"My *mother?*" enunciating just so, as if she were the devil incarnate.

"It will make it that much harder to say good-bye."

"I'm not thinking about my father or saying good-bye to you," I lied.

The coughing began again. He watched me watching him. Tubes were covering his body like overgrown weeds. I handed him some water to bring them to life.

"It must have been difficult for you."

I nodded, because I knew that was the expected response. I couldn't say this to him, but as long as he was alive and breathing, I knew that I was safe from the ghosts of my past. As long as I could keep the dialogue going, listen, smile, and dote, then he would remain on this earth. I foolishly believed, as most almost-sixteen-year-olds did, that I had control over whether somebody would leave.

"Don't be upset with your mother. She loves you very much. She worries about you."

I shook off the words of affection as if they were a contagious disease. I would deal with my mother and her flitting later.

"Please don't tell Jonas," I begged. "He'll just feel sorry for me and I don't want his pity."

"You don't know my son very well. He adores you."

"He has a funny way of showing it."

The door swung open and Dr. Missed Opp kindly asked me to leave. "Mr. Levy needs his rest," he said.

Adam Levy finished by saying, "You're like his little sister Amy; wait until you meet her."

I know he was trying to be kind, but the worst thing he could have compared me to was Jonas's sister. "I can't wait," I said, getting up to leave.

"Remember what I told you, Jessica, do something you love…"

But the door closed behind me, and his words were cut off, leaving me to wonder how this conversation took such a downward spiral.

Chapter 6

I knew my mother was angry with me before I even entered the house. Maybe it was the fact that I was an hour late for my own birthday dinner, the evening she spent hours meticulously planning to include all my favorite things—Beth, a handful of new video releases, and the radio on full blast. How could I explain to her that I would rather be at the hospital with Jonas and his family and that I had no desire to return to the world of the Parkers? Beth seemed insignificant to me; in fact, my life seemed hardly consequential enough to contain the thoughts and perplexities that burdened me. I had already celebrated with the people that mattered: Jonas, Adam, Rachel, and even Amy, Jonas's prized little sister. She was twelve years old and adorable. I liked her instantly.

Perhaps Mom was just angry because it was the day he left, the day our lives changed forever. My birthday was not a celebration, just a testament to my mother's loneliness.

The day started out unsettling. Adam's blood pressure dropped, and his breathing became rapid and shallow. It was my day off, being my sixteenth birthday and all, but in my new *profession*, there was no such thing as a day off. This new occupation did just that, occupied my living and my breathing. Beth wanted to spend the day together at Venice Beach going over our recent crushes, but I had an agenda that only included the hospital.

I was about to enter Adam's room when everyone was leaving it, the looks on their faces grim and foreboding. "What's going on?" I asked, first to Jonas, then to Mrs. Levy.

"Maybe it's not a good idea for her to be here," she said to Jonas, eyeing me at first, then lowering her head to Amy. I searched Jonas's eyes. Mrs. Levy was clearly worried. Amy resembled a Raggedy Ann doll, and not because of her red hair, but because of the way she reached for her mother's hand.

This can't be happening again, I was thinking, over and over in my head.

"It's okay, Mom," Jonas spoke. "I'll take a walk outside with the girls. You stay with Dad." He kissed her softly on the cheek and in a knee-jerk reaction, I brushed my own cheek with my palm.

Jonas, the den leader, led us out of the hospital and to a garden I'd never noticed before. There I was formally introduced to Amy Levy. Her fiery hair was a surprise, as was the unblemished complexion, not a freckle in sight. The green in her eyes was a shade close to her brother's. "Are you Jonas's new girlfriend?" she asked.

"No," I laughed.

"You're very pretty," she told me, rather matter-of-factly.

"Thank you. So are you!"

Amy was sweet and inquisitive, with a giggle that sounded more like hiccups. She loved her big brother and was protective of him just the same. If she weren't only twelve years old, I might have found my new best friend. An aspiring ballerina, Amy dared to go where I never could. I was a great athlete, I'd been told, but I was lacking the discipline, poise, and elegance that accompanied a career in ballet. Besides, a tutu was not my best look.

"You would make a great ballerina, Jessie," Jonas chimed in, just as I was teasing Amy about plies and those dreadful shoes.

"Never going to happen."

Amy followed as I walked out into the courtyard in search of the thickest elm I could find. Fingering its ample trunk, I steadied myself for a climb. Amy looked up, noting how tall this particular tree was. The gradual worry tugged at her face.

"Are you really going up there?" she asked.

"I've climbed a lot bigger ones than this."

My tennis shoes hugged the trunk as my sturdy arms embraced it in a tight-fisted grip. When I reached the first branch, I hoisted myself up, seeing Amy's face below me. She was toying with the idea of following, but I could see she was just plain scared.

The tree branched into a spray of lengthy fingers. When I found the right limb to climb, I continued to stretch my body in its direction. I was traveling higher than I'd ordinarily venture, but there was something about the two faces watching me that urged me on, lifting me up even higher. I've always had this unusual attraction to trees. Being up there, high above the world, it was like this energy would fill me up. I'd hear the leaves on each branch whistling in the wind, the sound as soothing as anything I'd ever heard. Up there I was free from the troubles below. I could literally sit for hours, and sometimes did. My dream was to one day have an enormous tree house, where I could sleep, watch movies, listen to music, and dream. No one could reach me, no one would bother me, except my mother, or maybe Beth, who would serve me meals via a pulley created from a basket and a strand of rope. I had it all planned out, with the exception of where I'd plug my TV in, and where I'd go to the bathroom, and, I guess, well, a lot had to be figured out.

I decided early on that trees were the only living things in the world that could give to the world without expecting anything in return.

"Watch it!" I heard from below, a voice of panic.

Before I knew what was happening, I felt the branch give way, my foot buckling, having nothing to hold onto. I didn't want to look down. I knew how high I had climbed. I felt my body slide against the rough bark, a searing pain gripping my left underside. At least my hands were safely around its torso.

I had fallen approximately four feet before my foot landed on another solid branch. My heart was racing. I saw that I was bleeding through my blouse, the red turning my white T-shirt crimson.

Amy was perched on the ground, hunched over with both hands over her eyes. She hadn't wanted to see me splatter. Jonas was there, and although I couldn't see him, I could feel his presence somewhere below, urging me to jump. "I'll catch you!" he cried out.

I had nowhere to go but down. The branch I was resting on was already beginning to waver. The second branch broke. I gasped, while my body dragged me down another two feet until I landed magnificently, and effortlessly, in Jonas's arms.

"Are you okay?" he asked.

"I don't know," I answered.

"That's not funny, Jessie. You could have really hurt yourself," he said. "What if I wasn't there to catch you?"

I hadn't considered that. There was something about Jonas that led me to believe he'd always be there to catch me.

"Look at you," he continued. "You're a mess." More blood had seeped onto his shirt.

"It doesn't hurt," I said bravely, pulling my hair back into a rubber band.

All this time, little Amy was still hovered over, afraid to look up.

"She's okay, Ames," he called out to her. "You can get up now."

I turned to find her beautiful green eyes peeking through the delicate fingers.

"You scared me, Jessie! Don't do that again," she said, running toward us, offering us a hug.

Sandwiched between the two of them lightened the load of my fears. My heart had been momentarily racing; it still was—beating stronger and faster than usual—when I realized it wasn't my heart at all. It was Jonas's.

He carried me into the hospital, where my mother begrudgingly cleaned my wounds and held back from giving me the third degree on my birthday.

Amy and Jonas were waiting when I walked out of the ER. They looked glum and annoyed.

"I'm sorry," I said, giving in to their shared displeasure.

"I don't know why I deal with you, Jessie Parker," came a frustrated voice from Jonas. "You've been nothing but trouble since I met you."

I surveyed this good-looking boy before me, remembering the way his heart was beating frantically against my shirt. "You were worried about me."

"Who wouldn't be worried about someone falling twenty feet out of a tree?"

"I'm not just someone, Jonas."

Amy Levy was gliding back and forth across the pine-scented linoleum floor practicing graceful ballet moves. I followed her with my eyes.

"You're right, Jessie, you're not just someone," Jonas said. "You're a little pain in the ass who thinks it's funny to shock people. It's not funny. Especially when something could happen to you. Isn't it enough I have to worry about my dad? Do I have to worry about losing you too?"

Amy was on her toes. Her arms were lifted high above her head. The sound of Jonas's voice brought her arms down by her sides.

"I'm sorry," I whispered, an attempt to shake the insensitivity out of me.

Amy had found her place beside us again, the measured stride replacing the fluid motions. Jonas's scolding had restrained both of us. Nobody dared speak as our sullen trio reached the nearest elevator.

The tree house debacle eluded me, as did the idea of owning my own personally furnished fun house. These plans were put on hiatus for now. When we reached his father's room, we were told that Adam was stabilized. I didn't know which made me happier—Adam's improvement or Jonas not wanting to lose me.

"Thank you for coming," Adam said to me, his words slow and hushed. Rachel Levy was writing the names of those who had sent flowers and gifts, Jonas and Amy were listening to a new album released by the label, and I was busy lining up the hundreds of cards from well wishers, taking my time to read the names of the famous rock stars. In my hands was a rare assortment of priceless autographs. I wondered what would become of them and how inappropriate it would be for me to ask to have a few of the signed inscriptions.

We had finished the cake and Adam had polished off a small glass of wine. The doctor assessed that it couldn't make Adam any sicker than he already was, so he toasted to his family, and to me, and we cheered.

"Why aren't you off somewhere celebrating *your* birthday?" he whispered.

"Shhh, it's your day today," I answered.

The doctor walked in and all of our heads turned in his direction. Sensing something about to happen, Mrs. Levy escorted Amy out of the room while Jonas engrossed himself in conversation with Dr. Missed Opp. I turned to Adam Levy and the words came flying out of my mouth. "He died today."

He looked at me like I had taken the wind out of his already lifeless sails. With an effort I hadn't seen in recent weeks, he took my hand in his. "So that's why you don't care about your birthday. Now I understand." He took a breath and added, "I'm not leaving just yet."

"I know," I said, and I believed those words because I never in a million years thought I could be so cursed.

"Your visits have meant a lot to me, Jessie, to all of us, for that matter. You've been the angel shining over us."

"I told you before, I'm no angel." I laughed, shrugging off his comment.

"And you and Jonas seem to be getting along nicely. I saw the two of you outside."

"Oh that, that was nothing. I was climbing the tree and lost my balance. Jonas caught me before I hit the ground."

"It looked a lot more serious than that."

"It was nothing, really."

"I saw. It wasn't nothing."

"He's okay," I said, my eyes resisting his. "He can be a bit of a nuisance at times."

"Are you talking about me again, Parker?" Jonas asked, taking a break from his conversation with the doctor.

"You obviously identify with the word *nuisance*," I called out.

Adam added, "You two are like magnets who can't get away from each other."

I turned to him. "I know what you're implying."

"I'm not implying anything. Unless you want me to."

I shook my head.

"Did you read our horoscope today?" he asked.

"Of course," I responded.

"No, this one," he said, pointing to the *New York Post* that lay strewn at the foot of his bed. I took the paper in my hand, turned to the last page, and zeroed in on *If Today Is Your Birthday*. I could have sworn it said the same thing in the *Times*, until I got to the last line. *The year ahead is one of great decision and great love. Search inside yourself, beyond wishes and dreams, for what it is you want. Only you have the answers.* That, I hadn't seen before.

"What do you think it means?" I asked.

"I think it means that a bunch of us Geminis have some soul-searching ahead of us this year." But I knew it was a sign of something that I didn't yet understand. I glanced down at my watch and took that as a sign that it was time for me to go. I kissed Adam Levy on the cheek and started to leave when I remembered. "Wait," I said, "I forgot to give you this."

I handed him the gift I had wrapped in tin foil. His weakened hands couldn't manage the paper, so I opened it for him. There were tapes, compilations of all my favorite songs. When he popped them into his boom box and heard the array of melodies I'd put together, he would then understand the part of me I wanted him to have.

When I ventured forth into my house one hour later than expected, my mother's face and her distinctive signs of being irate were predictable. Nor was I oblivious to Beth's forceful gaze—partly curious, partly agitated—for having to entertain my mother and her latest date. Others were there as well, there to celebrate my grand old sweet sixteen— Cynthia, a nurse my mother worked with who had sometimes babysat for me when I was a kid, and the Millers, this nice couple that moved in next door.

After surveying me in an accusatory manner, my mother motioned for me to go to my room and "make myself presentable," whatever that meant. I glared at the oversized man sitting beside her. Unable to ward off my stare, he turned his head away abruptly. If I had a paper plate, I would have written across the middle, "Zero."

I entered my room with a coolness and ease that had evaded me today, except for the time spent with Jonas's family. I was barely gone from them an hour and I was still going over the afternoon in my head, wishing it didn't have to end. Attempts at enjoying the rest of the day were failing, as I'd given in to the realization that maybe I didn't belong here, maybe I belonged somewhere else.

I flicked on the radio to drown out the absurdity of my thoughts. Swingout Sister was singing "Breakout" on the radio, and I sang along. I would have holed up in my room and watched *Sixteen Candles* for the seventeenth time, but I knew I was required to fulfill my birthday duties, which included eating cake and being merry.

The voices from outside my door were getting louder and louder, creeping their way into my personal space. I turned up the volume on the stereo and began rummaging for something to wear, when I saw myself in the mirror across the room. Clad in nothing but underpants and a bra, I studied my reflection. Mom said I had grown into my height that summer. I wasn't as gawky, "less like a filly," she said. My hair was the longest it had ever grown, layers of dark blonde passing my shoulders, and even my nose didn't jut out as much. Regal, I thought. Which brought the focus to my hazel eyes, speckled in green and gold. *The bra comes in very handy*, I laughed to myself. There really wasn't *anything* there to hold up, but it crossed my mind that if you wish for it, it will come. In this case, I just wanted to be prepared.

Settling on a white tank top and a long, blue skirt, I took one last look at myself in the mirror and decided that other than still being flat as a pancake, I didn't look so bad. I was tanned from the walks to the hospital, and with the white shirt against my skin, the tan seemed richer and deeper. I'd even thrown on some lipstick, something I never wore, but being sixteen now, it seemed like it was time.

My mother noticed my new look right away, and I could tell she was pleased with what she saw. I held up the watch she had bought me, wearing it proudly on my wrist. She had accomplished what she'd intended, the happy-go-lucky family complete with a man by her side. Seeing her seated there in her glory, smitten with her efforts, I felt guilty for not being able to enjoy myself. She did look happy though, happier than I'd seen her in recent years on recent birthdays. She noticed my gaze and smiled up at me from her seat on the couch beside the oversized man that resembled Paul Bunyan. She signaled for me to come join them, and it took much of my resolve not to defy her in her moment of pure bliss. I crossed the room. Then the doorbell rang.

My mother and I immediately found each other's eyes. Beth continued chattering with Cynthia. The song on the radio ended and cut to a commercial. Paul Bunyan sipped his beer, oblivious to my mother's uneasiness. Mom and I stared at our front door. I'm sure she was about to faint at the sound that had brought her to her knees twelve years before, so since I was closest to the door, I ran to it; and without asking who was there, I swung it open.

"Happy birthday, Jessie," they said in unison.

I was too amazed to speak, and the shock on my face propelled my mother across the room, no sign of any graceful flitting, until she saw who it was. "Jonas and Amy!" she called out.

"I'm glad someone's happy to see us, Mrs. Parker," said Jonas, in his smooth kiss-ass way. Ordinarily this would have rattled me, but I was happy to see him. So happy I couldn't even look at him.

"Hey, Amy," I said, welcoming them into our home that had now become even smaller than it was before.

"Why didn't you tell us it was your birthday?" she asked, stealing the question right out from Jonas's parted lips.

"Yeah, Jessie," he taunted. "Why did you keep the big birthday a secret? Being the attention seeker I know you to be, I can't believe you didn't want to bask in the spotlight."

"That's exactly why I didn't tell you, Jonas, all those stupid things that come flying out of your mouth."

"Happy birthday," he said as he swept past me, stopping only to lean in and offer a soft, delicious kiss on my cheek. "You mean stupid things like that?"

Amy joined Beth and Cynthia on the floor in front of the television, where they were watching one of my favorites, *Valley Girl.* The best part was coming up, when Nicholas Cage shows up at Deborah Foreman's door at the end of the movie.

"This is some party," Jonas exclaimed, managing to further humiliate me. "Where are all your friends?" he asked. "Is that Beth?"

I wanted to jump out in front of her so he couldn't see how beautiful she was, but he was too quick. He liked what he saw and so did she. I knew this because in an instant my best friend metamorphosized before my eyes, and the Jonas I'd known for the last however many weeks acted as if he'd never seen a girl before. After the introductions, I watched them flirt the way the boys and girls did at school, foolishly laughing in between nods of agreement. I don't think either one of them was fully comprehending what the other one was saying. People usually don't when they first meet. They're either too busy in their minds sizing each other up, or they're focusing on themselves and whether they have any likeability.

In just ten minutes, I learned more about Jonas than I had the entire time I'd known him. And you know what I mean when I say that. I *knew* Jonas, but how do I explain this, I knew him *mentally, emotionally.* It wasn't about words with us. It never had been. It didn't matter that I didn't know that he was a huge Lakers fan, because I knew things far greater and far more intimate. So, why'd it bother me that he was talking to Beth about their starting lineup and their mutual admiration for Kareem Abdul-Jabbar, and about her trip to London last summer, and how he had been planning to travel to Italy this summer—Italian food was his favorite—when his father got sick, and what a coincidence, Beth's parents just got back from Italy? I was fuming.

As if my birthday couldn't get any worse, a discouraging thought evolved, and I was starting to see that the larger-than-life *friendship* with Jonas wasn't a friendship at all. There were so many things about him I didn't know, things about him he never wanted to share with me. It felt like I had been punched in the stomach, hard.

"Why you so quiet?" he asked, finished with Beth and circling around me like a shark.

"Oh, nothing," I responded, thinking about how my best friend is flirting with this guy and I don't even *know* what he means to me, but he must mean *something* because this is really, really getting to me, not to mention that he's seven, well, now, six years older than I am and probably views me as nothing more than a prepubescent. "Nothing at all," I repeated again, willing myself to believe that with a smile.

"Sweet sixteen," he said aloud, in this acerbic tone I detested. "Does that mean in your case sweet sixteen and never been kissed?"

I glared at him, permeating such a look it didn't require any words to follow.

Then I couldn't resist, looking him squarely in the eyes. "Asshole."

"I guess I'm right about the never-been-kissed part. No one would want to kiss a mouth like that."

"Did you come here just to bother me?"

I noticed out of the corner of my eye that my mother was switching the station on the stereo. I had the inclination to run over and stop her, being fiercely protective of the radio dial; but Jonas was lurking by my side, and he was blocking my path. The short-lived attraction between him and Beth was evidently just that, and she had resumed her position in front of the TV. Maybe I'd imagined the friendliness between them, maybe I was freakishly jealous. I didn't know. I guess I'd hoped he'd disappear somewhere so I could collect my thoughts again, refocus, but instead he just stood there with this stupid shit-eating grin on his face. My mother had just turned off my favorite Bon Jovi song, and I wondered if she saw the look of fury I hurled in her direction.

"No," he answered, in response to the question I'd already forgotten I'd asked. "I'm not here to bother you, Jess, you know I'm only playing with you. You're so easy to rile up. I came here to dance with you."

"What'd you say?" I asked.

"I came here to dance with you."

"I don't dance."

"You do now," he said, reaching for my hand, while a stunned Beth watched as he dragged me toward the living room. This is what it means to be enthralled by a person who, at the same time, baffles you and requires that your guard be up at all times. I couldn't even make up resistance. Which is why I followed him into the other room, scared, yet excited. Besides, it was my birthday. Wasn't I entitled to simple acts of self-indulgence?

My mother continued to monopolize the radio with lousy choices in music, settling on a slow Elton John number as we crossed to the center of the room. Instead of the bubble gum pop that was playing seconds earlier, providing safe physical distance between us, Jonas was pulling me close.

"Are you okay?" he asked.

I nodded, knowing that my mouth would not be able to form comprehensible words.

With minimal space between us, my arms naturally and comfortably rested around his shoulders; and when I felt the touch of his hands clasp across my backside, we slowly began to move. Elton John was singing about two people in love. I figured if I could concentrate on the words to the song, it would diffuse all the dangerous impulses that were traveling from my head to my body at alarming speed. I mentioned the white tank top I was wearing, but I hadn't mentioned that the skirt I was wearing was as sheer and thin as the wind. I could feel *everything* through it; my body, unable to rebel, was warming to his touch. I had forgotten that minutes earlier I hated watching him talk with my best friend and likened him to an unpleasant part of the human anatomy. None of those things mattered when his arms were around me. It was easy to fend off suggestions and *what ifs* when we were across a table or in the same room, but to pretend that his touch didn't send screaming signals to every nerve in my body was impossible.

"What are you thinking?" I asked.

"How pretty you look tonight."

"And what else?"

"How you don't need this." And he brought his fingers to my mouth and wiped off the lipstick that I had spent hours applying.

"Why," he asked, "what are you thinking?"

I wanted to say *how soft your fingers felt against my lips and how this is sure to be the first song on the soundtrack of my life,* but I settled on, "Nothing."

"I think it feels nice," he said in a whisper so that my potentially eavesdropping mother and the Bigfoot by her side couldn't hear. "I think you do too."

His breath whipped past my neck like the whiff of a hundred kisses. It smelled like toothpaste, the yummy, minty kind. Is that what Adam Levy meant? Next time I'm at Vons smelling toothpastes, I'll be brought back to this moment?

Elton John crooned about taking his lover's hand in his. Jonas found my face and peered deeply into my eyes, while his hands heeded the words of the song and his fingers laced through mine. Something passed in those sweetest eyes I'd ever seen, a moment that I would never ever forget. All that I'd been pretending not to feel was staring me back in the face, his hands telling me what his words could not. My arms had no choice but to pull him closer, my head resting against his shoulder.

Words were hard for Jonas, at least, with me. He was always holding back something. When he gave, I'd soak him in, and when he closed off, I'd confuse myself into thinking it meant he didn't care. Tonight, he cared and when he tightened his hold around me, it didn't even bother me that Beth and Amy stopped watching the television and made no attempt to conceal their gawking at us. I think if it weren't for the fact that my mother saw this as a potentially heart-wrenching day, she might have intervened, but she didn't. Instead, she got up and danced, as did our neighbors Mel and Susan, and soon you might have thought this was an actual party; but for me, Jonas was the only guest.

"Did you say something?" he asked.

"No," but I'm sure what he heard was my heart pounding through my chest.

"Stop thinking so much," he said, interrupting the wail of my silent thoughts. "Relax and enjoy the moment."

I closed my eyes and tried. Being sixteen entitles you to few things, one, a driver's license in most states, and two, raging meddlesome hormones. The latter hit me with spellbinding force. All I wanted was for everyone around us to disappear so that when I opened my eyes again, it would just be me and Jonas and instead of his finger brushing my lips, it would be his mouth.

They were all still there. And the song dutifully came to an end as I prayed another slow number would follow, but like my previous prayer, that too went unanswered. With the song over, he stepped back, his arms and hands no longer around me, although remnants of his touch were left in secret, soulful places within. A look passed between us. He smiled. I smiled back.

"You have a great smile," he said.

"Thank you," I said, alarmed at how sappy I'd become.

The others kept dancing around us, thinking nothing odd of the attraction we had for one another. Since we were trying to figure it out ourselves and having nothing to do with all that displaced energy, we walked into the kitchen where my cake sat on a table. I looked at it with great fear, as if the numbers would scare him away, the reminders of the years between us.

"Are you cold?" he asked, noticing the trail of goose bumps down my arms. "A little," I said, confused, when only moments ago I was filled with heat. Jonas took off his sweatshirt with the Harvard logo and draped it around my shoulders. It was still warm; every hair on my arm seemed to stand at attention.

He wore a thin green T-shirt underneath. His arms were long and lean.

"Your shirt matches your eyes," I remarked, and his expression changed. As he reached for something, my mother called out from the other room, "Okay, gang, let's get the candles going…" I don't know what he was about to say, if he was about to say anything at all, but I was annoyed with the intrusion, and I think he was too.

Turning my attention to my mother, who didn't mess around when it came to candle lighting and had every year accounted for on my cake, I grinned. For all my lack of appreciation, the cake was beautiful. It had layers and layers of thick chocolate icing with pretty flowers surrounding a large candy tree. There was even a miniature figurine on one of the branches that Amy Levy took out and placed on the grass of icing below. She had everyone laughing, telling the incident of that afternoon, until we got to the part when Jonas saved me.

"Yes, I saved her."

"Yes, you did," I said, agreeing on something.

"He was like Superman," said Amy Levy, "swooping her out from under the tree."

"You hear that, Lois Lane?" he nudged me.

All the candles were lit; I closed my eyes to make my wish.

I was very careful about this particular wish. It had the promise of being different than years past.

"Come on!" they hollered, but I wouldn't let the pressure distract me from my goal. When the pictures I was searching for were there in my head, I pulled Jonas's sweater around me tighter, and released the wish into the air. All the candles blew out, except for one.

I blew again and watched as it disappeared, but the damage had already been done. I was deflated of breath, the sinking swell in me from lack of air, lack of hope. I already knew that my wish would never come true.

Sleep did not come easy. I was tired, my mind spent, my body needing to refuel. Jonas's existence was everywhere, his arms around me, his eyes before me. That my wish would not come true was only a small part of the worry that polluted my thoughts. He was looking at me, wanting me. I fumbled in the darkness for Sammy, my trusted bear, hugging him close to my body; but where he once consoled, there was a void that left me restless and unable to sleep. I tossed and turned in search of relief, my birthday long since gone by the steady accumulation of impatient hours. That's when I saw the ball of fabric that lay strewn across my floor.

Jonas had left without asking for it back, and I had casually thrown it on the floor of my room when I undressed for bed. I had forgotten it was there, caught up in the appraisal of my body in the mirror, sure I'd find some changes there, some small indication that I was now more of a woman, anything to contribute to the clamoring of sensations that cascaded down my legs.

I got up from the bed, my formidable opponent, and reached for it in the darkness. Holding it in my hands, looking it over, I couldn't resist raising it to my nose for a hint of Jonas, to smell him there on my bed. I pulled the tank top I was wearing over my head, tossed it on to the floor, and fit the sweatshirt over my shoulders. The fabric against my chest and arms did more than just warm me. Laying back on my bed, bikini underpants hugging my narrow hips, Jonas's sweatshirt was the only blanket I needed. Closing my eyes, it was easy to imagine that it was him there with me, Jonas on me, Jonas against me. It was simply a shirt, but it aroused me, teased me, fooled me into thinking he was there. I was creeping myself out a little and, at the same time, I was getting excited. This had to be the most intimate moment I had ever experienced alone.

I was feeling something.

I was feeling breathless.

I was feeling myself wanting to be touched by him, wanting more than the thin piece of cotton against my now hardened nipples. I yearned for something to extinguish the fire that was spreading between my legs. My body arched, my hips moved to a rhythm that defied me.

My hand found the dampness. *There*, I told myself, *just a touch*, feeling the slippery wetness of Jonas on my fingers. I was both ashamed and excited by my thoughts, but I didn't stop. It was my sixteenth birthday, and I fooled around with Jonas all night long.

Chapter 7

I only agreed to go to lunch with Jonas because he pressed me, practically bullying me into accompanying him.

"I didn't get you a gift..." he reasoned, "so let me take you out." I toyed with the idea of telling him that I had gotten from him a gift that I had gotten from no other boy.

When he found me in the hospital that afternoon working alongside my mother and the other nurses in emergency, he teased, "You don't look happy to be having lunch with me today."

"I'm in the ER, Jonas. Nobody's happy here."

"You two heading out?" my mother chimed in, astounding me with her lack of flitting.

I looked at him, thinking how cute he was, and then back at my mother. I was convinced they both could tell where my fingers had been.

"Is that alright?" I asked, in need of some necessary parental guidance.

"Go ahead," she said, without looking up from a chart. I untied the uniform from around my waist and followed Jonas to the parking lot.

"Where are we going?" I asked.

"Don't you worry," he said, "I have it all taken care of."

We got off the highway in Long Beach and headed toward the ocean. I was confused when we stopped in front of a marina.

"Can you swim?" he asked as he led me down a dock toward a large boat. "If not, you can wear one of these." He threw a bright orange life vest my way. I held it in my hand, still not exactly sure what was happening. When he got on the boat, shaking hands with someone who called himself captain, I was stunned.

"Come on," he said, helping me onto the vessel with a protective hand around my waist. My stomach was starting to grumble, and I wasn't sure if it was nerves or if it could have been actual hunger.

"Where are we going," I asked, "Gilligan's Island?"

"Fantasy Island," he answered with a laugh, because he didn't know I was there the night before.

I had a fleeting thought of my mother back at the hospital while I was whiling out the day on a luxury sea liner not much smaller than the Love Boat. Did she know what she had agreed to? Lunch was one thing. This wasn't a hospital buffet.

"I already cleared it with your mother, Jessie," he said, knowing instinctively where I'd gone in my head.

"You cleared it with my mother?"

"She knew I was taking you on the boat for the day. It was our secret."

"She agreed, just like that?"

"Yes, but there was one little hitch, one little catch."

"What's that?"

"I told her Amy was coming with us."

"Is she?"

"No, is that okay with you?"

He could have hung me from the ceiling and had me spit nickels out of my mouth, and it would have been okay.

"Come on, I'll show you around," he said, signaling for me to follow him.

In a matter of minutes, I could feel the engines humming below and the boat's placid movement beyond the harbor. I didn't know where we were headed. I had no idea what the day had in store for me, but I knew that I was with Jonas and wherever it was he was taking me, I'd be happy.

We walked to the bow of the boat, leaning against the rails, the wind twirling around us. It was highly improbable for me to sit for long periods of time with another person without spouting off something clever, but I deviated from tradition and relished in our shared quiet. Maybe it was the ocean, how its smooth humming danced around my ears, or maybe it was the thrill of the *morning after*, but I needed little more than the comfortable silence.

When a small island came into view, I asked, "Catalina?"

"Have you been?"

"No, only pictures," I said.

"Most people don't realize that the natives have been living on Catalina Island for thousands of years. They found silver on the west end in eighteen sixty-three."

Who could think about history right now? I was thinking about love; how much I loved being alone with Jonas, how much I loved that he'd planned something for me, how much I loved the anticipation that lay before us. All this love, by the way, was sure to kill me.

We docked on the island and the colorful postcards came to life. Catalina was a quaint and charming piece of land, with no visible similarities to its stepparent, California. A musical rhythm filled the air; merchants selling crafts and goods sprinkled the streets. Children were running and playing on the pavement, their laughter in tempo with the music. When you got higher into the hills, the trees were thick and lush.

Jonas led me to a scooter parked on the side of the road. "Hop on," he called out.

I swung my leg over, pulling myself up onto the shiny red metal.

"Hold on tight," he said, gunning the machine, leading us up a small hill that met a private road. The cobblestone street ended in front of a pair of wrought-iron gates, and a sprawling home was visible in the distance. That's where Jonas stopped.

I said, "Is that someone's house?" Sure, I'd taken star maps through Beverly Hills and peeked through security gates and over walls, but this was different. It might have been the way it was perched on the hill with the sea just behind it, or its considerable trees, or the ivy that crawled high along the French Victorian windows. It was impossible to pinpoint what made it perfect.

"You know, when I was a little kid…"

"Cause now you're such a big kid," he teased.

"When I was a little kid," I began again, this time more persuasive than before, the proximity of our bodies thrilling me. "There was a house around the corner from Beth's that looked almost like this. Every time I'd pass it on the way to her house, I'd pretend it was mine, sometimes following the walkway up to the door for a few steps. I wanted to know what it felt like to own it, to have it be mine."

Jonas didn't say anything, and I couldn't tell what he was thinking under his helmet. "Guess you never played make-believe," I said.

"You can have anything you want in life," he said, "if you want it badly enough."

"That's not always true," I said.

The mechanical whirring of the gates began, ceasing the passage of developing thoughts. The doors swung open and Jonas stepped on the gas. I hugged him closer, wanting to remember the exact detail of his body against mine.

The mansion turned out to be a charming hotel where Jonas and I would eat lunch.

"You've been to Disneyland, right? It's a Small World?"

I was ashamed to say I hadn't. Had I been, I might have known that you ride a boat through a magical kingdom where each room is a different country with its own decoration of color, costume, music, and song, very similar to the fairy tale land I was walking into now.

"How did you find this place?" I asked.

"A friend told me about it."

Each room of the restaurant was decorated in a color with a specific theme tied to the color. There was a blue room with a massive blue piano, a yellow room with a golden hammock to swing on after a long meal, a pink room with a dainty tea set for ladies who lunch, and even a red room filled with fresh roses for romantic evenings. It was like nothing I'd ever seen before, and I wasn't sure how anyone decided which of the many options to choose from. The hostess saw my confusion and said to Jonas, "There's no request on your reservation. Would you like to look around?"

"You pick," he said, "Maybe you know something we don't."

The hostess looked at us with interest. "Very well then, Mr. Levy," she spoke, without a hint of recognition as to his namesake. "Come with me."

We followed behind her, anxious to see the selection she'd choose. When we reached our destination, my mouth dropped open. She led us to the most spectacular of all the rooms we'd passed along the way. It was a corner space with floor to ceiling windows, giving the illusion of floating over the sea. Entering the brightly lit room to take a closer look, I studied the details, and something was noticeably off. "There's no color in this room."

"But there is," the hostess replied. "You'll find it."

We moved in closer, taking our seats at a wicker table with matching chairs. An overgrown mirror framed in gold rested against the solitary wall that wasn't a window, revealing the ocean in its view. I saw myself in the mirror, and Jonas saw my reflection too. There was no hiding the excitement across my face. Our eyes met and we smiled.

Everything on the table was white. The white napkins. The candles. The roses. The chairs were draped in white and the carpeting too. All of a sudden, I felt very grown up.

"White?" I looked across the table at Jonas. "White's not really a color…"

Jonas just shrugged. "Let's not debate that right now, okay?"

The presumptuous hostess left us there in amusement before returning with a white, wooden basket and a large roll of paper that was, not surprisingly, *white*. We watched as she unraveled the paper, cutting a piece large enough to occupy the space in front of us. She then laid the wicker basket beside the paper and watched our faces with a queer look of delight. The basket was brimming with hundreds of hues and colors—our very own Crayola crayons.

"You two get to create your own color," she said.

Jonas was noticeably thrown, but the fact that he wasn't getting up and trying to change rooms was a good sign. Maybe it was a woman's intuition, but the sweet old lady had picked the perfect room for two friends, not quite more, not quite less.

Like a kid in a candy store, I reached for the crayons. To sit beside a table draped in paper was all the inspiration I needed. Forget that they were the tools of a kindergartener. The crayons were a means to communicate without inhibition, to talk without being heard, to express all the delicious things I desired to say. Choosing the perfect color that would set the mood for our colorful conversation was a challenge. I searched for the exact shade of green, like his eyes, but settled on a deep brown instead. Brown was a strong, sturdy color, deep in hue, perhaps deeper in thought. Jonas watched, intrigued by the transformation in me.

"You finally look your age," he said. "The little girl happily playing with her crayons."

"I'm sixteen now, no more little girl jokes. Pick up a crayon and write me something nice." Then I started the interview I'd always dreamed about, the questions across the table I'd never been able to speak. When I peeked over at what he'd written, *me something nice*, I encouraged him to be more original.

"I'm just playing with you."

"Well, don't," I said, "just answer my questions."

And he did. Reaching for the red crayon, he wrote:

No, the waitress is not an ex-girlfriend of mine.

Yes, I take all my friends here on their sixteenth birthdays.

No, you're not a typical sixteen-year-old.

Yes, I liked our dance.

Yes, I'm happy to be here.

Thank u, u have nice eyes 2.

He was struggling with his responses, wanting to maintain the self-control that would prevent him from going deeper. He was trying to be tough, brown like me, but his words were red and impassioned.

And I like your lips, he continued, carefully drawing his rendition of red lips on the table. I lifted my crayon and drew a smiley face because I couldn't find the right word for a sentence that downright baffled me.

And you look pretty today.

It was a good thing she left the roll of paper in our possession because we had already covered the first with our thoughts, and I, for one, was ready for the interruption. By the time the second sheet hit the table, we were off.

Yes, I already said I was happy.

Harrison's my middle name, and then *yours?*

I'd written, *Pauline,* and then, *please don't laugh,* but he couldn't help himself as I cursed my mother silently under my breath. "It's not my fault that my mother's favorite group at the time was Peter, Paul and Mary."

"She couldn't have picked Mary?"

"She could have, but it was too biblical. We're not very religious."

I switched to a purple crayon, wanting to soften things up a bit, and began another thought. When the waitress was ready to take our orders, neither of us could bring ourselves to look at her. Now there were two of us playing in the sandbox.

His favorite place in the world was Hawaii; he hoped to take his wife there on their honeymoon someday. *Whomever she might be,* he added. He detested girls who cursed, put their feet up on the seats in movie theaters, and lied. He also didn't like a person with a big mouth. He wanted to be a doctor, that much I knew, but when he wrote *pathologist,* it was unexpected.

"Pathology? Why would you waste your talents there?"

"How is that a waste?" he asked, irked by the way in which I took the red crayon in my hand and vehemently crossed out the word that depicted a path different from the one I'd chosen. "What do you know about pathologists?" he asked, grabbing the crayon back from my angry grip.

"That's not really being a doctor. You're not *really* taking care of patients."

He stopped coloring the picture of a devil, clearly surprised that I knew that much about pathologists.

"I don't understand. I've watched you, I've listened to you. You talk of people with real diseases, and, yes, pathology is necessary, but you're the kind of person who needs interaction with the very same people you say you want to heal and protect. I just don't see where it fits into this whole pathology thing."

His eyes drifted out to the ocean behind us. "What?" I asked. "What's wrong?"

"Nothing."

"Tell me."

"You're nosy and opinionated. Let it go," he said, his eyes meeting mine.

"Not a chance. I can win at this game, Jonas. I always do."

He broke away, picking up the blue crayon and writing *I had a dream.* Then he added, *once.*

"So did Gypsy Rose Lee," I said, "and we all know what happened to her."

This didn't get the reaction I was expecting. Maybe he didn't know who Gypsy Rose Lee was. Putting the crayon down, he reluctantly began, "I was going to be a pediatrician."

"And?"

"It was first year and we had a gruesome experience in emergency."

"The throw-up thing again?" The words were out of my mouth before I could stop them.

"It's not a joke, Jess. I watched a four-year-old kid die right in front of me."

"I'm sorry."

"She was brought in after a terrible fall. Her face was a mess. We all knew there was no way to save her, but that didn't stop us from exhausting every option. When she died, I saw her parents' lives stripped from their faces. I don't have it in me to go through that again. Pathology is clinical. I'd be contributing to medical advances. At least that's what I'm told."

"Having seen what you saw, doesn't it inspire you to save lives?"

"I've heard all this before, I've gone over it in my mind a thousand and one times, and I hear what you're saying, but maybe this isn't one of those grandiose plans or dreams you're so infatuated with."

"'You can have anything you want in life.' Didn't you just tell me that on our way up here?"

"Fate swooped in and I had a choice to make, and I made it. Besides," he continued, "there's a lucrative business waiting for me when I graduate."

The words were upsetting. Up until this point, Jonas had been a man with courage—just like his dad—and now I was seeing this other side, this stranger creeping in. I said, "You should do what you love to do; someone wise once told me that."

His beautiful green eyes were asking me who, and when I didn't answer, he said, "Sometimes when you do something you love, the joy is great, but the pain is even greater."

I clung to that philosophy, letting the words wrap around the people and things that gave me joy. "But what if you never experience that joy? That love? What kind of life would that be?"

He was silent, his eyes taunting me with *what exactly are we talking about here?* He was searching the table for something, answers, insight, maybe my hand, but it was under the table, clasping the other one tightly.

The waitress came with our food and he turned to me. "What do you know about love?"

I took a bite of my lasagna, set the fork down, reached for the crayon, and wrote, *It stinks.*

"And what do you base that on, personal experience, or some after-school special?"

J. Giels, I wrote.

"What about you, Harvard? What's your experience with love?"

He sunk his teeth into his sandwich as I prepared myself to wipe the mustard from the corner of his mouth. "Does it matter?" The invisible door closed, a window slammed shut. He reeled me in close and then spit me out to sea.

"Yes," I said, "seeing that you know so much about it."

It's not so much what he said but what he didn't say. A red flag went off in my brain, a warning signal that permeated throughout my body and caused my senses to switch into high alert.

"You remind me so much of Amy," he said, "the way you wear your emotions for anyone to see."

"I do not," I countered, not caring about the lie. I never did have the power to hide things, at least not from him.

"It's not such a bad thing," he said, "unless you let people take advantage of it. You can get hurt that way."

"Are *you* going to hurt me?" I asked.

Never, he wrote on the table, in bright blue letters, all capitals, and then repeated the same with his eyes as he looked up from across the table. Could he possibly be preparing me for what was to come?

"You have stuff on your face again," I said, pointing a little to the left. "There," I said, as he dabbed it with a napkin. I was too afraid to touch him, afraid he might feel the electricity that was coming off my fingernails, afraid he might jump at my touch.

"It's still there," I said.

"Well, help me out."

I reached across the table, our fingers brushing as I wiped the yellow mustard off his face. "It's funny," he started, "how people come into your life. You meet them under strange circumstances, chance meetings, and all of a sudden there's this, this *thing* between you...how quickly it's determined if you'll be friends or not."

"You mean us?" I asked.

Yes, he wrote.

I wanted to say something fabulous and meaningful and sarcastic, but what? I wanted to ask him if he always bonded with young girls my age by puking on their shoes, because it was the only way I knew how to protect myself from his pursuit. If I divulged what was forming inside my throat, I would disclose too much, opening myself up to vulnerability. Could I let him have another glimpse, another peek below the surface, when he'd already seen so much?

"I like seeing you at the hospital every day," he said, pausing, waiting for me to add something. "You like seeing me too."

I asked, "How did your dad end up at Randalls Hospital when there are excellent ones in LA?"

"You're changing the subject."

"Cedars Sinai is one of the best."

"Okay, I'll indulge you," he answered. "Randalls happens to be the most innovative and comprehensive for my father's condition. Now stop changing the subject. You ignored me when I said I like seeing you."

"I was ignoring what you said after that."

"You didn't let me finish," he said.

"Finish what?"

"My thought."

"Which thought?" I asked.

"Why we ended up at Randalls…"

"You told me already. It was innovative and comprehensive."

"It was to find you."

Silence. I took the purple crayon and watched as a butterfly appeared on the one lonely spot of white on a page that told our story. Wanting more of his compliments, more of his attention, I ripped another page from the roll, moved our plates aside, and set the fresh, clean sheet on top. My heart, again, was beating at the vicious speed it always did when it was around Jonas.

I like you, he wrote on the vacant area near my plate. Just three small words, but they managed to take up the whole page.

Good, I wrote back, timid, excited, uninhibited. *I like U 2.*

No, not good, he added. Then, very slowly, he wrote, *my girlfriend.*

I recovered quickly from the blow.

I wrote, *we're only friends, right?* Did he notice my fingers were shaking when I added the smiley face?

Friends, he wrote.

The crayon became like a hot coal in my hand, so I flung it abruptly into the basket. Jonas took this time to casually finish off the rest of his sandwich. At this point, I didn't care if he got mustard up his nose and in his ears, I wasn't going to wipe it off. Remaining calm and balanced was a difficult task when the stinging of his admission was burning me up inside. Hadn't I seen that little inconspicuous red flag and failed to trust it? Weren't the signs evident? She was out there, someone beautiful and bright, and the envy, which would eventually turn into something larger and greater, incensed me.

"I know you're mad," he said, taking the last bite of his meal.

"Why would I be mad?" I asked, struggling to pick up a crayon and do something with my hands besides strangle him.

"I should've been up-front with you. It was never an issue because you and I were just friends."

"We still are."

"I know," he said, leaning forward, setting his hands on the table. It was better that he wasn't reaching for a crayon. What he was about to say needed to be said, not written on the paper. Now I knew how Demi Moore felt when she insisted Rob Lowe keep the lights on when he was dumping her, how they'd been in the dark for too long. "I like talking to you, and I liked dancing with you."

The mere mention of that dance brought an intimacy to the table that I was sure the whole restaurant could feel. I looked up from my doodle of a dog, pretending that the reference had nothing to do with Jonas.

He continued, unflappable. "I'm happy when I'm with you, this whole experience, the crayoned words. I've enjoyed it, and," he paused, hoping to lock my eyes into his, "there's something very sexy about writing you."

"You can't do this, Jonas. You can't just say things like that and pull me close and then in the same breath tell me you have a girlfriend and we're just friends."

"*You're* the one who said we were just friends."

"What did you expect me to say?" I questioned him. "How am I supposed to react when you tell me something like that?"

"I don't know. Why don't you just tell me how you feel? Forget twenty-two, forget sixteen, forget hypotheticals. Tell me what you feel."

"Does it matter?" I asked, throwing down an imaginary white flag. He knew what it meant. What did it matter what I felt when there were things more forceful than feelings between us?

"You're impossible," he said, rising to go to the bathroom, giving me five minutes to compose myself and grow up quickly.

When he returned, I asked, "What's she like?"

He took a sip of Coke. "She's nice."

"Nice? That's all you have to say?"

He thought about it for a minute, and then he began. Interestingly, once he got started, he didn't seem to want to stop.

"Her name's Emily. Emily Cohen. She's my age, and we've been close friends since the second grade. Her dad is an international banker, and he and her mom have traveled all over the world for most of Emily's life. She and her sister, Barbara, were pretty much raised by their housekeeper, Francie, and us.

"It's been Emily and me ever since I can remember. She's been like a fixture in our house growing up. I guess I've always taken care of Emily, from the very beginning." He could see how unimpressed I was with this story, pausing to see if he should go on.

"She's very pretty," he said, "different than you, cute, not as tall, serious and levelheaded…"

"I'm levelheaded."

"She's not as adventurous as you."

Big-breasted? I wanted to ask.

"Why hasn't she been to the hospital? Where's she been all summer?"

"She met her parents in Italy. We were supposed to go together."

"But instead you traveled all the way to the Valley to meet a fifteen-year-old."

"Yeah, I guess I did. Except now she's sixteen."

"What a difference a day makes. Is she smart?' I asked, thinking that was the one thing I might have over her.

"Let's just say that she finished first in our med school class, but we were neck and neck for a while."

"Oh," I said, deflated, "I didn't realize she was there with you."

"Yeah, we're both doing our pathology rotation."

I mumbled, "The friend who lured you from your dream," but he didn't hear me because he was busy explaining how he was going to work for her family's pathology lab—one of the most prestigious in Boston. *BrinkerHarte*, I heard him call it.

"That sounds really great," I said, hating Emily Cohen for keeping that last candle on my cake lit. "It must be nice to have everything so mapped out for you; no need to worry about any unforeseen obstacles."

He eyed me with what I now understood to be the *suspicious brow.* "I've always been very methodical, and I can deal with unforeseen obstacles."

"Qualities you'll put to good use when you're laboring over your research."

"Emily's uncle is one of the leading pathologists in the country," he lamented.

"You don't look like the type that gets swayed by other people's choices."

"I'm not being swayed. I want to do this. I'll be good at it, and I stand to make a lot of money."

"Do they even know you had a plan of your own?"

"It's important for the two of us to do this."

"Why?"

"It just is," he said, "I'm really all she's got."

"So you'll set aside your dreams to sit in a stuffy path lab to please your girlfriend and her family?"

He gave me a sheepish smile. "It's adorable that you care."

"I don't care at all," I snapped, moving away from the table and the close proximity of his charm. "I'm actually disappointed in you. You'll never be happy. Finding that place inside where you can sit comfortably in your skin is worth more than all that other stuff."

"You're going way deep on me," he said, studying my face, caught up by the depth of my emotions.

Then he wrote, *I like when you get all hotheaded.* On its own, this sentence would have had a profound effect on me, but when compounded with his spoken words, "That's something that nags at me and leaves me open to regret, not the regret of being a pathologist," I realized just how many levels were at work in our conversation.

"Besides," he continued, "your definition of happiness might be different from somebody else's." This wasn't what I wanted to hear. I wanted to forget ideology and have him write more insatiable things to me on the table, but he didn't. My words had reached a place in him that was tightly guarded. We were different people from different worlds. I couldn't expect him to understand the fragility of life and how something you love can be snatched away from you. I thought that his father's prevailing illness would have sensitized him to this, but maybe it was having the opposite effect. Maybe it was too much to bear, knowing that he was in the process of losing someone he loved.

"My father's dead, Jonas."

He moved around in his chair, both nervous and surprised, and then leaned forward with his head very close to mine.

"I'm sorry, Jess, I didn't know that. You never said anything."

"I know, I didn't want to, but you need to hear this now. When he died, it was an ordinary day like today. We woke up, we got dressed, we went about our business, with the exception of the special plans we had for dinner that evening, and everything was normal or appeared normal. We didn't know that this was the day our lives would be changed forever. We didn't know we would never see him again. And I know what you're thinking right now, and I *agree* with you—we can't live in fear of the unknown. But things *do* happen, and lives get turned upside down, and knowing that, don't you think life is just too precious to waste on something that doesn't make you happy?"

My disclosure rattled him. The otherwise smooth and confident Jonas appeared conflicted, torn, and dejected.

"I want to talk to you about your dad," he said. "It's important to you, but first I want to say something." Leaning back in his chair, he began again. "Everything you're saying makes sense. I can't dispute you're a bright girl—albeit a little outspoken at times—and you're aware of things on a deeper level than most; but I'm surprised with all your talk about happiness, you haven't taken a good look in the mirror. I hear it in your tone, in your comical sarcasm, the way you hide behind an insulated shell, pretending not to be interested when I know you're feeling things, things you don't even want to see yourself. What are you so afraid of?"

"I'm not afraid of anything," I said, meeting his powerful gaze. "Certainly not you or whatever it is you're implying."

"You should be afraid," he responded with a laugh while I glared back at him. Then he stuck his tongue out at me.

"You're really an ass," I spat out, exhaling, not caring that I cursed.

"Then why can't you look away?" he asked.

My face told him I didn't know how, that I was no longer immune to his cynicism. I could already hear the faint sound of the bell dinging in his favor.

"Tell me about your father," he said, freeing me from the urge to explode.

"There's not a whole lot to tell. He died twelve years ago yesterday, as a matter of fact."

"On your birthday?"

"You're quick."

"What happened?"

I looked up at him. He genuinely seemed to care. If we were going to be friends, real friends, I would have talked this through with him, but it was a place and a part of me I couldn't share. Just like the place and the part he couldn't share with me.

I wrote, *Can we change the subject, please?*

He had to know how serious I was, or he would have never obliged. We took the things we wrote on paper very seriously.

"Next time," he said, and then he got up from the table, so I did the same. When I took a step, I felt my foot buckle, losing my balance. His arm reached out for me, resting across the small of my back, intercepting my fall.

"I'm okay," I said, releasing myself from his grip and finding my footing, but I wasn't okay at all. And he knew it too. That's why his arm found me again, leading me out of the restaurant and toward the scooter.

I was sorry to see the magic restaurant disappear behind us. I would have liked to have saved the tablecloth, but I didn't want Jonas to know how much it meant to me.

The ride down the hill was a quick one. There was a warm breeze circulating around us, and I used the opportunity to hold him closer. When we boarded the boat, we sat on the deck and watched as Catalina became nothing more than a speck of sand in the distance. He turned to observe me every so often, proud to see that I'd been impressed with our little sojourn. I had worn the wide-eyed expression of disbelief across my face, but now it was faded, having seen things and learned things that could never be taken back.

"I think I finally got inside your head today," he said. "I think I know where you go when you're lost in your thoughts."

"Where's that?" I challenged him.

"Somewhere sad. And probably lonely."

I thought about this for a second, knowing that had our paths crossed at another time in our lives, we could have gone places together. The rest of the trip to shore was in silence, except for the purring of the engines and the sounds of the waves caressing the sides of the boat. I studied the view in front of me, knowing that when I reached land and took a step back on the ground, it was going to feel different.

Aware of his stare and how the pressure of serious thought made him look wistful, I asked, "What's wrong?" while twirling my hair in my fingers, something I did when I knew something big was about to happen.

"I was just thinking," he said, in a voice I'd never heard before.

"Me too," I said.

Thinking how nice it would be to stay on Catalina forever.

Chapter 8

"He's not here," Adam Levy's gravelly voice told me when I entered his room. "He's home sick with the flu."

"I came to see you," I lied.

"Maybe you should bring him some soup."

"Isn't that what girlfriends are for?" I asked.

Adam eyed me. He reached for a pen and paper and began writing. "Don't be a brat. Here's the address. He'll be happy to see you." Grabbing the piece of paper from his hand, I shoved it in my pocket and walked out of the room. My better judgment kept telling me to go home, but I'd never been one to listen to the echoes that sabotaged my rational thought. Instead, I picked up the phone, dialed the nurse's station three floors below, and called in sick for my shift.

I borrowed my mother's car at the hospital, planning to return it before she noticed its absence. Yes, I'd passed my driver's test, to everyone's surprise, including my own. Much to the chagrin of the other drivers on the Pacific Coast Highway, my foot was frozen on thirty-five mph the entire way to Malibu, afraid to venture any faster for fear of losing control over the massive machinery.

That wasn't the only thing that was massive. The house in front of me was even bigger than the hotel on Catalina. A security guard opened the gate, and I followed the road up to Jonas's front door. When I got out of the car, Mrs. Levy was leaving.

She said, "Jessica, how nice of you to come," in a tone that implied a whole assortment of conflicted thoughts about seeing me there. I wanted to blurt out, *He's just my friend*, but she would never believe it, knowing full well that a mother knew things when it came to her kids.

"He might be sleeping still," she said. "Amy should be back from ballet in about an hour. Maybe you can make sure he eats something."

"Sure, Mrs. Levy," I said, glad for her trust in me. "I'll get him whatever he needs."

"Gloria will show you to his room," she said, stepping into her tiny car. "I'm heading to Adam."

The sweet Spanish lady did just that, walked me up about thirty stairs and then down several hallways until Jonas's room came into view. "Gracias," I said to her as we entered the room.

"¿Tú hablas español?" she asked.

I wanted to say that everybody knows how to say thank you in Spanish, but settled on, "Oh, no, no," I repeated, "no habla español." She was disappointed. I could tell.

"Oh, okay señora, entonces adiós. Si me necesitas, por favor, llamame. Yo voy abajo."

"Okay. Adios, Gloria," I called back to her, talking in this voice much louder than my own.

Since Jonas was asleep, I took the time to survey the room and the artifacts that shaped his life. When the stale, germy air reached my nostrils, I walked over to a window and let in a fresh breeze. Jonas was right there, peacefully asleep on his big boy bed with mountains of pillows piled around him. His heavy breathing filled the room, his lips slightly apart, hair splayed across the pillow in a tousled mess. Taking a seat on the white sheets, I reached over him, smoothing the matted hair away from his face. Being this close to him, on his bed, making sure everything about him was in place, I'd almost forgotten how confused I was. I only thought of crawling under the covers and curling up around him.

He was smiling at something, so I smiled along with him. Was it possible he was reading my mind again, knowing the dirty secrets that lived there? My eyes grazed the space beside the bed when the picture on the desk caught my eye. Of course it did. She was really pretty, just like he said. The picture was small, in a simple little frame that she probably gave to him, but there was no mistaking the way she could let herself be known.

Staring at the picture of Emily Cohen forced me to evaluate why I was there. I knew there was a side to my friendship with Jonas that was just that—friendship—but I also knew that his overt display of come-hither when he puked on my shoe had to be indicative of something powerful, even if this impulse and desire lurked only in his deep unconscious. *Put that in your pipe and smoke it*, I whispered to the fine Emily Cohen.

Jonas's eyes fluttered before me, and I panicked that he had heard me. He rolled over and yelled into the pillow, *"Gloria? Hay quiero agua."* And then, *"Por favor."*

"No habla español," I said.

It only took him a few seconds to raise himself up, turn in my direction, and see that I wasn't Gloria.

"No hablo," he corrected me, *"mi reina."*

"Mi what?" I asked. "Is that some profane name in Spanish?"

"Wouldn't you like to know," he laughed, yawning, then stretching his taut body across the rumpled sheets. Gloria walked in with a fresh glass of water. When she left, I said, "I thought I was the kid here."

"You said it, I didn't, and no, it's not a profanity, it means, my queen." He said this, his voice deeper than I'd remembered it being. *Breathe*, I told myself, noticing his smell all around me, his sweat pervading the air. I inhaled.

"I feel like shit," he said, reaching for the cold liquid while I stole glances at his bare chest.

"At least you don't smell like it," I laughed, not able to help myself. "And you don't look like it either." Then, realizing I needed to be polite, I asked, "Have you eaten? Is there something I can get you?"

"My very own private nurse. I can get used to this." He touched my leg and I jumped, the move surprising me. "I don't need anything," he said, "Just stay here and talk to me."

I sat, very much aware of the proximity of our bodies. "I just saw your mom. I think she's wondering what I'm doing here."

"Jess," he said, "sometimes I wish you'd come right out and say the things you want to say."

"I can't do that."

"You're here because you're my friend, and in case you're wondering about that, I'm glad you're here, and lastly, I don't care what my mother thinks or anyone else for that matter. I know what I know and everything else is just speculation."

Silence fell between us while we retreated to our corners, he, blowing his nose, and me, reading into his words, scrutinizing each and every one until their collaborative effort resembled logic. "You were right about her," I said, nodding toward the picture beside his bed. "She's very pretty."

"Em?" he asked, the name slicing through the air like a butcher knife. It was the endearing way he said it; I had to change the subject.

"You must be hungry. Are you sure you don't want me to call down for Gloria?"

"I'm fine. You're nervous. Relax."

"I can't," I admitted.

"You missed seeing me."

I couldn't pretend I didn't know what he was talking about.

"I missed you too," he said.

Even with Emily Cohen's eyes staring me down, when I was alone with Jonas, there was just the two of us. Her name was the only intrusion. "How much longer?"

"These things usually last a few days, but I won't be going to the hospital for about a week. My dad's very susceptible, and it's best I stay away. I hope I don't get you sick, even if you'd make a cute patient."

I laughed. "The very worst."

"I find that hard to believe, Miss Parker. Thus far, you've been pretty good at everything—dance partner, eloquent prose, CIA operative, tree climber—and you've even managed to make me feel better just by looking at you. Besides, if you were my patient, I'd take real good care of you."

Jonas was saying too many nice things at once for me to look him in the eye, so I focused my attention on the view from the window instead. My eyes trained on the scenery while my fingers nervously fumbled, clasping and unclasping.

"Jess, I can't change this," he said. "She's real."

"I know," I said, finding the courage to meet his eyes.

"But so are you. To me, you're very real."

The suggestion that hovered around us was palpable. "I want you in my life. You need to know that. It's wrong, on so many levels, but I know what being around you makes me feel and I can't pretend it doesn't."

Stop, I was repeating, over and over in my head, but he didn't hear. I turned back to the window and began to count the leaves on the tree thinking that the repetition would relieve me from his words. *Eighteen, nineteen, twenty, twenty-one,* but he kept on going.

"You're always talking about life and how nothing is by chance, and there's no such thing as a coincidence, so I know you understand what I'm saying and I know you agree." I wouldn't turn around. "Jess, do you hear me?"

"Yes," I whispered. "And I think you drank too much cold medicine."

He grabbed my arm and forced me to face him. "I like being around you. I like teasing you. I like arguing with you."

My eyes pleaded with him to stop.

"I like seeing your face when you're glad to see me and how you turn away so you think I won't notice, and the way you squirm and fidget and twirl your hair when you're nervous." His fingers were searing through my flesh, much like his words. "I like watching you when you think nobody is, and the way you lick your top lip, and sometimes you bite on it too. See, you're doing it right now. In a way, it's like you're already mine, like you've always been."

How could I hate him when his words brought the steadiness of counting numbers to a screeching halt? They were words, I swear, but they could have very well been his hands, touching me all over. I didn't understand what was happening. There was so much we were feeling for each other, yet so much that was holding us back, and Jonas's obligation to Emily was only part of it. Let's be real here, he and I were from different worlds, and what kind of boyfriend could he be to a high school senior?

I said, "The scary thing is that I do understand. I know all about the lines we can't cross over. Things like feelings are harder to hold back."

"Remember that day I took you driving?" he asked.

"What does that have to do with anything?"

"I don't remember what street we were on. I don't even know if it was sunny or raining. I just remember you next to me, and I was responsible for you, and I liked it. A lot."

I began to feel afraid, the way he once said I should be. He would never hurt me, not in the physical sense. It was emotional vulnerability I was worried about. Beth once told me that power was the ultimate aphrodisiac. The idea of Jonas in charge excited me. "It's getting late," I said. "You need some rest."

"Don't leave," he said, "I don't want to be alone."

"Someone like you will never be alone," I answered.

"You're wrong, *mi reina*, and I'll tell you why. I met a girl this summer. She's beautiful, she's smart, kind, funny, and highly fanatical about her causes." Then, turning seriously to me, he added, "And this girl, she got to me," pointing to his chest, "in here, and you don't know how alone I feel when she's not around."

A knife was no longer the suitable weapon to slice the quiet in the room. A chainsaw would have been needed.

"How was that for going deep?" he asked, his success visible across his face. "Too much?"

Yes, I thought to myself, *No,* I changed my mind even quicker. It's one thing to hear those things and another to believe them. "Do you hear yourself?" I asked, needing to avert the attention he threw my way. "Does your brain have any control over your mouth?"

"I know exactly what I'm saying, Jess."

"Tourette's, that's it. Do you have Tourette's?"

"Not that I'm aware of."

"But it's wrong," I found myself stammering, the dam in my throat riddled with tiny holes. I had to get off the bed, had to be away from him, both the beautiful words he spoke to me and the horribleness of his germs. I was shaking my head back and forth, combating the idea that maybe Jonas cared. "You can't say these things to me and expect me to be unchanged by them. My mind can wrap around those words, but the rest of me can't. They're not mine to have." I got up from the bed so he wouldn't have to see the anguish on my face. There were some tissues strewn across the wood floor that I thought about picking up, but something else caught my eye. I bent down, picking up the shiny metal coin in my fingers, and laughed a boisterous laugh.

"It's not easy keeping up with your multiple personalities," he said.

"Fool's gold," I answered, holding up the sparkly coin.

Beth and I had sneaked into her brother's room one boring afternoon and read through all his love letters. John was eighteen and the type of guy that all the girls were in love with. There were piles of them. We were eleven then, maybe twelve, but it didn't stop me from stealing one of the letters. I just folded it up when Beth wasn't looking and stuck it in my pocket. I know it sounds awful, but there were so many of them, I didn't think he'd ever notice.

Jonas was waiting for me to share my revelation.

"You wouldn't understand," I answered, knowing that the tale of the miner in the unsigned letter would explain almost everything. I studied the coin closely. "Is this real gold?"

"I don't know. I think it's one of Gloria's kids. They're always playing treasure hunt, and besides, what does it have to do with what we're talking about?"

I placed it on the dresser, right beside the picture of Emily.

"There was this story I once read about miners and gold."

I'd oftentimes thought about what happened to the girl who wrote the letter. She was crazy about John, that much I knew, but I couldn't tell if the story was hers, or, like me, something she'd stolen. All these years later, and I guess it really doesn't matter if the story's the same.

"Miners and gold?" he asked. "Now you've lost me. Are you purposely trying to change the subject again? Did you hear anything I said before?"

I nodded. "I heard everything." But I was thinking about the letter. She had written to John how she loved him, that their story reminded her of the miner who set out in search of gold with his pan. After months, possibly years, of searching, the miner had found it flowing through a narrow stream; but when he crossed the stream to get closer to the valuable treasure, the pan fell from his hands and tumbled down the mountain, leaving the man with nothing but his hands to contain the gold.

I could still read the words on the lavender piece of paper, that John was like the gold sifting through her fingers. And although the miner hadn't wanted to be greedy—a few pieces of the precious metal were better than nothing—he still mourned for his loss and what might never be his.

It hurt just to look at Jonas. Like the miner's story, I could only have a part of him, a tiny nugget, and how was I going to accept these terms without losing myself, without being true to me? It was there, the limitedness of what Jonas could give me, being handed to me in my greedy little hands, his eyes, his words. I could have siphoned them in and tried to ignore the obvious truths, but how could I?

I searched his face for the answers, willing him to see my thoughts. "I don't know if that's enough, Jonas. I want more."

He was stuck somewhere in his head, my need swelling up around him.

"I don't think it's possible to give you anymore. I've already given you things I shouldn't."

Rochelle B. Weinstein

I fought the urge to console him, but then our eyes would meet, and the guilt he tried to hide would stare back at me, echoing my sadness, and I'd forgive myself, forgive him.

He reached for me, his bare arms drawing me close. "Can't this be enough?"

My gaze found the gold coin on his dresser. He said it again. "Can't this be enough for you?" And my heart could no longer fight the reasoning of my brain. I squeezed my eyes shut and let Jonas's arms find me.

Swallowing had become an entirely new experience; a response would be impossible to prepare. When I didn't answer, he backed away, seeking refuge beneath the sheets. The moment had passed, but as I found my voice again, it whispered, "You need your rest," and I got up from the bed. Before walking out the door, I turned to him and said, "Please get better." And I said it because it was all I could say without saying too much, and I said it because the idea of not seeing him for another day was intolerable.

I got in the car, making my heroic escape, and tried not to stall out in case he was watching through the window. I refused to turn on the music, knowing that Elton was in the cassette player and the combination right now would be lethal.

Thinking back to when Jonas and I first met, those first few days of innocent conversation, neither of us had any idea we'd be on the cusp of something larger than both of us. We didn't go searching for it. It found us. And now that it was here, what were we supposed to do with it?

I didn't see the road in front of me. I saw Jonas's face, the question in his eyes.

I whispered, "Yes." Then I repeated it again and again, nodding my head as if the word alone was not enough.

"This will be enough," I said out loud. "This will have to be enough."

Chapter 9

"He has a girlfriend. Do you know what they call people like you?" my mother said to me when she walked in the door that afternoon. "Not to mention the fact that you're sixteen and he's, what, twenty-one?"

"Twenty-two," I mumbled from the couch, legs propped up in the air along the cushions.

"That's statutory rape in California," she remarked.

"If we ever touched, it might be that. Does exchanging bodily fluids count?"

She didn't think I was funny. "Where did you go in my car?"

My legs now fell across the couch. "How'd you know?" I asked.

"You didn't show up for work today and you left this on the seat."

The sweatshirt I had taken to wrapping around my waist every day, I had forgotten in her car. She flung it at me, covering my face with the word *University*.

"It's not what you think," I said to her, tossing the hoodie aside. "He's sick. I went to see how he's doing."

She pulled a chair next to me where I had minutes before been watching an episode of Mason Capwell and Julia Wainright going at it on *Santa Barbara*, my now-favorite soap opera. "You know that he and the long-term girlfriend are planning to work together in Boston after they graduate," she said, her head bobbing in front of the television in such a way I had no choice but to zap my favorite characters off the screen with a touch of the remote. "Where do you fit into the pretty picture?"

"I guess there were exceptions, minor details that everyone overlooked."

"Yes, and what would those be?" she asked, rubbing her tired eyes as if she could wipe out what was happening inside of her daughter.

"Me," I said with a half smile.

She took a minute to filter through my sarcasm.

"Why are you doing this to yourself?" she asked.

I don't think I knew what I was about to say until the words were out of my mouth, part of my speaking-before-thinking problem.

"I've never felt this way before."

My mother sighed the sigh of a woman who wasn't prepared for this conversation for another five years. "You've always been special, you know that, Jess."

I wasn't sure what she meant.

"You've always been this strong, courageous girl, so independent, so mysterious. People have always been drawn to you. People have always liked you. Even if you never let them close. I've seen it, I've watched. There will be a hundred Jonases before it's your turn to settle down. I promise."

"One love was enough for you," I said. "Hasn't your track record proven that?" It was mean and hurtful, but in my need to defend myself, I was unwilling to accept the person she described. And she, being used to my remarks, ignored the slam, letting it float through the air and land against the wall beside us. I think I even heard it thud.

"Mom, I know I have nothing to compare it to, and I'm young, and there's the age difference, but I can't change what's inside. I can't just make this thing between us disappear or pretend that it's not there."

She stared at me, not trusting a word I said. So I tried again. "There's an energy that runs between us; Jonas feels it too. When we're apart in a crowded room, I can feel him there next to me. When I will him to be near, he walks through the hospital doors as if he heard my thoughts. When I look into his eyes, I know that he can read my mind and heart, and see things there that no one else can. It's like the moon and the earth. They don't touch, but they rely upon each other's presence. Just knowing he's somewhere, I'm less afraid, less alone."

"You've isolated yourself," she said.

"Let me finish, please." I was really on a roll here. Dr. Norton would have been impressed.

"I've thought about this, believe me, I have. Jonas isn't some cocky, thick-headed guy who plays on the high school football team and taunts the cheerleaders. He's always respected me and been honest, and I made the decision that I'll have to accept what he can give—whatever that may be."

"You're shortchanging yourself."

"Maybe I am," I said, the hypocrisy growing by the minute, "but if we're just friends, I won't get hurt."

"You're smarter than that, Jess. That's just semantics and you know it. *You're the Earth and he's the moon,* that's not friendship to me, nor is it to you. Call it what you want. Just because you haven't fooled around or kissed doesn't mean that what's happening between the two of you is right. Feelings are as real as actions, and their consequences can be just as dangerous. He's not single, and let's not forget that he's a lot older than you and goes to school thousands of miles away. There are more things wrong about this relationship and friendship than are right. It's hard to see it when you're standing in the picture, and Jonas Levy seems to be a nice person, but he's not for you, Jess. You deserve a lot more than he can give you."

Holding onto the term "friendship" made the evolution of whatever we became much easier. Jonas could justify the relationship without guilt, and I could conceal my disappointment through a foolish understanding of his limitations. "I'll never give up on Jonas," I said. "If friendship is all we'll ever have, I'll take it." Beth always said to be strong in your conviction and no one would ever doubt you. If I could verbalize conviction, maybe it would leak into my brain and other parts of me.

"I think you're scared to let anyone close, so you've accepted this as a way to protect yourself from getting hurt. I bet if Jonas gave you everything, you'd run the other direction."

I mulled over her words. I would never believe this ridiculous notion of my mother's. Jonas was in my heart. I felt him there every time I took a breath.

But my resistance was weakening. I was on the verge of attack when I remembered what Dr. Norton told me when I got in trouble for mouthing off to one of the kids at school. She said that when we argue with people, sometimes we get so stuck in our own heads, we can't be objective in our responses. She recommended that I take a deep breath and consider where the other person was coming from, what baggage he carries around with him. I looked at my beautiful mother and considered where she'd been.

"Mom," I said, "You didn't hear anything I said, did you? He could be on one end of the world, and I could be on the other, and we could have other people in our lives, but we'd still be connected. Do you understand that? *We'd still be a part of each other.* The bond is real. No words can change or minimize it. Call it anything you want and call me anything you want, and tell me how I'll act under certain circumstances and how I'm motivated by defense mechanisms, but none of it, none of it, is going to change what's real to me. None of it's going to change the way I feel about Jonas."

"You really need to cut out some of the television watching," she said. "I would love to be able to believe everything you're saying, and I want it all to be true for you, but age and experience have given me insights into things I just don't think you're able to grasp."

She took my hands into hers, and I noticed for the first time, we had the same hands, hands I'd always been able to count on for strength. "You speak like such a grown-up sometimes, but you're not. You barely know yourself. How can you be so sure of someone else? You deserve the same level of respect you give Jonas. I want that for you. You know that, don't you?"

A tear was forming in my mother's eye, and I think we were having our first *moment* together. I nodded my head, knowing she wanted the best for me, truly.

"I want you to have it all," she continued. "The crumbs and morsels he's giving you won't ever satisfy you. You're a beautiful, young girl turning into a beautiful, passionate woman. You'll have needs and desires, both physical and emotional, to be fulfilled. And about us settling, how we settled when Daddy died, it's entirely different. We had no choice. But you have a choice, and I can't help thinking that the wrong decision will leave you brokenhearted. There's someone out there for you who will give you everything, no sharing him with another. You'll fill up his life, not just part of it, and he won't need anyone else, because you'll be everything he wants."

I didn't think about what my mother said until I crawled into bed that night, and the sounds of her voice vocalized what my heart had been ignoring for weeks…*bread crumbs, selfish, uncompromising*. I was grossly misguided and I knew it, but I'd made the decision to turn a cheek and accept terms that would in no way satisfy me. It never occurred to me to ask Jonas why we couldn't be more. It never occurred to me to question the fact that he didn't choose me or what I might have been lacking. In some bizarre, distorted way, his devotion to Emily impressed me; here was this guy with morals and unwavering loyalty.

My science textbook was laying next to the bed. Flipping through the pages, I read aloud, *"Earth, which is our base from which we look into space, is constantly moving. The moon is the earth's only natural satellite. Its revolution period around the earth is the same length and direction as its rotation period, which results in the moon always keeping one side turned toward the earth and the other side turned away from the earth. This type of motion is called synchronous rotation. The side turned away from the earth is called the moon's dark side."*

I knew what I felt, and now scientific evidence supported it. I had no idea I was such a genius, coming up with the perfect metaphor for our love.

"Synchronous rotation," I repeated aloud.

That was me and Jonas.

Chapter 10

The things Jonas taught me those first few weeks were far more significant than anything I'd learned in school, books, or movies. I'd tackled all of those with ease, and still nothing prepared me for the splattering of emotions he left me to sort out. I'd never known that feelings alone could be so strong-minded; that like a planted seed, they can take root and grow, leaving you unprotected. Or that emotions were as equally consequential as the physical acts of touching and being touched. *If a tree falls in the forest and nobody hears it, does it actually make a sound?* If Jonas and I feel like this and nobody sees it, does that mean that our love doesn't exist?

Sometimes, when Jonas and I would be eating lunch in the cafeteria, our fingers would brush across the table. When we'd be sitting with his dad, close and confined in the narrow room, I'd feel his breath on my face, a shoulder rubbing up against me, and I'd shudder to think what it would be like if he didn't stop, if he didn't pull away. It would be perfect. I just knew it. He'd take my face into his big, strong hands, and we'd be staring at each other, knowing what was about to happen, and I'd say, "No, we can't do this," of course, not meaning any of it, and he'd say, "Yes, we can. I've been wanting to do this since the day I met you," and he'd pull me toward him, and his lips would touch mine, and his arms would draw me close, and I would give in to him, right there, with his tongue delicately probing the inside of my mouth.

And that's when I would wake up, because according to my mother, the dream was always much better than the reality. "Just like those movies you watch all day," she would say. "It's never like that in real life."

Well, I was determined to prove her wrong. I wanted the dream. I wanted the fairy tale. And if it existed in varying degrees, I had mine, albeit minus the white horse and a castle for Jonas to climb through the window and take me away.

Despite this realization, my summer surpassed all others before. Jonas filled my days and nights to where I needed nothing else; and with Emily frolicking around Italy, only the intermittent phone calls sent tiny cracks into our fragile exterior. On my days off, we would drive to the mountains with the wind on our faces, hair blowing in the breeze, and Bruce Springsteen crooning "Jungleland" on the radio. There were afternoons at the beach, swimming and sailing, when I clung to him for dear life after our boat capsized. Then we would go horseback riding in the hills by his house where he taught me to mount, trot, and gallop. His natural skill and unwavering patience made him an outstanding teacher. I, on the other hand, wanted to throttle my horse after five minutes on his back when all he wanted to do was fertilize the first mile of our trail. Sometimes we would picnic on the beach, watching the people, putting our detective skills to work, and then stretching our bodies along the sand, tanning ourselves. We'd go to the movies and instinctively I'd put my feet on the seat in front of me and Jonas would remind me, "You need to be a lady and take your feet down," but I'd always forget, and he'd spend the whole two hours kicking me, something I probably did just to get him to touch me.

Jonas's brain was an encyclopedia of information. He talked about history, he loved to predict weather, and he was obsessed with the fluctuations of the stock market. Whatever the subject, he was well-versed on the most relevant—and irrelevant—components. Take his obsession with presidential trivia. "Did you know that the Baby Ruth candy bar was named for Ruth Cleveland, President Grover Cleveland's daughter, who died in her teens? Most people think it was named after Babe Ruth."

Sometimes his mind astonished me in its ability to hold such a wide breadth of information. I couldn't help but feel a tinge of envy at the life he had and the people he would share it with in the future. I thought that if I could just remember every word, every detail of our time together, I would never be without him, he'd never be without me.

I knew in those afternoons that our time was limited. Emily would be returning from Italy, and he was scheduled to return to Boston in the fall, or upon his father's death, whichever came first. I selfishly prayed that Adam would hold on a long, long time.

Chapter 11

The phone was ringing when I stepped into the house. I ran into my room, reaching for the shrilling sound that bellowed from my bedside table. I knew instinctively who it was, picking up the receiver and saying, "You're going to get me punished calling this late."

"That never seemed to bother you before."

"Well, lucky my mom's not here. She's at Harold's."

"Paul Bunyan? Are things getting serious? Maybe I should come over."

"Very funny," I laughed, thinking there wasn't anything funny about that.

"Did you catch the bouquet?" he asked. I had gone to a wedding for one of the nurses at the hospital.

"I hid in the bathroom when she threw it. What a chauvinistic ritual, like we're all so desperate to get married. I'm *never* getting married."

"Never say never," he warned. "You'll have your choice of men."

I held the phone in one hand, his attempt at sweet talk muffled by the sound of the dress I was taking off. If he could see through the wire, he would see my nakedness, but I held onto the illicit thought and opted instead for a tumble on my bed, wrapping the crisp sheets around me, along with my little seductive secret.

"Did you dance with anyone?" he asked, trying to act nonchalant.

"You know I don't dance."

"I have firsthand experience that tells me you're lying."

"It's none of your business," I said, flattered at first, but hearing an intonation that bordered on territorial.

"No one's a better partner than I am."

Something inside of me was pleased and bothered by him saying this, but before I could analyze why, "Is that what all the girls tell you?" slipped right out my mouth.

"There's only one," he said, and before he could take it back, there was a deafening silence.

"Are you in bed yet?" he asked, ignoring the quiet.

"Maybe," I said.

"Let me talk to George. He'll tell me."

"He's not here. I gave him to one of the kids at the hospital," I lied, fingering the head of the baby monkey he had won for me at the Santa Monica pier.

"Give him a hug from me," he said, and then, "What's the matter, Jessie? You don't sound like yourself."

Unable to contain my agitation, I said, "What do you want? Why are you calling this late?"

"I was thinking about you."

Silence.

"Jess, are you there? What's the matter?"

I didn't know. All I knew was that I was majorly pissed off, and I got up from the bed, found my shirt and underpants in a drawer, and put them on.

"I'm just tired," I said, knowing I could never tell him just how much it ate at me, the longing to be everything to him.

"Well, then, Grace should get some rest."

"Who's Grace?"

"You, princess."

"I'm not a princess," I said, annoyed he would even suggest that, annoyed at myself for pushing him to want to hang up.

"You need sleep. You're very cranky."

"Good night," I whispered, and before I put the phone down, he said, "Let's go to Laguna tomorrow. I'll teach you to surf."

The boy had no clue, just oblivious.

"Good night, Jonas," I repeated.

"Good night, Grace, I'll see you in my dreams."

We ended up spending the entire next day together. It began with breakfast at Jerry's Deli (his idea), lunch overlooking the pool at the Beverly Hills Hotel (my idea to sneak in), and dinner in Santa Monica at I Cugini (a mutual agreement). In between, we walked along Melrose Avenue, where I bought a denim skirt and he picked out a pair of jeans. After, we stopped for some frozen yogurt at Humphrey's, and then paid a visit to Sharper Image, where he watched me test out most of the equipment while he stood back in horror, pretending not to know me. It ended with a beautiful view of the sunset along the coast.

We hadn't planned to do all that; the day just took hold of us, and we didn't resist it. On the drive home, we were talking about things we were afraid of.

"My biggest fear is to look out my window at night and see someone staring back at me."

"That's creepy," he said. "I'm afraid I'll screw up on some major important research."

"I'm afraid of driving." We both laughed.

There was a quiet pause before he said, "I'm afraid my father won't make it much longer."

"I'm afraid of that too," I said. "You know what else I'm kind of afraid of?"

"And here I thought you weren't afraid of anything."

I turned to face him, because before this thought I'd been watching the road ahead of us. "I'm afraid to say good-bye."

"To my dad?" he asked.

"Well, yeah, him too, but that wasn't what I meant."

He studied the road like I had done only moments before, not saying anything, just reaching for my hand and holding it in his own. He didn't look at me; he didn't have to.

Jonas was commended in Boston for some research he had done at Harvard. He flew out for the week for a special ceremony with all the other brainiacs. I only knew this because Amy had told me one afternoon at the hospital while we were bonding over chocolate milkshakes. I was proud of myself, though. She never saw the disappointment that crept its way into my face and down to my small intestines.

When he returned the following Sunday night, he called.

"Hey, Grace."

"Hey yourself," I said. "How was Harvard?"

"It was nice, actually. It was good to get away."

"I would have called to congratulate you, but I didn't know you were going away."

"It was unbelievable. I'm sorry I didn't call you."

I swallowed the hurt. "It's okay. You had a lot going on."

"We had the luncheon and then a few of us left for the Cape for a few days."

"You sound good," I commented. "Happy."

"I'm always happy when I talk to you."

"My mother got engaged."

"Already?" he asked. "That went awfully fast."

No, I thought, *for you, time always goes fast. For the rest of us on Earth, it travels at the usual, leisurely pace.* "This is what she's wanted."

"You sound upset. Are you okay?"

"Tell me about the award," I answered, changing the subject.

"Tell me about you. What are you wearing right now?"

It was always the same. In my hunger to be a part of Jonas's life, I was inquisitive, invasive. He, on the other hand, was seductive and charming. When someone makes you feel like the most important person in the world, it's tough to be angry at them. While your ego is stroked, you think your heart is full. Minutes later, or even hours, days, the emptiness returns.

"A ski suit," I replied.

We hung up the phone shortly thereafter, and I turned on the radio as a way to interrupt my inner banter. Jackson Browne was "Running on Empty," *not knowing what he was hoping to find*, and I whispered the lyrics as my head found my pillow.

Chapter 12

"Again!" the children cried out. "Tell us what happened to Buxbaum and Bixby and Bray!" I looked up, closing the book, and savored the smiling faces. Was Dr. Seuss preparing me for the importance of that night? Did he know when writing *Oh, the Places You'll Go!* how open to interpretation his message would be, how it transcended ages and stages of one's life?

"Come on, kids," Nurse Valerie said. "Time for bed. Say thank you to Miss Jessica."

"Thank you," they mumbled in unison, but not before little Sabrina cried out, "One more." She was seated on my lap, five-year-old legs hidden beneath two neon pink casts. I hadn't admitted it to anyone, but reading to the children twice a week was one of my most enjoyable responsibilities. I liked the way they followed my every word, as if I were the most important person they had ever heard. Sabrina, having been in the hospital about a month, was one of my favorites.

"Next week," I told her, stroking her silky brown hair. The chocolate eyes looked up at me. "Tuesday?" she asked.

"Yes, Tuesday."

"But I'll be going home on Friday."

"That's great," I told her. "Your mommy and daddy can read to you."

"I want *you* to read to me," she pleaded, crossing her tiny arms across her chest. When I set the book down on the floor beside us, she just tilted her head back and leaned up against me, making no effort to move; and I'll tell you, it wasn't so bad. She had this sweet-smelling hair and soft skin, and even though I wasn't supposed to, I slipped her a Hershey's kiss that smelled delicious on her breath.

The other children filed out of the room, some on crutches, some in wheelchairs. Nurse Valerie reached for Sabrina and helped her into her wheelchair.

"Can you come back to the room and tuck me in?" she asked, looking up at me with the most pleading eyes I'd ever seen.

Valerie winked at me and said, "Not tonight, Sabrina. Miss Jessie has to clean up in here, and you, young lady, have to get to bed." The little girl was distraught. I bent over her and told her a special secret, something funny that made her laugh out loud. She threw her arms around me, hugged me to her, and whispered in my ear, "I love you, Miss Jessie."

It was when I had begun the treacherous task of cleaning up the empty milk cups and foil wrappers that lay strewn on the floor that I heard a door behind me, and there was Jonas.

"What's up?" I asked with a smile.

"*Oh, The Places You'll Go!* One of my favorites."

I searched behind me, and then back at Jonas, the sly grin across his face. "A Seuss fan? Where were you hiding?"

"Right there," he said, pointing to the open doorway a few feet from where we were sitting.

"You're going to be a great mommy one day," he said.

The reference to a future that didn't include him was not what I wanted to hear. I straightened myself, the broom perched in one hand, the dustpan in another. He came close to me. I tried to maneuver, but he was invading my personal space, and as usual I pretended that was a bad thing. He just kept watching me, hovering, seemingly very serious. Then he took my chin in his hand and held it up so I had to see his eyes. "Sometimes I don't know if I should try harder, Jess, or if I should just walk away."

I began to sweep, rhythmic, premeditated motions that disguised the conflict within. He was waiting for *something*, as if that was a question and not one of the thoughts that happened to slip out of his mouth. When I finished, I set the broom down and took off my striper apron. He spoke again, impatient. "Can I drive you home?"

"I drove with my mom today. Why?"

"It's a yes or no question."

There was no pretending this time.

"I'll meet you out front."

We got in his truck without saying a word. There was something pensive and quiet about Jonas that night. Not in a bad way; I could just tell when he was thinking a lot.

"Let's take a drive," he suggested.

"Whatever you want."

We reached the top of Mulholland when he stopped the car. I had stared at this amazing view thousands of times before, but it was never as beautiful as it was seeing it with Jonas. He got out, walked over to my side, opened the door, and offered me his hand—a gentleman.

Tuesday night, I'd never forget.

"Hi," he spoke shyly to me, as if he were seeing me for the first time.

"Hi," I replied, staring up into his face.

We walked around to the back of the car, and Jonas lifted the hatch, telling me to climb in and take a seat. All of Los Angeles was spread out before me. I was feeling relaxed, less uptight, less prepared for battle, so I sat.

"Are you cold?" he asked, opening a can of Heineken.

"No, actually, I'm okay," I said, referring more to the range of emotions I was feeling than my body temperature. I was ready. I didn't care about my mother's recriminations. I didn't care about tomorrow, how it might make me feel. I cared about only "right now," the moment, and I was only sorry I hadn't brushed my teeth.

He started to talk to me about his day, about seeing his dad, how he was nearing the end. It was hardly the appropriate time to seduce him.

"He's just not the same man anymore. It's hard to see him like this, the shell where he once lived. Sometimes I just want him to go; sometimes I think it would be a lot easier to remember him the way he was, than the way he is now. And then I feel like such a jerk for thinking like that."

I wanted to say something meaningful, willing my brain to spout out the perfect response, but I was subsumed in my own sadness.

"I'm going to miss him…" he continued.

I was scared Jonas was going to collapse right there beside me. His head hung in his hands, the beer finished off in one bold gulp. I placed my hand on his shoulder, thinking that maybe I could reassure him, give him some of my strength.

"I'm sorry," I said. For him, for Adam Levy, for me, for all of us.

"No," he said, "*I'm* sorry. I shouldn't be laying this on you. You've had enough of your own pain."

Tuesday night. I'd always remember Tuesday. You think it's just one of those mundane days of the week, not Friday and not nearly as dreaded as Monday, but Tuesday.

"I'm your friend, and this is what friends do." I didn't want to tell him that he was wrong about my pain. He was the one who had time with his father. He was the one with stories. Without those memories, my pain was far less significant.

"He was always an amazing father. You should have seen him when we were kids."

Then he laughed. "But you weren't even born yet."

"Thank you for always finding the appropriate times to remind me of my youth."

If only I could have told him I wished I was twenty-two, like him, so when he touched me, it wouldn't be a crime.

"If it's any consolation," he said, "you make me feel a lot older than twenty-two."

"I'm sorry," I said, watching him open another can of beer.

"It's nice. You don't see it, but you look at me sometimes, when you're in one of your good moods."

"My Jekyll mood?"

"Yeah, that one. Your face changes. I can't really describe it, but you get this hopeful expression, like I have all the answers…"

"Don't you?" I teased.

"…like I'm everything…and it feels like I'm going to drown when you look at me like that. Not in a bad way. It's your eyes, they pull me in…"

He paused, the quiet before an influx of words.

"Sometimes," I began, "sometimes you *are* everything."

I stared at my fingers, needing to concentrate on something as benign as my fingernails. He didn't say anything and neither did I. We were both taking it all in. When he lifted himself up out of the truck and stared beyond the hills, I knew I'd never look out at this bluff without thinking of Jonas Levy.

I raised my knees to my chest and hugged them while he spoke. "It hasn't always been easy doing the right thing by you, Jess. Besides being wrong, I know it would be great, all of it, not just the physical part."

What We Leave Behind

"I'd never turn you in," I said, and he turned to grin at me. "Maybe it would be great, maybe it wouldn't. We'll never know."

"You really think we wouldn't be good?" he asked, searching my eyes for the truth.

"You can't ask me that," I whispered in his ear, knowing there was so much of life we'd never experience together. "Maybe we loved each other in another lifetime. I don't know."

"Maybe it was this life," he said, staring me in the face.

I'm sorry to spoil this moment with a reference to mainstream drama, but I knew just then how Molly Ringwald felt when she walked out the door on her sixteenth birthday and Michael Schoeffling was standing by his Porsche, waiting. We weren't sitting on a Porsche, but did it matter? When Molly walked out, I doubt she noticed anything other than how bright the world had become.

I was not about to avert my eyes from his. He might have said one hundred other profound sentences after that, but that first one was all I heard. He loved me. That was all I ever really needed to know.

"Our timing really stinks, doesn't it?" I asked, feeling strangely happy and sad all at the same time. "You're going to keep in touch with me, aren't you?" I asked, but he didn't answer. He grabbed my legs and slid my body down to the edge of the truck, pulling me close. His legs were touching mine, and his hands clasped around my fingers. "Are you drunk?" I asked, because Jonas never touched me like this before.

"I don't know, Jess. Truth? Maybe I just need to be closer to you." He crushed the second beer in his fist and threw it to the ground. Then he took my hands again and whispered dangerous, desperate words.

"Kiss me."

The symphony of innuendo that had defined us for weeks was playing loudly. There was no indecision here. His lips were on mine, his hands wrapping around me, his body pressing down against me. My legs spread further apart, and he moved in closer, my hands finding their way around his waist, tugging at his shirt, reaching for the smooth skin underneath.

There was no question of how Jonas felt about kissing me. His lips couldn't open wide enough. His tongue couldn't resist exploring my mouth. I tasted him, breathed him in, my fingers running up and down his back. It was like a drug—a force pulling us closer and closer together.

And when he kissed my face and my ear, and his lips brushed against my neck, I didn't stop him.

"I'm sorry," he whispered in my hair, abruptly stepping back, his arms pulling away. "I shouldn't have. It's wrong."

"It's not wrong," I said, out of breath, willing his eyes to meet mine.

He dropped his head down. "Jesus, what am I doing?"

"You're doing me a favor," I said. "No longer sweet sixteen and never been kissed."

I could tell he was torn. I held his fingers, lacing my own with his.

"Don't you want to be my first?" I asked, urging his hands closer, raising my head so our eyes would meet.

"Jess..." but that was all that came out. He grabbed my face in both his hands, and the confusion had all but vanished by the time his lips were on mine again. This time he didn't pull away. This time he stayed there, kissing me so hard, my lips were getting numb. I had to take a breath.

"Please don't stop, Jess," he practically cried out, but I had to massage my bottom lip.

I said, "It hurts."

"I never want to hurt you. Look at me," he said, cupping my face. "What do you see?"

What did I see? Beautiful eyes. Lips I wanted to keep on kissing, a boy I lost my heart to.

"What do you see?" he repeated, lifting my face up to meet his. "Look at me. Look in my eyes."

Everything I was feeling inside was staring back at me. I didn't care if it hurt. I couldn't stop myself. Reaching for him, I found his lips again, then wrapped my legs around him, securing him there, close to me. It had built up to this moment. There was no use fighting it any longer. Just the two of us, no rules. I could get hurt, yes, I could, but for one night Jonas Levy was mine.

We sat there like that, holding each other, Jonas running his fingers through my hair, and I was deliciously spent. In my adolescent longing, I figured that this was our defining moment and that everything would be different when I woke in the morning. Jonas wouldn't be able to resist having more of me. Was it wrong for me to think that this was the beginning of something and not merely a detour in the road?

"I love being with you," I whispered faintly into the hollow of his neck, "but it scares me."

If it were anyone else, I might have been anxious about the quiet that followed, but I'd gotten to know Jonas. He was examining the words that traipsed through his mind, careful to select the right ones. He tightened his grip around me. I understood his silence better than my own.

"I told you that would happen," he finally said. "And I was wrong for saying you should be afraid."

"Any time you let someone in, it's scary. But I'm also happy."

"This can't change things, Jess."

Jonas didn't know what he was saying. This—this moment we were in—was more than we could have ever anticipated. What we were feeling inside was bigger than both of us, and more important too.

"Everything's changed, Jonas," I said, "you just can't see it yet."

"Don't do this," he said, turning away.

"You can't tell me tonight didn't change everything. You can't tell me you don't feel what I'm feeling. I know I didn't imagine what I saw in your eyes, what I felt in your lips. Doesn't than mean something?" I asked.

"Yes, it does," he said. "And it's wrong."

"Do you love her?" I asked, then reconsidered. "Forget it, don't answer that." I should have just said, *If you really loved her, you wouldn't be here with me*, but something stopped me, rationale, perhaps or maybe the possibility that I didn't want to know the answer.

"I'm sorry," he said. "You'll never understand my reasons for staying loyal to Emily. She needs me. I'm her family. And you, you're just sixteen."

I got up from the perch I was seated on and walked toward the view, closely grazing the edge of the cliff. I could feel his eyes across my back.

"I used to have this recurring dream about a boy riding into my life, always on a horse, white horse, of course. And he'd lift me up onto this horse where we were safe from the world below, riding off along this stretch of beach. The faster he'd ride, the more exhilarating the journey. I'm not sure if it was happiness I felt, it was something unfamiliar—even for me. I couldn't tell you what he looked like, but I could tell you how large he was, how his physicality wrapped around me and I was, for a short time, unafraid."

He was standing motionless by my side. Turning to him, I said, "I never experienced that feeling in real life, Jonas, until you. You changed all that. I know you have another life, another plan, but when you think about all that had to fit into place for us to find each other, it has to make you stop and think."

"One day you're going to forget me, Jess," he began. "You'll be grown up, living successfully and happily off your addictions to music and movies. You'll be surrounded by men who want to befriend you, take care of you, love you. And all this will be the past."

My ears heard him, but my heart was wearing headphones.

"You know," he said, "you almost had me believing in fairy tales again."

"Fairy tales have happy endings," I reminded him.

"There will be a happy ending for you. Give yourself a chance. There's still so much of life ahead of you."

"You sound like you're saying good-bye."

"I'm not saying good-bye. I'm just saying I can't give you everything."

We drove back to my house in silence. There was really nothing more we could say to one another. Tomorrow would be different; Jonas and I would be different. He held my hand the entire time, and when I got out of the car, he was there waiting for me, leading me to the front door.

"Wait here," I said. "I have something I want to give you." When I returned, I handed him a picture. It was slightly worn from the years it spent in my mother's wallet, but I had no qualms about taking it; I'd stolen things before of far greater value than a picture. "Here, take this," I said, shoving it at him. In it, I had pigtails, but they were my only childish characteristic. I was seated in a chair with a book strategically placed on my lap. My face was serious, my body curled against the back cushion. He stared at it for a while before saying anything.

"Your eyes, my God, they look so sad."

"It's a couple of years after kindergarten. I think I was eight."

"What were you reading?"

"*Ruffian.*"

"Didn't he die?"

I nodded. "I thought you'd like it, the picture."

"I love it. You're adorable."

He tucked it into his pocket, pulling me against him, holding me as tightly as he knew how. Tuesday night. The night that everything changed. Then he kissed me, long, and wanting for more.

"We'll never say good-bye," he said, and I took a step back, forcing him to say those words while looking into my face. Jonas and I were taking a giant leap forward. Tomorrow we would analyze it to death—the right, the wrong, the how to fit it all together. Right then, I wanted to be present in every cell of my body. I didn't turn away. My eyes were locked on his.

"I'll call you in the morning," he said, and I mumbled something, *okay*, and he squeezed my fingers before letting them go.

I watched him walk back to his car, and then I turned toward my house and let myself in. I didn't head directly into my room, though. Instead, I stood by the window, masked by the hideous drapes my mother bought at a flea market, and watched him get into the truck. He didn't drive off as I had expected. I watched him take the picture out and hold it in both hands. He was looking at me and I was looking at him. I knew he would be staring into the eyes in the photograph, my eyes eight years ago. I knew he would see what I had already known. I knew he would understand how everything had led to this, that we were two people on the verge of falling in love, our lives now one.

And though I couldn't predict the future, I could feel its warm promise rising up inside of me. Jonas would no longer be able to resist being with me, and only me. His loyalties to Emily would no longer imprison him to old obligations. My love for him would set him free. I watched him stuck in a moment—a slice out of time, not part of the present, not part of the past. Time in that instant was a stolen fragment that belonged to us. Watching Jonas stare at a photo of me assured me that he was seeing pure love in my eight-year-old's eyes, and that our love, my love, was powerful enough to challenge fate. What did past virtue and morals matter when we shared a moment of pure love that could displace time?

Chapter 13

When I arrived at the hospital Thursday morning and found Adam Levy's bed empty, without any remnants of his ever having been there, I realized that I wasn't prepared for the inevitable—that people and things pass too quickly through our lives.

"What happened to Mr. Levy?" I asked Maria, the attending nurse.

"He's gone, Jessie. Late Tuesday night."

Tuesday night. I looked at the watch my mother had given me just a few days ago, or was it weeks ago, the face already scratched. The date staring back at me, encased in a clear, not quite plastic dome. I might have known, believing in superstitions and all. He died on the thirteenth. Tuesday, the thirteenth of August, the day that would eventually mark a series of extraordinary events.

"Where's all his stuff, his family?" I asked, hearing the panic in my own voice.

"They took everything this morning, cleared the place out."

Her words filled my lungs with a crushing heaviness. I ran out to the courtyard, the one where Jonas once held me in his arms. We had been kissing, being intimate, and Adam had just slipped away. Guilt consumed me for the obvious reasons, but mainly for spending the afternoon in bed on Wednesday relishing in the warm, cozy reminder of Jonas's arms around me. It didn't matter that he hadn't called. I didn't need to hear his voice to know what I felt inside my heart and what I believed he felt inside his.

I half expected Jonas to find me there, to put his arm around me, comfort me, but I knew he was with his family in Malibu. We had talked about what the end would be like, what the family's plans were. They were different than our plans, being Catholic and all. I had never been to a Jewish funeral. I was thankful I wouldn't have to look at Adam in that awful casket.

I wanted to cry. I did. I just didn't know if I could prevent the trickle from turning into a downpour. The ache was there in my throat and to unload right there, by myself, over someone else's father felt strange.

And as if I willed him to be there, I heard his voice beckon me from a very dangerous place. "Jess."

I turned to find Jonas Levy, the beautiful boy I'd fallen in love with in two months' time. He had been crying. I could tell by the splotches of red on his face. His hands were fisted deeply in his pockets. I wanted to run to him and take some of his pain away, but something about his expression made me stop. Instead, he walked over to me, his head held down, unable to look me in the eye.

"I'm so sorry," I said, unable to muster any other words.

He didn't say anything. He just stared out past me.

Then, "Look, Emily's inside, so I really can't stay long. We're just picking up some things."

He still wouldn't look at me. He gazed into the distance. "She's here?" I asked.

My question brought his eyes to mine. They were bloodshot. I saw a coldness in them I'd never seen before.

He said, "I think it'd be best if you don't come to the funeral. It'll just complicate things. My dad liked you a lot, I know, but it'll be easier for us, for me, if you just don't…I'm already feeling terrible about…"

I was starting to understand.

"Emily and I are leaving for Boston right after shiva."

"It wasn't your fault, Jonas," I interrupted. "Don't do this to yourself. You didn't do anything wrong. We didn't do anything wrong."

"We can't see each other anymore."

My head shook back and forth, resisting each sentence. *He doesn't realize what he's saying. He's upset. He's confused.*

"We can't be anything to each other anymore."

My body was racked with fear.

I tried to maintain control of my voice. "How could you do this? How could you do this to me?"

He didn't answer. He looked right through me as if I wasn't there at all.

Was he preparing me for this the other night? *This,* this ugliness? What I thought was love staring me in the face, was it something else? When he looked at the photo I had given him, he had said my eyes were sad, and they were. They were eyes that had learned that good-bye was no different than death, that good-bye meant never seeing someone again, never touching someone again. Didn't he know what his leaving would do to me?

The moment that had passed between us was now eclipsed by a cloud of distrust.

"You've been a very good friend," he said, as if he was signing my yearbook and sending me on my way. "Treasure the memory, 'cause it's never going to happen again." Then he turned and walked away, and that was it. Quickly, he entered my life. Abruptly, he departed. And I understood what it felt like to have the ground swallow you up and how agonizing and painful it can be when someone you love takes your heart, rips it out of your chest, and stomps it on the floor.

"Jessica," I heard my mother calling from outside my bedroom door. It was morning, but I didn't want to wake up. I didn't want to feel the rush of pain again. Its grip was paralyzing, choking me of life.

"Jessica," she said it again, louder. "Beth's here."

I rolled over in my bed, the sheets sticking to my legs. Beth poked her head through the doorway and entered the room. "Is it alright if I come in?"

"You're already in," I said, a statement I regretted before I had the chance to disband it.

I watched her open my drawers and throw a change of clothes at me. Beth was not about to watch me wallow in self-pity. "I'll be waiting for you outside in the car," she said. Then she looked at her watch. "You have eight minutes."

When I got into Beth's car, I slammed the door shut to let her know how angry I was by her intrusion.

"Slam away," she said. "Get all that anger out."

I didn't say anything. It was better for the both of us.

We drove through the neighborhood, and I looked out the window for a part of the familiar terrain to be whole again, to be recognizable. My neighborhood, that just yesterday was familiar, had morphed overnight into flimsy shades and ghosts, a land without substance.

Beth stopped at a red light. She slammed so hard on the brakes that it jolted me from my trance.

"Go ahead," she said, "blow on it."

I looked around. There were no other cars on the road. The clock on the dashboard told me it was too early on a Sunday for anyone to be out driving.

Neither of us moved. The light changed to green. Then it changed to yellow. Beth didn't take her foot off the brakes. The light changed back to red again.

"Blow," she said again; this time she demanded me to, and I couldn't ignore her.

"Why are you doing this, Beth?" I asked.

"Just blow, Jessie. Blow the damn light."

All I had to do was blow, and it would turn green. That's the way it always worked. That's the way my mother had taught me when we used to drive in her car. We'd stop at the red street light and she'd tell me when to blow, and the light would magically turn green.

"I'm not doing it," I told her. "I don't know why you're doing this." My hands wrapped around my forearms, protecting me from her response. Tears welled up in my eyes.

Beth put the car into park, took her foot off the gas. We were sitting in the middle of the road. She switched on the hazards. Its tapping sound was the only noise between us.

I looked up as the light switched again from red to green to yellow and then back around again. Red green yellow, red green yellow. The repetition of light and the beating sound of the blinkers unnerved me. Nobody was blowing. No cars were in sight.

I don't know how much time passed before she turned the hazards off and put the car into gear.

"And you don't have control over people leaving either," was all she said.

BOOK II
1994–2001

∽

*In everyone's life, at some time, our inner fire goes out. It is then
burst into flame by an encounter with another human being.
We should all be thankful for those people who
rekindle the inner spirit.*
Albert Schweitzer

Chapter 14

Today the ocean's waves are disorderly and unkind. I watch them fingering the shore—coming close and backing away. The sea is a grayish hue that I'd never seen, full of somber regret. I reach for the blanket I am sitting on and wrap it around my shoulders. The movement sends a sharp pain through my leg and up through my back. I'm almost certain it stops in my stomach.

Searching the span of beach, I see that I am not alone. A little girl—about five—and her mother are building a sand castle nearby. Other than myself, they are the only ones brave enough to venture out on this chilly afternoon.

The daughter is determined and playful at the same time. Her movements are controlled as she scoops the sand into her shovel and drops it haphazardly on top of the other piles.

I watch them for more than an hour. Shaping, smoothing, decorating. The little girl's patience is wearing thin. Her mother is executing the finishing touches.

I look away from this family to stare out at the ocean. I hear the little girl's cries first.

"Mommy," she shrieks, as I turn my head in her direction. "Mommy," she yelps again, as if her mother can stop the wave from beating down on her castle. I look up and see their hard work has been washed away with the tide. Almost instantly, the daughter bursts into tears. The mother desperately begins to rebuild. I know that however successful the mother is, the castle will never be the same for the child.

I want to rush over to them and tell the mother to stop. I want to take her hands into my own to prevent her from making a mistake. And when she turns to me with unyielding surprise, then anger, I will explain it all to her. I will tell her that if she builds a new castle, her daughter will never learn about loss, about mourning. She won't have the chance to move through her feelings and come out the other side, whole and recovered.

I don't say anything to the very young mother. Instead, I stand up, aware that it's time for me to leave and return to my son. I wipe the sand from my pants and hear the faint cries of the daughter as I fold the blanket. The mother is consoling her, rebuilding, frantic in her attempts to replace what's been lost.

I begin the walk up the beach toward my car and when I step in, I look at myself in the rearview mirror. I'm reminded of who I am and the various castles in my life that have been destroyed by the fateful waves of nature. I have been unable to stop the waves or rebuild the fortresses and dreams. I can tell you about the force of the ocean, but first, allow me to return to better times when my castle seemed to magically form out of thin air.

The ring of the doorbell roused me from such a deep sleep that I lifted up my head, thought I was dreaming, and put my head back down on the pillow. This commenced my twenty-second birthday. Then I heard it again. I looked at the clock, annoyed at what I saw, nine something or other. Some of the lights on the digital numbers were out, so it could have been 9:13 or 9:33. I didn't know, but I was sure I didn't want to be awake before eleven.

I was living in Santa Monica in a duplex I shared with two fellow UCLA film school grads. Mom had moved to Phoenix when a job opportunity presented itself at the same time that Harold broke off their engagement. Her sadness forbid me from saying, "I told you so," and reminding her that I was the one who had said that sometimes one love was enough. Beth had graduated from Boston University with honors and was moving to New York City to attend law school in the fall. I couldn't imagine why Kevin and Patricia weren't jumping up to get the door, but then I remembered the night before, and I figured they were both passed out, having partied until the wee hours of the morning. Some of us from film school had gone to Q's to play pool and ended up a whole lot intoxicated. It was the usual industry crowd, agents-in-waiting, mailroom contenders, aspiring actors, musicians, video promotion geeks, a small, incestuous group. Sure, we all had this untamed obsession for music or film, but you'd think sometimes we worked in the emergency room at Cedars Sinai by the seriousness in which we rubbed elbows. Then there were the A&R guys, Artist and Repertoire, a complicated group at best. One of my roommates, Kevin, well, he was aspiring to be just that and changing the world along the way. "We hear the music in our hearts and then it's our job to ensure the world hears it too. That's touching people's lives."

My June birthday always marked the completion of some milestone. This year, it was my graduation from film school, finishing a successful internship at Fox, and consulting with a local radio station on its playlist. "You should program, Jess. You're wasting your time in film school," they would tell me, but I shrugged it off, acutely aware of my goals.

The doorbell sounded again. I got out of bed, wrapped myself in something that lay strewn on the floor, headed toward the door, and with eyes half opened, peered through the peephole.

He was tall and gangly, with a face hidden from view beneath a mass of curls. I thought he was a delivery guy but couldn't figure out what he'd be delivering so early in the morning. Patricia, the aspiring actress, with enough drama in her life to fill an entire year of *General Hospital,* had promised me a strip-o-gram, joking that I needed a little loosening up. Could he be there for that? Or maybe it was one of Kevin's A&R cronies. This one I hadn't seen before.

"Who is it?" I called out.

"I'm here to see a Miss Jessie Parker."

I turned from the door. I wondered if this was one more version of the game my roommates played with me—drinks to get me to talk, a little pot here and there, smuggling guys into our house to see if perhaps I still had a pulse. I'd learned what kind of messes loosening up could get me into and saved the melodrama for the movies and the collection of songs I hoisted onto film, the backdrops to an oh-so-common theme: I love you and I can't have you and you're breaking my heart, but I love you anyway, still, forever, and hey, it feels great.

He knocked again and I turned around, searching through the door to see if he was carrying anything with him, nothing that I could see.

"What is this regarding?" I asked, slightly apprehensive.

"I have a delivery for a Jessie Parker."

"Leave it at the door," I shouted, seeing through the small circle that he was getting impatient.

"I'll just slide it under the door if that's okay with you, Miss." And I watched as the thin envelope found its way through the door without making a sound.

Kneeling over, I recognized the logo on the envelope at once, *SixthSense*. It was only one of the most well-known and successful production companies in the business.

My fingers were jumping, tugging at the sealed flap. The lone business card fell to the floor while I searched the remainder of the envelope for more, but it was definitely empty. The card with a Beverly Hills address was all that was there, and when I turned it over, it read, *10:30 sharp*, with today's date.

I opened the door, racing to find the messenger, shouting in case he couldn't hear me, "Who am I meeting there?" He was already out of sight. So I politely thanked him under my breath, closed the door behind me, and remembered, according to my misleading clock, how little time there was to get myself ready.

The ground floor reception area of SixthSense was silent and unassuming. I had given the receptionist my name. She eyed me coolly. I eyed her back, and when she told me to take a seat, I obliged. She didn't strike me as one that divulged *anything* to *anyone*, so I dismissed the idea of inquiring any further and waited patiently like the *anyone* I was.

When the waiting turned into an hour, I got up from the couch and scanned my surroundings, searching the walls for a sign of some kind. I'd been in enough entertainment offices by now to know what I'd find; the indulgent office with expensive art by some up-and-coming contemporary artist, or the self-promoting offices with giant life-size framed posters of their films or their artists, some housed with small-screen televisions of various videos or films that made them legendary. This office was different. There were no accolades garnering the walls, no self-serving tactics to lure in clientele, and no minimalist artistry, just tasteful, warm touches. Returning to the couch, I closed my eyes, and rested my head against the pillows.

"You must be Jessie Parker."

The voice came out of nowhere. I hadn't even heard approaching footsteps, but the words caused me to jump, seeking out the person behind the deep, penetrating voice.

"I'm Marty Tauber," he said, holding his beautiful hand out to me.

"Mr. Tauber," I repeated.

"Marty is fine," he said, his enormous hand engulfing mine in one hurried grasp.

"Call me Jessica," I responded, freeing myself from childhood.

"Jessica."

I couldn't believe I was shaking hands with Marty Tauber. He was, after all, one of the most famous producers in town and one of the top executives at SixthSense.

"I'd heard you were beautiful, and tall!"

I felt the blush crawl across my face, feverishly emerging from the place it had laid dormant for years. The pictures I had seen in the trades hadn't done him justice. Sure, he was good-looking, but there was a realness about him that the camera didn't capture, this energy that surrounded him and bounced off the walls. He wasn't much taller than I was, but his charisma added inches to his height. He was in the category of men who could have the leading role in a film, become the next big star, the country's sexiest sex symbol. When he walked into a room, people stopped talking and not so much because of his looks, but because of the way he carried himself, this elusive charm. I knew this because he had barely spoken, and I was riveted.

"No wonder my instructions were to leave you alone until you were of age," he said while appraising me.

"Do we have a mutual acquaintance?" I asked.

"I think we do," he said. "Does the name Adam Levy mean anything to you?"

Hearing Adam's name caught me off guard, and I wouldn't let the surprise unhinge me. "You knew him?"

"Everybody knew Adam, and I had the pleasure of working on different projects with HiTide for years. Adam's label always had the best repertoire in the business, still does, notwithstanding the fact that he was a close friend, a mentor, so to speak, and one of the few genuine guys in the business."

"Yes," I said sadly. "He was."

"Come, follow me," he instructed, waving me toward a back hallway and into a private elevator. His hand rested on my shoulder, and I smiled at him as we rode in silence. My composure had all but escaped me with the mention of Adam Levy.

We reached the top of the building, and I followed him down a narrow corridor through two large doors that opened to a sprawling office. "Have a seat," he began, as he found his way behind a massive mahogany desk, and I took mine on the espresso, suede chair across from him. A hoarse voice came over the intercom; I studied his features as he took the call. Marty Tauber was easy on the eyes with salt and pepper gray hair, steel blue eyes, and a strong, tanned face. I guessed him to be younger than Adam Levy had been. He was dressed in jeans and a white Lacoste, and the casualness of his clothes helped me to relax.

"I don't want any interruptions for the next half hour, Marla," he said to the intercom as he hung up the phone. Then he turned to me. "I'm sure you're wondering why you're here, so let's get to it. I've always admired Adam. He was a friend and his love for this industry matched my own. I started in music, hugely obsessed with it, and if not for my comparable interest in film, I would have taken him up on his several lucrative offers to work alongside him at HiTide, but I didn't want to pigeonhole myself at one record label when I could work with all the labels and their music. So, having kindly rejected his offers and pleas to come onboard, we started SixthSense, Jeff Walker and I, and well, you know, the rest is history."

Jeff Walker was only one of the most talked about directors in town. Every movie he touched translated into millions of dollars in box office revenue worldwide. The casual way Marty spoke of him, like he was a household name, was almost as jarring as hearing Adam Levy's name again after all these years.

"Adam thought very highly of you. He made that clear the last time we spoke."

"I never saw you at the hospital."

"That's because the old man wouldn't let me or any of his friends visit. However, we spoke on the phone often, and, like I said, he saw something in you, potential." He held up the cassette tapes I'd given Adam for his birthday, the ones with my favorite songs, the ones I'd emptied myself onto.

"You could sell these compilations in today's market. You picked an excellent blend of music. Maybe you weren't aware of it at the time, but he was. He knew you had talent."

Marty Tauber smiled, the corners of his lips turning upward. "Adam's lawyer drafted this document that I was to adhere to upon his death."

I eyed the suspicious piece of paper he held in his hands.

"In an unobtrusive manner, I was to keep close tabs on you, follow your education, watch behind the scenes as your career path unfolded. He'd always assumed you'd go into film and/or music, and as I witnessed, he was correct."

I fumbled in my seat at the idea of being followed, my life being scrutinized beneath a magnifying glass. I said, "He always told me to do what I loved."

"It's a good thing you did, because that's where I come in. Your dossier is quite impressive. Stellar reports from former employers, exceptional recommendations from your professors. What struck me the most were the two short films you worked on. They were decent stories, although similar in theme and tone. I was able to get my hands on copies without the music so I could watch your individual work, and then I watched with your music. I thought your music selections were perfect."

I took my time exhaling so as not to scare him with the tumult of anxiety I'd been holding in.

"I especially liked the lovemaking scene in *Butterfly*. All that pent-up sexual energy. The choice to shoot in black and white, showing the lovers' hands and obscure angles of their faces and bodies was a brilliant touch. It was tender and simple, naked, both literally and figuratively, and when I watched with the music, that Pavarotti song really brought it all together, with the man whispering the words in her ear, softly, erotically. I couldn't take my eyes off them. That's how all lovemaking should be."

They were actors and actresses in a tale I'd created, but hearing Marty talk about it, I was abashed and naked to his smiling blue eyes. He had described my most intimate moment, took a peek into my soul, and perhaps even at my body. "They say," he began again, "we create in art what is closest to us, what we think we know best. Is that true about you?"

I averted my eyes, avoiding the question that ignited forbidden thoughts.

"Nonetheless," he said, "you've accomplished impressive work, and that's what we're looking for—someone with your vision, someone who has her finger on the musical pulse, someone who can leave the audience captivated.

"What I'm offering you is an integral role at SixthSense." His long, smooth fingers clasped together and rested on the desk in front of him. "Music supervisor. You'll work directly with the executive in charge of music, overseeing all aspects of music for our films and their soundtracks."

I reflected over the pile of resumes I'd just finished printing at Kinko's, the unreturned phone calls, the stack of classifieds that had accumulated over the weeks, ripe with job possibilities, and the fact that Adam Levy saw something in me; with a souvenir from the past, doors were opening.

"Are you serious?" Even as the words tumbled out of my mouth, I recognized how adolescent they sounded. Things were moving quickly, so quickly one had to be guarded, cautious, and I still had my master's degree to think about, which paled compared to the opportunity that Marty was presenting.

"If you're going to work here, there are two things you'll need to know about me. One," he said, holding up a finger, "I never lie. Two," this time two beautifully manicured fingers, "I never go back on my word. I gave Adam my word, and I'm making good on it. There's one stipulation, though. I need you to start right away because we're shooting in Barcelona next week, and I want you to read the script before we leave. This could be the biggest film of all of our careers."

There was a mirror to my right I hadn't seen when I walked in. My likeness was reflected in it—the tailored suit, the self-assured smile. Marty Tauber dwarfed me in expertise, and for one split second, his expectations of me caused my eyes to question myself.

"What do you say? Can I welcome you to our team?"

I wanted to say let me think about this one, uh, yes, but I decided against mindless humor. "Thank you, Mr. Tauber. This is an incredible opportunity, one that I'm very grateful for. I'd be honored to join your team."

"Please, I told you, call me Marty."

"Marty," I repeated, already a good pupil.

"You're going to love your immediate boss, everybody does. He started out just like you. He's got passion, a hell of a lot of experience, and he'll teach you everything you need to know: conceptualization, clearance, negotiations, editing, licensing, distribution."

"I can't wait to meet him."

He smiled, a devilish grin mixed with amusement.

"You already have." And then he gave me that big, huge hand again, and I gave him mine. Of course he'd be my boss. He had commanded the room, hadn't he?

"Would you like to join me for lunch?" he asked.

It would have been terribly rude had I said no.

"Let's go," he said, "I'm starving."

A car was waiting for us on the street when we exited the building. Marty told the driver, "The Ivy at the Shore," and when we passed by my street on the way out west, I thought about how radically my life had changed since I left there this morning.

We took our seats at a table in the back of the restaurant, where at least half a dozen people stopped by to acknowledge one of its own. Most of them were curious. This was an envious town, a one-upmanship kind of business. Could I possibly be the next big star of one of his blockbuster movies, or, heaven forbid, his latest conquest? He introduced me to some of his friends, mindful of his words, not giving away too much. He seemed to know what they were thinking, and he played along with their carefully scripted inquiries, hiding their objectives beneath a bevy of baloney.

I said, "I can see why Adam Levy chose you as his protégé."

"The same can be said about you. You have vision Jessica. I've seen it. We're a lot more alike than you think. This business doesn't just occupy our lives, it lives in our bones."

"Adam and I talked about that, and here you are professing the very same thing. He warned me to be careful. He told me movies and music can become so much a part of your life, you don't know when the film or song ends and the real world begins."

"It's a dangerous place to live," he agreed. "You need to be careful about losing yourself."

"But isn't that what makes a great song, a great film?" I asked. "That passion, that marriage between the melody and the story?"

"Yes, to some degree. Filmmaking is a *tremendous* undertaking, from conception to premiere; all the parts are critical, and as long as every person I employ is as ardent and industrious with their craft as we are, the sum will be a stellar representation of its parts."

His mind moved me, my interest growing.

We talked about Marty's early days in the industry and how he moved from music to film in a rapid series of successes. He explained how the industry was different back then; budgets and boobs were inflated, and so were expense accounts. There was an *anything goes* attitude, and it extended way beyond business. "Those were the rated R years."

We discussed music, our likes and dislikes, trends, and the important role of the music supervisor. "The position has changed, now spanning from pre-production through shooting and post-production." And I asked the questions I'd always wanted to ask a producer: What was the most he was willing to pay for the licensing of a song? Is music another character in a movie? How much of the song influences the scene, or vice versa? I asked because it would be difficult for me to back down on a song that I thought completed a scene. His answers were thought-provoking and honest, and beneath the star-like existence, I saw something else. The labels the media had pinned on him were likely accurate: bad boy, womanizer, hot-tempered, but the Marty Tauber sitting across from me was so much more. Here was a man who was thoughtful, passionate, and comfortable in his skin.

We didn't stop talking until two plates of pasta landed in front of us.

"I hope you like it," he said.

"It smells delicious."

"Try it," he answered, eyeing me while I twirled the noodles on the spoon.

Uneasiness crept up on me, the kind you get when someone watches you closely. I lifted the fork to my lips and took a delicate bite. Marty wasn't eating. He was enjoying himself too much. "Am I embarrassing you?" he asked.

"It's a bit unsettling."

"Then you may want to put the fork down."

After taking a sip of his water, he began. "I haven't enjoyed a lunch like this in a long time. You've been a pleasure to talk with." This was what the trades meant by charming womanizer, and it didn't stop me from being flattered. I liked Marty. It was easy to be taken in by his compliments, but I was sensible enough to stay on course.

"You did most of the talking," I laughed.

"No, you actually said a lot, and your questions tell me you're not afraid to use your brain. You have a refreshing outlook. It's a pleasure to be around someone like you. Are you okay?" he asked.

"I'm fine."

"Fine means not fine."

"No, really, I'm okay. It's all a bit overwhelming." Yes, it was; with each bite, each gulp, I was letting someone get close to me. And just as my stomach would feel full and satiated, something was triggered, reminiscent of the hunger I could never abate. Marty felt familiar to me, but I wasn't sure how much of his familiarity was the reminder of what I'd once felt for someone else.

"I hadn't expected this," I said. "Adam continues to surprise, even now."

"Do you keep in touch with the family?" he asked.

"No," I said, probably with too much haste. "Not anymore. Last I heard from his son, he was at Harvard; and Amy and his mom, we lost touch a long time ago."

"That's too bad," he said. "Adam raved about Jonas. It wasn't easy for them when they found out Rachel couldn't have more children. They doted on Jonas, trying to compensate for the loss. They'd always wanted a house full of kids."

I wanted to turn off the volume so I couldn't hear, but Marty kept on going.

"When they adopted Amy. I had never seen a happier man than the one who showed me pictures of his new family. He was so full of pride and love for those two kids."

The news was shocking and hurtful at the same time. Jonas had never shared any of this with me.

"They're a special family," I said. "I'd love to know what Amy's been up to these years. She must be, what, eighteen now?" I pictured the adorable girl watching me hang from a tree.

"She's probably with Rachel in DC. There was nothing keeping them in LA anymore. They moved east to be closer to Rachel's parents. I usually get a card from them over the holidays."

I sat there talking with Marty Tauber about a family I had once been so enmeshed with, I might have considered them my own. I wasn't sure what Jonas told them. My absence had to have been noted at the funeral. I never expressed my condolences. I never got to tell them how sorry I was, how much Adam had meant to me.

Listening to Marty was upsetting. The Levys were strangers to me now.

The waiter came and cleared our plates. It had been an interesting and informative afternoon, and I stole a glance at my watch, convinced that at least one of us had somewhere else to be.

"Do you have to go?" he asked.

"I'm just thinking about everything I need to do to get ready for tomorrow."

"Well, there's only one thing you need to do today," and there they appeared, an army of waiters carrying a chocolate cake, singing loudly enough for the whole restaurant to stop what they were doing and join in, eyes feasting on us. Marty leaned back in his chair, smiling as if he had just beaten some worthwhile opponent.

"How did you know?" I asked him, but I already knew the answer. Burying my face in my hands, I hid the happiness that found its way across my cheeks. Twenty-three candles on the cake; I counted every one. Marty had made sure I got the one for good luck.

"Make a wish," he said.

"Maybe it's already come true."

"There has to be something else. Now close your eyes and wish."

I closed my eyes and did as he said, the heat from the flames warming my face, the uncertainty of wishes swelling around me.

When I opened my eyes, I exhaled and watched as the candles were doused with one plume of breath.

"Thank you. It's very kind of you and very unnecessary."

"It's my pleasure."

"You can't expect me to eat the whole thing."

"Of course I do," he laughed.

"You'll have to help."

"Nothing would make me happier."

We dipped our forks into the monstrous cake and didn't bother with the plates they gave us. Our hands covered in chocolate fudge, we knocked into each other playfully as we licked our fingers and wiped the messes from our faces. We hadn't even made a dent when he stood up.

"C'mon," he said, "let's get out of here." And he took my messy hand in his and led me through the restaurant, out the door, and into the warm California sun. "I want to show you something."

I wanted to ask about the check, but something told me it was already taken care of. That was the best way to describe Marty Tauber. He was a man in charge.

The car took us north along the Pacific Coast Highway for several miles before turning into a residential neighborhood and a sprawling home overlooking the ocean.

Marty looked at his watch. "We should be right on time."

Opening the door, we were met by a group of people, each wanting a piece of Marty. They followed us through the halls of the mansion, and when we reached the dining room, they dispersed amongst video monitors and equipment. Noise and movement filled the room. Makeup artists were touching up already-perfect faces. The fast-paced vibe was where I felt very much at home: a video shoot.

Marty led us through the room, introducing me to the director and then the artist. "Rylee, I want you to meet Jessica Parker. Jess, Rylee Matthews."

I shook the hand of the Grammy-award-winning, number one artist in the country, as if any introduction was necessary. "It's a pleasure to meet you," I said, pretending she was not the artist that topped every conceivable *Billboard* chart.

"You too," she said, bopping up and down while she spoke. "I hope you're staying to watch the shoot. The song's amazing! Marty, you're staying, right?" Then she leaned in to put an arm around his shoulder, and her lips found his cheek. The bouncing was worse than my mother's flitting.

"Jessica," he summoned me, "is it okay if we hang out here a little while?"

When I smiled, he led me to a sofa off to the side of the room, and we watched as sound checks and final preparations were made.

"Tell me what you think," he said, and the room fell quiet as Rylee began to sing. It was a ballad, her strong, rich voice filling the room.

The words described a girl in search of paradise, something she equated to love. Dancers were following around her, slow, rhythmic movements before an ornate dining room table brimming with glasses in golds and chartreuses. Food covered every inch of the table: rich cakes and pies, pastries, fruits, and cheeses. Bunches of hydrangeas were strewn about, deep burgundy wines, and candelabras afire.

"She wrote this?" I asked Marty.

"This part," he said. "Keep watching."

After the chorus, she began speaking in a hushed whisper. She was asking about paradise, whether it was a lie, a fantasy created about people and places as we would like them to be.

The words were recognizable. I'd definitely heard them before, but this was not their original context. "Charlene," I said. "Charlene Duncan, Motown Records, one hit wonder."

"Good memory," he said.

"Steel trap," I confirmed, pointing to my head. When it came to music, my brain was the most expansive catalog of tunes known to man. Ordinarily, I didn't like covers, but this was brilliant.

Rylee continued another verse and chorus before finishing on a note that left the audience mesmerized. "It's a wrap," the director called out, and his staff joined in a round of applause, while Marty headed his way. They were arguing, and Marty was adamant about what he was saying. I could tell by his posture and the way he pointed his decisive fingers. The director relented, calling over Rylee and someone from the record label. Marty summoned me.

"What did you think? Let's put that UCLA film school degree to use."

"I think the song is amazing."

"And? What else? Don't be afraid, enlighten them."

I began. "Forget we're in the nineties and how commercialized music videos have become, *and* that it's a moneymaking business. Let's go back to our roots. A good song is going to sell. *That* song is going to sell. You don't need all those embellishments. She looks cheap up there with those dancers. I see something more serious."

Walking toward the sliding glass doors, I surveyed the view outside. "That's paradise right out there."

Marty joined me at the window. The view was extraordinary.

"I'd plop her golden voice down there on the beach in and out of the water, shoot in black and white, dress her in all white, something loose and sexy, maybe on 35 mm film, giving it a family movie feel, this dream she wants for herself."

Marty was looking at me with an expression I could not read. "What?" I asked.

"I'm glad to see you didn't put any thought into that."

"That's just what I saw when I heard it."

"The amazing gift we share, to see things with our ears. It reminds me of *Butterfly*," he added. "I told the director the same thing. I told him to shoot outside, black and white, lose the riffraff."

"Great minds think alike."

"I'm interested in peering more into that brain of yours and figuring out why you didn't choose the director's path."

"I love music too much."

"One day, it'll break your heart," he said.

I didn't bother telling him that it already had. Asking, instead, how the director took to his suggestions.

"Bob's an old friend. He asked me to be here for creative assistance. If he didn't want my opinion, he shouldn't have extended the invitation."

"And Rylee?"

At the mere mention of her name, she appeared, hair flowing loosely down her shoulders and her eye makeup dramatically heavier. She winked at us before saying to me, "Has anyone ever told you that you look exactly like Uma Thurman?" Then she bounced away from us, heading toward the beach and the final hours of sun, leaving me to question how I'd never seen the resemblance before.

When we got in Marty's car, it occurred to me that we had just changed music history. The song was sure to go quadruple platinum, the video airing on every notable music channel for years to come, and I'd be driving in my car one late afternoon and hear the words on the radio, and remember this day and remember Adam Levy, the gentle force behind it all.

"I've monopolized your whole day, Jessica. What are your big birthday plans?"

"I don't think anything could top this afternoon."

"Do you," he asked again, "have plans?"

"No," I said. "My birthday usually isn't a big deal."

"Have you ever been on a helicopter?" he asked.

I looked at him strangely.

"I thought we'd take a helicopter ride."

"I know better than to ask if you're serious."

"You only turn twenty-two once in your life. Why not make it unforgettable?"

"It's already been unforgettable."

"You need to live, Jessica Parker. Forget where you're going and where you've been and concentrate on the now. Enjoy the ride, or you're going to miss out on the whole experience."

"You sound like an awful self-help book," I said, enjoying my sense of humor again. Then I smiled up at him, drinking in those soft blue eyes. "Where do you find all this energy?"

"It keeps me young."

"Don't you have somewhere to be, someone to win over?" I asked.

"I was hoping that would be you."

Chapter 15

It was the fall of 1994. *Pulp Fiction* was released, *Shawshank Redemption*, *Legends of the Fall*, and *Forrest Gump*, all of them strong contenders for the Oscar. The movie we were banking on was our Barcelona jewel, *El Pais*; according to early industry chatter, it had the potential to sweep the awards with its flavorful, foreign luster. The heartbreakingly tragic story followed an orphaned boy in search of his Spanish roots, who discovered that his peaceful, hard-earned life was far superior to the complex dysfunction of the wealthy, political family that abandoned him. The film was already being hailed as a masterpiece.

The music we worked with was mostly in Spanish, something I wasn't a smidgen experienced in, but rhythm knows no language. That's what Marty told me and it was true. When I dove headfirst into the Spanish catalog, it didn't take long for me to match the right music with the right scene. Marty was delighted with my choices. He said I'd become a Chiquita banana in no time.

"How's work?" my mother asked one afternoon. She had called to alert me of a pending visit. "Is it true what they're saying about you in the papers?"

"All of it," I said.

"You're happy. That makes me happy."

"It's amazing," I told her. "I love every minute of it." I'd been working with Marty for four months. He had become teacher, mentor, friend, and grueling drill sergeant.

"You sure spend a lot of time with that boss of yours."

"It's Marty, Mom. He has a name." But Mom was right. I had spent a ridiculous amount of time with Marty in the last few months, and it wasn't just limited to hours in the office. Sometimes our days didn't end until a new one began, spilling over onto the weekends. My roommates asked if they should find a new housemate. My absences were noted daily.

"Do you find him attractive?"

"Yes, and every day after lunch we go back to his office, climb on his desk, and screw like bunnies."

"Jessica!" she shouted, and while I was immensely proud that I could still shock the people closest to me, she added, "I hope you don't speak that way around him."

I should have told her he loves it when I talk dirty, but then I would have gone too far.

"I don't have to tell you to be careful, do I?" she asked, the insinuation as visible as her flitting. But I was saved from responding when the alarm sounded through the phone, and my mother yelled, "Code blue. I love you and be careful and keep making me proud," in one, quick, terminal sentence.

I hung up the phone and stared at the piles of paper strewn across my desk. It was late and most of the staff had gone home. *Prince of Tides* was playing on the stereo. I hummed along to the melodious sound, remembering the afternoon Marty dragged me to his house in the hills to watch it. I always knew when one of Marty's many dalliances ended, because he'd usually call me on a Sunday morning to discuss work, and then it would lead into what I was doing, which was usually nothing exciting except more work, and he'd ask me to go to a movie with him, or rent him some sappy, love story.

This particular day, I drove up to his house off Benedict Canyon with the video in my purse. It was a typical, gorgeous California day, clear skies, cool, sunny. Neither of us saw the change coming, how the afternoon shifted to something dark and threatening. We took our seats in the media room and watched while the screen brought to life a relationship that nearly everyone should experience and avoid. Passionate and complicated, the tale came with a sticker guaranteeing heartbreak. Marty kept looking at me, unable to comprehend why I was crying so hard. He even offered to go out to the bathroom and get me another box of Kleenex.

"I'm the one who just got dumped," he said. "Why are you crying?"

I shook my head, unable to speak.

"What's wrong with you?" he asked. "He was a good man. He went back to his wife and children."

"I know," I said. What I didn't know was if I was crying because his goodness made him more appealing or because I identified with

Lowenstein, the woman left behind. The movie was hard to watch. "They deserve something more," I cried out. "Both of them, or maybe it's that song, that 'someday when someone else's arms are around us' song."

"Jess, you're hysterical. I'm not going to let you drive down the hill like this, especially since it's about to pour. California drivers are the absolute worst in the rain." And by mere mention of the word, the skies opened up and down it fell, a hard pouncing on the driveway.

"I'm fine," I said, wiping the tears from my face and asserting what was left of my weathered confidence. Marty opened the car door and threw me into the driver's seat. He was standing in the rain, clothes soaked through, drops dripping down the sides of his face.

"I don't like this."

"Don't worry, I'll be fine."

"Call me when you get home so I know you made it in one piece."

"I will," I said, looking up at him. Then he bent over and kissed me on the cheek. It was a simple gesture, one showed by friends all the time, but it made me cry even harder.

Jeff Walker interrupted me from Babs's crooning by poking his head through my open doorway and asking, "You're joining us for Sharon's party, yes?" I composed myself and studied the man who had become a friend and colleague in a short amount of time. He was the antithesis of Marty, serious and soft-spoken, with nondescript features. His office was just down the hall from mine. "It's Halloween. You haven't forgotten?"

"Don't you find the idea of people hiding in costumes creepy?" I asked.

"Didn't you ever want to be someone else for a night?"

"I'm leaning toward no," I said, deciding that perspective was all about where you sat. Usually, people are never what they seem, only what we wish them to be.

"You have to go, Jess. As one of your bosses, it's my job to tell you attendance is mandatory."

"Of course," I said, reluctantly. "I wouldn't miss it."

"Now, go home. It's late. That too is an order."

Chapter 16

Sharon Walker's surprise forty-first birthday party was in full swing when I spotted Marty walking in. Actually, people like Marty didn't walk in anywhere. They saunter, carrying with them enough energy to ignite a room. Having the party a year after the big 4-0 was Marty's idea. He said she'd never expect it, and she didn't.

The event was held at a private home in Holmby Hills, and hundreds of important people were in attendance. Music and film executives, radio personalities, and a handful of actors and musicians decorated the lawns of the sprawling home. Sharon Walker was an über agent at William Morris. There was no profession in the entertainment industry not accounted for. And there was Marty, casually pacing himself through the cache of costumes: a mixture of the comical, the glamorous, and the common. He had no idea he was being watched, wandering through the crowd like a decisive animal on the prowl. Women flocked around him, oblivious to the way he kindly, and abruptly, brushed them off. When he stopped at the nearest bar and ordered himself a drink, I moved in closer.

"Hello, Marty." I heard Sharon Walker as she approached him at the bar.

"Happy birthday, Sharon," he said, leaning in for a kiss. "You look positively lovely, the most youthful Cleopatra I've ever seen."

I listened as he dazzled her.

"Who are you supposed to be?" she asked with a smile.

"Just me," he replied. "I'm not really into dress up."

"Why do I have a feeling that you are one of the few people in the world who can dress as yourself at a costume party?" He was as striking as I had ever seen him, and even more so because he didn't know it.

"I'd only wear one of these monkey suits for you."

"Let me fix your tie," she said, reaching up to repair the haphazardly strewn fabric. The dark jacket hugged his body, but the tie begged for help. "We need to find you a wife that can do these things for you. You can't be going out all disheveled."

Fastening the tie around his neck, Sharon Walker stepped back and surveyed her work, satisfied with the results. "Prince Charming, I presume," bellowed Jeff Walker from behind them. "I see you've already managed to squire away my wife."

"If she'd have me, I'd take her," he said, laughing at his old friend, who, I must say, looked terribly silly in his King Tut getup.

"She is a knockout, isn't she?" he asked his friend while placing his arm around her waist. The affection between them was rare. You hardly saw a devotion like theirs in Hollywood. Could they be the ones to threaten the validity of the married-couples-are-never-happy theory?

Marty said, "You two are an inspiration. Best friends, lovers, Sharon still laughing at Jeff's ridiculous jokes." Was he telepathic or was I standing too close?

"Jessica, is that you?" I heard Jeff say, a collection of heads turning in my direction.

"Is it possible that you're even more gorgeous than Cinderella herself?" remarked Sharon, heading toward me. Imagine my surprise when I opened the box from the costume store, and it wasn't Sandra Day O'Connor's robe in there.

"Who are you, and what did you do with Jessica Parker?" Jeff asked.

"Hopefully, she's under here somewhere holding onto her last shred of dignity," I said, noticing Marty standing there, not sure if he should laugh or pounce.

"Marty, cat got your tongue?" his friend quipped.

"Okay, little boys," I said, "recess is over."

"Thank you for coming, Jess," Jeff said, walking over to my side, filling the space between Marty and me and kissing me on the cheek. "It means a lot to me that you're here, to both of us."

"To all of us," Marty corrected him. Within a minute, Sharon and Jeff were off welcoming other guests, leaving the two of us alone. Marty inched closer, taking my hand in his, and in one gallant movement, raised it to his lips with a kiss. "Hello Jessica, or shall I call you Elizabeth, or Stephanie, or some other dazzling royal?"

"Jessica will be fine, Marty," I said.

"I'm Prince Charming," he teased. "My crown dropped on the way in."

I tried to avoid his eyes. "I figured you to be a king. Henry, maybe?"

"Then you must be one of my many wives. You look stunning."

The dress I wore was everything I hated—girly and feminine, white and satin. It was strapless with long layers of itchy tulle that dragged across the floor and caused me to trip. The kicker was the sparkly tiara that rested on my head. "All the reasons I hated dress-up as a kid."

He said, "I like your hair down like that."

"Thanks," I said, instinctively reaching for the hair that was free of its customary ponytail. I appreciated that he noticed something other than the ridiculous outfit.

"Can I get you something to drink?"

"I think I'll have some champagne."

"Don't move. I'll be right back."

I laughed. The slightest step could be life-threatening.

While the band played Frank Sinatra, Marty and I sipped our drinks and watched the others dance. He ignored my pleas to sit this one out. Instead, he grabbed me by the hand, leading me to the dance floor.

I could forget that he was my boss, but not about the crowd of people who were watching us and formulating gossip, which would end up on *Access Hollywood*.

He maneuvered me across the dance floor, taking the lead, like he did everything in his life. His persistence inhibited me from resisting. Some people in the world just evade the laws of gravity, pushing you in directions you normally wouldn't go. When our arms found each other, we danced as if we had been partners for years. Closing my eyes, I let the music circle around me. I was not the same girl who danced all those years ago with a boy she hardly knew. I was a woman, a lady, and Marty was definitely a man.

"You're good at this," he commented, a whisper in my ear.

I lifted my skirt and showed him my real secret: Converse high-top sneakers.

"You need that glass slipper," he said, pulling me closer.

"Such a romantic."

"Stick around, and I won't disappoint."

"I have no doubt."

"Shit," he called out, "Dori's headed our way." I turned to see the attractive woman Marty had been dating the last few weeks making a beeline in our direction. Her costume was the sexy, vixen kind. He grabbed my hand and led me to the guesthouse adjacent to the pool.

"What did you do now?" I asked

"Nothing," he said, watching through the window as Dori stomped off into the crowd.

"It must be something. She looks pretty pissed."

"You women get too sensitive about these things."

"What things, Marty? What did you do?"

"I was supposed to pick her up tonight."

"You were supposed to bring her here? She was your date?"

"You can call it that," he said, with a sheepish look plastered across his face. I didn't find it amusing. Throwing his arms up in the air in defeat, he said, "You're right. I know. It was terrible. I'm sorry."

"Don't apologize to me. Go out there and apologize to Dori."

"What?"

"You heard me," I said. "Go out and there and apologize."

"Why would I do that when we can stay here and play spin the bottle all night?"

"Go!" I said. "Now! Out, out," I repeated as I opened the door and scooted him down the cobblestone path.

It was hours later when I watched the two of them sitting in a lounge chair. She was rubbing his back, he was smiling, and I climbed into my pumpkin and drove home.

Chapter 17

The next morning a large package was delivered to my office. It wasn't until I completed a grueling four-hour meeting with a composer and read through two scripts that I remembered it was there. Opening the brown paper, I noticed a smaller box within the box. Lifting up the final top, I studied its contents closely.

I'd never seen anything quite like it, other than in books and film, and I didn't know who would manufacture such an impractical item, but it was interesting. The note included was written on stationery with Marty Tauber's name printed boldly across the top.

Next time, don't forget your slipper.

Perching the glass shoe on my left hand, I marveled at its sparkle. It could have been my exact shoe size, but I didn't dare put it on. Instead, as the bearer of such unprecedented adulation, I giggled to myself, like a schoolgirl.

Picking up the phone, I dialed Marty's office. "Mr. Tauber has been expecting your call, Jessica," said his secretary, Marla.

"Shocking," I blurted out to the loud music that played while I was on hold.

"What took you so long?" he asked.

"I just opened it."

"But I sent it priority to arrive first thing."

"It was here. I just hadn't gotten to it."

"Your boss is working you too hard."

"Shamelessly."

"Then you like it?"

"It's clever."

"What happened to you last night? You didn't say good-bye."

"I couldn't find you," I lied.

"Want to get a bite to eat?" he asked.

I looked at my watch. "It's five o'clock."

"And that's a problem because…"

"My grandmother eats at five o'clock."

"Then give me her number. Maybe she'll eat with me."

"I'm not that hungry."

"Then watch me eat."

I shook my head from side to side. We'd been through this a dozen times before. Marty had a hearty appetite. He ate at all hours of the day. Breakfast all morning long, lunch at four, dinner sometimes five, then again at ten. It's amazing he wasn't grossly overweight from all the food he inhaled.

"Where to this time?" I asked, eventually stepping into the car.

"Mexican," he said. "I want some tequila."

It was daylight outside, but in the darkened recesses of Casa Vega, you couldn't tell. Without any windows, the place was dark, cramped, and crowded. When my eyes finally adjusted, I caught the full Mexican regalia covering the walls, the Mexican men pacing the room with their violins in anxious hands. One of them stopped his fiddling long enough to seat us at a table in a far corner in the back. "Sombrero?" he asked us.

"For the lady," Marty said.

"No way." I shook my head as Marty went ahead and placed the oversized, colorful hat on my head.

"You don't expect me to wear this all night, do you?"

"Are you giving me all night?" he asked.

I pretended not to hear him and threw the hat on the chair beside me, which was fine, because he didn't even wait for my response. He was busy telling the waitress to bring us a round of tequila shots. "Let's get hammered," he said as she walked away. "Let's get stupid drunk and silly. It's only five thirty. We'll be sober well before work tomorrow."

I said, "I have a dozen meetings tomorrow, and I have to meet with the attorneys about the fine print on Daisy Duke's contract."

"Oh, come on, Jessica, lighten up. I'm your boss, for God's sake. You won't be fired if you sleep in, and I won't dock your pay."

I'd seen this reckless behavior before. "She dumped you, didn't she?"

It took him a split second to answer. "Like a hot potato."

"Marty, for someone so full of spontaneity, you really are predictable."

"What about you?' he asked. "You're the least impulsive person I've ever met. As predictable as I am with women, you're about as predictable with men."

"What men?" I asked.

"Exactly the point. When was the last time you even went on a date?"

"Sex isn't everything, Marty."

"Obviously," he laughed.

"It's complicated," I said.

"Spoken by someone who's still holding a torch," he teased.

"Whatever," I said.

"I'm right, aren't I?"

"No."

"Who is he? I'll kill him."

"I'd like to see that."

"Come on, you've heard all about my women. Who's the guy that broke your heart?"

"This is ridiculous."

"That bad?" he asked.

I peered directly into his eyes. He said, "Tell me."

I shook my head over and over, knowing I shouldn't say his name out loud, but it emerged: "Jonas Levy."

He hesitated a minute. "Adam's son, Jonas Levy?"

I nodded.

"Now that I wasn't expecting."

"It was nothing, really."

"It was way more than nothing. Don't tell me a pretty girl like you hasn't found a way to move on."

I silently prayed for amnesia and that his compliment wouldn't feel so nice.

"You look surprised. I'm not all about boobs, you know. If I wasn't your boss…" he began, stopping himself just as the waitress dropped the shots on the table, which was excellent timing because I didn't want to hear the rest. Or maybe I did, and the tequila would help me digest what he was saying. My eager palm wrapped around the smooth cylinder closest to me, and the cold liquid slid down my throat. Glass down, lime to the mouth, all this while Marty watched with amusement before downing his, flawlessly.

"Impressive," he said.

"Likewise."

"What else can you do?"

"Lots of things."

"Tell me."

The tequila went straight through me. There were parts within, warm and tingly, flirtatious and chatty, that prohibited any type of censorship over my mouth. I said, "What do you want to know?"

"Why don't we start with what happened between you and Jonas?"

Something about hearing his name always felt like a freight train slamming into me at full speed.

"Nothing."

"Again, with the nothing," he said. "I must be on to something. Waitress," he called out, "we'll need another round." And then to me, "to get to the bottom of all this nothing."

The liquid was traveling at ridiculous speed. "What do you want to hear? I felt a zillion things for him. I think he felt the same for me, but it ended there. Nothing happened. It was never really able to progress."

"Why not?"

"His girlfriend."

"He had a girlfriend?"

"That's what I said."

"I cheated on every girlfriend I ever had back in those days."

"How upstanding," I said. "What's your excuse now?"

"I'm not married. If I was, I'd take it a little more seriously."

"Just a little?"

"I take marriage very seriously. That's why I've never done it."

I pondered this before raising the next shot to my lips. I wasn't merely talking about sexual cheating here, and I think Marty knew that too. That's why he said, "Little Jessica Parker, still lovesick after all these years."

"Your empathy is astounding."

"I'm sorry," he said, straightening up. "It couldn't have been easy for you."

"No, it wasn't."

The waitress brought Marty's food and another round of shots. I didn't have to be coaxed into it. He raised his glass to mine, and we toasted to fidelity.

"Jonas Levy, the first boy you ever loved. Hard to believe."

He said boy like we were in the eleventh grade, but it didn't matter because I was already there. It was like being on automatic pilot. A gear switched, and I was catapulted through time. I could only nod.

"Are you feeling okay?" he asked. "Why don't you have some chips or something to absorb the alcohol?" I'd become ravenous, as if my body knew that it was about to become depleted of vital nutrients. When the waiter approached, I ordered nachos loaded with cheese, sour cream, and extra jalapenos.

"And there's been no one since? How long ago *was* that?" He looked repulsed.

"Six years," I said, knowing the number by heart.

"That's a long time to be living without love, without letting anybody close."

I brushed it off. I'd been living without love long before that, long before Jonas.

"I thought I'd never get over it, but I did, and you're wrong, I'm not still pining over him."

That's when the tequila kicked in, speaking on my behalf. "We don't always leave someone we love, or forget them, or get over them all at once. Every time they hurt us and every time we cry, we're saying a partial good-bye until the person is eventually gone. Believe me, I'm much better off now."

"Adam never said anything. He must have meant a lot to you."

"Hasn't anyone ever broken your heart?" I asked.

Marty leaned forward, hands clasped. "People have never broken my heart, Jess. Films and songs, now they've broken my heart. Sometimes their words, their plots, leave me as flustered as a person might leave others. I don't think I've ever allowed myself to love someone the way I love my work."

"There's something sad about that."

"Yours is sad. Mine has been a lively road marked by great triumphs. I don't just create and watch films with my eyes and ears. I observe and listen with what's in my heart. I've experienced grief. I've felt pain. I've known loss and betrayal, and on the upside, I've felt great joy and even love."

"But you've experienced all of that alone. Those are the types of emotions we're supposed to share with other people, the kind that connect us."

"I guess I never had a relationship with anyone that made me feel all that. If I had, I might have been encouraged to make it last." I savored this about him, and then he said, "All the guys in the office have crushes on you."

"You're just trying to make me feel better."

"It's true. I told them you're off limits."

"You've really become my knight in shining armor, haven't you?"

"Isn't that what every girl wants?"

The fourth tequila shot landed in front of me. "I used to think that was what I wanted," I started, but I didn't finish. I'd seen how far away I can be carried.

The plate of nachos arrived, and I realized how nicely the cheese and the sour cream could coat my belly. I was ready for the next shot. Marty's eyes were red and still a beautiful blue. He wasn't outwardly drunk, but there was a definite loss in gross motor skills, and his guard was down—the way he was casually flirting with me and making me feel beautiful. I didn't even try to pretend that I wasn't charmed by him.

We talked about men and women and relationships, and although I'd had a very limited amount of exposure to the jerks that women complained about, I still had to agree with Marty that most of the time, women could be tough, scheming, and spiteful. If the men were guilty of anything, it was weakness, but the women, they could be utterly daunting.

"There *was* a love," he blurted out.

"She must have hurt you real bad. It only took five tequilas to unrepress her from your past."

"Her name was Michaela. She was South African, a model, and we were seventeen and mad for each other. I thought I was going to marry her, and then she went away for a shoot, and I, being the quintessential bastard, ended up in bed with one of her best friends."

"You piece of shit," I said.

"It's not what you think. She played games, all the time, loving me one minute, keeping me at arm's length the next. She was painfully insecure. I think she pushed me away to protect herself. There were rumors she'd slept with one of the photographers on a shoot."

"But her best friend?"

"I had to do something to get a rise out of her."

"And presumably yourself."

"She didn't talk to me for years. She'd forgotten her participation in our demise."

He reached for my nachos. I watched as he rolled a black olive against his tongue. "And then she fell in love, this time for real, and we've been close friends ever since."

"How come you don't drag her to your Sunday movie break-up club?"

"She lives in South Africa. Gave up modeling, has three kids, lives on a farm or something," he laughed. "I thought you enjoyed our movie dates."

"I never thought of them as dates."

"Semantics."

"No, it's okay," I slurred, putting my hand on the table close to his. "You've been amazing. I don't have many friends, and you've become one…" I didn't go on because the words forming in my head weren't for Marty, my boss, but for the man sitting across from me, the one who had me tiptoeing closer to possibility. Marty was giving me *something*, call it relationship, friendship, whatever it was. The seed was being planted, and it didn't have to be hidden from the world or even from ourselves. Opportunity was before me, and I was allowing it in. Or maybe it was the tequila. God, I was feeling horny.

The emotions mixed with the shots, and as though he was watching a movie, Marty watched my face change. How the things he made me feel took over and frightened me. "I've never had this effect on a woman before," he said. "Usually they're ecstatic to be around me, and the last thing they want is to be my friend." He said this with such a straight face it made me chuckle.

"Laughter. That's good. I want you to be happy when you're with me."

"What's with you guys?" I asked. "Does a little vulnerability scare you?"

"Only when I'm feeling a little vulnerable myself," he said, which made me think twice about my next sarcastic reply. "I didn't mean to pry about your past," he went on. "Your sadness makes you who you are today. I'm enjoying that person, and I want to know her more and understand her better. The last thing I want is to be the person who makes you sad. So let's leave the past where it belongs and concentrate on other things like tequila and glass slippers and fidelity and maybe," he teased, "making out a little."

He was right there in front of me. My lips could have reached his and let him inside. I felt out of control. Fortunately, the Mexicans intervened, arriving at our table for a mariachi session. I listened to the music, but my thoughts were swelling. When the trio finished, Marty handed them a nice wad of bills, and I observed him. This was a different type of man—secure, honest, candid, a breed of man that came with age, experience, and no false pretenses. He was himself, not a pretender.

"You never fell in love after Michaela?"

"Oh, I fell in love with hundreds of women. They just didn't last very long."

"Why doesn't that surprise me?"

"You make me sound like some animal."

"Aren't you?"

"We're all innately animals," he said.

"Some of us."

"I just never found the right one," he confessed. "If the relationship was good, the sex was bad, the sex hot, the conversation cold. I have strict criteria."

"Hot, voluptuous, with a penchant for music?"

"That's what you think of me?" he asked, almost sadly. "You're just saying that because you know exactly what my type is, and it scares you."

We were officially hammered. I knew this because when my eyes met his, the room around me began to spin.

"I don't know what I think of you," I said, finding my voice. "You're forthright and mysterious. It's a contradiction."

"What are we doing here?" he stopped me, unexpectedly.

"What do you mean?"

"What are we doing? What are we really talking about here?"

I was silent. I'd never been with someone so direct before. My adrenaline was pumping, and with each impulse, my body was becoming more and more alive.

"Tell me why I'm a contradiction."

"You're this cool, detached womanizer. You crave the wild, crazy nights, the women, the booze, possibly the drugs, but I think you're just waiting for the next Michaela, the woman who will steal your heart away."

"And you think that might be you?"

I didn't want the tequila to speak on my behalf, but against my better judgment, my mouth opened, and "I never said that" shot out.

"I'm serious," he said, searching my eyes.

"No, you're not," I refuted. "That's just the tequila talking."

His words stopped me from reaching for my glass.

"I like you, Jessica."

"I like you too, Marty."

He repeated it again. "And if I have to, I'll find you a job at another company so I can be with you, but I'm selfish and I don't want to lose my best employee."

"You'll chew me up and spit me out in less than two months, and then I'll have no job."

"Two months?" he asked. "I'll take it."

"That's not what I meant."

"I know what you meant," he said. "It's hard for you to admit it, but you like me."

I looked up at him. Did I really need to respond to that?

"Maybe you're not used to men like me," he said. "I don't play games. If that's what you're looking for, I'm not it."

This was what I'd wished for and avoided for years, my heart skipping multiple beats, my judgment clouded. I was on a cliff about to jump off, the feeling that I couldn't breathe, the drama, the longing, and all the other terrible things that got me into trouble in the first place hovering around me.

"Would you be opposed to going on a date with me?" he asked. "And just so we're clear, a real date, not as friends, not as your boss, not because I'm paying you, but because you want to be there."

He was challenging all my existing pretenses. I couldn't comprehend that we could just come together so easily. It didn't fit into the schema I'd invented in my head. Love was supposed to be a struggle, dramatic and leaving you wanting for more. Love wasn't supposed to be so *simple*. 'Cause then it wouldn't make sense when it got to the part when someone leaves.

"My chatterbox has suddenly gone mute. What's wrong with you, Jess? What are you so afraid of?"

"I think I'm helplessly drunk," I garbled.

"Think about it. I think we'd be good together."

"You make it sound like a business proposition."

"I'd never be this forthcoming in business."

This was a sobering moment for me. His hands had found mine on the table, and he was touching them. His fingers were soft; they were strong; they were heating up my entire body. "Do you want to get out of here?" he asked. It was an invitation and a question all rolled into one. "I already called Julio. The car will be waiting for us out front."

I stood up, because to say yes was admitting how impossible it was for me to say no to him. Grabbing me by the arm, he led me out of the restaurant. Julio was there, as promised, opening the door first for me, and then holding it for Marty, who took the seat beside me. The sun glared in my eyes, and I squinted from the brightness. I was trapped in my head, replaying the conversation again and again.

We didn't speak as the car drove up the hill toward Los Angeles. The sun was beginning to set and I wished for darkness. Marty reached for my hand, and I allowed his warm, caring fingers to encircle mine. Happy, scared, and caught up, I was a combination of many dangerous sensations.

Julio was driving well above the speed limit, and I felt something unpleasant filling my throat.

"I think I'm going to throw up."

"No, you're not," he said to me reassuringly. "You'll be fine. Here, put your head on my shoulder."

I rested my head there where he said, our bodies cozied up to one another across the backseat. I swore to myself I wouldn't get sick. Partly because he sounded so convincing, I didn't want to disappoint him, and partly because I didn't want this to be the way he remembered the night.

"Make this louder," I heard Marty say to Julio. I grasped onto the tune, the lyrics a rope that grounded me, restraining me with its words. It was a Tesla song. I could tell any song in three notes or less, even when I was drunk, and Tesla was easy with the shrill of their distinct voices. Marty had a penchant for rock bands. It had something to do with this long-haired phase he went through. He was into the rhythm and the noise, and although I enjoyed the music, I was a *word* girl. In business, I could pick a tune better than anyone, but when I was home alone and flipping the stations and listening to demos and there were no pressures to enlist a song to a particular movie, I was all about the words. Words always told a story.

Tesla was singing to me tonight. It always happened that way, it seemed, but then again, there are statistically more songs about love than any other subject on the radio, which means if you're a love junkie, it's not hard to find one that mimics your life.

"Did you hear that, pretty darlin'?" He was stroking my hair. My shoulders were sinking into his chest. His arm was wrapped around me. I was falling.

I nodded, because if I opened my mouth, more than just a word would come out.

Being there on Marty's shoulder, how could I describe it? If I wanted it, I knew he could take care of me forever. This caused me to hyperventilate. Breathe, I said to myself, breathe. I knew if I could just take breaths, I'd be okay. And when I did, the air filled my lungs and bits of Marty were sneaking in. They were the masculine scents, the mix of sweat, cologne, booze, and a cigarette that would remind me of him when I smelled him on my clothes days later.

I must have fallen asleep, because my eyes opened, and we were in front of my apartment in Santa Monica.

"Here, let me help you out," he said, lifting me up, careful not to let my skirt rise past my thigh. His hand reached inside my bag for the keys, and in one fluid motion, he was inside my apartment; thankfully, my roommates were nowhere to be found.

I pointed to the bedroom, where he laid me on my bed. "Do you want some water? Coffee?" he asked.

"I'm fine." I looked at the clock. It was either 8:13 or 8:33. I did need to get a new clock.

"You don't have to come in tomorrow if you're not up to it."

"Have faith," I heard myself say.

He was sitting on the edge of my bed, Marty, in his sexy jeans, white oxford, bloodshot blue eyes. The room seemed smaller. "I'm gonna go now," he whispered.

"Don't," I said, leaning in closer, "Stay."

"Are you sure?"

"Don't ask me that, or I'll change my mind."

He got up, and I heard the front door open and close. I was glad I didn't have to see Julio's face when he told him he was staying. When he returned, he handed me a glass of water and then went into my bathroom in search of some Tylenol.

"Take these. You'll feel a lot better."

"Please tell me you didn't go into my medicine cabinet."

He laughed. "Nothing I haven't seen before."

He sat beside me taking my hand into his, touching each finger. "The alcohol hasn't spoiled your judgment, I hope."

I shook my head. "I don't know why it was so easy to give myself to someone who only wanted part of me. Here you are, everything a girl could want, and I'm struggling with letting you in, letting you close."

He watched me and didn't say a word. He squeezed my hand even harder. That's how I knew what he was thinking, by the strong, careful grip of his hand.

"You make me want to be that person," I continued. "That person you think I am, that person who's like you, in search of that one great love, but I don't know if I'm her. I'm scared."

He moved toward me in slow motion, or it just seemed like that because I was in sluggish, tequila time. He gathered me in his arms and hugged me. It wasn't sexual. It wasn't friendly either. It was meaningful and kind, and I knew I wanted to hug him back, really, really hug him back. We sat like that for a few minutes. He, stroking my hair, rocking me in his arms; me, lapping it up like a lovesick puppy.

He pulled away first, brushing my cheek with his palm. I leaned into him, feeling the smoothness of his fingers across my face. I wanted to curl my whole body into his hand.

"I want you to trust me," he said, just as a barrage of thunder resounded throughout the room. Within twenty seconds, it was pouring rain, the hammering sounds drowning out the swelling in my heart.

I nodded, resting my head against his hand, listening to the swells accumulate outside my window, wanting to tell him more.

"Trust hasn't always come easy to me," I said. "Not when I lost my father at such a young age."

"I'm sorry," he said. "That explains a lot."

"It was eighteen years ago."

"That's a tough thing for any kid to deal with."

"He was leaving work early to be home for birthday cake. It was a perfectly beautiful June day. I was playing in the yard when clouds had hovered overhead and a stretch of rain was ready to unleash itself from the sky. It wasn't ominous at the time, but when I think back to that afternoon, there was something chilling about the way the wind swept in, hugging my hair and neck, wrapping itself around my dress and shoes.

"My mother called me in, and at first, I hesitated because I always loved the sky before the rain fell, the moment before the water leaked from the clouds, the way they were thick and full. And I always tried to catch the first drop in my mouth, closing my eyes and stretching my neck back, feeling the rain on my cheek or on my forehead. And I remember being so happy that afternoon, so free, so light. I had to catch just one in my mouth. Only one.

"He died that afternoon. The rain on my tongue—because I did get that drop in my mouth—was the same liquid that stole my father from me. I was eyeing the cake and the pink frosting when the officers arrived at the house. I didn't see them, but I heard my mother's wails in the kitchen and knew. "It was *me*, Marty," I said, searching his eyes to make sure he heard me correctly, understood how deep were my wounds.

"What was you?" he asked.

"It was *my* fault," I said, the power of my words appearing before me, words I'd never said to anyone, not my mother, not Jonas, not Adam, none of them. "It was me. He was rushing home for me, my fourth birthday, and it's my fault he got killed."

Marty was no longer looking at a twenty-two-year-old, but a small child, frightened and ashamed. Taking my face forcefully into his hands, he said, "It wasn't your fault."

"Yes, it was," I said, turning away from him, realizing what I'd done. "I'm sorry. I'm sorry to unload this on you." I noticed how my voice had changed. Either I had aged many years or the tequila was wearing off.

He didn't say anything else. He just reached forward, pulling me close to him again and I squeezed him hard, clinging to his outstretched arms and ridding myself of the guilt that had paralyzed me most of my life.

"I won't leave you," he whispered in my ear, kissing me lightly there with his lips. I believed him because it's what I hoped, and all the things I'd been warned against seemed so meaningless. His kisses found my cheeks, then my lips, covering my mouth with his own. I didn't hesitate, even with the stale taste of tequila on my breath. I didn't pull back. I gave in to Marty's tenderness. It's what I wanted, what I waited patiently for, and what I rightfully deserved.

Once I'd given in to his kiss, his hands found the rest of me, touching me, holding me, sweeping the fingers across a body that was ready to be explored.

"I won't leave you," he said again, this time staring into my eyes to be sure that I felt what he was trying to say.

"Hold me," I said.

"I'll hold you all night."

"You can," I whispered back at him. "It's still early."

And his arms were around me again.

Chapter 18

Sunflowers. I love sunflowers. Their name precisely describes the sunshine, and their strong, sturdy stems and colorful petals make me smile. Friday morning a big bouquet of them appeared magically on my desk. The card read, *I miss you already.* I surveyed the offices to see if anyone had noticed, if anyone knew who sent them, if anyone could see that I was lit up from within like a firefly.

A week had gone by since that night, and I could still feel Marty's hands on my body. We hadn't slept together, but there are tender moments far more intimate than sex that left me feeling as if we had.

The morning after, as he so eloquently termed it, reduced my office demeanor from professional to absurd. Marty was much better at the love game than I was. He was cool and reserved when we were around other people, while attentive and boyish when we were alone.

The flowers arrived as he boarded a flight to New York. When I brought them home to my new apartment in Century City, I watched as the petals fell one by one onto the table, leaving me to question their meaning and what was going on in my life. Reaching for the yellow pages, I located a Dr. Norton, Dr. Deborah Norton. Her office was in the valley, a child psychologist. Could it have been the same woman? Dr. Norton obviously had a profound effect on me, this woman who both irritated me and enthralled me. She did. She was consistent. I could always count on our Fridays at three.

The phone rang, dispelling any thoughts I had about calling the number. It was eight o'clock.

"Hi, Beth," I said, knowing who it was because she always called when the rates went down on the East Coast.

"Hi, darling," he surprised me.

I was so happy to hear from him. I was sure he could feel the vibrations through the phone.

"I missed you today."

"I missed you too," I said, fingering the yellow petals in my hand. "How are you?"

"Busy, lonely. We just finished dinner, and we're heading to a club for a showcase. I'll try to call you to say good night."

"Don't worry, I'm fine."

"I'm not worried," he said, "I want to hear your voice. How's the new place coming along?"

"I like the quiet, the privacy."

"You should've moved in with me."

I smiled inside, letting the suggestive offer warm me up. Music was playing loudly in the background. He said, "They're playing our song."

"What's that?"

"DaVinyls, 'Touch Myself.'"

"You're twisted," I laughed. "Sick and perverted."

"You like that."

"Maybe I do, maybe I don't."

"Then I'll call you later and we can talk about it."

"Good-bye, Marty."

"Bye, beautiful."

The book was there on the table, the page opened to where I'd left it. I picked up the phone again and dialed the number. It was late, so the likelihood of her being there was slim. I should have been unloading the boxes from the move the day before, but decided this was more important.

"Hello."

"Hello," I said, if not by complete accident.

"Who's this?" she asked.

"I'm sorry," I said, "I must have the wrong number." It was her. I would recognize that nasal voice anywhere.

"Sorry," I said again, hanging up the phone, hoping she didn't have some modern mechanism that enabled her to see who was calling.

I stared at the phone, now my enemy, when it started to ring. Please don't be her.

"Hello."

"You sound disappointed it's me," said Beth.

"No, I'm actually relieved."

"What's going on? I haven't heard from you all week. How was the move?"

"Fine," I said, her voice a temporary relief. "What's up with you?"

"I'm a freshman all over again, the low man on the totem pole."

"You're at one of the top law schools in the country; there's no such thing as a low man. I bet you can find the loophole in my artist's contract quicker than our in-house guys."

"Another licensing headache?" she asked.

"The worst kind."

Then she laughed.

"What's so funny?" I asked.

"You. I love to hear you talk like a grown-up, your own apartment, a high-powered job with clearances and deadlines and legal jargon, serious stuff. Why don't you come out here and visit before the leaves have fallen?"

"You can actually see trees from your window?"

"No, but we'll go to the park. You'll love it. Besides, all your record labels are out here, and you can combine it with a business trip." Beth had been beckoning me to visit her in New York for a while now. New York was close to Boston, and since the entire Northeast had always been an area occupied by Jonas, it was one which I deliberately avoided. Only because he had once loomed so large was it possible that he might stretch across the entire eastern seaboard. Now he appeared smaller, a bleak spot on a map. Maybe it was time to take a trip.

"Marty's there now."

"How *is* Marty?"

"Fine."

"Now that's a vague response. Do tell."

"I think I like him."

"Your boss, the womanizing philanderer?"

I nodded, but she couldn't see. I squeezed the phone tighter in my hand.

"We kissed last week."

"He's not harassing you, is he?"

"It's nothing like that, entirely consensual."

"Do you think it's a good idea to stay there, working with him and dating him?"

My voice of reason had spoken. "If it gets serious," which it already had, "then I'll make that decision."

"Six years, and you've finally managed to move on, a miracle. What's with you and these Jewish boys anyway?"

She didn't say his name. She never did.

"Let me clarify one thing. Marty is nothing like the last Jewish boy."

"Then I suppose I can tell you."

"Tell me what?"

"They got married."

I processed this carefully.

"Are you there?" she asked.

"Yeah," but I wasn't. I was on a hill atop Mulholland Drive with wind whipping through my hair.

"I'm sorry. I shouldn't have said anything."

"How do you know?" I asked

"I read it in the paper…last year."

"A year? You kept this from me for a *year?* The effort you put into protecting me makes me want to jump on a plane and come give you a big hug."

"Well, you may have to be coming out soon, because he's not the only one with marriage on his mind."

"Paul proposed? How long have you been keeping *that* from me?"

"Just a few days."

"Well, it took him long enough."

"Doesn't matter, I'd have waited forever."

Beth had fallen in love the first day of college. There she was carrying her suitcases up the steps of her dorm at BU, and he appeared, offering a hand. I'll never forget the day she called me and said, "It's better than the movies. One hundred percent."

"I'm so happy for you, Beth. You deserve this."

"We haven't set a date but as soon as we do, you better book a ticket. You have a big job to do."

"What's that?"

"Maid of honor, and don't make that face I'm betting you're making, because I won't have it any other way."

"Do I have to wear a dress?"

"Yes, and it won't be pink or peach, I promise. Oh shoot, Jess, that's probably Paul's parents clicking in. I'll call you tomorrow."

"You better. I want to hear about the proposal. Knowing Paul, I'm sure it was something extravagant."

"I love you. I miss you," she yelled before the phone went silent.

"Me too," I said, putting the phone down, the impact causing a whole new spattering of petals on the Formica. When I finally exhaled, I knew the air would never feel as compressed as it once had, and my heart, once heavy, was now lighter than it had been in years.

Chapter 19

It only took me three days to accept Marty's proposal. When you're that sure about someone you've known for such a short period of time, the decision is easy. It's the explaining to everyone why you're jumping into something "so quickly" that's the cumbersome part. So even though my heart had said an impetuous yes when he proposed, it took another two days to convince my mother and Beth that I was doing the right thing.

"It's simple," I told my mother, who picked up her telephone as she heard the word *marriage* reverberating from my mouth and bouncing off her answering machine.

"I thought you weren't there."

"I was screening."

"Screening from whom?" I asked, knowing that my mother loved to gab on the phone with *anyone* who bothered to call.

"Does it matter? Did I hear you say you're getting married? You've only known this man a few months."

"Eight," I corrected her.

"That's not enough time, Jess. You can't possibly know him that well, and marriage, it's a whole different game, a whole new set of rules."

I could hear the concern in her words, the mother's need to protect her child, but I wasn't a child anymore.

It was a surprise, to say the least, but I'd come to rely on Marty's direct and innovative approach. He took me to dinner under the guise of discussing this lawsuit that had the capacity to complicate things for SixthSense, some confusing breach of contract thing that could have several employees in the company subpoenaed as early as next week. He tried to assure me that these types of lawsuits never panned out, but the idea of Marty being questioned and scrutinized terrified me; and because I worked so closely with him, would I be subpoenaed also? Marty just came right out and told me not to worry.

"How can I not worry?" I asked. "I might have to testify *against* you!"

"I have it all taken care of." But I wasn't a believer.

"Jess," he said, and I should have noticed the twinkle in his eyes, the way his lip seemed to curve a tiny bit as if stifling a smile, "they can't question you."

"How do you know that?"

"A wife can never testify against her husband." And with that bold statement out of the way, the fear that had gripped me turned into something else, something happier. He then placed a perfect diamond on my finger and asked me to be his.

"You're not using me to stay out of jail?" I said, before kissing him square on the mouth.

"That's a low one, even for me, but since there's no case, you won't have to worry about that."

"There's no case?"

"I had to figure out a way to trick you, so you wouldn't see this coming."

"You made that all up?" I said, before giggling and grabbing him in my arms.

I thought it best to leave the details of the proposal out of this conversation with my mother. She was saying, "Marriage is hard enough, and statistically you're reducing your chance for a good one by jumping into it with someone you barely know."

"I'm in love," I said.

"I've heard this before," she said, unconvinced.

Marty was what I had been looking for all this time and it did manifest quickly, but I wasn't about to question what felt so nice and uncomplicated. I had paid a high price for allowing myself to love again.

"Can't you just be happy for me?" I asked. "Can't you just, for once, let me relish in the moment? Haven't I earned this? Don't you want me to spend the rest of my life with someone who adores me and only wants to please me?"

"Well, it would be nice if I could meet him."

"Is that was this is about?"

"Maybe."

"Geography's the only reason you haven't met him," I said. "Trust me, you will love him."

It was over a family dinner at Marty's home in the hills that I finally and officially gave Marty the affirmative answer that he was waiting for.

He empathized with my mother's concern and set out to make things right. In less than twenty-four hours, she was squired away on a plane headed west to meet the man who had stolen my heart. He also invited his parents, a couple in their seventies who talked endlessly about their time in Palm Springs. The warmth of family around us eased the answer out of me, and when I saw my mother flitting around Marty, practically stepping over herself for his attention, I knew I'd made the right choice. Selma and Ezra Tauber were welcoming and kind, and I watched them lost in deep, loud conversation. There was no doubt we would have a full and happy life.

"Where are you right now?" Marty asked. He was seated next to me, nudging me with his shoulder. "You're off somewhere."

I faced him, seeing his eyes as they appraised me with a kindness any woman would envy. "I'm with you."

"Where are we?" he asked, a faint smile crossing his lips as his hand dropped into my lap, caressing my bare leg. I searched the table, but my mother had now joined Marty's folks in conversation, and no one appeared to notice that the host and hostess had gone off to a secret, private world. His fingers grazed my skin lightly.

"In a good place."

"Yeah," he continued, softly stroking my inner thigh, "and what happens in that place?"

Nothing about Marty inhibited me, and I would have shouted this across the table if it were just the two of us, but it wasn't. I didn't want to share with anyone the emotions he brought out in me, the things he made me feel. I whispered in his ear, running my fingers through his thick hair, relishing in the ownership of that gesture, knowing that it would always be mine. "We love each other and we're happy and some R-rated material I'll tell you about later."

He may have kissed my cheek, or maybe I brushed my lips against his. It was a light, promising touch, and when I turned my head, I sought the eyes of those seated around us, and they were staring at us, awed in part by the moment we were sharing and the embarrassment at being caught. They couldn't turn away. Their illicit stares were of envy and joy. When Marty kissed his hand and touched it my chest, an act both private and protective, the embarrassment turned to appreciation.

"I love your heart," he said to me. And I understood the raw affection was nothing less than pure devotion. My heart had once betrayed me, the disconnect between its needs and its desires as vast as the pain that proceeded it, but it all made sense to me now. I could feel the gentle, consistent beating in my chest. It had been waiting for Marty Tauber to hold it in his generous hands.

We got married on a clear spring afternoon on a Polynesian beach surrounded by nothing but sparkling ocean and the sound of the man officiating. We were going to have the large, lavish affair, but in finding Marty, I needed nothing more than to recite vows and make him legally mine.

"I do," he said.

"I will," I decided, because I would.

We spent two weeks devouring and discovering each other. I couldn't figure out how such a delinquent little kid ended up luxuriating in so much happiness. I asked myself if I had ever known happiness *at all*, and the answers would come to me in memories, times I thought I'd been happy, now faded, fragmented. Life had changed me. My work was going well. I was professionally where I wanted to be, and with that came a healthy identity and well-defined purpose. I needed Marty in my life, but that need was overshadowed by the pure *want* to have him there. There is a big difference between needing and wanting, especially when it comes to subjects like love.

We walked on the beach for hours, talking about everything and nothing. When we weren't making love or talking about making love, we were venturing through the islands hand in hand, feeding each other with our bare hands, listening to music, lounging lazily in the hammock outside our villa. I did not miss my work. I did not miss the telephone. I did not miss life. That is, the life before Marty came along and the one that was existing around us.

I was disappointed when the two weeks came to an end and we had to return from paradise. I didn't want to share my husband with the world again. We boarded the plane, and as I reached for the overhead compartment, my pocketbook dropped to the floor; the contents spilled across the carpet. Kneeling down to pick them up, I placed the personal bits of my life back in the bag and found my seat.

The flight attendant popped her head in our row. "Miss, did you drop this?" It was my gold compact, a gift from my mother. It must have rolled across the aisle. "Yes," I heard myself say, opening the clasp to see if the powder had crumbled.

It didn't, but when I saw my shattered image in the broken mirror, I froze.

Marty said, "We'll buy you a new one when we get home," and returned to his magazine.

I quickly closed the compact, pretending I hadn't seen it, pretending it wasn't there.

It was a silly superstition anyway.

Yet, it nagged at me the whole way home.

Chapter 20

We were celebrating our two-year anniversary and were at the top of our game, having racked up award after award for our work on several major motion pictures and their soundtracks. SixthSense was plastered across most every entertainment trade magazine; if I wanted to learn something new about the company or our current status, all I had to do was open a magazine and there would be the information I was searching for. It was surreal to be so sought after, eerie to be so closely watched. Marty and Jeff were the high-powered household names, but I'd found a niche for myself that was spreading across the industry. I was told I was an *expert* in the field of music, that I was the authority for hit songs, and with that, doors opened. Radio stations loved me, film studios courted me, record labels wanted me on staff, and songwriters pursued me at every turn.

And then the subject of kids.

I was twenty-*four* years old, almost twenty-five as I liked to say, and the question of children had come up on numerous occasions. Actually, every time Beth or my mother returned my phone calls, it was with the assumption that we were announcing our impending pregnancy. "Marty looks amazing for his age," they'd tell me, "but he's not getting any younger."

We had decided to forego protection and have fun. If it happened, it happened.

Therefore, it was no surprise when a doctor's appointment confirmed what my usually punctual and now excessively tardy period had already conveyed to me—I was pregnant. Marty was working late, again, negotiating yet another deal, this time for the rights to the remake of *Hair*. Swarms of attorneys from the label side and the production side were in the office that afternoon, and I'd snuck out early, feeling tired and weepy. The label wanted close to a million dollars for some of the songs. Nowadays, that wasn't entirely unheard of, but led to continuous debates over commercialization versus art. Marty could spend hours on that topic and apparently had been for the last few nights, picking up where my queasy stomach had left off.

"I wish you'd come home," I bellowed into the telephone, fretting at the thought that I had become one of *them*, one of those wives that complained for her man to come home early.

"I'll be home soon, babe. We're almost finished here. No more than an hour."

"Okay," I found myself relenting.

When he walked in the door, I noticed that the man I loved was no longer just my husband. By day's end, my secret had changed him. He was as handsome as ever with his grayish hair still thick and full, his eyes as warm as the first day we met in his office. Even when he was exhausted after a long day, he always had a smile for me, ready to talk and share his day.

I wanted to make love to him right then and there. I wanted to undress him at the door and feel him inside of me as if everything were the same, and it was always going to be just the two us.

"What's gotten into you?" he asked, as I started to kiss him urgently on the lips.

Raging hormones, I almost let slip out of my mouth. "Are you complaining?" I asked, taking off his jacket, wrapping my arms around his neck. "I've missed you terribly today."

"You say that every day, Jess," he said, laughing at the attention I gave him.

"I know, but today was different."

I wanted to tell him, I did. I wanted to look into those questioning eyes, the ones I had trusted enough to give this part of myself to, but I stopped myself before the words could dislodge themselves from my mouth. I did not want him to look back at this moment, when he found out he was going to be a father, and remember standing in our foyer. I wanted a tale that he could later tell our children, something that would embarrass them to think of their parents that way.

"Different how?" he asked, as I continued to seduce him, first with my hands, then my mouth.

We did make it up to our bedroom. His question still hung in the air, but it was clear to both of us that the answer didn't really matter anymore.

I slept with our little secret safely cradled inside of me and thought of nothing else for the next forty-eight hours. It was Sunday by then and it was time. While Marty dozed beside me, I sneaked out of our bed, threw on my robe, and headed for the kitchen. I was a novice in the kitchen, but Marty loved having breakfast in bed, so I threw caution to the wind and began to prepare his favorite coffee and French toast. When I wheeled it into our room, he was startled awake by the wheels on the cart.

"And here I thought you didn't know where the kitchen was," he joked, wiping the last remnants of slumber from his eyes. He was at his best in the morning, pure sex appeal. Pulling me next to him on the bed, he planted a tender kiss on my cheek.

"What's this?" he asked, when he saw the wrapped package on the tray. "I didn't forget my birthday, did I?" he laughed

"Your birthday's in January, Marty. It's June. Open it," I called out.

I watched as the fingers I loved scratched the surface of the paper, tender, like the way he handled the important people and things in his life. It was fitting for the moment we were about to share.

The silver frame fell from the loose paper and landed on the tray, so he didn't notice the engraving across the bottom. When he picked it up, I watched how his face changed. The metamorphosis occurred right before my eyes. The engraver had chiseled into the precious metal *Happy Father's Day*. The photo was the sonogram, a tiny dot on a black and white screen. How something so important could be so infinitely small.

It didn't take but a millisecond for Marty to realize the extent of my gift. I whispered into his ear. "You're going to be an amazing daddy."

His arms flew around me, the tremendous stretch of his grasp, unable to contain his happiness. *"Are you serious?"* he asked, and not because he didn't want this, but to the contrary, he wanted to be sure that I was sure.

"Very," I beamed.

"I love you, honey." He looked into my eyes, and we both were crying, and I could hardly tear myself away from him, until I realized that I didn't have to. I could lie there beside him all day. He was mine to keep, and now we were bringing our baby into the world. Nothing warmed me more than that prospect. So much hope, so much joy.

I wanted to make love with him again, but now he was afraid. I had become this delicate doll, and his concern for us endeared him to me even more. It is an interesting phenomenon with men. On the brink of becoming fathers, they revert to childhood, frightened, worried, impossibly thick-headed.

"I'm not being a child," he responded to my mockery. "I think I'm being rather fatherly—worried about my wife and unborn child, wanting them to be safe and healthy."

"Well, making love is how they usually get in here. It can't be that dangerous."

"Is that how it happened?" he teased, sitting over me on the bed, kissing my neck, my chin, my lips. His hands found my belly, and although there was no bloating that would indicate my secret, his hand touched it lightly, possessively, proudly. He then lowered himself so that his face was aligned with my belly and even though he was whispering, I could make out the words perfectly. "I love you, little one. I love you."

The pregnancy was not an easy one. Just as I had announced the news to Marty, the nausea began, accompanied by some of the worst vomiting I had ever experienced. It was difficult to cover up such sickness, and before long most of our friends knew, including Jeff and Sharon. "I know someone that vomited the entire ten months," Sharon told me one afternoon, while visiting.

"What are you talking about?" I asked, "pregnancies only last nine."

"It's more like ten if you take into account the two weeks the doctors tack on to calculate the baby's due date. They're probably too afraid to tell the mothers that."

I would never have thought that my body that was at one time so strong would react like this to the growing of a life in my womb. I couldn't picture another day of vomiting, let alone practically an entire year of it. Marty was as supportive as I would have expected. Every morning before I'd wake up, he'd leave a plate of crackers and a glass of ginger ale by the side of the bed. Sharon said it would calm my queasiness to eat it before getting up, but it was difficult to swallow when I knew it was just going to come right back up. I worried that the baby wasn't getting enough nutrients. I worried that I wasn't getting enough nutrients. I worried that I was going to be throwing up when the baby came out of me, that I'd be throwing up on the first day of Mommy and Me.

"I thought it was supposed to be only morning sickness?" I asked her, noticing the time of my last upheaval was well after noon.

"Everyone's different. It'll get easier. You'll just get used to it. And you know what they say? You're probably having a girl."

I waved off her remark without further discussion. The thought of getting accustomed to vomiting every day was too frightening.

"You do look beautiful, Jess," she said.

"Well I feel disgusting and fat."

The months passed slowly, uneventfully. I was working full-time, as well as consulting for a local radio station on their playlist, and found the work helpful in taking my mind off my burgeoning belly. Each month that passed, Marty would send an arrangement of flowers to the house commemorating the time drawing nearer; but for me, it was a celebration of survival. By the eighth month, despite the daily vomiting, I was huge and uncomfortable. I had gained at least fifty pounds, but everyone would swear up and down that I looked great.

"Radiant," they'd say. "Positively glowing!" Was I the only one that noticed the veins that colored my legs like a Spiderman comic and the tree trunks that had replaced my otherwise slender calves and ankles? The whole experience bewildered me. I felt trapped in my body, taken over by this life growing inside of me.

"You must be having a girl," this kind woman in the grocery store told me, joining in the consensus that predicted the sex of babies. But I was certain, Marty and I were having a boy. It would contradict everything we were told, everything my body suggested, but it was going to be a boy. Without question.

It was a crisp, February morning when we welcomed Ari to our world. He weighed in at eight pounds, six ounces, with a head of curly dark hair and a smile that challenged those that claimed the birth canal was a traumatic experience. He was the spitting image of his father.

"I never thought we'd see this day, Jess," Jeff remarked. "You've finally made Marty an honest man," He kissed me on the top of the head and then baby Ari, who squealed with delight.

My mother flitted around the room in her best flitting style, keeping track of the flowers and presents that filled the hospital room while touching up her hair in case some of our industry friends showed up.

Beth and Paul flew in from New York. The hunger in their eyes was apparent. Beth did her best to hide it, but I knew it was there. They'd been trying to have a baby for a while now. She was happy for us, though, and I sympathized with her sadness.

I held Ari in my arms closely.

"You're a natural," Marty would tell me, although I didn't feel like one. It was awkward and strange, yet at the same time one of the most important things I'd ever done.

"We created him," he'd whisper to me, after the others had gone, and I'd look down at the tiny figure in my arms, overwhelmed by my purpose in life, the voracious need to protect. My heart was brimming with something that could have been love, but even that wasn't enough.

"You make beautiful babies, Jess," Marty said, hurling me away from the enormity of what we had just delivered. When I turned to face him, the only thing that came out of me were tears.

Marty was a wonderful father, and that was partially due to the fact that Ari was such an easy baby. For the first couple of months, he ate, slept, and pooped on cue without so much as a cry or whimper. He smiled, watching us with his big blue eyes, delighting in his new surroundings. We were enamored by him, and we thought, he of us.

The months that followed were filled with getting Ari on the proper schedule, helping him with his crawl, providing a hand when he started to stand on his own, and supervising, basically, his life. He tackled each milestone with grace and deliberation. I watched as he grew before my eyes, no longer a baby, but a remarkably sweet little toddler. I gave up work altogether those first two years, saving my time and energy for the documentation of an endless list of firsts. I delighted in his growth and discovery, relishing in the time we had to share with one another.

It wasn't long before I became pregnant again. Ari was just two and a pure joy. He had become Marty's shadow, following him aimlessly around the house, begging his daddy—in only the way a two-year-old knows how—to accompany him to the office, and oftentimes winning the battle. Marty had the forethought to convert an entire area of the building into a children's play area, and this was helpful to me, because as expected, I re-experienced the wrath of my first pregnancy.

"It could be a girl this time," Marty told me. "You never know."

But I knew instinctively that we were having another little boy. It made things easier in a lot of ways, and I was equally as excited about his arrival as I was about Ari. I even knew his name was going to be Josh.

"I hope he looks like you."

"I hope he looks like *you*," I repeated.

"We already have a mini me," he laughed, referring to Ari, who despite having brown hair in contrast to his father's salt and pepper, was an exact replica of his father.

"I like that he looks just like you," I said.

"Yeah, why's that?"

"Because it makes him that much easier to love," I said.

Accustomed to the strain on my body and the vomiting, I decided to attend a music convention in San Francisco. It was the largest music convention in the business, and I was approached by the head committee to serve on a panel of soundtrack and music supervisors. I was eight months pregnant.

As anxiety provoking as it was for me to leave Ari for the first time, Marty was anticipating spending three days alone with his son. He had taken the week off work to prepare for their adventure.

For me, it was a hectic week in San Francisco. I was so busy meeting with label executives and artists, new and old, that I hardly had a moment to acknowledge my incessant vomiting. "You look fantastic," they'd say—more lies—thinking the flattering words could somehow translate into their songs being added to radio playlists.

Returning to the game, I enmeshed myself in the music and the latest controversies in the business. I felt a refreshing autonomy—rejuvenated. But at night, the craving for my child would envelop me. I would hear the call of Ari's voice or feel the flutter within my underside, and assume my role again as mom.

When I would lay in bed in my hotel those nights, I understood what it meant to be blessed. I had a husband who was my best friend and an exceptional father, a healthy child and another one on the way, and a career I loved. Never did I believe it could get any better than this. When you're feeling that good about something, so content with life, you don't stop to think it might improve. We are taught not to expect too much, to be so greedy for goodness.

Nothing could have prepared me for what happened next.

The accident occurred just south of Santa Barbara. A young man on a motorcycle saw a car ricochet off the steel barrier along the perimeter of the Pacific Coast Highway and was sensible enough to stop and see if the driver was okay. That would be me, and no, I was not okay.

I was airlifted to Cedars Sinai Hospital, where the doctors prepped me for surgery. In and out of consciousness, the damage was done; a fractured pelvis, broken arm, wrist, concussion, and massive internal bleeding. I only know this because Marty later gave me the details. What he didn't mention was the baby.

Being alive was something I remembered being grateful for, yes, definitely grateful, but then I thought about the baby, and a life without him seemed deplorable, unacceptable. I couldn't speak. Grateful turned into something else, something ugly and threatening. If not for Ari, I would not have been able to go on. It was as simple as that. I closed my eyes, not ready for what was to come, thinking that maybe I was better off not knowing. At least not knowing allowed for some minor glimmer of hope. With knowledge came finality. I didn't think I could stand the alternative.

In between the bouts of pain and hysteria, the medication and procedures, my mind wandered aimlessly to where I had been, where I had traveled, why San Francisco. My body writhed with a pain far more excruciating than the physical when it latched onto the notion that this was my penalty for enjoying my work, for feeling that moment of separation from my child. But there was something else weighing on my mind, something lurking in the distance. I knew a shadow was blocking out my memory of what caused me to veer so carelessly, because if there was one single thing I could be sure of in that hospital bed, it was that I was to blame for this.

It was almost three weeks before words would escape my mouth. Three weeks passed of watching Marty watch me with desperation in his eyes. I wasn't afraid. Living with my loss would be my punishment. Death might have been a lesser sentence.

The doctors said I very well could have died, but I was hanging onto life by a short, delicate string. "I'm sorry," Marty said to me, as if he could possibly take the blame for my wrongdoings. I knew what those two small words meant. He shook his head, tears rolling off his cheeks. I wouldn't let it in, I wouldn't hear of it. My hands reached for the protruding mound I hadn't been able to touch since arriving in the hospital. The emptiness in my belly was there. My hand touched the folds of skin my fingers detested, vestiges of the baby I'd never hold, the child I would never know, that one moment snatched from me.

"He was beautiful."

My mind clutched onto the words. I wanted to reach out and stroke my husband's pale face and wipe the tears that had fallen down his cheeks, but my arms resisted, my hands lifeless.

"I did this," I said.

They were the first words I uttered in almost a month's time, the ownership for my crime. He reached for my face, swollen and tear stained, and I recoiled from his touch. My body grieved for its lost companion, and the writhing guilt that began at my unresponsive toes ended atop my throbbing head. I hated him for loving me. I hated that he wanted to be close to me, to touch me. He should have been angry. He should have been shouting and ranting, but he was not. If he would only punish me for my sin, I thought. I did not deserve his love. I did not deserve anyone's love, but his eyes, however broken, told me not to push him away. And I saw the man he was, the one I had learned to love, and now he lost his son, our son. I had let him down.

The next few weeks were a blur. I was confined to the tiny bed with monitors and devices that I was told were correcting the damage, repairing the cracks. We all knew there was no medicine for the area of greatest damage, no device for the irreparable hole. Marty was with me every day, and every hour I was reminded, at the sight of him, of how I cost us, what I had done. I only smiled when they brought Ari to see me. For him, I would live again.

"What can I do?" Marty would ask. He would bring flowers, my favorite movies, write me beautiful cards, but it didn't change anything, and eventually, he just stopped asking. I waited for his anger, for the recriminations and the accusations, but they never came. For the rest of our lives, I knew I would live with the belief that I have failed him, and he would know it. One day he would burst with hate toward me.

It was fitting that Marty arranged for me to come home from the hospital on Christmas Day. It had been six weeks, and I was ready to be home, eager to be near Ari again. Things were strained between Marty and me. We walked on eggshells around each other; or rather, he walked on the eggshells, as I was confined to bed. He was sensitive and kind and nurturing, yet I awaited the big blowup. There were times the heaviness of our loss felt an impossible burden, and I wanted to reach for him or hold him while we lay side by side in the bed we once shared together, but I dispelled the urge, knowing if I gave him that part of me, I'd be vulnerable to his eventual attack.

Eventually I stopped counting the weeks, stopped predicting what he would look like right now, stopped touching my stomach for what I believed was a flutter, a kick, a life, and boxed up all the clothes and toys and books I'd set aside for his arrival. Instead, I threw myself into motherhood, the very thing that had caused me the intolerable suffering in the first place. My legs were still in a brace, so Ari and I spent a lot of time watching Nickelodeon and Disney Channel. We built castles over the metal and a bridge to connect them in between. When he'd nap, I'd pass the time by flipping through the channels. The movies I'd once found appealing no longer held my attention, their plots bland and boring. The radio was off-limits, part of my disconnect to pleasure, and I puttered through the house in search of someone to blame. The hours vacillated between self-absorption and Romper Room with Ari. When morning came, I would wake up, and the rotation would begin all over again.

Chapter 21

"I can't do this anymore, Jess."

It was a late Tuesday night in January. The new year had come and gone without any celebration, and our marriage was no different. There were no fireworks. There were no explosive revelations when the clock struck twelve.

Marty had returned from a business dinner, where he had obviously imbibed too many drinks. Finding me in our bed reading a magazine, he took a seat next to me and touched my leg affectionately. I looked up, taken aback at how good-looking he was, even messy with his tie undone and bloodshot eyes. I knew how those dinners evolved from business to pleasure before appetizers were served, and my appraisal of him turned to suspicion. Could he have returned to his old skirt-chasing ways? I wasn't sure, but my leg reflexively moved away from him. His fingertips on my flesh left a mark of defeat. His eyes poked at me. I knew what he wanted, but I wasn't ready.

"I can't do this anymore," he repeated.

"Do what?" I asked.

"This," he replied. "We haven't talked in weeks, months, for that matter. My wife," he hesitated, "where's my wife?" It was clear that he was upset. Upset and very drunk.

"I almost lost everything important to me in that car, Jess, *everything*. I don't know what I would've done if I lost you too, but shit, it feels like I did." He took a breath. "I need you to come back. I need my wife back."

The tears spilled down his face, Marty crying openly for our lost baby, for me, for his wife who had disappeared in the crash, leaving him with an imposter. He didn't even try to wipe them away, and neither did I. There was a wall between us that I couldn't climb over.

His head hung down in his hands. I could have reached out to him and stroked the hair that I loved, kissed the cheeks, tasted his tears in my hungry mouth, but I was paralyzed. I believe I had finally become the horrible person I always imagined myself to be.

"I'm sorry," I managed to say.

He looked up, the sadness turned into anger. "I don't want to hear that, Jess. You need to talk to me. You need to tell me what's going on in your head.

"Look at me!" he demanded. I had turned to face the wall. "We have a life together. We have a child. He needs us. He needs us to love each other. He needs to see that his parents are still there for him."

"I'm there for him," I stammered, but I knew Marty meant that our team had dissolved.

"What happened to my girl? Where'd she go?" He reached for my hand and I let him hold it. "Talk to me, please."

"I can't," I whispered. "I don't know what to say."

How could I explain that I didn't feel part of an *us* anymore? There was just me, the pariah, alone on a hilltop, banished from the rest of society. There was an ocean separating us. If I tried to swim to him, even if I had a miniscule urge to do so, I would never have made it across.

"Then let me help you," he said.

Shaking my head, I said, "My child died inside of me. You have no idea what that does to a woman."

"He was my child too. Damn you for being so selfish."

He could have just slapped me across the face; his words left a similar sting along my cheek.

Marty left the next morning for work, and I did not see or hear from him for four days. He called my mother in Arizona to come to the house to assist the nurse that was taking care of my wounds, and I was furious. On the fifth day, he resurfaced.

Genuine surprise appeared on his face when he saw that I was walking, but I was too angry to see anything but betrayal. I didn't ask where he'd spent the last few nights, convinced he'd regressed to his previous immoral behavior.

He appraised me with his eyes, observing how self-sufficient I'd become. If I could have reached across the room, I would have shoved him away, slapped him, ordered him to stop looking, and just as quickly, I'd retreat. My response to Marty was conflicted. The anger alienated me from the sadness, the sadness from the regret, and what remained was a drained, unemotional well. If I loved Ari, there was nothing left to give Marty. If I loved Joshua, I could not love myself.

"You're walking?" It was more a question than an observation.

"Yes."

"Sorry I wasn't here to see it."

"Yeah, me too," I replied, searching the space around us so I wouldn't have to meet his eyes.

"What's your problem?" he asked, noting my sarcasm.

"I don't know, maybe you should be apologizing for other things, like what you've been doing the last four nights."

Marty searched the same wall as I did, as though the way to make us whole again would appear in the crevices of Venetian stucco. "Does it matter?"

"You look like shit."

"I'm surprised you noticed."

"It's hard to miss."

"You still look the same. You still look beautiful."

We stood like that, facing each other in the hallway. I knew I was a frailer, paler version of my old self, and Marty was thoughtful enough to overlook the obvious. Even when he pretended not to see the changes in me, I could vouch for the ugliness that sprang from deep within. It had to have transformed me, inside and out.

"You don't have to say that."

Then he surprised me, heading toward me, his arms extending around my shoulders.

We stood there like that as the vacancy between us became as noticeable as the silence. Before the accident, he would hold me in his arms, and life in my belly would brush against him, and we would smile as the convergence of our bodies fed love to the child inside. If I had gained any wisdom at all, which at this point in time was debatable, I would have concentrated on the solid arms around me, representations of viable, caring things I still had to be thankful for, but I could not. Instead, I honed in on the barren place within that I shamefully could not protect and retreated from his touch.

"Do I repulse you that much?" he asked

I didn't answer.

"I love you, Jess. I'm not going to give up on us. You're not going to walk away from me that easily."

Even in moments of weakness, Marty could be strong. Even in the darkest hour of his grief, he could still love me without anger or blame.

A man like that was rare to find, and although his strengths would be the very things most appealing about him, they were also the things that left me in a tangle of inadequacy. In the giant presence of his virtuous character, I had become diminished, overshadowed by his goodness.

I wanted to cry, the gnawing ache rising up through my neck, but I just held it in; at first it hurt, those few seconds, but after awhile, it felt better than the pain that accompanies the unleashing of tears. I realized how good I was at this game of pretend, how easy it was to hold it all inside and make believe that none of this was happening. Just like I did in Dr. Norton's office.

BOOK III
2001 – 2002

❦

All changes, even the most longed for, have their melancholy;
for what we leave behind is part of ourselves; we must die to
one life before we can enter into another.
Anatole France

Chapter 22

"Ari," I said, "you have to hurry up because Mommy has an appointment today she can't be late for."

We were in his favorite toy store. It was wall-to-wall activity, and he'd gotten hung up on a particular aisle.

"Don't know, Mommy," he said, his nearly four-year-old body hunched over and defeated by the inability to make this important decision.

"Star Wars or Pokemon," I said. "Pick one."

He studied both boxes, holding one in each hand. They were the last on the shelf.

"Can't I have both?" he asked, his eyes beckoning mine with their hopefulness while I quieted the desire to answer *yes, you can have anything you want.*

"One," I told him again, firmly, realizing that I was definitely going to be late.

He was eyeing Pokemon closely. I could see how he was struggling with choice, as if not picking Hans Solo would result in a quick, painful death for the intergalactic hero. He put the boxes back on the shelf and studied them. He dragged out his decision as long as possible.

I checked my watch again. I didn't want to be late. Not today of all days.

We were interrupted by a little boy of six or seven. He stepped right in between us and reached for the Star Wars action figure. He didn't waver, didn't deliberate, just snatched Hans Solo from off the shelf.

Ari quickly followed his lead. "I'll take this," he said with confidence and handed me the lone Pokemon toy.

"Are you sure this is what you want?" I asked.

He nodded. "That's it," he said. "That's the one I want."

Later, after I had dropped Ari off and was heading east toward the office buildings of Century City, I was reminded of my son's struggle.

My mother once told me that decisions are difficult because by making a choice, we're forced to give up something. How lucky for my child that a little boy with a few more years on him could help him make a decision, could free him from being responsible for the death of Hans Solo.

"But that's life," my mother would say. "Life is about making choices."

How could I have known it would all lead to a choice? And the thing about choices is that they can be influenced by things we aren't even aware of, things stuck in our subconscious that have a louder voice than our gut instinct. How could some decisions be so clear, and others so unmistakably ambiguous, like the cryptic imprint that loved ones, whether present or absent, leave on our souls, charting the course of our lives?

Yes, my mother was right, as she often proved to be. Life is about making choices. But it's also about re-embracing the things you gave up. And it's learning that there are some things, and some people, you can't live without.

I had made choices before, but none more important than this one. And even though something is lost, there is a spirit that moves me and encircles me and leads me to a clearer path.

I know this now because I understood that fated day when my phone rang that there are some things that never leave you at all.

It was a rainy morning when Marty was at the office and I was home alone in the house. My mother had flown in from Arizona and had taken Ari to the library, and I had nothing I was working on, except dawdling. I had become good at dawdling. Kind of like my mother and her flitting. I lay on the bed where Marty and I had just made love a few hours before and wrapped the sheets around me. In some ways, I had become his wife again. I smiled when it was required. I talked to him when it was necessary. I got dressed and went to dinner with him when it was mandatory, and we raised Ari together, however stiff and contentious. Having sex with him was merely going through another obligatory set of motions.

Essentially, I had fulfilled his basic needs—wife, companion, mother, but he wanted more and I wanted less, and the disparity kept us from recognizing the darkness brewing around us.

It was similar to the man who jumps to his death, leaving a trail of shock and betrayal behind. Weeks later, days even, you hear the ripples, the slow-moving chatter disguised in whispers and hushed sounds, how random strands of odd behavior suddenly come together and make sense. No one wants to see something that he doesn't want to believe is there. It was a lot easier for those closest to me to pretend that everything was going to be okay.

The phone rang, plucking me out of my head.

"Ms. Parker?"

I was not used to being called by my former name while lying naked in my husband's bed. "Yes?"

She said, "Please hold for Mr. David Stevens." I wrapped the sheet around me. I had no idea who David Stevens was.

"Ms. Parker? David Stevens here. I'm an attorney in Manhattan."

"Yes?" I pulled the sheet tighter.

"Ms. Parker, it's not customary for me to make a phone call like this. Ordinarily, I would insist we speak in person, but under the circumstances…"

"How can I help you?" I grumbled at him, all his niceties annoying me.

"I'm representing a husband and wife, the Sammlers."

"I don't know any Sammlers."

"But I think you do. Your daughter, they are her…"

"I don't have a daughter, Mr. Stevens. Are you sure you have the right Jessica Parker?"

"Birth date June fifteenth, nineteen seventy-two, resides in Los Angeles, California?"

"That's me," I sighed, "but I don't have a daughter."

"Yes, I know that. Excuse me, let me clarify. I know that *legally* you don't have a daughter, not anymore, but the Sammlers, the adoptive parents of your little girl, they've been desperate to find you."

I could barely make out his next words.

"Ms. Parker, are you there?"

I hesitated for a moment, remembering the shattered glass.

"Yes, I'm here."

"The adoptive parents, they've been desperate to find you. Michelle, their little girl, has leukemia."

I stood up from the bed, latching onto the name. "She was diagnosed a few years ago and underwent an aggressive chemotherapy treatment, but recently relapsed. Ordinarily, patients with this type of leukemia recover with chemotherapy, and I apologize in advance as I'm not a medical doctor and don't have specific details to give you, but the relapse is serious. In all likelihood, Michelle's going to need a transplant in order to survive. Finding a match is of the utmost importance."

My voice couldn't be found. It was somewhere stuck in the restricted up and down motion of my chest.

"Ms. Parker, I understand this is upsetting for you."

"Yes," I whispered, and then he continued in his fixed professional manner. "Her adoptive parents realize that you might be paramount for her survival. I know this is difficult for you. It's difficult for everyone involved."

There had been no one else to contact. I had told them that day that there was no father, that he had died, because he had, at least to me.

"The parents are here with me now, and they'd like to speak with you. You can understand, Ms. Parker, they are desperate to save their daughter's life. I know there are provisions regarding your anonymity and laws protecting your privacy. We can discuss that later. Until now, they've been very respectful of your rights."

The forms I had signed long, long ago did not prepare nor protect me from this type of call. "What will I need to do?" I asked.

"Just talk to them."

Nothing was making any sense. "My husband doesn't know about her." I wasn't sure if I voluntarily spoke it aloud or if it jumped from my mouth.

"Ms. Parker, I understand the delicate nature of this matter. Protecting your privacy is of the utmost concern to all of us. The parents would never have contacted you if it weren't a life-threatening situation. You must know that and do what you think is best."

I'd already lost enough. I said her name out loud, *Michelle.*

Chapter 23

"What do you mean you're leaving?" Marty asked, the thought occurring to him that maybe the charade we called a marriage had busted wide open.

"I'm going to New York for some work. My mother will stay here with Ari. It's important."

"Last time I checked, wasn't I your boss?"

"It's a consulting gig."

"And it's so important you need to leave your family again?"

The reference to San Francisco released a slew of hurt I thought I had buried with other human emotions. "I have to start somewhere; sitting in this house is killing me."

"Are you ready to travel, physically ready?"

"The doctors say it's fine, as long as I'm emotionally up to it."

He sized me up and down, my own personal barometer.

"Are you sure you're not just running away from something?"

I said, "You mean you?"

"If that's the first thing that comes to your mind."

"It's not always about you, Marty. This is something I need to do for me."

"Why so cryptic?"

I turned to him, thinking back to the four mysterious nights we never discussed. "Can't you just leave it alone? Can't you just give me the space to figure some things out?"

He was angry. "My wife tells me she's leaving for New York, and I can't ask questions? When did our life together become solely about you? When did you decide that I shouldn't be included in major decisions?"

"Since when is a business trip a major decision?"

"Since I had no idea you were even going back to work."

I had thought of telling him about the phone call, but was afraid our weakened relationship didn't have the emotional muscle to withstand more damage. He would understand my wanting to go to New York, yes, but the dishonesty of what I've withheld all these years, never. And to part with this information now was too hard for me. At sixteen, I held onto it because it was all I had left. At almost twenty-nine, I wanted to keep it in my heart, where it had lived for so many years, untouched, a chapter in my life that was mine alone, a song in my soul that belonged to memory. I could not, not now, give that up.

The plane ride to New York was nerve-racking, marked by a ruthless turbulence that bobbed the plane up and down in a hysterical frenzy. The man next to me appeared not to notice while my fingernails dug into the armrest that divided us.

"Don't worry, it's just a little turbulence," he said to me.

"I don't really like to fly," I replied, unsettled by the movements.

"This plane isn't going down," he assured me, although the captain had already asked the flight attendants to return to their seats and resume beverage service after the pocket of wicked air was behind us.

I said, "How can you be so sure?"

"Planes don't go down because of turbulence. It's nothing more than a bump in the road, like when you're driving your car down a potholed street."

"Well, it feels like a lot more than a bump in the road."

"It's an analogy," he said. "If it brings you any consolation, and at the risk of being cliché, lightning doesn't strike twice. My mother died in a plane crash. God wouldn't do that to my family again."

In a prophetic way of looking at fate, I drew some comfort from this, and for the first time in minutes, I permitted myself the freedom to relax between the diving motion of the plane's insulated walls. Until a thought occurred to me and I said, "I'm sorry to hear that, really, that's awful. I'm surprised you'd get on a plane."

"I told you, lightning doesn't strike twice."

"Don't you think the reason lightning won't strike twice is that the same place isn't there anymore? The plane your mother was on is gone." The insensitivity of my comment was glaring.

"Lady, I was just trying to make you feel better," he said, clearly perturbed and turning to the book he was reading to signal the end of our conversation.

After twenty more minutes of terrifying dips and bumps, the pilot came on and told us we would be making our initial descent into Kennedy Airport and landing in about thirty minutes.

With the receding miles of air space, the plane decided to calm its queasy stomach. The skies were full and gray, like the way they look before a snowfall. I had read that the weather in the city was freezing, and I wasn't looking forward to the chill. The magazine I had planned on reading was still strewn on my lap with Darva Conger and Rick Rockwell on the cover. Did anybody really care about their sham of a marriage, or was what bothered me that it reminded me too much of my own?

I counted the years in my head. She would be approximately twelve now.

Did she have his eyes? His smile? She was an enigma to me, this child, having passed in and out of my life like the coupling that had brought her to me.

You hear stories about kids who try drugs for the first time, only to find that the first, innocent taste would be the last. These poor souls had grappled all their lives with the idea of experimentation, patiently waiting, only to find that their one experience would cost them everything. That's what happened to me that fateful summer night. We live in a world defined by instant gratification. The consequences of my actions never crossed my mind.

After having read *Forever* one hundred and sixteen times, being able to recite the back cover in my sleep, and resisting the gnawing desire to feel what Katherine had felt for Michael, I gave myself to Jonas Levy. It was as pure and sweet and perplexing as page eighty-five with one added component: I got pregnant. Where was *that* chapter in Judy's book?

Jonas never knew he had a child.

I found out I was pregnant after he'd gone back to Boston, and by then, I didn't want him to know. The last thing I needed was for him to think I was trapping him. Remember, he was practically engaged to another girl. As for me, I was as equally unprepared for a child. I was *sixteen*, in high school, with little to no understanding of how children operated. Besides, I had hoped that one day I could do it in the order that has always been of tradition: meet the man, get married, enjoy a few good years, and *then* have a baby. On the other hand, there was absolutely no possible way that I would have aborted Jonas's baby. With two diametrically opposed scenarios tugging at me, I did what I thought was best. Mind you, this was a time of great strife and sadness for me.

If my decisions were faulty, they were on account of the heavy load of grief I was lugging around with me. As much as I wanted to let go of that boy and that life, this child was all I had left of him. I could not destroy that too.

Jonas and I kissed Tuesday night on that mountaintop, but that's not all we did. He took me in, all of me, devouring my mouth, exploring my lips with his tongue, probing deeper and deeper until I did, at some point, tell him to slow down.

Jonas was unnerved by this. What he wanted from me, I could feel in my fingers and toes. He didn't slow down nor did he stop the rush that was exploding inside me. I couldn't think of right or wrong. He might not have been mine to kiss, but when our lips found each other, there were no two people who belonged together more than we did.

"Jonas, stop. Look at me," I said, pulling back, not too much, needing to stay close. "What do you want?" I asked.

"I can't tell you that," he said.

"Yes, you can. Just say it."

He was shaking. His hands were reaching for me.

"Tell me," I said.

"I don't want to stop."

"Then don't…"

"But…"

"No buts," I said, stepping closer, until he had no choice but to take me into his arms. And that's when I permitted myself to give into everything I'd fought so hard to keep under control: Jonas's arms around me, Jonas's lips kissing my hair, then my face, Jonas touching places I'd saved just for him, places that when he finally explored would let him know how badly I'd always wanted him. And it wasn't like I was the only one who couldn't hide what they were feeling. He was holding me so close, I could feel every inch of him against me. Now that I could finally have him, I wasn't about to have him stop.

We were standing there up against that car when he helped me into the back. Facing each other, he didn't kiss me this time. He just took his two hands and lifted my top off over my head. My first reaction was to hide myself from him, but I couldn't because he was already starting to unbutton my jeans. And it wasn't like the movies. They didn't just peel off me and drop to the floor. We were sitting, so I had to lie back while he attempted, gracefully, to pull them down. All the while, I was holding up my underpants to afford myself some small token of decency. It was intimate and personal and awkward, but I loved his hands running down my legs. I loved how they were warm and somewhat sweaty.

There I was in the back of his car, no bra, with an inch of fabric separating us. He touched my shoulders, tracing their shape, and then he touched my breasts, cupping them in his hand. I watched him, knowing exactly what he was doing, memorizing every detail.

"No one's ever looked at me the way you do," he said, his finger tracing my nipple. "Your eyes…they're hard to turn away from."

"Is that bad?" I asked.

"No, it's not bad," he said, pulling me near to him, straddling my legs around him.

He lifted his shirt and then took off his jeans. He'd done this before. He did it a lot better than I ever could. He leaned into me, my legs holding tightly around him, and he kissed me, this time his hands touching me, tugging at my panties until they slipped off in one single motion. That's when his fingers found me, slipping inside smooth and gentle. I was as embarrassed as I was turned on.

He lay me down beside him, kneeling before me, watching me there in the darkness.

"Is this the way you thought it would be?" I asked.

"Better," he said, tenderly touching my body, stroking my arm, my belly. "You were wrong about us not being good together."

I nodded, reaching for him to come closer, sure that if my mouth opened, an overflow of words would tumble out.

He resisted me, saying, "I just want to look at you a little longer, Jess. You look so pretty in this light, your body…"

And when he leaned toward me, his grip was more powerful, his kisses more hurried. Finding my breast, he kissed my nipple, touching, tasting, teasing it with his tongue. My back arched at his touch, and my fingers reached for his head, tugging at his hair. He found the wetness again, lightly teasing, until I couldn't stand it any more, so I reached for his hand, guiding him, urging him to probe deeper inside, begging him not to stop. But he enjoyed teasing me, he always had. I could barely compose the noises that were escaping my mouth, wanting to feel more of him inside of me, but he'd only continued to tease, lightly touching and then stealing himself away. I remember thinking I needed something, but it's not like I even knew what it was. I only knew that there was an ache where his fingers were, a throbbing that wanted more. *This* was what Katherine and Michael had wanted too. I reached for him, Ralph or whatever his name happened to be, and I felt the soft, smooth skin under my palm, knowing the effect I had on him by the way he writhed beneath my touch. I was just a girl, but I knew the tremendous power I held in my hand. I could make it so he would never forget this night, that he would be left with a want for me so insatiable, one night would never be enough.

I guess we both were left with something we would never forget.

It wasn't long before he was on top of me, and we were staring into each other's eyes. The wetness between my legs was now against his leg. I could feel him coming closer.

"What do you want, Jess?"

I could have rattled off a list of things, but only one thing came out of my mouth and it was, "You."

He didn't blink. He just entered me as Phil Collins sang "This Must Be Love" on the radio, and I knew I'd never forget what it felt like to have Jonas Levy inside me or what Phil meant when he said *words can only say so much.* I tried to turn my face so he wouldn't see me wincing from the pain, but his hand reached for me, forcing me to stare him in the eyes.

"Look at me, Jess," he breathed. "I want to remember your face right now. I want to close my eyes at night and see you there on my pillow wanting me like this, what you look like with me inside of you."

"You've always been inside of me," I said, taking his fingers in my own, pulling him closer.

"I don't want to hurt you," he whispered, but it was too late, so I ignored him and the pain between my legs, because there was something else stirring inside of me that didn't hurt at all. A tear found its way down my cheek. My legs held him tighter.

His mouth bit at mine just as his body seemed to shudder. I think I felt the waves that passed through him emanate from his body into mine. And just as he finished, my body seemed to ignite with something I'd felt before, a quivering that was building with each second. I heard myself cry out his name in the darkness, only now, for the first time, he was right there with me.

The pilot came on the loudspeaker. "Flight attendants, please prepare for arrival." I gazed out the window, New York coming into view, the triumphant buildings in the skyline. I fastened my seatbelt tighter around my tummy and remembered the pregnancy.

Unlike the recent two, it was an easy one. The first couple of months, I was queasy and highly emotional, but I never threw up, not once. If I looked tired or sad, it was attributed to my broken heart, and the bump was conveniently concealed beneath my clothes. No one knew about my secret.

I was a walking contradiction. Inside of me, life was blooming, a new start, the beginning of endless possibility, and on the outside, the shell that cocooned the life was hardened, lifeless. I went to school each day, an under-functioning teenager, with an over-functioning belly. My height, fortunately, hid the secret well, and I dared not disclose my news with anyone until my mother found me sobbing in my room one afternoon. She knew, had suspected, like most devoted mothers would, and held me close in her arms while I cried. She was understandably broken up about this, but she resisted discipline and became my fiercest ally. Wasn't the pregnancy punishment enough? She was the one who found me the trusted doctor. She was the one who explained my options. She was the one that eventually located the right adoption agency.

She never once asked me to say his name. She never asked how long we'd been having sex or any other detail. She wouldn't have humiliated me like that, and after that first day of initial disappointment, she never let me see the dissatisfaction in her eyes. I was no longer alone. She assured me that we would be handling this matter *together*, as a family.

"Mom," I said to her one afternoon, wanting to tell her I was sorry for the distress I'd caused her, but we were so attuned to one another, she cut me off before I could begin. "Don't you dare apologize to me, young lady. With what you're dealing with right now, I'd say you've learned a great lesson. I won't shame either one of us with this conversation."

I'd never known my mother to love me this way before. Even her flitting didn't get on my nerves anymore. "You're my child," she said, "and I'll do whatever it takes to protect you."

"Thank you," I mumbled.

"Don't thank me, either," she said, "just use protection next time."

I almost laughed, but I didn't dare. My mother had overcome great adversity in her life. Her strength overshadowed any sign of weakness. Not even her child having a child could make her come undone.

A day did not go by without my thinking of that little girl and how beautiful she looked when they took her away from me, all wrapped up in that pink blanket. I had grieved for her long after I had grieved for her father, and yet they were so undeniably connected to one another, I'd be forever connected to him. That is why I had such a difficult time for so long and why I couldn't trust again, open my heart, for fear of losing all the people that I cared about. That was why a memory could take me back to him at any given moment—on her birthday, when I'd hear a song on the radio, when I'd breathe.

I stared out the window of the plane, relieved to see the ground below us. I asked myself why this was happening. Was this more punishment for my thoughts, or did it mean something else? The extent of the atmosphere made me believe that perhaps there really was a higher being who orchestrated our every move.

Before my car accident, I might have shared this with Marty, and we would have gotten through it together. Now we were separated by lies and the miles that buried them from view. I was alone, and the touch of the plane's tires hitting the ground severed the ties between us even further.

Chapter 24

I arrived at New York's Memorial Hospital the following day for the meeting with David Stevens, the Sammlers, and Dr. Phillip Greene, head of pediatric oncology, and the one presiding over my daughter's case. I had slept fitfully the night before, and by five I was wide awake; I headed out, not sure what to do with myself. I ended up at the hospital around seven. The parties involved were scheduled to meet at nine o'clock. Did I really think if I got to the hospital early, I would be able to see my daughter sleep?

I sat in the coffee shop while the hospital slowly came to life around me, remembering a time when the milieu transformed me too. When I headed to Dr. Greene's office on the third floor, I was ushered into the stark white room by a plump, middle-aged woman. My daughter's parents were going to be joining us. I was a mess inside, but I wore my distress beneath the layers of clothing I'd chosen for the occasion. They arrived shortly, apologizing for the delay, and were accompanied by a little man with a horrible toupee. His briefcase was larger than his body.

"There was terrible traffic on the Tappan Zee," the pleasant-looking blonde woman said, as if she owed me some type of explanation. "Thank you for coming on such short notice," she whispered, "for coming at all."

The man, my daughter's father, was less apologetic, eyeing me with cautious disregard before extending a casual smile.

"David Stevens," the tiny man beside them said as he offered his hand. "I'm glad to see that you're taking this as seriously as we are. Thank you for being here." We all took our seats in the now-crowded office.

I watched them closely. The husband took his wife's hand casually into his own. I admired the open display of affection.

Dr. Greene was a pleasant-looking man, probably in his early fifties. He seemed anxious to get right down to business, while I was busy appraising my daughter's parents. Mrs. Sammler had these sad eyes I empathized with and understood. Just because I didn't raise the sick girl didn't mean that I was incapable of feeling strongly about her. I once believed I cared for her enough to give her the life I couldn't. I loved her in deep, subtle ways, the ways that mothers experience when they nurture a child in their womb and watch it enter the world.

I had selfish reasons to be here, to save my child, but I also didn't want another parent to lose what Marty and I had lost.

"You're familiar with leukemia?" Dr. Greene began, directing his question my way.

"Probably not to the degree I need to understand it now."

"Leukemia begins in the marrow of a cell and is characterized by the uncontrolled growth of developing marrow cells. There are two major classifications: myelogenous or lymphocytic, which refers to the type of cell involved. Of these two forms of leukemia, either can be acute or chronic, giving us four types of classified leukemia. Michelle has what we call acute lymphocytic leukemia, ALL for short."

I nodded.

"ALL is the most common form of leukemia in children, accounting for eighty percent of the cases. In acute cases, we have a rapidly progressing disease. It begins with an accumulation of immature, functionless cells in the marrow and blood; the marrow eventually cannot produce enough normal red and white blood cells and platelets, causing anemia, and eventually, the inability of the body to fight off infection."

My brain was processing the ugliness of this disease.

"Michelle was brought to us when she was eight. We treated her with chemotherapy, and she went into a normal remission. In the majority of cases, children whose cancer is in remission live long, healthy lives, but Michelle's recent relapse indicates a more progressive and perhaps life-threatening form of the disease. Even with another course of treatment, the odds of a relapse are greater and her long-term survival rate is poor. In cases like this, we'll do another round of chemotherapy and hope for an extended remission, but a bone marrow transplant is her best option.

"When Mr. and Mrs. Sammler initially told me Michelle was adopted, it was reasonable to say that our chances of either of them being a match were remote."

I was buried in details that stretched from bad to worse. This is where David Stevens chimed in. "Ms. Parker, while California law prohibits a birth parent from looking for or contacting their child until they are eighteen, there are also such laws that protect the birth parent from being contacted by the child, and in this case, by the adoptive parents.

"Adoptive parents of a person younger than twenty-one can receive information on the birth parents if there is a medical necessity or extraordinary circumstances that justify the disclosure. We would all agree that this situation falls within the range of medical necessity and extraordinary circumstance." He didn't wait for my opinion. "The Sammlers were particularly concerned as to how you might interpret their phone call."

I felt Mrs. Sammler's eyes on me, studying me. She had to see the good in me, that I would never have fought for my privacy on this matter.

"What's the likelihood that I'm a match?" I asked.

"It's not that simple," said Dr. Greene. "See, how it works, and I told the Sammlers this before they phoned you, a full-blood sibling, meaning a child created by you and the person that fathered Michelle, could be the match we're looking for."

I vaguely remembered Mr. Sammler asking if I had other children. If I had said yes, I meant Ari.

"She doesn't have a blood sibling, a *full-blood* sibling."

The worry that passed between Mr. and Mrs. Sammler was hard to take in.

"I thought you said you had other children." Mrs. Sammler glared at me.

"Yes, I have other children, another child," correcting myself, "but not with Michelle's father."

With that, Mrs. Sammler began to cry.

"I'm sorry," I said. As if it were my fault. As if I gave her a damaged good and couldn't fix it.

I tried to say more, but she stopped me. I had given up my child. She didn't know what kind of person that made me, not then, and not now. That was when Mr. Sammler began to wipe his eyes and openly cry. He didn't even try to hide his whimpers or cover his face. He was a man that was visibly humbled by the threat that crept into the room. Glancing at Dr. Greene and Mr. Stevens, my business sadly finished here, I slipped out the office door.

I returned to the hotel after four that afternoon, and before taking off my coat, picked up the phone and dialed our home in Los Angeles. It was one there. Ari would be napping, and I was irritated that I didn't get to speak with him before he went down. My mother answered on the first ring.

"I'm worried about you."

"I know. I'm sorry. I had to make an early start today, and I'm just getting back to the hotel. How's Ari?" I had a feeling my mother didn't believe any of this, that she knew everything that was going on, but I was too tired and too jet lagged to argue.

"Do you want to talk about it?"

"No. Is Marty coming home for dinner with Ari tonight?"

"He has a business dinner. I thought you spoke to him about that. Should I have him call you when he's done, or will it be too late?"

I pondered this. Every day that went by, this secret and its power to destroy us became stronger. I hated more than anything keeping things from him, but I was frightened by his reaction. If I told my mother I didn't want him to call me, it would open up an entire new assortment of problems.

"Sure," I mumbled, "have him call my cell."

"I love you, Jess."

"I love you too, Ma." I hung up the phone before she said anything else.

The ringing startled me from a deep sleep. It felt like three in the morning when I groggily whispered hello into the receiver, but it was just after twelve. It was Marty.

"It's good to hear your voice," he said.

"Hi," I said.

"I miss you."

"You too," I muttered.

"How's the mystery assignment coming along?"

"Good. Busy. How's Ari?"

"He misses his mommy. So do I."

"Give him extra kisses and hugs from me," I said, aching for my son. Leaving him had never been part of the plan. One day I would tell him why, and maybe he would deem his mommy a hero.

"Are you okay?" Marty asked.

"I think so. I will be."

"Do you want me to come out there? I can always visit a few people in the city."

"You don't have to. I'm making arrangements to fly out tomorrow."

"Okay. Well, go back to sleep. You sound tired."

"I'll call you in the morning."

"I love you," he said.

"I love you too." But I never ended up calling him. While I slept that night, a thought formulated in my head. At first, it was merely a whim, then it turned into something larger, a plan, a scene from a movie, and I had the starring role.

Dialing Boston information, I jotted down the number that the monotone recording gave me for BrinkerHarte, the name I heard for the first time in Catalina when Jonas and I shared words on a white table. When Beth informed me he had married Emily, I assumed the rest of his plan was in place with their picture-perfect little pathology lab.

Don't get me wrong. I had thought about Jonas over the years. There were times when I'd recollect the way he touched me, not in the biblical way, but the lasting way, the kind that leaves an impression without actual touch. I would awaken from a dream, and he would be all around me, so near I could feel the palms of his hands. Songs, in particular, brought him close. They'd play, and I'd be back in time connected to him again, feeling how deeply he once cared and believing that that alone could ever make me complete. I often asked myself, on those occasions, how we could have felt so deeply and yet have so much separateness between us? I used to worry that time would eventually erase my memory altogether, that slowly I would lose parts and pieces until there was nothing left. But I was foolish to think that Jonas, and what he left with me, could ever disappear.

I didn't like that he was intruding on the life I'd created with Marty and Ari. He had always been the past, the great lesson I was supposed to learn. He was the lanky boy I'd met as a kid, the gentle one on a cool summer night, and that's where he remained, never growing older like the rest of us, a timeless picture in my mind. I forbid myself to create an image of him today, Jonas coexisting somewhere with everyday issues and problems. I was mad at him and life for the intrusion, mad that he could so easily slither back into my world and uproot it. I wondered if he ever thought of me, of that summer. Was I merely *a passing fancy* like my mother used to say to her friends when she thought I wasn't listening, or had I been what he had been for me, the great love of my young life?

I knew what I had to do, but I was frightened. It was after nine now, and I had spent the better of the last hour ruminating, going over my options. I presumed the best place to find him at this hour would be at his office, so I set forth on my mission.

My fingers were trembling. I was a grown woman with a husband, child—two children, I corrected myself—yet he could still unglue me, take everything that was once solid and secure and turn it into mush.

Yes, Jonas had resurfaced from the past, and it was time, I'd decided, for the past to meet the present.

"BrinkerHarte," the receptionist echoed into the phone.

"Uh, yes, I'd like to speak with Dr. Levy, please."

"One moment, please."

A few seconds passed before I was transferred somewhere, and another monotone voice came on the line.

"Dr. Levy's office."

I looked down at the pendant that hung from my neck. It was moving up and down, up and down, in rhythm with my beating heart.

"Yes, is Dr. Levy available, please?"

"May I ask who's calling?"

"Jessica Tau—" I stopped myself. "Jessica Parker."

It was so close. Jonas was so near. I could hang up and tackle this on my own like I intended; but I pushed onward, holding onto the phone as if it were a flotation device, and I was the sinking ship.

"This is in reference to?"

"I'm a friend, an old friend."

"The doctor's in a seminar this morning. Would you like to leave a message?"

"Yes, I mean, no, no, thank you. I'll try back later."

Chapter 25

"I hope it's okay I'm here," I said to Mrs. Sammler. "I thought maybe I could see her before I left."

She was in the hallway outside Dr. Greene's office when I arrived at the hospital the next day.

"You're leaving?" I don't know why she acted surprised. We both knew I was of no use to them.

"Soon," I said. "There's something I need to take care of first. Then I'll be going."

She took some time answering; then like an old friend, she reached for my arm and said, "Come on," and led me down the hall. Her courage left me speechless.

I followed her through a maze of hospital corridors before we settled on a group of elevators. She was shorter than I was, and her blonde hair a mass of tight curls. I saw through the heaviness in her eyes an appreciative hazel green.

"I'm sorry we have to meet under these circumstances," she said to me in the sterile elevator; gone were the misgivings from the day before.

I said, "You needn't apologize. It would have been worse had you not contacted me, and there was a chance I could help."

She nodded her agreement. "Michelle has always been an easy, spirited child, so full of life. I think about what we could have done to prevent this." For whatever the reason, Mrs. Sammler felt the need to talk with me, and I didn't mind. It felt soothing to concentrate on someone else's pain, even if it so closely hinged upon my own.

"You can't blame yourself."

"Then who should I blame?"

I know she didn't mean to point fingers when the accusation came out of her mouth. The question had been raised before. Dr. Greene had assured us that leukemia was not a disease passed down to children, but I think we all could agree that some things were easier to believe than others. She was asking, I think, about her faith.

"Looking for answers distorts the truth," I said. "It tricks you into believing you have some control over the situation. We'll never be able to understand why bad things happen to good people, so don't do this to yourself, Mrs. Sammler. Don't punish yourself for things that are beyond your control."

"How do you know all of this?" she asked me, seeing for the first time that I was a person and not some teenager who had a lapse in judgment. I couldn't tell her that my husband once said the same thing to me, that my advice to her was easier to give away than to keep for myself.

The doors of the elevator opened, and we stepped out onto a floor that resembled a children's playroom, not a hospital ward for terminally ill children. I was nervous for a dozen reasons, each one causing the steps in my daughter's direction to falter. I was about to see her for the first time. It could very well be my last. The irony of it all would cause anyone to lose her footing.

"Are you okay?" she asked.

"That's a question I should be asking you."

And then she did something wonderfully bold. She took my hand into hers.

Michelle was asleep when we reached her door. Mrs. Sammler poked her head in and found her clutching her favorite teddy bear, whose name I learned later was Benjamin Owen.

"Come take a look," she said to me.

She led me into the room, and there I was, standing over her. This was my daughter, Michelle. My eyes took her in all at once, leaving little room for the tears that were forming. She was as beautiful as I'd remembered. The Sammlers had to have seen the resemblance. Maybe that was the reason they couldn't look away when I first walked in the room. To see the adult version of their little girl had to be startling. Ari never resembled me as closely as this precious child did.

"She's beautiful," I spoke, feeling the tightness in my throat.

"She looks like you."

"Thank you, but I was never as pretty as she is."

"She's a terrific kid," she said. "You'd be very proud of her."

"You're the one that should be proud."

"We are."

You couldn't miss the stacks of cards that filled the room, the hand-drawn artwork from her friends, the get-well wishes too serious for such a young girl. Mrs. Sammler adjusted the wires connected to some important-looking apparatus and then turned to me. "Take as much time as you need. I'm going to step outside to speak to one of the nurses."

The door closed behind her, and I was alone with my daughter, Jonas's child. She was a stunning eleven-year-old with long, golden hair, a tiny, perfect nose, and a heart-shaped freckle on her cheek. Resting peacefully under the covers, a narrow foot emerged from beneath the sheets, revealing toenails polished in pink. She didn't look sick. To the contrary, everything about her looked alive and peaceful, with the exception of the tubes and wires that were connecting her to lifeless equipment. Her red lips forced what resembled a smile. I was grateful that her dreams were giving her the satisfaction that the real world could not. Did she know I was there? Did she dream I would come to her?

My fingers grazed the colorful toes as my mind shuffled through the years, resting on the only time I held her. I zoomed in on the memory and how my hands once dwarfed the tiny parts of her. They say it goes by fast, but this was a blink, the years in between nothing more than a blur. Her skin was cool, so I pulled the blanket over her and slipped the foot beneath.

I would have liked to have held her again. If I did, she would feel all the reasons I gave her up. She'd know how much I loved her, and how I would still do just about anything to save her. Instead, I watched her sleep, listened to her breathe.

Mrs. Sammler returned.

I said, "Thank you for letting me see her. I know this isn't easy for you. It's not easy for me, and I don't even know her."

"You're a mother, and you know there's nothing we wouldn't do for the sake of our children."

"True."

Then she said, "Michelle doesn't know she's adopted," and with a sigh, she took a seat next to me. "We wanted to tell her, we did, and we were waiting, always, for the right opportunity; and then she got sick and it didn't seem right or fair to tell her just then. We thought it was best, under the circumstances, that she not be exposed to any further stress, especially emotional."

I didn't disagree, but I was skeptical. "If she sees me, she'll know."

"We're not saying that we'll never tell her. We just don't want to tell her right now, until, unless, she gets better."

"Mrs. Sammler…" I started, but I was interrupted by the sounds of the monitor, a succession of beeps that told us Michelle was awake. Had she heard the tension escalating around her?

We watched as her eyes began to open, a moment years in the making. I wasn't sure what I would say. We moved toward her in unison, and when she saw her mother there, her face brightened and she smiled. Then she turned to me and asked pointedly, "Who are you?"

I stared back into the eyes that had haunted me for years.

"This is Jessica Tauber, Mich," Mrs. Sammler said in a voice that signified their closeness. "She's a friend of mine," she added, looking at me for approval.

I heard myself say hello to her and ask how she was feeling, but I was having trouble focusing on her responses when I was so struck by her face. She was awake and real and eyeing me without a hint of the attachment we once shared. She had no idea she was the baby growing inside of me, the reminder of a desperate, loving moment. I could tell she bore no scars from that night, her face pure and kind. Neither of them saw it, but Jonas was there with us. He was floating around the room. My compulsion was to touch the freckle on her cheek.

"How are you feeling?" her mother asked.

"Good. How are you feeling?" She smiled.

"Are you cold? Do you want something to eat?" She took a pair of socks from a drawer and placed them on her feet.

"I'm fine, and I'm starving. Can we have a pizza delivered?"

"How about something healthy? Can I get you a turkey sandwich?"

"I can't get any sicker," she quipped.

Then Michelle Sammler turned her attention back to me. "My mother's never mentioned you before."

I delayed answering by pretending to cough. Mrs. Sammler followed my cue.

"Remember when I worked for a few years when you started school?" she said.

"At the museum? Yes, you and all those terribly old people."

"Well, we weren't all terribly old. Jessica was there too, and we've kept in touch over the years."

"You don't really expect me to believe that, do you?" she asked as Mrs. Sammler and I stared at each other. "A bunch of fuddy-duddies worked at that museum."

Her humor reminded me of being in the sixth grade again. I saw traces of myself in her sarcasm. I could only stare.

"Where's my CD player?" she asked.

"I thought it was attached to your head," Mrs. Sammler answered.

"Here it is," I said, picking the portable player off a nearby chair and handing it to Michelle. I'd been a passive audience, watching their exchange.

"Thanks," she said, staring deeper into my eyes than I'd expected, hurling me to the forefront of the stage.

"What are you listening to?" I asked.

"What doesn't she listen to?" Mrs. Sammler laughed. "She's a music junkie."

I smiled, and Michelle answered, "It's *Two Rooms: Celebrating the Songs of Elton John and Bernie Taupin*. It's awesome, one of my favorites."

"I met them, you know?"

"Really?"

And wanting nothing more than to share my dreams with her and the career she would have idolized, I remembered my role here and began a different explanation. "Yes, really, they came into the museum one afternoon together for some kind of meeting. They were scouting out venues for a party."

It had really been at the Grammys. Marty and I had stayed away that year reveling in our pre-matrimonial bliss. Later in the evening, we had met up with some friends and artists at the after-parties. I think I even shook Elton's hand that night without thinking of the past. Now, here he was again, completing the circle.

"Do you still work there?"

"Yes, I'm still working there. We miss your mom, though."

Mrs. Sammler's gaze thanked me for abiding by her story. I could tell she found my tale as interesting as her daughter. And then, just as casually as she discussed her favorite music, Michelle asked, "Have they found a match for me, Mom?"

I looked up, about to respond.

"They're working on it," Mrs. Sammler answered, brushing Michelle's hair, seeing to it that it fell softly around her face, the face that Jonas and I had created. "You're on the donor list, and first we have to do another round of chemo. This is a process. It's going to take some time."

Michelle put her earphones over her ears and dismissed us. It must have been easy for her to shut the world out that way. I looked at my watch. It was just after eleven. I wanted to try him again, becoming increasingly anxious with every minute that passed. I didn't want to postpone this any longer.

"I think I'll leave you two alone now," I said, grabbing my purse from off the chair. To Mrs. Sammler, I said, "Thank you for letting me see her." This good-bye was much harder than the first. "I'd like it if you could call me and let me know how she's doing. You have my cell phone number."

"You don't have to go, Jessica," she said. "You don't need to leave New York so quickly. Michelle needs love around her."

I thought about how hard those words must have been for her and thanked her. She looked like she wanted to give me something else.

When I searched for Michelle's eyes, they were closed, sealing her off from us. "She'll be asleep in a few minutes," she said. "The music always puts her to sleep."

I held onto this thought so I wouldn't cry. "Good-bye, Mrs. Sammler."

And she didn't offer me her hand, just said, "My name is Jill. Call me Jill."

Chapter 26

Standing before the complex that Jonas had probably walked through hundreds of times, my instincts signaled me to run. Thirteen years ago, I hadn't wanted to burden him with a child; now, not only was I burdening him with the news, but with the gravity that we could lose her.

I stared at the intimidating structure that made up the cluster of hospitals and care facilities throughout Boston. Jonas was a grown-up, living in a highly sophisticated world. He had fulfilled his goal of becoming an important pathologist, a huge leap beyond our discussions on the physics of farts, and the memory of our talks made me smile. With my coat pulled tightly around me for the extra support, I stepped inside the glass doors that read BrinkerHarte, the renowned pathology lab for Boston's leading hospital.

The building housed several labs and a bustling staff. I approached the receptionist's desk, gave her my name, and asked for Dr. Levy. She proceeded to call the office and relayed the same message as the day before. "Dr. Levy is in a seminar. Was the doctor expecting you?" she asked.

"No, I'm in from Los Angeles. It's urgent that I speak with him. Do you know when he'll be back?"

The receptionist eyed me strangely. Within five minutes, I was being escorted through the tumult of lab equipment to an obscure office. There were files all over the place—on the floor, on top of each other, leaning up against the walls. Somewhere, beneath the chaos, was a chair and a desk.

"Excuse the mess," she said. "Believe it or not, we know where everything is. Just have a seat, and someone will be right in."

She closed the door behind her. I was left alone with my nervousness until I heard his voice, almost unrecognizable, say, "Ms. Parker, how can I help you?"

My body began to slowly turn to face Jonas when he repeated again, "Ms. Parker?"

His formality perplexed me. I willed myself to look, and when I did, the breath I'd been holding in streamed out. To a man who wasn't Jonas, I exhaled, "You're not Dr. Levy."

"Yes, my niece isn't here right now, and the gal at the front said this was important. I'm Dr. Cohen, is there anything I can help you with?"

"I meant Jonas, Jonas Levy," I said, about to clobber the tall, clumsy man with the shrilly voice I mistook for Jonas's. He had a receding hairline so precise it could have been painted on with a stencil, and thick, black glasses that overtook his whole face. An image of the absentminded professor came to mind.

"Jonas doesn't work here," he said. "Emily's the only Levy on staff." He said all this while observing me closely, unclear as to why a woman would need his niece's husband so urgently. I wondered if Mr. Magoo would be able to help me with my escapade, but thought better than to get the funny man involved.

I said, "I thought he worked here. When I called information for Dr. Levy..." but I stopped myself midsentence when I discovered my mistake. "It was all he talked about back then."

"How do you know my Jonas?" he asked.

"We were friends in LA when his father was in the hospital. My mom worked there. I did too." I would spare him the throw-up story.

"You knew Adam?" he asked.

"Didn't everyone?"

He was still standing before me, sizing me up like a science experiment he wanted to fling under his microscope.

"You must have lost touch with him."

"Nineteen eighty-eight," I said, knowing the year indelibly by heart. "Is he alright?"

We exchanged worried glances. "Jonas is fine, Ms. Parker, but he's no pathologist."

"He's not?"

For this, he took off the glasses. "He changed his specialty. Damn near broke my heart."

"Then we have something in common," I whispered, unable to stop myself.

"What's that?" he asked, returning the glasses to their perch. I could swear he could see through me with them.

"Nothing," I muttered. "You must have been very disappointed."

"I was, for selfish reasons, but I wouldn't argue with Jonas's logic. He's a smart man, and he didn't enjoy it like the rest of us. Just look at him. A guy like that was made for human contact, the interaction with patients. Jonas has always been that way, always touching people's lives. People like me stay behind the scene."

I was starting to feel sorry for Magoo. "I remember that about him."

He started to say something else when the door swung open and an attractive woman burst through. "I just got in from the USCAP meetings. You need to read this article in the journal about hepatitis C and hemochromatosis gene mutation." Shoving the papers at Magoo, she continued with no indication that she was interrupting. "We have to incorporate it into the iron labs that Rick is working on. They're onto something. This could be huge."

"Have a seat," he beckoned to me, as I sat on the lone chair, sipping from a cup of water.

The woman managed a limited glance in my direction, remaining focused on her discovery. Dr. Cohen read through the article and sifted through another file while she leaned over his shoulder. Offering an opinion, he handed her back the papers and she turned to leave.

"Thank you, Em," he said, "nice work, as usual." She smiled and closed the door behind her. It was then I felt the glass of water slip through my fingers and onto the floor.

Without missing a beat, Dr. Cohen called for somebody to assist with the floor, but I was right there, picking up shards in my bare hands.

"Ouch," I said, feeling the thin glass slip through my skin.

"Let me see that," he said, taking my left hand into his, eyes stopping on the finger that housed my diamond wedding band. "That's a beauty," he said, and I didn't know if he meant the ring or the glass wedged in my finger. He pulled a tweezer-like apparatus out of his pocket and tugged on it, enjoying himself in a quirky, methodical way. "I take it you hadn't met Emily before."

"No. I saw a picture once. She looks different than I remembered." Or maybe I simply hadn't wanted to remember.

"There, that should do it," he said, and then he wrapped my finger with a bandage from a nearby cabinet, patting my fingers with his own.

"Thank you," I said, noting the tender way in which he took care of my wound. The mess, although gone from our sight, was still hovering in the air around us. "What's so important? Is Jonas in any trouble?" he asked.

If only our kind of trouble could be tended to with a topical and reassuring hand. "No," I said, but he was scribbling something on a piece of paper; when he handed it over, he said, "This is where you can reach him, but please, I've never seen you before in my life."

I looked up at my latest ally and thanked him. "I really appreciate this, Dr. Cohen."

"You're welcome, Ms. Parker," he said, and he stood up to lead me out of the building.

"Good luck," he said, as if he knew my mission required it.

I whispered back, "I think any patient would be lucky to have you for a doctor."

He smiled and thanked me shyly. I walked off with the piece of paper burning a hole in my hand.

The next morning I flagged a cab to New York Memorial Hospital. Instead of climbing the stairs to Michelle's floor, I walked through the main entry foyer and passed through to the medical building adjacent to the hospital. When I found the name I was looking for on the directory, I headed toward the elevators and pushed the number twelve, taking a second to catch a glimpse of myself in a mirror as the elevator doors closed before me.

Maybe I had read the words wrong. Maybe I was seeing things I wanted to be there but weren't. My jittery fingers pulled the tattered paper out of my pocket. *Dr. Jonas Levy, NY Memorial Hospital Professional Building, Pediatrics.*

The doors opened, and I searched the walls for Jonas's office number. Was it possible he had at some point passed Michelle in the hallway?

"Can I help you?"

I stuffed the paper back in my pocket and turned to the woman behind the desk in the crowded office. "I'm looking for Dr. Levy, please. Dr. Jonas Levy," I corrected myself.

"Do you have an appointment?"

I almost said *do I look like I need a pediatrician?* "No, I'm an old friend and was visiting a patient in the hospital and saw his name on the directory."

"He's finishing rounds in the hospital. He'll be back in a few minutes, if you'd like to have a seat."

I scanned the parade of boys and girls hurling toys across the floor and asked, "Can I use your bathroom?"

"Here's the key to the one down the hall," she said. "It's a lot cleaner."

I took the key and thanked her, leaving the sounds of children behind me.

The circumstance was exhausting me. My arms and legs dragged far behind my brain's determination. I had spent the last two days so close to him, we might easily have run into each other. He was here, saving people's lives, unaware of the fact that his daughter was in need of the very thing he had to offer. At the same time, I couldn't help but feel honored and prideful that he had listened to my advice all those years ago.

Stepping out of the bathroom, my cell phone rang. Like a vacuum cleaner, it slurped the clutter out of my head, forcing me to concentrate on the voice of my precious son.

"Hi, Mommy."

"Hi, Ari! What are you doing?"

He mumbled something that resembled "cookie" and "Gammy," the name he uses for Grandma, and I said, "Are you having fun with Grandma? Mommy loves you, sweetie. Mommy will be home real soon. Big kiss, big hug." And then the phone clicked as my little boy hung up on me. As I began to dial my home, a voice from behind me said, "I told you you'd make a beautiful mother."

My body stiffened. The voice was unmistakable. I didn't know if I had the energy to turn and look at him. One single step, and Jonas Levy would be in front of me.

"Grace, it's you, isn't it?" His voice came closer.

I stared at the door to his office, searching the dark wood for something to concentrate on other than him.

"Grace?"

And with the help of my racing heart, I turned around, and there he was.

"It's me," I said.

He smiled. The same smile I'd seen a thousand and one times, the same smile that told me he was genuinely happy to see me.

"What are the chances of this?" he asked. "Wow, I can't believe it's really you."

"Yeah, it's been a long time."

He leaned in to place his arms around me, a friend giving an old friend a hug, but there was nothing friendly about the way my face rested on the space between his shoulder and his neck and how his scent crept into my nose and other places. I saw how time had changed us and what remained exactly the same.

"You look great!" he said, pulling back faster than I'd expected.

"You too," I said, noting he was no longer the lanky boy but a broadchested man. Gone was the tan, but the skin was as smooth as ever. His hair was the same; there were traces of gray. Time had been kind to him. Although aged, he now possessed a distinguished quality I hadn't noticed when we were kids. I inhaled.

"How long has it been?" he asked.

"Thirteen years," came racing out of my mouth.

"I can't believe it's been that long. What are you doing here? Is everything okay?"

Doctors and patients traipsed by, oblivious to the reunion between two intimate strangers. "I'm fine, I'm here visiting someone." And then I stopped, or he interrupted me. I wasn't sure which happened first.

"You live here in New York?"

"No, I still live in California."

"This is too much." He appraised me with those eyes. "How have you been?"

"Do you think we can go somewhere and talk," I asked, "alone?"

Without answering, he possessively took my arm and led me to a door adjacent to his waiting room.

"You still fidget," he said, unlocking the office and offering me a seat.

"Here's the key to the bathroom," I said, handing him the ring while he paged one of the nurses to pick it up.

When I got comfortable, he asked, "Did you know I worked here?"

I contemplated my potentially explosive response. There was nothing fateful about our meeting today. Having a sick daughter in this hospital had been scripted long ago. We were players in a much bigger story that bound us together. It could be argued that we had never parted.

"I had no idea. I always assumed you lived in Boston."

"I commute. I still can't get over this," he added. "You're so not 'almost sixteen' anymore, and you're much quieter than I remember."

My heart hurt, and I didn't want to cry. Not yet.

I said, "A pediatrician. Dare I say how much it suits you?"

"You were right all along. This is where I belong. You can say it. You told me so."

"If only it were that simple," I said. "Was it hard to give up pathology, the years you invested?"

He turned serious and said, "It was way harder giving you up. A lot harder."

I wanted to stay in the present, but he was guiding me back to the courtyard. "You made it look so easy."

"I know," he said, not disagreeing, studying his hands and the platinum band that circled his left finger. "It's what I had to do."

I thought about symbols and what they represent, and the ring on his finger prohibited me from pressing on. Seeing Emily was opening the door and stepping into a scene in Jonas's life I never knew. Mostly, because I chose not to look. Had I been wiser in my youth, I might have known that everything about her affected me, and if Jonas knew that too, maybe things could have gone differently.

The interminable silence passed, as we made our way back to the present. There was so much I wanted to say to him. I wanted to hear about his life; I wanted to share stories of mine. I wanted to know him again, feel close to him again; but I was worried that once I shared the news, there wouldn't be anything but accusations and blame. If only I didn't have to tell Jonas news that would change his whole life. Then I would have told him how good he looked, how at peace he seemed with himself, how in a brief encounter in a hospital corridor, years hadn't passed, and we were the same two people who once were in love.

"Jonas," the only thing I could muster was, "it's good to see you again."

"Something's wrong, Jess. Tell me what it is." His hand rested on mine; the bands between us touched like concrete fences.

I said, "I know you're busy, but there's something I need to tell you."

"Anything. What is it?"

"There's a patient here," I started, while the fragments of the story turned into logical sentences. "She's almost twelve years old, a little girl..."

"Is she yours?" he asked. "Is she sick?"

"Her name's Michelle Sammler."

"I remember that name. She came in with bruises all over her body. Initially they thought it was a case of abuse, until the doctors diagnosed her with leukemia. She's back in the hospital?"

"She had chemotherapy, went in to remission, and just recently relapsed. She needs a transplant. It's her best chance for survival."

I was reminded of our childish medical bantering, and ironically realized that this medical discussion was as profound as we would ever discuss. Rebellious tears formed in my eyes. I could feel them pooling, willing them not to spill over. An awful silence permeated the room, making what we weren't saying louder than the quiet.

My face was now in my hands, resting in my lap, hiding the evidence of my distress. I hadn't wanted him to see me cry. I didn't want our reunion to be like this. It should have been a tender meeting, not news of a child whose body was ravaged by a killer disease. The crying kept me from having to speak the truth; and while it bought me some time, it couldn't obstruct the dam from bursting, and the droplets of deception from floating out of my mouth. The words poured forth; I had no opportunity to censure them.

"She's yours, Jonas."

"What?"

"She's yours."

"I'm not sure I understand."

"She's ours. The little girl in there dying is our daughter, Michelle. I gave her up. I didn't know, I swear..."

"Jessica, this isn't funny."

"You had left for Boston by the time I found out. It was weeks after you'd said your good-bye. I never heard from you again, and it was over and you were clear about what you wanted, and I loved you so much, enough to let you go, and I hated you too, but I knew I couldn't get rid of it. I couldn't abort our child. She was made with so much..." I had to stop myself from saying the word again. "I thought about telling you, but

I didn't want you to think I was trying to trap you or keep you. My God, I was sixteen. I didn't have it in me to be that malicious or selfish, and I knew I was too young and too irresponsible to raise a baby on my own. It was the hardest thing I ever had to do, but, the baby, she was matched with a very nice couple and on the day I gave birth to her, they took her from me and I never saw her again."

I didn't want to look up, afraid of what I'd see on his face, so I kept my face buried in my hands, hiding the shame, hiding the agony, hiding the mess that was dripping from my nose. When I finally did look up, his face was a mix of anger and regret. He hovered over me, ready for battle. Maybe if I continued to speak, he wouldn't lash out at me.

"For years, *this, you*, it was all behind me, until I got a phone call from this lawyer acting on behalf of the family, talking about privacy and parental rights. He said my daughter was here, and they'd consulted with Dr. Greene about her options; when they found out she was adopted, they asked if there was a chance she had a blood sibling, and I said yes, because I have a son. I thought that's what they meant, and I was on my way from LA. When I got here, they told me they needed a full-blood sibling."

He still didn't say anything. He just sat there. His accusatory eyes glazed over.

"I have a daughter?" he spoke, the words hollow and barren. "And you're telling me now, all these years later? You didn't think it was something I had the right to know?"

I looked him square in the eyes, "No, I didn't."

There was another silence between us. It was only a few, insignificant seconds, but it felt a lot longer.

"How could you do this?" he asked me, searching my face for something, whispering to control his venom. In loving him and trying to protect him, I had betrayed him.

"Does it matter now?" I asked. "Hadn't you said to treasure the moment? You think I planned this? You think I wanted it to be this way? This wasn't what I wanted, none of it."

"Why didn't the attorney contact me?"

I looked at my shoes, studying the intricate lines that held them together. "I didn't write down a father." I cowered.

"What did you write?" he hurled at me.

"Deceased," I spat at him. "Deceased. There, does that make you feel better? At the time, you *were* gone. Not just vanished, not just missing or lost, dead. Don't you get it, Jonas? You broke my heart. I thought I'd never recover. You were this boy I thought I knew, and then you became a stranger. Maybe you always were. Did I ever know the baby's father?"

This is when he turned toward the wall and threw a punch right through it. When he faced me again, he fumed. "Do you have any idea what you've done, what your lies have cost? You can't play God, Jessica. It's not your right. I have a wife and…"

"Emily," I said.

"Do you know what this is going to do to her? Do you know how many lives you've disrupted?"

"I'm sorry."

"*I'm sorry?* Is that all you can say? *I'm sorry?* You have my child, and you keep it from me…you lie to me…"

"I didn't lie to you."

"A sin of omission, what's the difference?"

I shrugged.

"And you tell me now, thirteen years later, that you gave our child up for adoption and the only reason you're sharing this bit of news with me, this otherwise insignificant information, is that I'm expected to share in your grief? What about my rights? What about what you took from me when you made a decision without consulting me first? What kind of person does this?"

"I lost a lot too," I spat back. He wasn't looking at me. He was holding his bruised hand. Blood was starting to drip onto the floor. "Hate me, curse me, but don't forget what I gave up. Don't forget what this did to me and how it changed my life. It didn't have to be this way, Jonas. You were the one who walked away. You were the one who never looked back. If you had even called one time, just once, maybe I would've told you, maybe it could've been different, but you didn't. It still doesn't change anything. She'd still be here, and she'd still be sick."

"She doesn't even know us. How do you know her parents even want us around? Legally, she's not our child. We have no obligation to her. Besides, we can't help her."

Jonas was beaten. Gone was the adoration in his eyes, the place I used to occupy. He had once been my harness. Now I was floating in the air.

"They wouldn't have contacted us if they didn't want us here."

"They contacted *you.*"

There was no fight left in me. "If nothing more, I just wanted you to know about her. I wanted you to know how much I once cared about you, how I couldn't bear the thought of giving up that part of you. What you want to do with that is your decision, but please don't hate me." My eyes pleaded with him. "If you saw her, you'd understand. She's beautiful and smart and…"

"I think you should go now." His hand was getting worse, and he was wrapping it with some tissues on the desk. "You've done enough damage, but that's always been your way. You've always been trouble, Jessica. Just get the hell out of here."

His words were like a dagger. They ripped into me as I walked from the room.

I stayed away from the hospital the rest of the day, walking the streets of Manhattan, barely noticing the casual snow that flurried from the sky. It was a cold day, dark and cloudy, and I pulled my coat close to me as I walked distances with little care about direction or destination.

Seeing Jonas after all these years brought back a tidal wave of emotions. The freedom to love him was overshadowed by the responsibilities that were now mine. I yearned to be young and fifteen, to love again as though love was all that mattered.

I stopped in front of a store window and saw a different face staring back at me. So much for the preparation I'd put into making myself presentable, desirable. I studied the woman in the glass and the sounds of Asia's "The Smile Has Left Your Eyes" were escaping the open doorway. It was the perfect song for this depressing scene.

Before the accident Marty would have been the person holding me close, assuring me that things would turn around; but I'd failed him, and before him I failed another man I had loved. I witnessed the disapproving looks in both their eyes. My self-destructive behavior was as potent as the wreckage that I had created. Could I have willed all of this to happen? Was this how love always worked?

I deliberated my next move. I had given my daughter life, and I was helpless to its revival. Then there was my marriage, in need of similar resuscitation. I worried how Marty would react if I told him that I had a child with Jonas, the only man besides him that I had ever loved. But the betrayal and the dishonesty is what Marty wouldn't be able to forgive. He cherished all the firsts he believed we shared together: our first pregnancy, our first delivery, our first child. They were not, in fact, firsts at all for me. I thought if somehow Michelle could be cured, I could redeem myself. But if she lived, would I be able to play a role in her life? And would the burden be too much for my marriage to bear?

It was late when I returned to the empty hotel room. My hair was wet, and my fingers were frozen inside my gloves. I'd felt even emptier than I had when I'd left that morning. Jonas's disdain had turned me inward. I'd become disengaged from everything around me. The hole within me was gaping wider and wider. I half expected to see it there when I undressed for bed, evidence of the mistakes I had made. Every direction I turned left irreparable damage. Maybe, I thought, Michelle was the one thing I could save.

I didn't clean my face, brush my teeth, or even call home before I got under the covers. I was angry at the world, angry at myself. None of it seemed to matter anymore. Acne and bad breath were the least of it.

Chapter 27

The message light was beeping red when I woke the next morning. I hadn't even heard the phone ring. Jill Sammler's voice was on the machine, something about a development, and if I could meet them tomorrow at Mr. Sammler's office in the city. When I arrived, they were all in there— the Sammlers, and Jonas. It was like walking into the principal's office. Learning that Dr. Levy was the father had to have been a shock to all of them.

"Is Michelle alright?" I asked.

"She's fine," Mr. Sammler said. "I suppose an introduction isn't necessary. You know Dr. Levy." I murmured something, trying my best to conceal my shame.

"There's something I'd like to discuss," he began. In his office surroundings, high above Manhattan, Mr. Sammler located his voice. I might have guessed he was an accountant.

My eyes urged Jonas to look my way, but he made a point to ignore me.

Mr. Sammler continued, "Since Michelle doesn't have a blood sibling, we're looking for matches in the national registries. The chances are slim that she'll hold on long enough for us to find a match."

"What about my son?" I volunteered again. "There's no possibility of his being a match?"

Mr. Sammler responded emphatically, "We need that blood match. Presuming Dr. Levy is not the father of that child, your son won't qualify."

Nobody spoke as Jonas and I independently wrestled with a fate of which neither of us could speak.

"Which is why I'm glad you're all here," he continued. "I've been researching an option. It's a pretty hot topic today, wide debates on both sides of the bioethical spectrum, but it's been done in similar cases when a child's life is at stake."

Something unthinkable was about to come out of Mr. Sammler's mouth. I knew it before he even breathed his next word. "I read about a family recently that was about to lose their eight-year-old son to a disease called Fanconi anemia. It's a rare genetic disease that causes bone marrow failure. Without a bone marrow transplant, their son would die. His sister was not a match, and there were none in the national registry. The family had always wanted a third child, so they moved their plans up."

"Having a child to save a child?" I interrupted.

"Precisely. In this case, the cord blood from the baby's birth·was collected, and it was an exact bone marrow match. The baby boy saved his big brother's life."

The hunger in Jill Sammler's eyes tore through my heart. My initial reaction was that this was a preposterous resolution and ballsy of Mr. Sammler to ask, but he kept right on talking as if this was something Jonas or I would participate in. "Assuming Michelle's blood work comes back normal this afternoon, and we can continue with the course of chemotherapy, we'll buy ourselves another year. A match might come up in the registry, but we all know there's no guarantee. The possibility of a full-blood sibling, again, is our best option."

"Parents choosing this option when they're married is understandable, even commendable, but this is by no means the case," I said. "Our situation is radically different. How can we create a baby, two unmarried strangers?"

"We're hardly strangers, Jessica," Jonas regrettably spoke up, for the first time looking in my direction.

Ignoring him, I continued my rant. "We bring a baby into the world for medical reasons, and then what happens? It's not like a bottle of medicine that gets thrown in the garbage when we're done with it. It's a life, a living, breathing person."

"That's right," Mr. Sammler said, "it's a life, and a life that has the potential to save your daughter's. We can all agree this is an insane proposition, but we're getting desperate here. How far are you willing to go to save Michelle? That's the question you need to ask yourself."

She was my daughter, my child; the ties to her were undeniably there. I resented him for implying otherwise and told him so. "I'd do anything to save my child, but *this*, *this*, is crazy."

"To some people, yes, it's crazy. To us, it might be her only chance to live."

"I don't understand," I said. "Does conceiving a child with him guarantee a one hundred percent match?" I stopped talking, because I was entertaining the idea.

"Ms. Parker, that's a very good question…"

"Mrs. Tauber," I interrupted, becoming fiercely defensive of my family.

"Mrs. Tauber, in the case that I just referred to, the parents underwent IVF treatment, in-vitro fertilization. A pre-implantation genetic diagnosis was performed on the embryos to find a suitable match."

"Suitable," I repeated, "that sounds open to interpretation. What exactly do you mean?"

Jonas spoke up. "One in four embryos will be a match. With the pre-implantation genetic diagnosis, the embryos can be tested to ensure that a match results."

"They also perform a human leukocyte antigen test," Jonas went on. "It tells us if the cell markers within the embryos are an identical match to Michelle's. Every cell has markers that need to match. If they do, we can use the stem cells from the cord blood immediately after birth, and the procedure would not affect the baby at all."

My head wasn't grasping something. "Have you thought about what happens to the embryos that are rejected? The ones that aren't selected?"

Nobody dared respond, not one of them. The blank faces around the table just waited for the question to go away.

"That's why pro-lifers are adamantly opposed to these kinds of tests," Mr. Sammler said. "There are legitimate concerns. Maybe you should take a look at the some of the articles I've read, see what other families did under similar circumstances. There's a controversial component to this type of practice. I can fully appreciate your apprehension."

I couldn't control what came out of my mouth next. "Similar circumstances? I doubt anyone is on record with this type of circumstance. Do you have any idea what you're asking of me, Mr. Sammler? I'm a married woman with a family, and you're suggesting that I create a baby with him, just like that."

"No," he interrupted, "I'm not asking that of you. I'm merely offering you the only option that will guarantee my daughter a life…IVF is a non-invasive procedure."

"Like having another man's baby inside my body, other than my husband's, isn't invasive, or disruptive?" My personal life had fallen under public scrutiny, and Jonas, well, he was just sitting there mute.

"Jessica," came a voice from the back of the room. It was Jill Sammler. This turned all our heads, because up to now, Mr. Sammler had dominated the conversation. Her voice was steady and strong, her eyes fixed to my own. "You loved her enough to have her," she said. "Can't you love her enough to save her?"

Chapter 28

"Can we meet for dinner?" Jonas asked. I was at the library on the computer when my cell phone rang.

"I'll think about it," I said, abruptly hanging up, wanting to get back to my studies. It was the same empty response I'd given to Jill Sammler when she looked me in the eyes and pretty much begged me to help her child. In both cases, I spoke the truth. I was willing to think about it.

Mr. Sammler encouraged me to research, and I did what was asked of me: I researched. I researched acute lymphocytic leukemia. I researched bone marrow transplants. I read about probability and life expectancy. I even found a few articles on the ethical and moral debates pertaining to *having a child in order to save a child.*

My research wasn't limited to leukemia. I found myself in a library researching the Internet for Fanconi anemia after I had stumbled upon a Web site devoted to these children and their parents. Intrigued, I began to read.

Jared Thompson was his name, the one who stood out from among the thirty or so others who were written about on their site. He was diagnosed with Fanconi anemia, and as I read his mother's personal entries, I became engrossed in his ordeal, as if in her words, there was a message of some kind. Her journals had been kept for years, documentation of the heartache and frustrations that a life-threatening disease has on a family. I had lost a child, a baby boy who had not entered the world, while Jared's parents had lost life that they intimately knew. They lost baseball practice and holidays, Jared's body curled around them at nighttime, the smell of his breath, the wisps of his hair, and the sounds of his voice and laughter. They lost years of loving each other. They lost time with their healthy children, and life was reduced to hospital visits riddled with anger and fear. No one who hasn't experienced it knows what it is like to lose a child, I realized, or even what it's like to discover your child is afflicted with a life-threatening disease. These people understood, and my heart ached.

As I read through Jared's mother's blog, I saw the words *bone marrow transplant* across the screen. He was almost eight. During the months following, he seemed okay, even if okay meant losing his hair and not being able to leave his house because of the high risk of contracting random illnesses. I learned that children that have transplants are depleted of their regular immunizations, leaving them susceptible to most germs. Even the most common everyday activities can be life-threatening.

But then Jared's ANC dropped (a subset of the white cell count that fights against infection), and what followed was swollen lymph glands, fever, elevated liver levels, but not all these things at once. No, for these parents, it was far worse. Just as they had seen a tiny spark of light at the end of a lengthy tunnel, darkness would descend. A day of good spirits and positive test results could end with part of his stricken body malfunctioning, or even worse, death. It was a roller coaster. Jared's story haunted me. And although I could have skipped weeks of past entries and learned the outcome, reading the heartfelt passages delayed the inevitable and gave me an indication of hope.

Blood cultures, pneumonia, hospital stays, antibiotics, chest x-rays, stool cultures, infection, kidney failure, loss of appetite, and other unpleasantries continued. Jared's mom was not alone in rooting Jared on. I believed maybe he would survive. And with each dated entry, I prayed he would tackle just one more hurdle. But finally he couldn't fight any longer.

Less than a year from the day he had his transplant, Jared's little body gave out. The reality was crushing. This was someone's life and not a story one reads or hears about from the friend of a friend of a friend. I searched the page for the date of Mrs. Thompson's last entry and saw that it was three months ago. Three months. For me, Jared died today, but a mother had now lived three months without her child.

My cell phone rang again, momentarily tearing me away from the horror on the page.

"It's about the baby, isn't it?" my mother asked.

I turned from the computer, cradling the phone between my shoulder and my ear and flat-out answered, "Yes." How could I deny my mother the opportunity to once again be right? She said something in response, but it was hard to hear with the printer shooting out pages of information I'd bookmarked. I think I started to cry. Either for Jared, or the release of truths, or for mothers everywhere who feel their children's afflictions as their own.

Seeing what happened to Jared Thompson's family helped me open up to my mother. When I told her what had happened, she cried with me.

"She's my granddaughter, Jessica. What can I do?"

I told her what I knew and prepared her, and myself, for the things we didn't.

"You mean she might die?" my mother asked.

"She could. We just don't know." Two teenagers caught my attention, hiding behind one of the bookshelves. They were laughing loudly, without a care in the world. I'd been so stuck in my head the last twenty-four hours, I had forgotten the simple pleasures of life. Look how close we can be to joy; look how close we can be to sadness.

"Mom, do you think it's a sign?"

"A sign?"

"You know, Jonas being here, and Michelle. Marty, he's off doing God knows what."

My mother said to me, "This is life, Jess, and looking for signs isn't going to give you answers. Have you considered life is testing you? You have to answer the test."

"It's too coincidental—all of it."

"Magical thinking makes it a lot easier for you, doesn't it?"

I didn't know. I was staring at the young couple groping each other and then said, "Yes."

"You figure you don't have to be responsible for your choices. You can just blame fate."

"It has to mean something, doesn't it?" I asked, "that I'm here, and he's here, and we…" But I didn't go on, because I hadn't yet accepted my feelings. I'd been fighting them for hours, years.

"You need to tell Marty about this," she said. "You can't just put your marriage on hold and expect to come back to it like nothing's changed. He's your husband. He loves you, despite all your imperfections. Didn't he prove that after the accident? Talk to him, be honest. He'll support you. He always has."

"I can't," I said. "We're not strong enough."

"You have to learn to find your way back to each other, some way to trust again."

"What if I don't want to?" I sighed, my eyes following the young couple out the door of the library. "What if I want to walk away?"

"That would be a mistake."

"I think I can handle what's happening between Marty and me, but I don't think I'll ever understand why God would make a little kid like that so sick. I just can't wrap my arms around that."

"It's horrible," she agreed. "No one should ever have to go through something like that, nobody. I don't even know what to say, but I do know you need the support of your family around you, and that includes Marty. Talk to him. Tell him the truth. He's your husband; he loves you."

"I don't mean to sound pessimistic, but I'm not buying into that happily-ever-after crap, not now, not anymore."

"You never believed in happily-ever-after, Jess."

"What are you talking about?" I asked, getting irritated.

"You've always found a way to sabotage things, the good things."

"How did I sabotage Jonas?"

"He was hardly a good thing."

"And Marty was?"

"Marty *is*, and Marty's *willing*, and Marty's *capable* of giving you everything you've ever wanted. Just let him. Let him do it."

"Whatever," I said, brushing her off because I simply wanted the conversation to come to a close. My mother didn't understand.

"*Whatever* is not going to put your life back together."

"I love you, Mom," I said. "I do."

"I know," she said. "Let me know if there's anything I can do." And we said good-bye, and I returned to Jared Thompson and his mother's pain, so that I wouldn't have to think about my own.

Chapter 29

When you're dealing with sickness, I learned, life as you once knew it is barely recognizable. Instead of doing the things you had done before like going to work, laughing, and sleeping, you find yourself in a trance, robotic-like. Each day blends into the next, a merging of the mundane: waking up, brushing your teeth, dressing in the dark, and seeing what you've become in the mirror. Sadly, a stranger stares back. Your hair isn't combed. The lines under your eyes grow more defined. The clothes you put on are the same you wore the day before, and still you walk out the door and head toward the hospital. When you're finished there, you head back home, and you remember that you haven't eaten all day, and the mail has piled up, and the newspapers, and you get into bed to sleep and are awakened by dreams. You don't know which are worse, the ones with your loved one sick or the ones that feel even more nightmarish, where they are well, and you awaken to the truth. I walked into New York Memorial after a two-day absence, tired and angry. I couldn't recall if I'd brushed my teeth. I ran my tongue across them and reached for a Tic Tac.

"Jess, what happened to you?" asked Jonas when we ran into each other in the hallway. "You haven't answered my calls."

"I turned my phone off." He did not need to know that I had cried myself to sleep the past few nights, dreaming of Jared Thompson, stifling the urge to call Mrs. Thompson with my condolences.

"I think I'll take you up on that dinner invitation," I finally said, reluctant to deal with the issues at home. "I want to talk to the Sammlers." I had questions for them. "Can we grab something to eat after that?"

We agreed to meet outside Michelle's room in an hour, but my visit upstairs was cut short when Jill Sammler grabbed hold of me in the hallway to tell me that her daughter had been having a bad couple of days. I saw through the door that the machines were pumping chemo into her veins.

"You look terrible," she told me.

I said, "No worse than you," and a laugh escaped us, drawing comfort from our shared unease.

I could see the black bags under her eyes, the deep worry that burrowed its way into her hollow cheeks. She was tired and going through everything that parents of sick children go through.

"I miss her," she said. "The chemo's exhausting her body. She's either sleeping or throwing up." I reminded her that there were machines pumping supplements into her, not just the life-saving toxin. I had seen the alternative. This was nothing compared to that.

"She'll be back," I said.

"We have to accept that one day she might not. Maybe these little absences are preparing me for that."

I wanted to tell her that nothing ever prepares you, not for that, but I didn't, because it was accepting an inevitability I didn't want to think about.

"Be strong, Jill. Michelle needs that from you."

"I'm trying, Jessica, I'm really trying."

"I'm so sorry you have to go through this, really, I am."

"She's all I've got."

Mr. Sammler approached with some people that could have been friends or relatives and steered his wife away. I could tell she wanted to stay and talk to me more. I liked her. It was improbable that we'd ever be friends, in the broader definition of the word, but I would have liked to have known my daughter's mother. If friends were an option, I would have explained the reasons I had to give her up and then maybe she'd tell me why she couldn't have kids, why they didn't adopt more children, and what it was like the day they brought Michelle home.

"I'll be back tomorrow," I told her, and she thanked me in a way that reminded me I held the life of her child in my hands, and that I wasn't wrong about her wanting to stay.

Jonas came up from behind me and started talking. We were standing there in the stale, sterile hallway while the hospital players in the drama called disease walked by. We were standing so close to one another, I could feel his breath on my cheek. He was saying something. His lips were moving. Did I smell toothpaste on his breath? I had to stop myself from reaching for that hair that fell in his face, hiding one of his eyes.

"Are you listening to me at all, Jessie?"

This time I looked up at him. I wasn't.

The tone of his voice was what grabbed me, the familiar way he said my name, *Jessie*, firm, but forgiving, telling me his anger had passed. He heard it too, and the silence was laden with ambiguity.

"Are you ready?" he asked.

"Yes."

I followed him down the hallway, watching his hunched-over shoulders, knowing better than to ask where we were going. We reached the elevator without uttering a word. When the secluded space filled with other passengers, we didn't let on that we had once mattered to each other. We were strangers like everyone else on the elevator, which is a phenomenon that has always fascinated me. You think about the millions of people in the world and amid a crowded elevator of people, two souls can be standing side by side with this *thing* between them, this *I know what you look like with your clothes off*, and no one else knows. It's your secret. And it happens every day, in office buildings and darkened movie theaters—there's someone we were once connected to, and we pass like strangers, and no one could ever guess that we had once meant so much to one another. It was terrifying to me how life could go on without acknowledging what I had invested in, just masking what had once been the true love of my life.

I searched the eyes of the other passengers looking for an indication that one of them was on to us, some recognition, but there was none.

Only when we reached the lobby floor did Jonas address me, and it was to tell me to wait out front, that he would bring the car around and pick me up. I found myself wanting someone to have overheard the dialogue. *There*, I'd say, *see that? We're not strangers.*

The cold air sidled up against me as I walked out the front door of the hospital. It was a refreshing change from the stagnant air of the building. Staring up at the stars in the sky, I found the biggest and the brightest, and quietly said a prayer.

He honked, on purpose, scaring the life out of me.

"You didn't have to do that," I said, settling into the car. He just laughed and pulled away from the hospital. Old habits urged me to look over my shoulder as I had years before, this air of mystery and discretion that followed us; but I resisted it, reminding myself that we were older now, different, changed, married, with children. There was nothing to hide from anymore.

"There's a great restaurant right outside the city. Do you mind taking a ride?"

"That's fine."

He fiddled with the radio station until I grabbed the dials and found what I was looking for. "You still love your music," he said.

"Uh huh."

The barrier was there between us, even though neither of us could see it. I crossed my arms closer to my chest, prompting him to turn up the heat. I could have told him that I wasn't cold, just protecting myself, but I was waiting for him to say something first. I didn't want things to be like they'd been that summer, with me doing all the talking and Jonas filling in blanks with vague inconsistencies.

"Fill me in about your life," he finally said.

"Besides this mess?"

"Besides this mess," he repeated.

Phases of my life flashed in a fleeting montage. Was I supposed to sum that all up?

"We live in LA. Our son, Ari, is three." I paused and then told him his father knew my husband. I didn't tell him what Adam had done for me, how he carried me on his shoulders and led me to my husband and career, only to end up back where I started.

"I think I met Marty once, a long time ago," he said. "Which did you end up in, film or music?"

"I'm a music supervisor. I'm the one that puts the music to the movies."

"You get to do both. How lucky for you."

"Lucky," I said, "Now there's a word I've never been."

"I don't get out to the movies very often these days. If I'm not in the hospital, I'm commuting back and forth to the hospital."

"You're missing out."

"You're probably very good at it."

"I was, but I've taken some time off."

He drove down 34th Street and parked in a lot adjacent to the water.

"The ferry's here. We've got to hurry."

"Where are we going?" I asked, as we ran across the street and boarded the small vessel, but he didn't answer. Not until we reached the other side and he was guiding me through the doors of the restaurant did he finally say, "You'll like it here."

It was loud and noisy, packed with people and a piano player. From any window, there were dramatic views of the city.

"Dr. Levy, it's so nice to see you," said the hostess. "Will your wife be joining you tonight?"

"No, Marcella," he said, stepping aside so she could see that I was there and I wasn't his wife. "She's back in Boston. Are there any seats at the bar? We can eat there."

Marcella nodded and led us to two seats at the end of the bar. The bartender dropped two white napkins in front of us. I immediately asked for a glass of white wine.

"Water for me," he said, and then to me, "I have to go back to the hospital tonight," as if he needed to explain.

"I'm sorry about the other day," he continued.

"You had every right to be mad," I said.

"You caught me off guard. I didn't know how to react. Having a daughter all this time…it incensed me that I didn't know about her."

"I thought I was doing you a favor. I didn't want to spoil your plans."

"It was only a matter of time," he said, gulping the water. "Maybe I will have a drink," he said, calling the bartender over and ordering a glass of red wine. When it landed in front of him, he brought it to his mouth. "What's the difference," he asked, "messing my plans up then, messing my plans up now?" His elbows rested on the table. He seemed tired, apprehensive. "We're ready to order," he called out to the server who walked by. I hadn't even picked up the menu.

Reading through the entrees, he stared at me until I told the man what I wanted.

"I'm glad you agreed to meet me," he said. "I thought I had forgotten how much I could miss you." Then he finished the wine in one last swig while I reached for the basket of bread to help absorb what he was saying. "Jessie Parker. It seems like yesterday…"

"It was a long time ago," I said. "Who even remembers?" He turned to me, to be sure I meant what I was saying; when he saw that I was, he let what he was about to say disappear into the air and reverted to a role he was accustomed to, the revered doctor.

"What's the bottom line?" I asked.

"Like Mr. Sammler said, our best option is to consider having another child, a sibling for Michelle."

"I was afraid you were going to say that."

"If you want to maximize the possibilities for a match, she needs a full-blood relative."

"I can't," I responded. "I won't do it. It's unethical. It's immoral."

He eyed my defiance with interest. "I agree with you, but it's not a question of ethical. It's how far are we willing to go to save Michelle?"

It was a proposition I hadn't wanted to explore.

"Put away your moral compass for a minute," he said. "There's a gray area, and I think it's worth looking into."

"Moral compass?" I asked. "Fortunately, one of us has a moral compass."

"What's that supposed to mean?"

"If the baby's a match," I said, ignoring his response, "and again, that's a big if, what happens to him? Do you take him? Do I? Does he have a relationship with Michelle? Do we tell him why he was created, for what purpose? And what if we end up with twins? Or triplets? How exactly does it work?"

He sat stonefaced silent. I hadn't even mentioned to him what I knew happened to kids after bone marrow transplants. Then he shook his head. "I don't have all the answers."

"You don't even have one of them," I snapped back, angrily. "You have a family. Have you thought about what it's going to do to them?"

"It's just me and Emily."

My detective skills had not seen this coming. "No kids?"

The monosyllabic response was full of regret. "No."

"Let me get this straight. You don't have kids, and you claim to know how I feel or how Jill Sammler feels, or how you're *going* to feel about a baby?"

He shuddered; he did. For one hurried moment, he dodged what probably felt like a bullet to his normally guarded exterior. Wanting to discuss anything other than the idea of our procreating, I honed in on this delicate subject.

"Did you forget to have them?" I asked.

"I love children," he said.

"According to your plan, you should have had about three or four by now."

He was getting angry. I was treading on thin ice, and I didn't care.

"That's none of your business."

I laughed. "You want to have a child with me, but it's not my business why you never had any of your own?"

It would have been much nicer to hear that he had never loved her and that he never had children with her because I had always been the one he wanted to practice being fruitful and multiplying with, but he didn't. I couldn't tell if I was saddened by that or relieved. Whether he couldn't, or she couldn't, or they couldn't, wasn't my concern, lest it were he couldn't, but that was impossible. Jonas finally blurted out, "Emily didn't want children," and put an end to the string of questions.

This required another sip of alcohol. I was astonished, galled, not that she hadn't wanted children—*that* I understood, having witnessed firsthand many friends in our business, happily married couples who made a conscious decision *not* to spawn when they realized their lifestyles and personalities would be crippling to a child. I couldn't fault Emily for that. What stunned me was that Jonas, who had always wanted children, fell in love with a woman who didn't.

"I can't believe you don't have something witty and sarcastic to say."

This was not the time for sarcasm. My eyes found his, and the exchange passed between us, that momentary glance that said, *I know you so well that I can feel your skin unfurl around me.* We just sat like that, him looking at me, me looking at him, until our food came.

"I know what you're thinking," he said, breaking the silence. "I know you, Jess, better than you know yourself. I messed up. I made a huge mistake. Are you happy?"

Hollow words that once would have changed my life now left me feeling sorry for Jonas. Inside I mourned for his losses, as I know he might have mourned for mine. This was finally his chance to have a baby. That it wasn't with his wife and was with a girl he had once loved seemed to make sense to him. Was I happy? Of course, I wasn't happy.

"A little," I blurted out.

"There's the girl I used to know."

I asked, "You'd really do this for Michelle?" It flew off my tongue from somewhere within, a place that hadn't wanted to see the outcome. I hadn't thought until that moment that maybe there was some shred of good in this.

He nodded that he would. His eyes were amazingly bright and clear and focused on me.

"What will you tell her?" I asked.

He hadn't bothered asking whom. She, her, we danced around her name just like when we were kids. I watched as he fingered the fork in his left hand. It amazed me that he could even swallow at a time like this. He was looking at it, and not at me, when he finally answered. "It won't matter."

"Yes, it will. You think my husband's going to accept this without a fight?"

"We're separated," he said.

I reached for my glass to steady me.

"We were both in Boston, and I got accepted to a residency program in New York, so I commuted back and forth and it worked for a while; she'd come here, I'd go out there, but then it stopped working. I just signed a lease on an apartment here."

"You still wear a ring."

"It's hard to let it go. I've been waiting for the right time."

I said, "I knew if you were getting everything you wanted from her, there would have never been a need for me. But I see it differently now, more clearly than I could with my sixteen-year-old eyes. Sometimes we have to stay with people we love even when we don't like them very much. You taught me that lesson. You showed me how to be loyal and committed."

"Oh yeah, I'm the poster boy for deep, meaningful relationships. If I had really known about loyalty and commitment, I wouldn't have made so many mistakes. If I had appreciated what you said, really listened and understood, I wouldn't have had to let you go."

"We were just kids."

"We weren't kids that night."

The food was still sitting on my plate, but who could eat when you're naked on a barstool in a packed restaurant? "Look where that got us," I said.

"It may have been adolescent at the time, but it mattered to me. Even with my dad being sick and dealing with losing him, there was you and your adorable face. I enjoyed every minute of being around you."

Thank God we weren't facing each other. Thank God I was staring straight ahead, and it was the bottles of wine lined up that I was looking at and not Jonas, not Jonas Levy saying these things to me. "That's got to mean something, Jess."

My hands reached up toward my face, to cover it from view, but he moved them away, forcing me to say something. "You gave me these glimpses into your life," I said, "and sometimes I felt like I mattered, and sometimes we were miles apart. All I wanted was to be close to you. I think that's why I let that night happen. It was the only way I knew how to be close to you."

"You were as close as I could let you."

"Why'd you let me go?" I asked, turning to him, wanting to see the answer. "Why'd you let me walk away? Where was all the love back then?"

He started to answer, but I saw the ring on my finger, and I was reminded of who I was, whom I belonged to. He was saying something about our age difference and his commitment to Emily, the loyalty he felt toward her and his guilt. The excuses for what he let slip away were starting to disturb me. We were forgetting who we were at that moment and the reason we were having dinner, so I raised my hand and stopped him from confusing me with a sixteen-year-old any further. "We don't have to do this, Jonas. We don't have to get into all of this now. Bygones." I had always wanted to use that word and actually mean it.

"But I need to," he prodded.

"It's too late," I said, finishing off my wine and already thinking about another glass.

"When I saw you in the hospital that afternoon, when I heard your voice," he began, "time stopped. I honestly thought that somewhere in that astonishing coincidence, you were there to find me. I thought only fate could work in such a remarkable way, bringing you to the hospital where I worked. And when you told me about the baby, I was pissed, really pissed, but not for the reasons you think.

"I wanted to hate you, just like this small part of me has for years, for all you represented, for all I blamed you for. You left me with so many feelings I couldn't get rid of. What you did, it couldn't have been easy, but I love that you didn't want to get rid of that part of me. I love that about you.

"What I was angry at the most was myself, for letting you go, angry because when I saw Michelle and how beautiful and smart and funny she was, I knew if I had just handled some difficult decisions more carefully, we could have somehow prevented this. Maybe we could have loved her so much, she would have grown immune to a disease like cancer."

He looked sad and silent and lost. "You're a doctor," I said. "You know better than that." It was meant to comfort, nothing more, but my hand slid across the bar and found his, holding onto it tightly, staying there longer than it should have. "We don't know what would've happened, Jonas. Our relationship..." and then I corrected myself. "Our friendship was never entirely real. All the pieces were just bits of stolen opportunities, nothing permanent, nothing truthful, based on 'what ifs' and 'if only.' Hell, I don't even think we would have known what to do if reality came knocking at our door."

"Are you saying that you don't think it could have worked?"

"I don't know the answer to that. I just know there were too many obstacles back then. I never had the privilege of seeing beyond the small window you let me peek through."

"But the things we saw together, Jess. You know how amazing they were."

He was squeezing my hand tighter. "You can't do this, Jonas. I can't do this with you again." The exterior around me was crumbling. "I'm not that person anymore. I've moved on with my life. I've grown up. There's someone in my life now, two someones, and they're everything in the world to me. Can't you see that?"

"You know what I see?" he said. "I see you. I see you seeing me just like you did that summer. Your eyes still dance. Your body still shakes when we touch."

I backed away, taking my hand along with me. "You don't have that power over me anymore, and you're wrong to even suggest it."

"I see it in your eyes, Jess. It's there. Don't tell me you don't feel it too."

"It's wrong, Jonas," I said, shaking my head, shaking out the contents of what he was saying.

"We're just talking, Jess."

"But it's wrong," I said again, hearing myself practically shout.

"Is it?" he asked, "or are you just afraid of what you might find out?"

"I know everything I need to know."

"Really? Then where's your husband? Why isn't he here with you in New York? I bet he doesn't even know you're having dinner with me. I bet he doesn't even know about Michelle."

"That's none of your business."

"But you're not denying it," he boasted.

"You don't know the first thing about my marriage," I snapped.

"I know you're here with me. I know you can barely look me in the eye. I know the sacrifices we made for each other…the ones we're still making."

"I made all the sacrifices."

"Do you know what I gave up for you?" he asked. "Do you have any idea how the wrong choices destroyed my marriage?"

"It doesn't matter now, Jonas," I said, as if understanding why his marriage fell apart would make us even. "I'm not the same person I was back then. I don't need all the answers." I was a little curious; *that* hadn't changed in the last thirteen years, but if I was going to be a grown woman, I couldn't return to living in the past. The check was sitting on the bar, and I ignored the bait as he paid cash for the meal I barely touched. I was about to get up when he grabbed my arm.

"I'm not done," he said. It was more a command than anything, so I stayed rooted to my seat. "You know I gave it all up because of you."

At first I wasn't sure what he meant. Did he give up Emily for me? That was a great presumption on his part.

"The pathology residency, the chance to run the entire lab one day. You walked away from me that afternoon. It took me weeks to recover."

"*Just weeks?*" I asked. "It took me *years* to get over that day and all the things that preceded and followed it. And just so we're clear, I didn't walk away from you, Jonas. You walked away from me. Actually, you ran."

"You didn't try to stop me…"

"And what would you have done if I did?"

"That time was the worst for me. I left your house, and I was torn, confused, drifting toward you and feeling the tug from Emily. I didn't know what I was going to do, not with you, not with her. Then we got the call that my father had died. I couldn't even tell you."

"Instead, you blamed me," I said.

"After the funeral, Emily thought it would help me to focus on other things—the boards, our apartment, our engagement. 'Our plan,' she'd say to me, 'let's stick to our plan,' and it was all I could do to get through the day, to go along with 'our plan.' Don't get me wrong, for a while that's what I wanted. In time it was easy to pretend I was happy, at least as happy as I thought I could be."

I stared at him blindly, unsure of who he was, someone who closely resembled Jonas. I had known his backbone had failed him before, but as he was talking, I imagined that the strong, vital man I'd once believed him to be was turning into a weak little rat.

"And then there was you," he said, reaching across the bar, urging my hand to curl around his fingers again. "I didn't go looking for you," he said to me, his eyes penetrating into mine, "I didn't seek you out. I didn't even know I was vulnerable enough, capable enough, to be drawn in. You were never part of the plan. Even when I tried to keep you somewhere safe and special, I failed miserably, hurting both of us.

"Back then it wasn't just about giving her up. *That* would have been the easy part. It was much harder living with letting her down. Emily was never as strong as you. Your father dying made you self-sufficient; Emily's parents' absence made her needy. It taught her early on to depend on other people to take care of her, and one of those people she depended on was me. I was responsible for her."

"You could have bought yourself a puppy," I said.

He laughed, adding, "I'm glad to see you haven't lost your cruel wit."

"Yeah, well, fortunately some things remained intact; others are lost forever. What does this have to do with me anyway?"

"When I realized that you were gone, really gone, and I was never going to speak to you again, life just changed. It became dull. You always told me to follow my dreams, to do what would make me happy. If I couldn't have you, I thought maybe I could fill that hole with something else. Do you understand that?" he asked me. "Do you understand what I was going through at the time?

"I wasn't thinking about that when my period was three weeks late, Jonas. You stayed with her when you had a choice. What I thought was your loyalty to her sounds a lot like plain old weakness. People like you deserve what they get. Haven't you ever heard, 'Weakness of attitude becomes weakness of character?' It serves you right that you never had any children." I was being hurtful and I didn't care.

"I should have known I'd receive a rant out of you. Not answering the questions, just jabbing me with your twisted insults."

"It's twisted because you don't understand me."

"If that's what makes you feel better, Jessica," he said, leading us back to formalities, "relish in the idea that you are wiser than I am. You're right, you've changed in a lot of ways, but in some ways you haven't grown up at all."

"Maybe it's too late for this conversation," I said. "What needed to be said should have been said all those years ago when you were the center of my young universe."

"And now?"

"What about now?" I asked. "What difference does now make?"

"All the difference in the world, for Michelle, that is."

He got up and I knew I had to follow him if I wanted to get back to the hotel. We sat in silence, the night air close to freezing, and he didn't offer me his jacket. When we got off the boat, he walked ahead, expecting me to continue following until his gait doubled mine, and I was left with his coattails in front of me. He walked with purpose and pride, even when I knew he had to be seething inside. What was I supposed to have done? Tell him that just being there eating with him was like being sixteen again?

Chapter 30

"Hi, Marty," I said into the phone.

"Jess."

I could tell he hadn't expected to hear my voice. It was almost six on the West Coast. Ari would be eating dinner, throwing rice and macaronis at Elmo on the television.

"I'm checking in." As if that's what husbands and wives did when there was an impasse and thousands of miles between them.

"How have you been?" he asked.

"Good. Busy. How's our little steam engine?"

"He's right here, eating dinner. Looks like he might have stepped in the blender. Do you know how nicely carrots and noodles affix themselves to a television screen?"

I laughed at the visual. Yes, I knew.

"I miss him," I said, my son's laughter in the background taking me away from all the madness.

"He misses you too," he said, and then, "so do I." When I didn't respond, he said, "When are you coming home?"

"I don't know. I was thinking maybe you could come out here." I didn't know that was going to come out of my mouth. It was partly a reflex, partly an admission of guilt, and then it felt like the right thing to say.

"Hello?" I asked. "Marty, are you there?"

"I'm here."

"We really need to talk."

"About what?" he asked, pressing on.

"Not here. Not on the phone. I need to see you."

"Then I'll be there tomorrow. I'll call you when I get in."

"Okay," my voice said flatly. "Let me talk to Ari for a minute, please."

His little voice crowded the empty space that was left between his parents. The sweet, innocent laughter, the way he'd enunciate the word *Mommy*. Children had a power that flowed from their little mouths. My heart was divided in so many different ways, but with Ari, it was whole.

241

I felt one thing, love, no conflict. His declaration placed me under a deep spell. The next thing I heard was the familiar recording, *"If you'd like to make a call…"* This woman was heard all over the country, yet probably sat in her estate home in Greenwich counting her fortune. She would have never gotten into a mess like this.

The television sat before me, begging me to turn it on. I flipped through the channels. First CNN, then MSNBC, next Fox, and when I saw there was no breaking news, I turned to the lighter channels, HGTV, Discovery, TLC, Animal Planet, VH-1, MTV, and that's where I stopped. Marty was on the screen. I couldn't believe he hadn't told me, but who was I to complain when I'd had enough secrets to fill a week's worth of *Divorce Court* episodes?

I pressed the button for the volume, and for some reason it wouldn't go any louder. It was mute. I watched as his lips moved up and down, probably discussing a new film or a soundtrack's video. Smiling before a crowd of millions of viewers worldwide, my husband was doing what he did best. His gray hair was longer than usual, and his tan made his eyes burst from his lids. He looked good. The silence became louder. His name was imposed on the bottom of the screen, but the once familiar words were those of someone I did not know. I recognized the sweep of his tongue, how his eyes blinked just so. Yet, he looked different than I remembered. The cameras panned on a scene from a recent video he had produced. It looked like one of those mansions we had visited when we first met. The artist was Stella, no last name, just Stella. I knew this because her name was there across the screen where Marty's once had been. No last name was required when you had the looks, body, and voice that this barely twenty-something girl possessed. When the camera returned to Marty, he was discussing something of great importance. His eyes lit up, and then Stella was back, standing in front of her high school graduating class. "Valedictorian" the sign read. "Brown, here we come!" but the word *Brown* was crossed out and someone had written *Hollywood* instead. Maybe it was her friend, the girl she cavalierly had her arm thrown around.

And then I noticed it. It was subtle at first, but when it became clear, it became very clear. Marty touched the back of his neck. He sometimes did that when it was hot and the wisps tickled his skin. There was no way

I was mistaken. He *never* took it off, never, but I got up, moving closer to the screen, and I waited, waited for the hand to reappear; and when it did, it confirmed my disbelief. The finger was bare. His wedding band was gone. All I saw was the imprint of the best years of my life, the white circle of skin that paled in comparison to the deep brown that covered his arms.

The talented MTV editor panned back to the video shoot, while I positioned myself in front of the screen scouring the footage for evidence of what remained of my marriage. With no one else to lash out at, I narrowed my eyes on the young, talented, and obviously intelligent Stella. I felt like Ari, who insisted he could talk with Big Bird on the one-way screen. He was too young for me to explain the whole television thing, how Ernie wasn't *really* in the big box. Why did it seem like Marty and Stella and the rest of the crew were in there and could see me staring at them?

I saw him again. This time he was watching the shoot from the rear of the room. The lights were shining brightly on Stella. He was supposed to fade into the background, but he didn't. His eyes were following her up and down the stage.

I'd seen that look before. I recognized it at once.

"Fuck you, Big Bird," I screamed at the screen. "I know you can hear me in there!"

I climbed into the bath recalling Marty's face. He had the same look as Santa Barbara, the first time we made love, and the beginning of all the lies. I didn't want to go there, didn't want to retrace the memory, but the bathroom was dark, my eyes drifted, and I let myself go, just like I did on that trip.

I had driven up the coast for a scene change when shooting ran late, and I was forced to spend the night at a local hotel. I wanted to leave, but Marty was in my ear insisting that I stay put until morning. Our relationship had turned serious, and the newness of each other drenched the days with anticipation and longing for the sensation that came with the first kiss, the first touch. We were on the brink of going further. Walking into the room, I should have guessed that something was going on around me. My CIA skills, however superior, were tested and they had failed me. I canvassed the room, and it was spectacular—the champagne flutes, lingerie, fresh fruit. They should have been the first clues, but I assumed the hotel management provided these treats for all their high-powered guests.

Lingerie? I backtracked, picking up the silky material in my hands, laughing at the people that wore this stuff. Marty had said he would call the hotel to take care of anything I needed. "You need to sleep in something," he said mischievously, "unless, of course, you're the type that sleeps naked. Are you?" he asked.

I fingered the beautiful fabric, feeling silly and feminine all at the same time, and then decided to take a bath. My clothes were strewn at the foot of the bed, so when the knock at the door came, I *should've* known, but I didn't.

Grabbing the hotel's plush robe, I wrapped it around me, and there he was, walking into the room like he owned it.

I stepped back. "What are you doing here?"

"What do you think?"

"You sneak, I should have seen this coming a mile away."

"But then it wouldn't be nearly as fun seeing that expression on your face."

He looked good. He looked better than good. I pulled the robe tighter, keenly aware that there was little between us. He walked around the room proudly, like an artist, surveying the masterpiece he had created. "You're not going to make me drive all the way back, are you?" he asked.

I eyed him suspiciously. He moved closer to me, standing right in front of me. "I've missed you," he said.

"I've missed you too."

He turned toward the bar, opened the champagne, and poured it into two glasses. I watched how easily he handled the things around him, taking the glass he offered into my bare hand. There was no second-guessing, no speculation. I never thought it could be so easy to feel something so right, because that's what it was like, being with Marty. We toasted to each other, sipped the champagne, and then he finally started kissing me, his hands up and down the thick robe. And then he stopped.

"Don't be mad," he said, backing away from me with a teasing grin. "It was a long drive, and I *really* need to go to the little boy's room."

"When I come back," he whispered in my ear, "I want you to be naked."

We didn't indulge in the chocolates or fruits that lay before us, instead choosing to indulge in the things we had been anticipating for months.

"Have you thought about this?" he asked.

"Yes."

"How much?" he asked. "Tell me," he demanded. "Say it."

I looked him in the eyes and said, "Make love to me," and there was little time between my words and his body on mine.

I remembered the morning, how I woke up exhausted. We barely slept, but when I rolled over and found him there next to me, the desire for more found its way between my legs and spread throughout my body. I touched the smoothness of his back, kissing the birthmark on his left shoulder. I wanted him to wake up and take me there again, but it was embarrassing, the insatiable urge to need someone like I needed him.

I whispered, hoping he would hear the longing in my voice, but he lay lifeless, enjoying the game of teasing me. So I took matters into my own hands, literally. I reached for him under the smooth sheets, feeling him stir, coming alive beneath my touch. He was soft and smooth and still evading me with silence, but I knew he wanted me. It was unmistakable. The arch of his back, his fingers running through my hair, the heavy groans that fell from his mouth.

I watched as his eyes fluttered open, transfixed on my body. He didn't say anything. He didn't have to. He just smiled at me with the most satisfied eyes I'd ever seen. And as romantic and peaceful as it all sounds, my patience was beginning to wear thin. "I want you inside of me."

The words were enough, because I could see his look change from gentle to something else I wasn't quite sure my body could handle. I wasn't afraid. He got on top of me, holding my hand in his, staring deep into my eyes. And when he unleashed himself inside of me, he cradled me in his arms until I almost couldn't breathe. He found my eyes again and said, "I'm falling in love with you, Jessica Parker."

And it was pure and it was beautiful and it spoke volumes about what he felt inside about me. Except it was the same look he gave Stella tonight.

Chapter 31

The phone rang early. I didn't know the exact time, but it was somewhere between the sound of early-morning rush-hour traffic and the calm slumber that follows. When my eyes adjusted to the light, I saw that it was 6:46 a.m.

"Hello," I muttered into the phone.

It was Jonas.

"I don't want to fight with you, Jess."

He sounded hoarse and serious, as if he had slept as little as I had.

"You couldn't wait an hour to tell me that?"

"No. I've been up all night with a patient. I waited as long as I could. I just left Michelle's room. I sat there watching her sleep for the last hour. She looks so much like you. She's so beautiful."

I was too tired and stubborn to argue with that, so I held the phone to my ear, hugging it close while he rambled on. "You know how much I always wanted children. I just assumed she wanted them as much as I did. I mean, we never discussed *not* having them, even if every time I brought it up, she managed to change the subject. Maybe I never noticed."

There was more. Jonas wasn't finished. The clock said 6:49.

"When I decided to quit pathology, I suppose that was the final straw. She never got over it, and for a long time, our discussions about kids ceased. Quid pro quo, I spoiled her dreams, she could spoil mine.

"I never stopped hoping she'd change her mind. I never gave up on the possibility that maybe she would get pregnant—even if by accident. I'd be ecstatic, and she knew it, but she never once missed a day on that pill. It's a little ironic, since I had a child all along."

Maybe I should have said something right then. Maybe I should have interrupted. I was always so good at interrupting. But how could I tell him that Emily Cohen not wanting a child had nothing to do with him and more to do with her parents' absence?

"Are you there?" he asked.

"Yes," I said, "I'm here."

"It kills me to see my child like that, Jess. I feel so helpless. I feel like there's something I could have done to save her, to stop this from happening. I feel like I failed her, and I don't know how to make it right."

"I don't know either," I said. "I don't know how to make any of it right," and I didn't. I was busy trying to soak up his words, the way in which he poured himself out for me to drink.

"I don't know her," he began again. "She's a stranger to me, but I look at her, and I feel as if I've known her all of my life.

"I understand," I said.

"It's killing me," he continued. "And I'm a doctor. I was trained for situations like these, but nothing, nothing, prepared me for seeing my child laying there on a gurney with tubes helping her stay alive."

He was talking to me, but it sounded as though he wasn't talking to anyone at all, that he was just thinking out loud, and that if someone would hear what he was saying, they'd recognize the suffering. He was hoping, I figured, that they would make it all go away. In another time, another place, I would have dropped everything to comfort him and given him exactly what he had been asking for. I wanted to be there for him, but much was out of our control. I had given him everything once, and he hurt me more than any one person has the right. I didn't want to let him know that I cared, that I was barely hanging by a thread when I heard his voice, that if I could, I'd do just about anything to save her, to save him, anything. I didn't trust my words. The sheer size of the conversation threatened me, the anger toward Marty's betrayal brewing.

"I'll come to the hospital. We can talk then."

"I have patients at ten. Meet me outside Michelle's room around eight."

The clock told me I had about fifty-five minutes to get myself ready. I had become obsessed with time. If I kept looking, maybe it would stop, maybe it wouldn't keep traveling at such ridiculously fast speed. "That's fine. I'll see you there."

"Alright, and Jess, thank you for listening," he added.

I hung up the phone and walked to the bathroom. I needed a lot more than minutes to reduce the puffiness that marked my face. The mirror saw tired eyes, an aging reflection, and something else not easily recognizable. I opened the cabinet that housed my cosmetics and crèmes, searching for something in there that would help me to dissolve feelings.

I skipped breakfast altogether, feigning disinterest. The sight of any type of food would make me nauseous. I did have some coffee, the warm liquid flooding my bloodstream like a temporary drug, and was out the door by seven thirty.

Had I stepped from the building one minute later, we would have passed each other on the street like two random commuters. Instead, the doorman opened the stately brass door to a brisk Manhattan morning, and there was my husband getting out of a limousine in front of the hotel. My heart leaped at the sight of him. Revelation turned into fear, completely passing over joy, and headed straight to anger. I had forgotten that he had the resources and connections to maneuver about the country quickly and unconventionally. He must have hitched a ride with an artist or a friend, flying late into the night. That was typical Marty, efficient in the face of adversity. When he wanted something, he got it. Had it only been the night before that I'd seen his face on TV?

Whoever termed the phrase *carpe diem* had never stepped into my shoes. How was I supposed to seize the day when it entailed repairing my marriage and saving my young daughter, who happens not to be my husband's, but the result of a one-night stand with the ex-love of my life? I could not seize the day, and I certainly could not seize that particular moment. John Keating was going to have to come up with something a little more manageable for people who make a habit of messing up their lives and the lives of those around them.

"What are you doing up and about so early?" he asked, cheerfully. "I was hoping I'd sneak into your bed and curl up next to you."

My body stiffened at the thought. I wanted to throttle him with my pocketbook, even if he looked more gorgeous than he did on MTV. He had that bedhead thing going on from the plane ride. It was sexy, and I wanted to stroke it, but I held back. I was angry at his timing, and angry for what I knew was his guilt trying to work me. I mulled over the options in my head: go to my sickly daughter or bicker with Marty?

"I have an appointment. I need to be there at eight." My words were stunted. I sounded like one of the artists we worked with who could carry a tune, but not a sentence. Which reminded me again of Stella and why I sounded so disjointed and why I wanted to beat him in the head with my pocketbook, which I clutched tightfisted in my eager hand. "I didn't expect you so early."

At this point, he was watching me with a doubtful, guarded expression on his face. I thought I heard him say something about how skinny I looked, which he knew would offend me because I don't find exceptionally thin women to be appealing. I was sorry I had skipped breakfast, and I was even sorrier for the week's worth of breakfasts I had skipped, contributing to my cadaverous figure.

"I'll take a ride with you," he blurted out; and it was a blurt, because I had one leg in a cab, hoping to be on my way, and in a Concorde-like movement, he was right up next to me on the torn leather seat, and we were heading to the hospital. The hotel and the idea of revenge had all but disappeared in the exhaust that streamed behind us.

"What did you want to talk to me about?" he began.

"Not now," I said.

"Yes, now," he said.

"Trust me, not now."

"Jessica, tell me. There's nothing you can't say to me."

"This is different. This is complicated." I said.

"It doesn't have to be."

"I don't have much time, Marty. I'd rather discuss this with you in private," I said, glancing at the overanxious and overly friendly cab driver who kept remarking about how gorgeous the day was. "It's too long and convoluted a story to tell in ten minutes of traffic."

"Just say it, Jess."

My mouth wouldn't open. He reached for my hand.

"It's hard."

He squeezed. It was his way of letting me know he was there for me, that he could help if I'd let him. I could push him away, but Marty could see beyond what was in front of him. He'd witnessed me at my weakest moment and still found it in his heart to love me. That was the exceptional man he was, and the kind of woman I had wanted to become, but somewhere along the way I got lost. Misplaced, I like to call it.

"I just don't know if I'm ready. It's a lot to deal with, and I'd never hurt you, not purposely, but these things are complex and they're going to change us. I'm not ready for the blame and accusations."

"Why don't you let me decide how I'm going to react?"

"I'm telling you all this so you know that I've thought it through. I know what it'll do to you. I'm preparing you for something you could have never made up yourself. It'd be a lot easier if you did, if it were one of your twisted plots."

"I would never make up something that would hurt the people I love."

The taxi driver finally gave up when he realized neither of us cared about the beauty of the day. Even if there were an earthquake outside, we wouldn't have noticed. I was sure through his silence, he was eavesdropping on our every word. I didn't care. We'd be out of his car in a minute or two. We, Marty and I, had a lot to uncover and learn about each other.

"This is my stop," I said.

Marty's face changed. He seemed to understand what I needed from him. "What time will you be done?"

"I don't know."

"Call me and we'll meet somewhere."

He let go of my hand as I climbed out of the car, his fingers slipping away from mine in one determined motion. I had the driver let me off at the corner, and when the cab was no longer in sight, I walked the few streets to the hospital.

Chapter 32

When Jonas taught me to drive his car, I'm sure he didn't know at the time how shifting gears would be useful to me thirteen years down the road. I've since learned that shifting gears is not limited to driving cars and machines on life's highways. It is an innate ability that fortunate ones are borne with and steers us through life's other highways, the complicated issues of people and problems. I was shifting gears as I approached the floor that housed Michelle. My husband would take a backseat for now, while I dealt with the other bumps in the road.

The Sammlers were nowhere to be found, and Jonas was standing outside her door conversing with another doctor.

When he saw me approach, he gave me a nod and headed in my direction.

I don't know if it was the apprehension of the last couple of days, or plain relief, but when he finally reached me, he stretched his arms around me, pulling me close. I willed him to stop, but he didn't, and the shrinking space between us was almost as conspicuous as all the other things we were trying to pretend weren't there. My mind was tired of analyzing everything. Switching gears would be virtually impossible.

"Jess," he whispered in my ear, the voice like a visit from the past.

"Don't," I said.

He lingered a little longer, and then he pulled away. "You seem to be doing alright."

"I've learned to hide things a lot better than you. I've had more practice."

We stepped over to the side of the hallway so that other doctors and nurses and visitors could pass by, and then we peeked in on Michelle again. She was sleeping after a round of treatments, her face peaceful, remarkably unharmed.

I watched her breathe, deep breaths, and an unspeakable ache formed inside of me, a dull throbbing that made it difficult to watch someone else's sluggish movements when your own are so hurried, so desperate. It didn't matter that I hadn't seen Michelle take her first few steps, and it didn't matter that I hadn't held her hand on the first day of nursery school. I had loved her from the day she was created, even before then, because I had loved her father so much. The promise of what she would become had always lived deep within me. To watch her in that bed was insufferable. If someone had plucked my heart out and put it there to rest, the pain would be no different.

"She really is incredible, isn't she?" he asked.

"Like mother, like daughter," I joked.

"I know, Jess. I was there when you were a kid."

"Not entirely a kid," I said.

Then I noticed Michelle's movements: first, her hand, then her head. Her eyes fluttered open, and they caught me looking back at her. She raised her hand, waving me in.

He asked, "Do you want to be alone with her?" I shook my head no, thinking it better to have him there beside me. He followed me in, checked her vitals, and asked her if she was in any pain, but our daughter was a lot smarter than either of us.

"You two sure spend a lot of time here," she said with a smile, unaware of how astute she was, and how tired, how pale, and possibly how sick she was. We waved off the remark, attributing it to a child's imagination, and I took a seat next to her on the bed. Jonas continued to read her charts and then took a phone call at the other end of the room.

"What time is it?" she asked me, as if in her condition it was something that mattered, but I answered her, "Eight thirty in the morning."

"My parents won't be here until nine. There's bad traffic again on the bridge, and they're running late." She told me this directly, as if it was pertinent information I was waiting to hear.

"How are you doing?" I asked my daughter, the answer more important than her parents' whereabouts.

I watched her face as she struggled to tell me. Her red lips and bright green eyes were a sharp contrast to her pale skin. Golden hair fell around her face. Most of it would be gone, possibly as soon as the next day. I had already seen thin strands of it on the pillow.

"I'm a little scared," she answered. The overwhelming need to touch her resonated off my fingertips as I reached for her soft, little hand.

"You've already been so brave," I told her, knowing that she never once shed a tear, never complained, never asked God *why?*

"Why do you keep coming here?" she asked. "I know you're close with my mom, but is there any other reason?" The room became cold, and a chill slithered down my back. Her questioning eyes searched my own for answers. It was like staring into Jonas's eyes when we were kids; they mesmerized me, making it impossible to turn away. I thought that maybe Jonas could sense that I needed him at that moment. My eyes traveled to where he stood, and I saw in one single second what our lives might have been, the family we could have had. But he was immersed in conversation with another doctor. They were discussing a little girl with an irregular heartbeat. He was focused and articulate. I didn't have it in me to interrupt.

I had seen Michelle's question coming. The last time I visited, I half expected her to come right out and ask me. I saw how she would watch me when I'd be in the room. The way she noticed things—how my eyes seemed to mist over when she'd call out *Mom* and I'd turn, just so, unknowingly, revealing my regret.

The silence stretched between us, like the distance and years that had eluded us.

"I know that I'm adopted," she started. "My parents don't want me to know, but I found out two years ago, and I waited for them to tell me, and they never did. I've never felt unloved or unwanted, but it's always been this big, huge *thing* between us. It's as if they took me away from me or a part of me. I know that sounds confusing."

"No," I almost shouted. "It's not confusing at all." Even if it wasn't the truth, even if I doubted what she was saying, I'd never let her know it. Better to let her feel that she could trust someone, anyone.

"You're her, aren't you?"

"Who?"

"My birth mom."

She said it just like that. A simple sentence with complex repercussions.

"Michelle, I don't know if your parents…"

"Just tell me," she said. "Tell me you're not because I think you are, and if I'm wrong, I just want to know."

Jonas was oblivious. I focused on my daughter and gave her the acknowledgement that would change everything. "Yes," I said, "I'm your birth mother."

The ten seconds that passed felt like the years since I handed her off to a stranger. This was the same girl only moments earlier I had never seen cry, the same one who never complained, nor questioned her fate. Now she was openly crying and asking me, "*Why?*" I know that I hadn't imagined it. I know that because I wiped a tear that had rolled down her cheeks and crushed it in the palm of my hand.

Jonas's beeper went off, and before we knew it, he had thrown the phone down and was rushing out the door. "Bye, Dr. Jonas," she called out, and my eyes met his, and I told him I'd see him later. He didn't notice the desperation that passed over my face, or he might have stopped to intervene. Instead, Michelle's father was gone, out the door, leaving the two of us to again sort this out.

Michelle's question was lingering in the air. *Why?* Before I could answer, she continued, "A kid in my class is adopted. His parents told him when he was like five or six. They are white and he's black, so there was some explaining to do.

"He used to walk around the classroom talking about it all the time, and we all thought he was kinda weird. I used to wonder what it must be like, until that afternoon I found out I was adopted too. Damien, that was his name, came to our house the next day after school. I thought I could learn something about this whole adoption thing if I invited him over. He was such a happy kid. He told me his birth parents were part of some royal family in Africa, and when he turned eighteen, he was going to meet them. I never told him I was adopted also. I was too ashamed of it.

"I found out I was sick a little after that. At first I felt tired all the time, and then my nose would bleed every day, and then there were the bruises, even when I didn't fall. When they told me how sick I was, I went in my room and slammed the door, and I blamed you. I thought it was you who poisoned my blood. If what Damien said was true, that he'd one day get his parent's palace and land because he was their son, then maybe I could get leukemia from you."

"That's not the way it works."

"I thought, just maybe, if things had only gone the way they were supposed to, if you hadn't given me up for adoption, if you hadn't given me to someone else, then maybe I wouldn't have gotten sick, maybe everything would have turned out just right."

I recalled the day I found out my father was dead, and how I blamed myself, how if I hadn't been born, this would have never happened. A child doesn't think like an adult. A child doesn't understand circumstance or chance, only the abrupt silence of a door that's been closed to her for reasons belonging only to her.

"Damien used to say to me when we had a school assembly or something, 'Even though King and Queen Omalara of Africa aren't here, they love me just as much as my new mom and dad.' But I never believed him."

"Your parents have done a terrific job with you, Michelle, much better than I might have done. You need to understand the circumstances that led me to my decision. It's not that I didn't love you, God, I loved you too much. Things worked out for the best. You'll understand that better when you get a little older."

"What about my father?"

"First, I want to explain something to you. *I loved you.* I loved you long before I ever gave birth to you. You were created from a love that some people never experience. I cared about your father very much, but there were reasons we couldn't be together, reasons I still don't understand today, but you have to know that there was always love. Whatever else we were missing, whatever it was we didn't have to make it last, we always had that feeling between us."

Now probably wasn't the time to ask if she knew how babies were made.

"What happened to him?"

"Your father never knew about you. We couldn't be together. We'd had a fight, I guess you can say, and we parted ways, and then I found out that you were growing in me. I thought about calling to tell him, but I didn't want to make things complicated for him. There were other options, and they were as limiting as any. I would have never gotten rid of you—*that* was never an option—but I also knew that I was just a kid and how could I give you the life you deserved? I wanted you in this world, and I wanted you to have everything you would ever dream of, but it wasn't possible for me to be the one to give it to you."

She interrupted my logical explanation to say, "I had all that."

"I know you did," I said with a smile, relieved by her perspective.

"I did," she said again, trying her best to hold back the tears, wiping at her nose with the hospital sheet.

"I'm so glad because that's all I've ever wanted for you."

"I love my mom and dad. Even when I couldn't make sense of adoption, I didn't want it any other way."

"I know that," I told her. "Grown-ups, mothers, we have a way of understanding those kind of feelings."

"Can you tell me about my father?" she asked. The girl was as relentless as her mother. "Does he live in New York like you?"

I had almost forgotten the lie that Jill Sammler had thoughtlessly bestowed upon her daughter.

"I live in Los Angeles."

"But I thought…"

"I know what you thought, and I'm sorry. We weren't ready for your questions or your intuitiveness."

"Does he know about me? Does he know I'm sick? Does he want to see me?"

I bit my lip and gave her the answers, "Yes, yes, and the last part's tricky."

Her little head was at a loss.

"He doesn't want to see me?"

"He does," I said, watching her head turn just so, unable to hide her curiosity.

"Don't tell me," she said with renewed energy. "He has green eyes."

"Yes," I nodded.

"And he's smart and he's funny and he's a famous actor like my friend Polly's dad."

I laughed at her little game, knowing that there was nothing humorous about this type of guesswork, even if observing her piqued interest was fun and the truth would never amount to the expectations we place on idealized fantasy. She had probably dreamed of this moment, dreamed of him, as I had over the years, and now he would no longer be an apparition.

We were so engrossed in conversation that neither of us noticed the door swing open and the entrance of Jill Sammler. We were talking about something important. She could tell from the looks on our faces, the exchange between her baby girl and me. I watched as Michelle tensed up just so; the gentle spirit that only moments ago had welcomed me into her heart had closed herself off. She was trying to tell me something with her eyes, with the effusive glare. It didn't take me long to figure it out. I would never betray her trust. The secret would remain ours.

"Hey, honey," Jill said, leaning down to kiss her, touch her hair. "Is everything alright?"

"I'm fine, Ma. Mrs. Tauber came in here looking for you." *An actress*, I thought. *My daughter would be an actress.*

"Yes," I said, "I wanted to check and see how you were doing, but it can wait. I'll leave you two alone."

I lightly tapped Michelle's wrist before I turned from her bedside. She would know that it meant she need not be afraid.

When I closed the door behind me, I knew that a bond had just taken form. Years from now, I might not remember the date, though I might remember it was a beautiful day by the insistence of a New York City cabdriver. I would remember the way it felt when my daughter first trusted me, the moment when we began our relationship.

Jonas was finishing up rounds before heading back to his office and said, "Let's take a walk outside."

"I have to get back to the hotel."

"Come on, a quick walk. You can use the fresh air." We ended up a few blocks down from the hospital at a park, where we took our seats on adjacent yellow swings. There was something soothing and comforting coming from Jonas.

"My husband's in town," I blurted out.

He nodded, staring at the brown ground beneath him, not really swinging but dragging himself back and forth.

"He doesn't know about any of this. I'm going to tell him tonight."

He looked up from his frozen gaze, turning to face me.

"Jess," he began in a way that first stopped my breathing. The word might have been fine on its own, but the face...I didn't have any more strength to hide from it. "I think we should have this baby."

Hearing those words after days of tap dancing around them took a minute to process. All discussions regarding Michelle's treatment had led to this. I watched my shoe as it dipped beneath the sand in front of me, unable to meet his stare.

I knew what he was proposing was in response to saving Michelle, but I wasn't sure what having another child with Jonas would mean to me. I had once believed I was destined to love Jonas for the rest of my life. I chalked it up to old loves, something about how we never get over the first one. But over time Jonas faded into the background, a place I seldom visited, somewhere distant and grainy. When I'd come across his name or a memory would flicker, I'd gain access to the fuzzy picture, unclear to the human eye, but there and very real. I often equated it to a cavity. Sometimes my tongue would brush across the sensitive tooth, a system of checking, to see that the pain was still there. And even though it would hurt badly, just brushing up against it like that, there was an equal amount of comfort in the movement. The familiarity of the feeling was the sensation I was searching for, the comfort that it hadn't left. The thought of extracting it was far more severe. And slowly over time, the pain diminished, as did the cavity, but the sensitivity remained.

Marty gave me the Novocain to upend the wound. Through his eyes I saw a different world, one filled with joy and possibility. I opened my heart in a way different from before, storing everything related to Jonas Levy, all the pieces of the puzzle that never quite fit together, in a place where no one would ever find them. And for a long time, I didn't go searching for them either. It was a part of my history, what I had left behind. I was both proud of it and ashamed of it.

But what was I feeling now? I couldn't get a grasp on it. In managing difficult times, I had always found the ability to compartmentalize. This over here, that over here. But this, this whole thing, there was only blurred vision, no light leading me toward a clearer path. Loving Jonas yesterday was getting mixed up with loving him today.

He was staring at me, awaiting a response. I was off somewhere important and he knew it. The eyes beckoned me for an answer. I could see in between the blinking motion that they were sad, worried, and hopeful all at the same time.

"I don't know if I can do that," I answered, hesitant to say any more.

"I know," he answered. "I understand. I've thought about it as much as you have, and it's more than a little outlandish. But I can't sit here and watch my own flesh and blood deteriorate before my eyes. I took an oath."

He waited a few minutes before beginning again. There were more reasons he had to explain.

"I love you, Jess. I've always loved you. I don't know what I might have done at the time, when we were kids, but if you had come to me and told me that you were pregnant, I'd like to think I would have made some radical changes in my life. But you didn't."

"That's unfair," I said. "You know why I didn't tell you. I cared about you too much."

"I want to have this child with you to save our daughter. I would request custody, and that way you don't have to worry about your husband. He won't have this situation rubbed in his face."

He had taken the reins, and I hadn't even gotten on the horse yet. "If Michelle reaches remission after this second round of treatments, and assuming we get pregnant immediately, we could witness a transplant by the following year at around the same time."

"Doesn't that all depend on this child being a match?"

"I'm hopeful, Jess, aren't you?"

"How do we know she'll even survive a bone marrow transplant?"

He looked so convinced, so sure, so Jonas. It was hard to imagine the years that had passed us by. Being so close to him, his hands gripped around the swing's chain, there were memories of my youth flooding my pulse—his hands on my leg, his arms around my shoulders. I saw in that split second that his mind was already made up. It was my turn to decide a fate that would again change everything around me.

I stood up from the swing. "Marty's waiting for me at the hotel." I owed my husband the truth, and maybe then we could go back to the life in which I once had a peaceful existence. Maybe there, speaking with Marty, I'd find the answers.

"Think about it," he said, standing next to me, so close I could see the lines on his face. Then he turned to walk in the opposite direction, and I watched him and thought about how easy it would be to run after him and beg him to hold me again.

Chapter 33

Dialing the hotel, I reached Marty on the first ring. We agreed to meet at the Seaport in half an hour. I took my time, knowing that things would never be the same, wanting to freeze the passing of that moment.

He was waiting when I approached the pier, leaning against the stone wall adjacent to the Gap. A cigarette dangled from his mouth, something I hadn't seen him do since we had Ari. The pillow of smoke formed above his head as he exhaled a foreboding steam. He had to know that I was nearby, turning around abruptly, throwing the butt on the floor, and stomping it with his boot.

"Hey, pretty lady," he said, as I moved in closer.

"Hey, yourself," I smiled back. His arm weaved itself around my shoulders, dragging me in one smooth gesture to his side.

I didn't waste any time. I figured I had waited long enough. He deserved to know the truth. He deserved to know the direction we might be headed. As we tiptoed along the water's edge, hardly noticing the cloud of cold air that wrapped us in its hands, I told my husband my story.

Marty already knew about my love for Jonas. He knew how we'd said our good-byes and that a part of my heart was closed off to anybody's reach. What he didn't know were the much larger truths. I filled in the blanks. Mulholland. Tuesday night.

"There was a baby, a little girl. I was sixteen, Marty, my choices were limited. I couldn't subject her to a life without a father. You know what living without mine had done to me." He sat there stonefaced. If I had wanted him to sanction this, it didn't look promising.

"Jonas never knew about her. I didn't tell him."

He saw I was capable of lying to the only two men I had ever loved.

"It was a part of my life I wanted to be over, forgotten."

Marty's reaction at first was calm, but as accusations flew from his mouth, the calmness dissipated. "I can forgive the act, Jess, and the decision you made, but I don't know if I can live with how easily you looked me in the face and lied. You turned the things we shared together into bullshit. From the start, we were based on a lie, and the firsts that we shared were all lies, *fucking* lies." I winced at the words. Marty had never spoken to me like this before. I had to turn away. "How did you look at me every day, Jess? How'd you sit there as we marveled as the baby grew inside of you? The excitement, the nausea? It was all bullshit, all of it."

"Just because it wasn't the first time didn't make it less special."

"You lied to me. The whole time you were lying, and it was a lie that just got bigger and bigger…this thing…it's not something you can hide from. It's a person."

"I'm sorry." It came out as a whisper.

"You should be," he chastised. "*You* did this. *You*. I never asked for this. *You* did this to us."

Words did not come easily, even for me. Shattered glass would be easier to imagine. One piece was Marty, one piece was Jonas, one piece was Michelle, one piece was me.

"Is she here in New York? Is that why you made up that bogus story about work? God, Jess, I would never have thought you were capable."

"There are things I needed to take care of out here."

"*Things?* What the *hell* does that mean?"

He lit another cigarette, and I told him how she was sick. I told him she might die.

The terminal facts were the only things that had the power to freeze time and reactions. His voice sounded changed, but it was still Marty saying, "I'm sorry to hear that, but what does it have to do with you?"

I outlined Michelle's options and what a full-blooded sibling would mean.

"Is there another child?" he asked. "Is she the only one?" The way he asked me was insulting.

"Damn it, Marty. I'm trying my best to make this thing right. I could have been any one of those girls you screwed who wound up pregnant, any one of them. Who knows for sure if there aren't any little Martys running around Los Angeles right now."

He grabbed my arm, "But you're not one of those girls, Jess. You're my fucking wife, the mother of my child."

"And that hasn't changed," I said. "I'm still all those things…I still want to be those things."

"You've been gone for five months."

"What do you want from me, Marty? So much has happened. It hasn't been the easiest time. My head's really messed up." I wasn't about to throw in his face what I'd seen on MTV the other night.

He was slipping away. I would have preferred his hand around my arm again, even if in anger. "I know you're upset, and just as I made that time in my life disappear, I wish I could make this go away, but I can't. This little girl needs me. Her life depends on it."

It was painful to watch the slow and subtle transformation on Marty's face as I continued talking, the way his tightly controlled jaw and eyes turned sad, how he first felt empathy, then shock, and finally anger. The cigarette went flying.

"So what are you telling me?" he asked, his fury no longer containable, rage taking over. "You're going to screw this guy and have another baby so there's a full-blood sibling to save your daughter?

"You have to be kidding me," he said as I turned my head down, staring at the pavement, looking at anything but his face. "This is a fucking joke," he shouted, as his arms reached for his head, shaking and nodding in disbelief.

"I wouldn't joke about something like this," I remarked.

"You're considering *fucking* Jonas Levy and having a child with him?"

He backed away from me as if the close proximity would spread the insidious disease that had taken over my brain and disrupted my rational train of thought.

I tried to think of something to say, anything to ease the tension, but what he was implying was correct. I was asking for my husband's blessings to do the unthinkable.

"I wouldn't be actually having sex with him."

"Have you lost your mind?"

"What if it was Ari?" I asked. "What if he was the one fighting for his life? Wouldn't you do anything to save him?"

"It's not Ari, not even close, and other than blood, what's your responsibility to this kid? You don't even know her."

"How can you say that?" I spat at him. "How can you minimize this? She's my child, and even though I didn't raise her, she's part of me, and you, of all people, should respect that."

"I can't believe you are deluding yourself into thinking this is logical. It would be one thing if you and I were faced with this and decided to have a child again, a married couple with a foundation where it's legally and morally acceptable."

"I told you it was complicated. It affects a lot more people than just us."

"Jonas. I'm assuming you've spoken to him?"

I figured it would be best to forego anymore dishonesty. "I've seen him."

Marty took a deep breath. I watched as the air filled him up with thoughts he couldn't put into words, accusations he wasn't ready to hurl. A boat hurried along the river, releasing a loud horn into the air, giving him time to think it through.

"Do you love this guy?" he asked. "I mean, has this been going on? Have you been carrying on with him all this time?" He was humbled, and there I was, unsure if this made me sad or somewhat satisfied. "Is there something else you're not telling me?" Marty asked, cross-examining me with his eyes, "something that would help me understand why you'd risk everything we've built together to save his child?"

"I love her," I whispered. "Already, I love her. She came from me, my body, and there might be a part of Ari in her, or a part of my mother or maybe even my father. That's my life, Marty, a piece of me. You can't ask me to turn away from that."

"You didn't answer my question," he said, pausing so the words had time to sink in. "Do you still love him?" he asked. "Because if you do…"

"That's not what this is about, Marty. It's about a girl with little hope, and there are two people in the world who might be able to change that. I know you'd do the same, I know you. You'd be able to put that other stuff aside and do the right thing because that's who you are." I had to take a breath before adding, "And, no, there hasn't been anything going on all this time."

"Is this about the baby?" he asked.

"You mean Joshua? He has a name."

"Maybe you're trying to compensate for his loss. This isn't going to bring him back. It's only going to make things worse. It's going to pull us further apart."

"You've done a good job of that already."

"How you can say that is an outrage," he said, shaking his head back and forth. "I've tried for months to save our marriage. This is such bullshit."

He started to walk away. I wanted to follow him, but his walking away from me packed me with so much fear, the only way I could diffuse it was to be angry. When he had reached a safe distance, he turned around and said, "I understand why you're doing this, I do, in theory. You're an amazing, strong woman with a huge heart, but in practice, in the context of our life today, I don't see any way we'll get through this together. You're not even capable of answering a simple question."

"I answered you. I told you it hasn't been going on all this time. I haven't seen or spoken to Jonas Levy in thirteen years."

"That wasn't the question I was referring to."

He began to back away from me again.

"I asked you if you loved him."

I returned to the hotel, and he was gone. There was no sign of him having been there at all. The bed was made. The place was in perfect order, and Marty was nowhere to be found. I lifted my cell phone from the table and began to dial his numbers, but they went directly to voice mail. I called down to the front desk. They said they hadn't seen him since this morning when he got into a cab with me. I looked out the window and the darkness that descended over the city and knew he was gone. Not just from the hotel, gone from New York. I could no longer feel him there.

I picked up the phone again, this time dialing our home in California. There was no answer. When I saw it was four o'clock there, I figured my mother had taken Ari to the playground. I was alone and exhausted. The bed lay before me so I slumped myself down, nowhere else to go but beneath the warm comforter. I hid beneath the crisp folds, remembering how many people before me had lain across the fabric. The germs were rampant, and I didn't even care. This was my refuge, and I shared my sorrows with the soothing pillow. I ached for the baby I had lost, for the baby I gave up and now might lose again, for the love I once shared with Jonas, and for a marriage that was probably over. I racked my head with the unborn possibility of hope, the symbol this baby would stand for, the gift I could give Jonas, the gift I could give Michelle. I wasn't sure if I could ever learn to separate the two.

I didn't hear from Marty that night. My mother called to tell me that he was home, asking what was going on between us.

The decision I faced quieted her, quieted me. I was being pulled into a deep, dark sea with no more strength to ride the oversized waves. At least, if I were in a river, there'd be some direction, some range of motion. I was anchored down by the stillness of indecision. "I feel so stuck, so limited," I said. "Any direction I move in, someone is going to get hurt."

"This is a bigger decision than anyone should have to make, but please try to figure out a way to make it work with Marty, or that little boy of yours is going to inherit all your problems." The thought of Ari suffering stayed with me the duration of our conversation.

"I wish I could be there for you," my mother said. "Are you sure you don't want me to come out to New York?"

I was sure. I hadn't even called Beth yet. This was something I needed to do alone. "It's more important you're there for Ari," I said.

"I'm worried about you."

"As you should," I answered her, not making any bones about the fact that I was a complete wreck. "I always screw things up."

"You couldn't have predicted any of this would happen."

We hung up and I closed my eyes. There are people who spend years behind bars for unspeakable crimes, their physical constraints visible. Others commit sins, and although not punishable by law, their sentences are as confining as those in jail. The burden of my sins was condemning me, emotional constraint was my punishment. The lie that had sprouted out of love had turned into something that I realized might destroy an innocent child, a decent marriage, a good man. These were the nooses I carried around with me.

I had to face the unthinkable, conceiving another child with the one who had been the great love of my life, the one who still swore he loved me, only this time, for reasons barely a handful of people would understand. Hester Prynne had better move over, I thought. I was starting a new breed of adulteress women, one that combined heroism with a dash of betrayal. Was there not a more sympathetic name for that character than Hester?

The sound of loud music made me jump. It came from the clock beside the bed. I hadn't remembered setting the alarm. Fortunately for me, it was only eight forty-five at night. When we were in the seventh grade, Beth and I went to Palm Springs with her family. The morning that we checked out of our hotel, we set the alarms on the clocks to go off at three in the morning. We thought it was funny to wake the people up, but there was nothing funny about it at all. I was about to lower the clock radio, change the channel from the country music, but the song's lyrics stopped me. Keith Urban was singing one of his wistful songs about a woman he loved, and it hooked me right away. There was the night in LA when Marty and I were in our almost-dating stage, hanging out in his office after everyone had gone home, talking about what would bring us to our knees, and I said, "A man singing an original love song to me in a crowded, dark, smoke-filled bar."

The next night, I was whisked off to the Whisky a Go Go on Sunset with Jeff Walker when Marty walked onto the stage and proceeded to sing "Mixed Emotions" by the Rolling Stones. It wasn't original, and it wasn't a typical love song. Although Mick Jagger joined him midway on-stage, it was Marty singing the words that told me what he wanted from me. It brought me to my knees.

The telephone rescued me from further nostalgia. There was a voice on the other end I didn't recognize. She called me by name, as if she knew me, but her matter-of-fact drawl did not belong to anyone I knew.

"It's Amy, Jessie, Amy Levy," she said, and at the sound of her name, I stood up from the bed. "I'm in the lobby," she said. "Can you come down?"

Chapter 34

The elevator doors opened and there emerged Amy Levy, all grown up.

"Jess, it's so good to see you!" she said, and we hugged each other as if time hadn't passed at all.

I would have come right out and asked why she was there, but I already knew. "I heard you're training to be a famous surgeon. Look at you all grown-up."

"I had to do something with all the precision and poise I learned in ballet. Gosh, it's so great seeing you again. You're still so tall," she said, looking up at me. "I think I stopped growing in the ninth grade."

"How old are you now, twenty-five?"

"Good memory."

She wasn't twelve anymore, that was clear. Her hair was straighter than I'd remembered—cut short—and I admired the same gorgeous shade of red. Her face had matured. She was sophisticated and self-assured.

"Can we sit for a minute?" she asked.

"Sure," I said, taking a seat at one of the couches off the lobby and not wasting any time. "I know why you're here."

She crossed her legs and straightened her skirt. "It's none of my business, I know."

"It impacts all of us, Amy. Michelle's your niece. Your mother has a grandchild."

She had a far-off look in her eyes. "It must have been hard for you to give her up." Then she brightened and said, "She asked that I say hello. She wanted to be here."

Neither of us brought up her own adoption and what all of this stirred up in her.

She said, "Mom always liked you."

"How is she?"

"She's okay. Losing my dad, she just never got over that. It's been hard for her."

"Did she ever remarry?" I asked.

"She gets proposed to a lot, but she swears she'll never get married again."

"Your dad would've wanted her to be happy."

"She is. She started an organization for underprivileged kids in Boston that gives them access to music and the arts. Almost every record label and film studio from LA to New York has contributed to the fund, and the center should be completed in the spring. She's on the board and very actively involved."

"The Boston Center for the Arts?"

"You've heard of it?"

We had recently made a donation, but I didn't tell her that.

"What about you?" she asked. "Is it true you are married to the legendary Marty Tauber?"

"Guilty."

After hearing Amy rank my husband as one of the most eligible ex-bachelors in California, I said, "I'm good, under the circumstances. I'm learning to take each day as it comes."

"Have you decided what you're going to do?"

"Not really."

"Maybe you should climb one of those fabulous trees in Central Park, and the answer will appear."

"Those days are long over," I laughed, but I liked that she remembered.

"I know I was a kid back then, and I didn't understand everything going on, but I know what I saw that summer. We all did."

"Your family was very generous to me."

"I'm talking about you and Jonas. You were important to him. You know that, don't you?

None of us ever understood why you weren't at the funeral. We thought it was Emily, and Jonas never said a word, until now."

"I wanted to be there. That was a hard time for me. Your father was a special person in my life. He still is."

"He'd be a grandpa. He would have loved that."

"I went to see him," I told her.

"You did?"

"It was about a year after he died." I remembered it vividly. Michelle was already with her new family, and I knelt on the ground to feel closer to him, to make sure that he could hear me. "I spoke to him, and I apologized for not saying good-bye." I also read him the article they wrote about him in the *Times*.

"I told him there was a part of him still in the world with us."

I didn't finish the rest of the story. The memory of that day was so powerful that I didn't want to share it with anyone, not even Amy. I didn't tell her how I shouted at the ground, "You always told me to do something I loved, and I loved your son and look where that got me," and how I grabbed a handful of grass and threw it, looking around to see if anyone had seen me. I didn't tell her how the rabbi came that afternoon and found me sitting there and that he was waiting for the family—for her and for Jonas and the rest of them to arrive—and that the unveiling happened to be that afternoon. When I told him I didn't understand, he explained that the unveiling was for everyone, that it was *symbolic*, an acknowledgement of death a year after the burial, and by placing a stone at the gravesite with your loved one's name, there comes finality, and an acceptance of that finality. The ceremony was to say good-bye and to begin again. I had memorized the words.

If I had told her any of this, she would have thought I picked that day to visit Adam on purpose, that it wasn't just a coincidence in which I interpreted, at the time, to be another sign. And she would have never understood why, when I saw the black limousine turn the corner toward me, I ran.

"That was very thoughtful of you," she said and acknowledged how close we almost came to seeing each other that afternoon. And then she got right down to business, looked me straight in the eye without an ounce of apprehension, and said, "Give him that child, Jess. Give Jonas that one thing he wants more than anything in the world, what no other woman can."

"Amy…"

"Listen to me," she said, "He's so torn up about Michelle. I've never seen him like this. The idea of saving her life and having a baby of his own is all he talks about. I know no one can make this decision for you, but I saw the two of you together and how you felt about each other. Even when he went his separate way, he never got over it. He never got over you. If you believe that everything happens for a reason, then you have to question why all of this is happening now. If you had told him the truth all those years ago, Jonas would have done the right thing. He would have never let you go."

My ears were taking in the words, the lush tones and delicious sounds, but my heart was unsure of what to trust.

"You can never tell Jonas I told you this, please. She came to see me."

"Who did?"

"Emily. They had just gotten married and settled into their new house, and I guess she found that picture of you. You know which one I'm talking about?"

I nodded.

"It was in his wallet, Jess. She found it in his wallet."

Amy continued. "She had asked him first about it, and he screamed at her for going through his things. She said it was the only time he ever raised his voice, and when he was finished scolding her, she realized he never gave her an answer. Needless to say, she was upset."

"What did you tell her?"

"I was caught off guard, and I'm the worst when it comes to thinking quickly on my feet. I told her it was a patient of his. She knew right away I was lying. She said they'd gone to med school together, and she knew about all his cases.

"You have to know Emily. Her brilliance is her biggest downfall. For some reason it inhibits her from containing hurt and managing emotions like jealousy. She drove Jonas crazy for months about it. He was even mad at me for a while for saying anything."

"Did he ever say anything more?"

"He didn't have to. She knew she'd intruded on something important, and she worried incessantly about him leaving. If he was mixed up that summer about leaving her, he was more mixed up the year of the picture fiasco. He saw how weak and desperate she was. He honestly didn't think she had the coping skills to handle a breakup."

But I wasn't listening to Amy anymore. I was thinking about what Jonas had told me about his relationship with Emily and how he'd left this part out. I was seeing Jonas with that photograph in his wallet all those years later. I was seeing him staring at my face long after good-bye and long after years had dragged us apart. I was tired of obsessing over what could have been and how I underestimated how much he cared about me. It was time to make a change. It was time to do something radically different, because the way I'd handled things thus far wasn't working.

The words rolled off my tongue the way I knew they would. She would know before anyone else.

"I'm going to do it," I said.

Amy jumped off the couch and took me in her arms.

Whether it was relief that filled my deep sigh or atonement for my betrayal, the calm resounded around me. I had never been as sure about anything in my life.

Chapter 35

Jill Sammler was the one who ultimately made the decision to introduce Michelle to her birth parents.

Mr. Sammler was understandably hesitant. He hadn't wanted to delve into this thorny area, but it was at Jill's insistence that the truth come out. Their secret had been blown wide open the day they prompted us back into Michelle's life. By our consenting to do this, there was no proper way to hide our identities, the people who were willing to endure life-changing circumstances to save her.

"Mom," Michelle said, making specific eye contact with her mother, "I knew you didn't meet Jessica at the museum."

"I'm a terrible liar."

"You were, for a little while," she continued. "I knew I was adopted, not because you weren't good parents, you were the best anyone could have ever asked for, but I found out another way. You're going to be mad."

"Michelle, you didn't," her mother said.

We all watched as she hugged Benjamin Owen to her chest.

"You did. I can't believe it."

Mr. Sammler finally spoke up. "What did she do?"

"She read my journal."

Michelle nodded her betrayal. I sucked in my breath, knowing I'd have done the same thing, when Jonas whispered to me, "Wonder where she learned that from?"

We all had to be careful, tread lightly, and keep our distance from one another even as we came together in a united cause. These were Michelle's parents. These were the people who nursed her and ran into her room when she cried at night. These were the people who clothed her and fed her and made sure she was immunized each year, even when they had no idea of her fragility—that even the best intentions sometimes couldn't prevent bad things from happening.

Jonas and I, although her birth parents, had to take a step back and allow this family, this other family, to deal with their history without outside interference. She wasn't ours to reminisce about. She wasn't ours to debate similarities or differences. We'd lost those rights a long time ago.

"I'm sorry," Michelle said, "that was wrong." I saw the bold contrast between her conviction and the fatigued figure on the bed. She was hidden under tubes, and her hair was strewn across her pillow, most of it no longer rooted to her head, but she was honest.

Jill Sammler didn't say anything. She just knelt over her daughter and took her into her arms. The two of them stayed like that for a few minutes when Jill spoke, "I'm sorry, honey. We didn't want to bring this up now, but it's important for you to understand how Jessica and Dr. Levy are here to help you. They're our best chance for a match, and you know how hard we've been praying for a miracle. This could be it, honey. This procedure is so important."

All of our faces were fixed on the bond between mother and child and how painfully it can be tested. Michelle was almost twelve. She wasn't a kid who didn't yet understand death. She got it, and she knew what a match would mean for her. It took a gutsy parent to look her child in the eye and lay out the facts. What makes a parent, I understood at that moment, is not so much genetics, but all the other things you give. Anyone can be a parent, but to be a mom or a dad, that takes years of giving with no thought of getting.

Michelle narrowed in on me and Jonas. I said, "We're so happy to know you. We're so proud of the young girl you've become."

"Thank you," she said, and I know she was thanking me for more than the nice things I was saying, for keeping her secret and for the sacrifice I was about to make in her honor. Her gaze shifted to Jonas, who watched her like we had just given birth to her.

"How about you get some rest?" Jill Sammler said.

"I don't feel much like sleeping, Mom. I want to talk to Dr. Levy and Jessica. Can I?"

She hesitated, but when her husband touched her hand, she softened. The threat was gone. We were no longer the people who could take her child away. We'd become far more than that. We were the ones who could bring her back. Mr. Sammler wrapped his arm around her shoulder and led her from the room.

"I love you, Mom and Dad," she called out, reassuring them before they were gone from sight.

"We love you too, honey," they said and walked out the door.

Jonas and I circled around her. "Isn't this just like being on *7th Heaven*?" she smiled, but neither of us was feeling comical. "*ER? Jerry Springer*?" She could see we weren't going to laugh. I was worried she'd inherited my defense mechanisms.

"I can't believe you didn't tell me it was him."

"I couldn't. Look at those eyes, though," I said, directing her gaze to a subdued Jonas. "They're exactly the same."

"Tell me," she started. "From the beginning."

She seemed to be more interested in the two of us than in anything else.

"She was fifteen…" Jonas began.

"Almost sixteen," I corrected.

"Yes, almost sixteen, and I was twenty-two…"

"A big shot with a sensitive stomach. He puked on my shoe. A memorable introduction."

"Guilty. But it made a lasting impression, so I'm not sorry about that."

Michelle was listening and smiling almost as much as we were.

"And then he asked me to dance…"

"She tried to act all cool and standoffish like she didn't want to… until we actually danced. It was her sixteenth birthday, and after that she agreed to have lunch with me, and I whisked her away to Catalina to my favorite restaurant…"

"Which, he failed to inform me at the time, was owned by his family…"

"And we colored, and played games on the table…"

He continued, but I wasn't following anymore. He'd gotten to the part about climbing a tree, and I was already there, back in California, with Jonas, loving him like I'd never stopped. There was no time or distance between us, just the freedom to be together. It worried me that someone could walk back into your life after so many years and rattle you as if they had never left.

"And then my father died," he continued, which was the intrusion I needed. Had he not, I might have gone on daydreaming all afternoon.

"And I went back to school, and your mom, I'm sure she did all sorts of wild things in the eleventh grade, staging anti-smoking demonstrations, crashing the Oscars, eavesdropping on anyone's conversation she felt entitled to…"

"How did that weak stomach handle medical school?" Michelle asked.

"It was something I had to get over."

"Like my mom?" she asked, a question wrought with grown-up innuendo.

There was Jonas, standing over our daughter, trying to be composed, me fidgeting, and a cloud of suspense pummeling through the air thick with truths or non-truths that would spill from Jonas's mouth.

"Some things you never get over."

I started to tug on a cuticle that was hanging from my finger, not even attempting eye contact with Jonas, when Michelle blurted out, "How come you never got married?"

Jonas just shook his head back and forth.

"Do you think you will now?"

I sought Jonas' eyes.

When neither of us could give her an answer, Jonas began, "Michelle, I think you're getting caught up in the details of right now, but we're all thinking about your future. You have to trust that we have your best interests at heart."

"I *was* thinking about the future," she said, crossing her arms. I noticed how skinny they'd become, marred in color from purple to deep shades of blue. "You have no idea about what's in my best interest." She was changing. Something inside her was stealing the strength from her face.

"I think we do," said Jonas, turning to me for agreement. By then, her lips were quivering, and she was holding in a whimper. "You have no idea," she stopped herself, shaking her head. "You just don't know."

It didn't matter what she was about to say because she was right. We didn't know anything. Sure, there was literature for us to read, a how-to guide for understanding leukemia and bone marrow transplants, but third-person accounts are never as poignant as the first. For Michelle, the facts were the life she lived every day. We had no concept of what it was like to wake up being prodded by a needle, to find your hair in clumps across your pillow, to be happily watching your favorite television show and realizing you won't live to most of the characters' ages. We didn't know what it was like to worry incessantly about pain, about being separated from our parents, about making up all the missed work at school, about friends looking at you as though you've become *different*. Jonas and I laughed for weeks about his vomiting on my shoe, and our daughter didn't go a day without unwanted bile. She was correct. We had no idea. All the pamphlets, brochures, and guidebooks couldn't spare us the worst possible outcome—how to survive life without her.

I reached for her hand. It was cold and clammy. I could practically feel her bones through the thin skin, but she held on tightly, squeezing my palm in her own. Her resilience amazed me; and although she might have worn me down with her resolve, I knew a different path, remembering the grave sadness of the day a little boy was taken up to the heavens. My daughter's courageous battle had now become my own.

Chapter 36

Beth looked more beautiful than when we were kids. Her brown hair was pulled back into a tight knot, and she was wearing John Lennon frames that suggested sexy schoolteacher. I don't know what it was. I couldn't put my finger on it, but when she approached me with her casual smile as I stepped out of the cab the next day, all I could see was her glow.

"I finally got over you not being at our wedding, but being in New York without calling is unforgivable," she said, wrapping her arms around my shoulders, hugging me close. It was comfortable and nostalgic to be with Beth again. She pulled away first, stepping back, reaching for my hands and studying my face.

"Where did the time go?" she asked.

"Have I aged that much?" I scoffed.

"A little skinny. Let's go fatten you up," she said, taking my arm in hers as we strolled down Cornelia Street to one of her favorite lunch spots.

Beth has always had a gift that I have never been able to master. She can sit through a glass of wine, a basket of bread, conversation about marriages and careers, a Cobb salad, and then dessert without letting on that she already knows what I'm about to tell her. It was only when she returned to the table after a trip to the little girls' room that she looked at me pointedly and said, "I already know about Michelle."

I leaned forward in my chair, clasping my hands like an obedient child. The need to protect everyone was exhausting and ineffectual. With no wine or food in front of me as a distraction, I had only Beth and her wide-eyed expression to face.

"How come you couldn't tell me?"

I shook my head. "I don't know."

"You're my best friend. How could you have kept something like that from me?"

If I could have just stared at the table and not looked into her eyes, I wouldn't have had to see the disappointment there. "There are some things you can't even tell your best friend," I said. "Or a gossipy mother," I added.

"She's worried about you."

Beth got right to the point, just as Amy Levy had. Everyone I cared about seemed to hold a position. "Are you really going to have this baby?"

"Either that or a nervous breakdown, whichever comes first."

She sat there not saying a word, her arms crossed in front of her. "This must have come as a real shock to Marty."

"Let's just say he wasn't expecting it."

"He loves you."

"I'm not so sure anymore."

"Even in Marty's fast-paced, playboy-driven life, everyone knows he's crazy about his wife. Everyone."

"I doubt Marty cares about the sanctity of our marriage vows right now."

"You don't mean that," she said. "You're just feeling badly about what you feel you need to do."

I looked up at grown-up Beth, the other half of the *Be Fri* necklace I kept locked up in my jewelry drawer. *St ends.* She was always reliable *St ends.* This was going to tear her heart out. "Needing to do this is logical. Wanting it as much as I do is what's breaking me up inside."

"How *is* the infamous Jonas Levy?"

I turned from her when she said his name, while the giant elephant in the room sat between us. "Don't say it like that."

"Like how?"

"Cynical, untrusting."

She sat there, mouth partially open. "You're still protecting him. After all this time, after everything he's done to you, you're still putting Jonas Levy before you and what's important."

"That's not true."

"Yes, it is. Why are you so blind when it comes to him?"

"And why are you so misguided when it comes to him?"

"I was there, Jess. I saw how he destroyed you. Everything about you changed."

"I knew what he could give me, and it was my choice to expect more."

"Naïve words spoken by the other woman."

"We were different," I said, thinking we were distinguishable from the thousands of star-crossed lovers in the world.

"I can't believe you haven't gotten over him," she shook her head. "You find a good solid man who worships you and supports you through the most hellacious times, and you fall into your old patterns."

"I thought you were a lawyer, not a psychiatrist."

"You could use a good psychiatrist."

"It's not what you think," I refuted.

"Then explain it to me."

I told her about the signs, thinking they would be enough to convince her, but she shook her head in disbelief, dismissing the string of coincidences with a wave of her hand. I said, "He looks so good. He's so much more grown-up than when we were kids. He's this deep, caring doctor, and he says these things to me."

"Does he know he's gotten under your skin again?"

"Maybe. I'm doing my best to hide it."

"Just like you did at sixteen," she said.

"Which reminds me," I said, reaching into my bag and handing her the book she'd given me that summer when Jonas left, the one she thought would comfort me. "Here," I said, shoving it in her direction.

"If he comes back to you, he's yours, and if he doesn't, he never was," Beth repeated, like she had a dozen times before. "Are we going to argue this point again?" she asked.

"It was a bird, Beth. How could you have compared what happened between us to a bird?"

"It was a metaphor," she said. "The bird was analogous to people. Why are we rehashing this now?"

"Because I want to know what it means when the bird comes back after all these years. I want to know what the other bird would do."

"Look," she said, "whatever it is you're feeling, you're not going to find the answer in a book or a movie script. You've got to find a way to look inside yourself and figure this out, because this affair, whether it's mental or physical, is not going to wind up being some widescreen romantic comedy. It's going to end up ugly for all of you."

The waiter dropped our check on the table, the escalation of our voices sending him scampering away.

"But wasn't your whole point that if the bird came back, he was yours to keep?"

She was getting annoyed. "The rule only applies to the good birds, not the ones that have pooped all over you."

"It was vomit," I hit back.

"Even better." And with that, she stood up and announced she was going to the bathroom.

"Again?" I asked, and she was off, leaving me to pay, something we'd always fought about in the past.

When she reappeared, I observed her as she walked toward me and took her seat. I had put the book back in my bag and had forgotten how unsettled I was. "There's something different about you," I said. "When did you get glasses?"

"I've had them forever."

"Somethings's different. Did you change the color of your hair?"

"Jess," she said, resting her chin on her hands as she ignored what I was saying, "Please be careful. Think about what you're doing and why you're doing it."

"You're pregnant!" I shouted. "That's it! I can't believe it. How could it have taken me so long to figure out? You're definitely pregnant. I'm right, aren't I?"

Her face burst into a full-toothed smile. "Someone hasn't been refining her detective skills." I jumped up and ran to her side of the table while she raised herself from her chair. "Hello in there," I bent down to her tummy, introducing myself and then, taking its mother in my arms.

"Sixteen weeks today," she said.

"Talk about secrets," I laughed.

"We were waiting for the results of the amnio. It's a healthy boy!"

Beth looked perfect and happy, and I made it my business to tell her so. I hugged her again, while she detailed every symptom and every craving. When she was finished, I threaded my arm through hers, and we left the restaurant. For a brief time, neither of us thought about birds or secrets.

Chapter 37

The house was quiet when I entered, except for the sounds of Ari frolicking in the bathtub and my mother begging him to simmer down. It was seven thirty and I peeked in on them, marveling at how beautiful he looked, how much he had grown in the short time I was gone. My attempts to speak with him every day were thwarted by time zones and unforeseen events.

He looked so much like Marty, it was uncanny. When he saw me there, his full-toothed grin was all I needed to feel at home and joined to him. I ran over, throwing my arms around his neck, and nuzzled the sweet bubbles that saturated his body. If I thought I had made the right decision before, holding my son further validated my cause. Life was too precious to turn from our children.

My mother could have pretended to be happier to see me, and if I weren't so exhausted, we might have engaged in some raucous banter. There would be plenty of time to discuss my marriage with her, or lack thereof, and plenty of time for the world's critique of my state of affairs.

"Where's Daddy?" I asked, disguising my annoyance that he wasn't there to bathe his son.

"He's working late," my mother called from the other room. "He got back from New York, and we haven't seen much of him since." My mother eyed me scrupulously and questioned me with perilous eyes. I would have preferred the flittering.

Getting Ari squired off for bed was delightful. I so enjoyed this time with him, reading to him, lying next to him on the floor, smelling the fresh scent of his warm body. He was a real chatterbox and loved to talk. We were going through the "why stage." Everything beginning and ending with why. "Why do I love you?" I answered his last query. "That's easy, because you're the sweetest most delicious boy in the world." He clasped my hand in his, resting his head on my shoulder, and I kissed his forehead, happy to be there sharing in our special ritual.

Watching him climb over the railing into his big boy bed, I sighed, aware that the insulated days would soon be over. His blankie was his comfort now, and he curled the delicate blue fabric in his arms until the heaviness of the overactive day pulled him into a deep sleep. I patted him softly on the back, feeling each breath he took, knowing that each one was as special and significant as the last. My eyes lingered a little while longer on the nape of his neck, the round cheek, perfect little nose. He was an angel, for sure, an angel sent to me from heaven. I was amazed that the creation of someone unique was so universally known to all mothers.

Marty never came home that night. I was in the shower when he called to check on Ari. My mother had presumably told him that I had returned. Whether or not that was why he chose to stay away, I wasn't sure. Perhaps he had made that decision sometime earlier in the day.

I got into our bed, large and empty without him there, and closed my eyes.

The streaming smells of my mother's cooking woke me in the morning. By the time I made it downstairs, she had a complete breakfast awaiting me. I could hear Ari through the monitor talking to his animals, asking them what they were doing and why. When the babbling turned into a loud, wailing "Mommy," only then did I head to his room to retrieve him.

Walking into the kitchen with my son straddled around my waist, I said, "Mom, you've outdone yourself with breakfast. Thanks so much. Thanks so much for everything." Ari released himself from my grasp, finding something on the floor to play with. As I spoke to my mother, I reminded myself of Michelle. Then I asked, "Are you sure you're going to have a job to go back to in Phoenix?"

"Don't worry about me," she said, kissing my cheek and smoothing my rumpled hair with her hands.

We ate together like that, Ari in his booster seat fingering the eggs, patting them into shapes he would then toss onto the floor, while my mother remarked on how much weight I had lost. Hunger found its way back into my starving body as I finished off a plate of eggs, a stack of bacon and sausage, two biscuits, and two cups of coffee. Food was fuel, and I hadn't remembered the last time I had replenished. Ari wanted out of the kitchen, so I let him run off to the playroom, where he busily played with Legos and toy trucks, which left my mother and me alone to discuss my decision to get pregnant.

"I'm disappointed in you," she said.

"It's not the first time."

"You're destroying your marriage."

Whether she was waiting for my response or giving me a moment to digest my food, I didn't know. I wasn't ready for her criticisms, her partial, uninformed accusations.

"This has nothing to do with your decision and all to do with how you're handling Marty. I would do the same thing for my child. I would…"

"You would?" I asked, becoming the little girl who had leaned on her in the past, the one who had needed her mother's approval.

She nodded yes, as if knowing that if she opened her mouth, the vastness of it all would come rolling out.

"I just worry that your marriage won't be able to sustain it."

"What can I do?" I asked, relying on my mother's insight to guide where I'd somehow lost my way.

"First it was the baby. Now it's Jonas. Find something that will keep you and your husband together instead of pulling you apart. He loves you, Jess. You just have to reassure him, love him, listen to him, and pay attention, because he's giving you signals I'm afraid you're missing."

"Everyone's so sure he loves me," I said. I was convinced that they were wrong. I saw the missing wedding band.

"No one knows how they'd react under these circumstances. I'd like to think we'd all find it in ourselves to do the right thing, even if it's not always the best thing. He'll come around. You know why? Because you're everything to him. You and that little boy in there."

I wanted to believe that, but it scared the shit out of me.

"I think he's seeing someone."

"I don't," she answered, giving absolutely no credence to the possibility.

"I know things about him, you don't. I've seen things."

"And I've been practically living in your home with him, and I'm telling you, he's not being unfaithful."

"Don't be so sure," I said.

"Even if you have to do this, you should be here with him, and your son, and you should be figuring out a way to reassure him."

"I'm taking Ari back to New York with me."

"That's ridiculous this time of year. Let him stay here where he's comfortable."

"I think he'd be most comfortable with me, regardless of the weather. Why don't you come with us? Michelle can meet her maternal grandmother."

She mulled it over in her head, watching Ari across the room playing attentively with his toys.

"You go. It'll get more confusing if I show up out there, but you have to make me one promise."

"What's that?"

"You'll bring me back a picture of her."

The next morning I got my period. Whether it was a sign or an omen or something else deeper, graver, I wasn't sure, but I knew what the crimson represented—and it wasn't just a trip to the drugstore. In approximately fourteen days, I would be ovulating, and I could conceive a child with Jonas Levy. I quickly dialed his cell phone in New York, and after he gave me an update on Michelle, I told him the news about the day's arrival. There was an awkward silence on the other end, yet I felt closer to him than I had ever felt to him before. We were finally, completely on the same page about something, a common goal.

Marty was not seen or heard from until late afternoon. He called as Ari and I were returning from the park. I didn't care to ask where he had been. My head and my heart were somewhere else. I sent Ari to the playroom, shielding him from our words.

He couldn't hide the revulsion in his voice when I told him my plans. I could have filed for divorce, and it would have been a lesser blow than the scandalous events that were unfolding.

"This," he told me, "I *cannot* understand, will *never* understand." I had to hold the phone inches away from my ear. "My wife," he said, "with another man's baby inside of her. Do you get that? Another man's baby will *be inside* of you, *not mine*. What do you expect me to say, congratulations?"

"It's not like I'm being unfaithful to you, Marty. I'm not betraying us. You have to believe that."

"Don't make it sound so clinical, Jess. There's more to it, and you know it. Maybe I don't want to share you with him. Maybe I don't want you having this kind of bond with another man. Is that so unrealistic of me? You're my wife, for God's sakes. What about our family? What about our having another child?"

"I have to do this, Marty."

When a few seconds passed without a response, I looked at my cell, and the call had been disconnected. I had already set the deed in motion. There was no turning back.

When we reached New York three days later, Ari was full of questions. I tried answering them as honestly as I could.

"Mommy needs to work in New York for a little while, and it's so close to Aunt Beth. We can see her every weekend if we want."

"Why?"

"Daddy has to work in his office."

"Why?"

"Yes, we'll go home again," I said, unsure of this one. I didn't know if home would ever be the same.

Same response. "Why?"

He was inquisitive about the extra layers of clothing, and why a cloud formed when he spoke. He would try to grab it with his mittened fingers, to no avail. And when it snowed that first afternoon, I saw the marvel and delight in his innocent eyes. It made me wish for my own personal innocence to be returned to me, that I could feel that wondrous delight again. And I wished Marty could see Ari's face too.

We settled into a hotel near Times Square. It was a little too touristy for my taste, but it was nearby a children's museum and a stone's throw from the new Toys R Us. Ari became fixated when he caught sight of the life-size ferris wheel. I could see MTV's offices from my window, a reminder of Marty. If I turned in its direction, there was a mammoth billboard with Stella emblazoned across the front, a reminder of things gone wrong.

Marty would call to speak with Ari, and I'd give him updates, but he and I never talked for long, the conversation more an exchange of insults—short, empty words meant to hurt. His pricking insults stayed with me throughout the day, further affirmation that he'd given up on us.

The day before the procedure, I had been visiting with Michelle—she was completing the second week of chemo using one of the newer anti-cancer medications. She was tired, her joints ached, and all of her hair had fallen out. I brought her a baseball cap, the Yankees, her favorite. Her maturity on many levels astounded me. I didn't remember ever being as brave, though I'd never faced the battle that she was caught in. "I'm not so brave," she'd tell me, and the commonality between us grew more apparent. We had grown close to one another in such a short time. She knew what I was sacrificing for her. But I was as insistent as she was defiant and not nearly as optimistic.

"There's a one-in-four possibility this baby will have the identical tissue type necessary for the transplant. The odds of matching an unrelated donor are one in a hundred," I'd tell her, having studied the donor registry, memorizing the essential statistics.

She'd listen to the numbers, and I'd remember she was just a kid, a fragile bird with a lot more than a broken wing. Her loyalty to her parents was admirable, yet the friendship she offered me filled the twelve years we were apart. My daughter was a deeply intoxicating person. I wished for more years to share with her, to learn all I could.

"Tell me about Ari," she'd ask. "Do we look alike at all?" And before I'd finish describing him, before the picture was out of my wallet, she was asking about her grandmother, wanting to know if she could meet them, if it would be okay. We left out the parts about the man I was married to. I didn't bring him up and neither did she.

Jonas entered the room as I was walking out the door, explaining how he had to see his girl. I heard Michelle whisper, "Which one?" and I shot her a look before walking out. We were both pretty taken by our daughter. Neither of us could escape the remnants of that summer when the end result, this precious child, was the reminder of what we had once shared.

"What's so funny?" he asked, when he stepped from her room and saw me there with my hand cupping my mouth. I always laughed when I saw Jonas in his fatigues with his Looney Tune stethoscope around his neck. Today he looked even more grown-up and more handsome in his getup. Whether it was cheerfulness or Michelle's stable status, I wasn't in the mood to be distant. "You look cute," I said.

"Then why don't you have dinner with me tonight?" he asked.

Beth and Paul had offered to take Ari to Washington, DC for a couple of days to test out their parenting skills, and Ari couldn't have been more excited. I wanted to say no. Everything told me to resist, but I answered, "Okay." The alternative would have been room service, which I was growing tired of. Besides, Jonas was going to be a part of my life. We were publicly stepping out, addressing the world with our association. There was no more hiding what we once felt for each other.

"Good," he answered. "I just need a little time with her. Why don't you meet me downstairs in the lobby in fifteen minutes?"

"Make it thirty," I said. "I need to make a call."

After settling downstairs, I found my cell phone in my bag and checked my watch for the time. It was two o'clock in LA. I needed to hear his voice. Maybe he would be calm. Maybe he would reason with me. Marla answered on the first ring. She never had a reason to be discreet with me before, and now she was dancing around something that sent warning bells off in my head.

"He's out of the office for the next two days," was all she said.

I knew better than to ask the poor woman for more. She was already uncomfortable enough. So I dialed his cell phone, but he didn't pick up.

As further confirmation of what I'd already believed to be true, I got up from the chair, found the nearest bathroom, and prematurely threw up.

Jonas found me pale and upset in the lobby. I contributed it to nerves, and he believed me, but then he became worried. I wasn't up for dinner, but he was adamant, dragging me to his car, taking me to the hotel, and insisting that I get cleaned up and changed while he waited downstairs.

"Miracles don't happen that fast," I told him.

"Get going. I'll take a ride around the block if I have to. With this traffic, you'll have plenty of time." He was probably right. I felt too depressed to care.

I went upstairs and tried Marty again. No answer. I called Beth and Ari in Washington and found them in good spirits, which peaked my mood, somewhat.

I headed downstairs, unaware of what the night would bring. How could Marty do this to us? Even though I'd always known what he was capable of, jealousy and distrust never interfered with the life we built together. When we found each other, two halves became whole, and it was always enough. Had I pushed him to it? Losing Joshua had cost us a lot. I guess some people grieved in one way, others grieved in another.

Jonas was waiting for me downstairs, as promised, a grin stretched across his face. I wanted to accept the smile and send him one back, but the suspicion I was holding onto prevented me from having any control over my facial muscles. Instead, he helped me with my coat, and we took off in his car through the streets of the city.

Chapter 38

Dinner was at a quaint restaurant in Chelsea. The food was delicious, and I even allowed myself the luxury of a glass of wine to loosen my stiffened body. We discussed Michelle at length, and then turned our attention toward the supremely "out of the ordinary" mission we would be embarking on the next day.

Jonas began. "I know I said I wanted to raise the baby, but I don't think I can do that to you. Listening to the way you talk about your son, watching my patients with their mothers, a bond between a mother and a child is sacred."

"What about you? Dads are just as important."

"We'll figure out visitation, weekends, summers, whatever it is."

"Should I be hiring an attorney?" I laughed. "We sound like a couple that's getting separated."

"Only there's no requisite sadness."

"We had that first…"

"It won't get contentious," he said. "I promise."

"It can't," I said. "This baby represents too much hopefulness."

"And she'll be loved by both of us, no matter where we are."

"She?" I asked.

"I'm a sucker for my girls. You know that."

Sitting there at that table, we were sorting out the leftover questions thrown at us—Would we tell her what she did for her sister? Why her parents are not together?

"Who needs to know?" he asked.

I said, "She will, people, the press."

The important questions had already been asked through the handful of articles we pored over—skeptics challenging us like we were harvesting corn and not a live human being. Condemning our decision only united us further in the pursuit to save our child. If there was any doubt on either of our behalfs, we hid it well. Understanding the ramifications of our actions, we were prepared to defend our cause publicly—if it got to that point. The broad spectrum of issues spread out before us.

The moral and social implications raised all kinds of red flags. "Selective breeding," said one article, "is debatable, even for married couples. Divorced couples producing a child to save the child from their previous marriage exceeds the definition of unethical." Jonas and I didn't fall into this category either. Imagine what they would think of us then. And yet, other articles supported what we were doing. "What better reason to bring a child into the world than to save a life? People have children to save bad marriages or by accident. Aren't those reasons for conceiving just as questionable?"

There was also the issue of prenatal testing. The Center for Bioethics and Human Dignity had the strongest argument. When I pulled up what they had to say on their Web site, it opened up the whole debate between viable and non-viable: "Prenatal genetic diagnosis involves the intentional destruction of nascent human life and is therefore contrary to the principle of the sanctity of human life. It cannot be disputed that the embryo is human and is a human. To destroy an embryo is to cut short a human life that has already begun."

A number of psychologists in the fertility office outlined the long-term effects, one being the burden the children carry with them when they are told of their conception and the role in their sibling's life. Others expressed concern over the possibility of Michelle's relapse and how the new child would be further burdened with the responsibility of partaking in another medical procedure to save their sick sibling a second or even third time.

And still we moved forward with the testing.

The response I found the most interesting was a baseless remark by a hospital staffer who said that we were treating this child as a pawn, acting selfishly and "Orwellian." Jonas looked at this woman and said, "Reproduction between me and my future wife has absolutely nothing to do with you." Then he put his arm around me and we walked away.

That's when it became impossible for me to continue living in denial about the harder questions, the ones I wouldn't discuss with anyone. Was this child the beginning of something more between Jonas and me?

After dinner, we decided to go for a walk. Jonas said, "You'll have to have that serious mother/daughter conversation with her to explain sex and relationships and why protection is a must."

"You'll have to explain to her why sometimes loving someone isn't enough."

"Maybe she'll never have to go through that," he said, before adding, "You're very brave to do this."

"So are you."

"I don't have a husband and another child at home," he said. "You're making a tremendous sacrifice."

If it were on my tongue all those years, I hadn't been aware of it, but it slipped out simply and without reservation. "I would have done anything for you."

"This is for Michelle," he said, a casual arm thrown over my shoulder.

He was right in reminding me. I was doing this to save our daughter. Jonas, the man I had once loved with every fiber of my being, just happened to be her father.

"You know," I said, "I didn't plan to have sex with you that night. I didn't think it through. I never thought it would actually happen."

"Neither did I. And I didn't need it to feel close to you either. I felt close to you long before that night."

If I spoke right then, everything I'd been trying to hold in would have leaked out.

He said, "It happened because I wanted it to happen, and because I loved you."

Something about the way he said it made everything complete. The uncertainty that plagued me for years dissipated and flew off into the air.

I said, "I remember when I found out I was pregnant. I didn't know whether to be ecstatic or miserable. I thought about the life we could have had together. I didn't think it was possible to love someone the way I loved you. It was this feeling that was just there—no matter how hard I tried to fight it, no matter how much I knew it was wrong. You were this part of me that took up all this space inside."

He stopped walking and turned to face me. "I'm glad you didn't give her up," he said. "I'm glad there's life in this world because of us. I'm glad there's a part of you and me that is still together, even if we can't be."

His eyes bore into mine, the way I used to love staring into them, pulling me closer. I didn't know if it was the wine or if I was finally allowing Jonas back in. I wanted him to hold me. I wanted him to touch me. There were words for what I was feeling, even though they weren't readily accessible to me. I could feel them in the tightening of my chest. "That's why it means so much to do this for her," I said. "The thought of losing her, the thought of her dying, it's unacceptable. If she dies, who will attest to all those feelings we had? How will anybody know how important we once were?"

I hadn't really expected an answer. Jonas was never really good at giving them, and I was a woman who needed understanding and solutions. When loving me wasn't enough, he walked away, and everything he'd been meaning to say was hidden inside him.

"She's not going to die, Jess. We're going to see this thing through. I promise you, and I know I haven't made you many promises in the past, none more significant than this one, but I'll do whatever it takes to save her." He took my hand into his when he said this, and I didn't pull away. Instead, I allowed his fingers to clasp around mine, just like I had when we were young and I was in love. "Michelle exists, but she didn't have to for me to know what you meant to me. What we shared was better than anything I'd ever had. However short a time, however limited, it was something I keep close to my heart. It existed, Jess. Nothing will ever change that."

I'd been waiting to hear those words for too many years.

"I'm sorry I couldn't give you what you wanted," he said. "I'm sorrier for myself because I know now what I lost. You were all I wanted and I blew it. I spent so much time worrying about failing Emily, I didn't see how I'd failed myself and you."

"You were the first boy I ever loved. I don't know what went wrong with us. Maybe it was just bad timing," I said, looking him in the eyes, no longer intimidated. "I don't know that I'll ever get over that; parts of you have stayed with me even when I wish them gone."

I didn't let go of his hand. I hadn't wanted to. I wanted to be close to him, close to someone, to feel safe and loved, like I hadn't in too many months.

"I lost a child before."

He didn't say anything. He didn't have to. When a parent loses a child, there are no words.

"I was almost nine months pregnant."

"You don't have to do this."

"I know," I looked at him, "but I want to. You were there with me that day." Before the words were even out of my mouth, I realized what I was doing. I stopped the rest from coming out.

"You were always starting a thought and never finishing," he said.

"I could say the same about you. You started a lot of things you didn't finish."

"Finish the thought," he said.

"I don't know, Jonas. I'd been living with this thing inside of me, this premonition of doom. When I was leaving a music convention that I really had no business being at, and you know me with the music dial, there it was, that song, playing, just when I'd least expected it, just when I thought there'd be no possible way it could affect me."

We reached an empty park and stepped inside. He was close to me and edging closer, waiting for me to go on, knowing what I was about to say. "I'd long since forgotten, really, I had. My life was different, better. Years had even passed without me thinking of you. When I heard the song on the radio, everything came back. Even in my *better* life, you were never really gone. I only learned to hide you better. That's the last thing I remember."

He was watching me, and it occurred to me that he might kiss me.

I wasn't sure I'd turn away.

"It was a little boy, a beautiful baby boy. I didn't see him, but that's what they told me."

Having his lips on mine might have eased the burden of my mistake. If only I hadn't been there in the first place. If only I hadn't turned the radio dial. If only I hadn't happened across that song that set my mind in motion. If only I had been anywhere other than on the road and in a heavy machine that was cradling my unborn child and me. If only…a whole host of details that could have been different, and Joshua would be alive today.

"This baby's not going to bring your son back."

"I know. My husband already reminded me. Somehow it feels better hearing it from you."

"Jess…"

I knew what he was about to say. I knew what he wanted from me. I saw it all over his face. I felt it in his grasp. He was twenty-two and beautiful, and he was loving me and filling up every hole in my body.

He was considering this was his last chance to give me the life I had once wanted, with him, and it was hard to walk away from that when the memory of what we shared, what we had once meant to each another, made me shiver. If I thought the pull toward him would diminish over time, I was wrong. No time had passed since that night.

He leaned in, and his lips brushed my lips. I felt the familiar softness. I tasted Jonas again. He tried to get closer, opening his mouth wider, but I pulled away, turning my face to the side. It would turn out to be one of the most difficult movements I ever made.

"Don't," I said.

"Why not?"

"Because," I said, trying to come up with a better reason. "I can't…"

"I'm not going anywhere, Jess. I didn't fight for you before, but I will now."

"Please don't," I said. "I don't have the strength."

An airplane sounded above us, the roaring engines causing both of us to look toward the sky. When it passed and quiet returned, Jonas turned to me, but the moment had passed.

He said, "I'll transfer to a hospital in LA. That way we can be close." His eyes lowered, trying to find the words that wouldn't cross more boundaries. "I don't want to put a strain on you and your family, but I want to be near my child."

"That's your decision," I said, knowing that I was disappointing him by my necessary lack of enthusiasm. That I wanted him close was not the issue.

"I'm sorry," he said, an apology that covered a lot of terrain.

"No," I whispered, "I'm sorry."

Chapter 39

It was summertime, and I still had not become pregnant. Ari and I were back in Los Angeles. I would fly out to New York once a month for the awkward appointment where I was poked and prodded and injected. The interest and anticipation flurrying around our undertaking had died down when the first couple of months my body didn't produce a matched, healthy embryo; and when it finally did, my body continually rejected the embryos. It never occurred to me that my body would reject anything connected to Jonas. The doctors chalked it up to flying or other things.

"Are you stressed?" they asked me. What kind of question was that to ask a woman who was having a baby to save another child?

Michelle was in full remission again, living her life outside the hospital as normally as a now terminally ill twelve-year-old could. She felt so good, she didn't understand the need for a bone marrow transplant, but we all knew it was only a matter of time before her body would begin to fail her again. We spoke often from her home in Rockland County, and our relationship was growing and taking shape. I didn't know how I had lived my life without her for all those years, but this new baby was reassurance that I wouldn't have to anymore.

Marty had all but moved out of our house, unable to accept the duplicity of my actions. The walls that separated us weren't just stucco and concrete either. The emotional barriers were far more obstructive. He had taken up refuge in an apartment nearby owned by one of the big studio heads. It was lavish and spacious; I was sure he wasn't alone.

Although absent, Marty remained a devoted, loving father to Ari, having breakfast with him every morning, then going off to work, and returning at the end of the day to bathe him and put him to bed. Ari's life had not been disrupted at all. Weekends were full of zoo visits, afternoons at the beach, and trips on Marty's brand new boat. Sometimes I went along. Sometimes I didn't. I was angry at Marty, and he was angry at me, but there were concessions we had to make to keep it from our son. There were times when we were together when I'd resume the role of his wife, accepting his attention, complimenting him, and showing the slightest hint of interest in his work. The tiniest bit of affection would seep into the darkened crevices we created, and then he would leave, go back to his cave, and I would find solitude in the aloneness of it all. We had allowed things to go too far. There was no turning back.

Jonas would call to check in on me, and we'd talk for hours at a time. I had grown accustomed to his voice on the line before I'd go to bed. He'd whisper, before hanging up, "Sweet dreams," and his voice would warm up the cold space beside me. I would imagine the kiss that never quite touched my lips.

It was late August when the doctors were getting concerned. Michelle's health was beginning to show signs of deteriorating again, and I wasn't pregnant. The registries still had no match for her, and the pressure was rising, contributing a heightened level of stress to our situation. At the doctor's urging, I made an appointment for a round of tests and a comprehensive evaluation. They told me, "It's likely your inabilities to carry this baby are due to the accident last year, but the additional stress is a mitigating factor."

"What are you saying?" I asked. "I can get pregnant with less stress, or I can't get pregnant at all?"

"We'll have to wait for your test results, but understand that we oftentimes don't know why IVF doesn't work. You've done pre-implantation genetic testing, so it's likely that your embryos are healthy. It could be your uterus, and we won't know that for a few days." Whatever it was, it didn't sound good. As sympathetically as she could, she told me to hold tight and have hope, but I had already expected and prepared for the worst.

Marty showed up that evening to bathe and read to Ari. I couldn't mask the anguish I was feeling, so I kissed my son good night and let Marty put him to bed. Something of this magnitude would have shaken both of us. Only now, I had to bear the burden alone. I hated to consider what news like this would mean for him. Would this be yet another reason for him to move further away from me? I wasn't one to bask in wasteful self-pity, even if it felt damned good to do so, but Marty wanted loads of children. Somewhere en route to that number, things had gone astray.

I knew Ari was asleep because I heard the door slam and Marty's tires screech in the driveway outside our window.

When I woke up the next morning, it was late, and I was alone. Marty must have come and gone, leaving the newspaper propped up at the foot of the bed. I should have known this day was going to be different, the way the shades were drawn and the sun seeped through and the air just felt heavier.

I grabbed the paper and began to read; and when I did, the lifestyle section fell to the floor, opening to the page with advice and movie listings. Reaching for the pages, my eyes fell on today's horoscopes. I'd long ago stopped relying on the psychic medium to give me the direction and answers I was looking for. Not since Marty entered my life and my career took off and things were solid and complete had I felt the need to check my "sign." *Confidence*, I thought. People who relied upon horoscopes needed more self-confidence. They weren't in control. Words on the page told them what they needed to hear.

And here I was, twenty-nine years old, a mother and a wife, and my horoscope was calling out to me.

There is a shift in your sign right now. Take a sensitive approach to your goals and the obstacles that may be inhibiting you from achieving them. Sometimes it's better to let someone or something go. Release yourself from old wounds, and you will find that anything is possible and is very well within your reach.

That night, Ari was snuggled under the covers and Marty was beside him reading *Goodnight Moon*. I hummed along to myself the words, hoping they might slow down the thoughts that were running through my mind while I picked up some of Ari's toys from the floor. *Barren. Infertile. Empty.* These were just a few of the adjectives that prohibited me from concentrating on the brush, the mush, and the old woman who was whispering hush.

I kissed my son on the cheek, inhaling Marty's scent, the one his lips had just left behind on Ari. It was the closest we had come to any shared intimacy in months. I tasted him on my lips, the memory nudging me awake.

I turned the light out while Marty closed the door behind us.

"What's wrong with you?" he asked, sounding more like a concerned husband than the estranged spouse he had become.

"Nothing."

"Nothing doesn't usually put you into this kind of state."

"What state?"

"Quiet. Careless."

"Careless?" I inquired.

"You didn't tell Ari you'd see him in the morning. You always say that, every night, without fail."

I hadn't known that Marty was aware of the superstition that had begun in childhood and now infiltrated my adult life. I drew comfort from saying those words, probably more for my benefit than for Ari's. That Marty noticed it, tonight of all nights, interested me. Even with the gulf that widened the space between us, there was an intuition amongst couples that hindered their efforts to truly separate. There were nuances and quirks that you learned over time and through everyday closeness that a physical separation, alone, could not dissolve. It was this one piece of information, this one ritual that held Marty and me together.

"What's on your mind?"

I looked at him across the room. He was the same man in many ways, probably even better looking than when we first met, but I could feel the subtle change in him. Was it me? I wasn't sure. I was aware of the way our bodies reacted to one another—something guided them close, then far, then near again.

How could I explain my fertility problem without hurting his feelings? Or even worse, how could I explain them without activating that part of me that *wanted* to hurt him?

"I see you're not pregnant yet," he said. "Is that what this is about?"

I wished it were only that. The doctor hadn't gotten back to me with my test results, but I'd become convinced they would indicate an immense problem, and punishment for the sins of my youth. Something was wrong; I felt it in my bones. Rather than discuss my inadequacies with Marty, I decided to bring up a whole different topic. He had taken a seat on the couch in our once-shared living room. I sat across the room in a lone chair. It was fitting.

"I used to say the same thing to you."

He was clearly puzzled. "What?"

"When you used to be here, when we'd be in bed together, I'd whisper in your ear, 'I'll see you in the morning.' I don't know if you ever heard it, but I said it, every night. It was my assurance that you'd never leave."

"I never left you, Jess."

"No?"

His eyes turned sad and regretful. "Your heart hasn't been with me since Joshua died."

I said, "My heart was ripped out of me that day. There was nothing left to give."

"What's motivating you now? What's motivating you to have this whole life planned without me in it, with someone else?"

To hear it laid out like that, straightforward and raw, any explanation I could offer seemed almost inhuman. Marty's indifference to my desires had made it easy to justify what I was doing. When I'd cling to the idea that he was betraying me and betraying our marriage, I wouldn't need to empathize with him. But my need to be right resurfaced and I said, "It's not like that."

"Explain it to me."

"My daughter's life is at stake here. I'm not trying to fill some selfish need. I'm not trying to hurt you."

"I never would have stopped you from helping your daughter. I'm just sorry you never felt you could trust me. I'm sorry for the brother or sister we won't be giving Ari. I gave you everything, Jess, all I had...I thought it was enough."

"What about Stella?" There was no sense avoiding it. If we were going to have this conversation, right here, right now, why not air out all the dirty laundry?

"What about Stella?" he repeated. Something in the way he spoke her name made me regret asking.

"Are you sleeping with her?"

"I'm not going to dignify that with a response."

"It's me, Marty," I said. "I saw you on TV with her. I saw the way you looked at her. You could barely keep your eyes off her. You weren't wearing your ring. I saw your finger."

"She's the next Madonna, Jess, everyone watches her like that."

"Not you, Marty."

"And what about that weekend?" I continued, a series of allegations I couldn't quiet from my mouth. I called your office, and Marla had no idea where you were, or at least she acted like she had no idea where you were. I tried your cell phone for two days, and no one answered. Where were you? Were you with her?"

I thought my accusations would leave him repentant or eager to fire off a defensive response, but he just smiled. And the smile turned into laughter as he cupped his head in his hands, nodding back and forth, taunting me. "Jess, you have some imagination."

"It's well-founded."

"It's cute."

"Don't even try to charm your way out of this, Marty. You were always a cheat. I should have never expected you to change."

"Really? Then what can we call you?"

"How dare you turn this into some cheap affair."

"Is there another name for a wife's relationship with her ex-lover?"

"We're not in a relationship."

"Then how come you haven't been able to answer my question?"

"Answer me, first," I demanded. "Where were you?"

Marty faced me with the little fight he had left. He spoke rationally and calmly. "Don't accuse me to justify your actions. Saving your child, I'd never take that away from you, but I didn't bring our breakup on, you did. Don't blame me. Whatever's going on with you, whether you know it or not, is destroying us, so you better be clear about what you want. I know what I want. I want our life back, I want you, but I won't accept you back with missing pieces. If you won't give all of you, our marriage isn't worth saving."

Marty walked toward me. The tight thickening of my heart had begun to weaken as he came closer. Standing before me, he watched me and I watched him. "I didn't cheat on you, not with Stella, not with anyone. I've been faithful to you since the day you walked into my office."

"You were dating seventeen different women," I said, tears welling up in my eyes.

"And I got rid of them all for you," he professed. "Listen to me," he continued, taking my hand into his, his voice hoarse and dry, "That week, when you couldn't reach me, I was with Ari and Beth in DC. I missed him. I wanted to see him, so I flew out and met them all. I didn't want you to know. Marla must have been confused when you called, because naturally she assumed I was with you. I haven't told her what's going on. Nobody knows, not even Jeff and Sharon. If I talked about it with anyone, the actual separation, there would be a finality to it. I was hoping we could work through this…and my ring, Ari insisted on showing it to his playgroup, so I had to take it off for a day. Other than you, he's the only person I can't say no to."

His confession of innocence flooded through me, and when it reached places torn and battered, a calm rushed over me. I clasped harder to his hand; the smooth skin welcomed me like an old friend. We had lost a lot over the last year. With all that anger and hurt, it was hard to see a way for things to be right again, but I found some comfort in knowing that there was still love. Marty kneeled before me and cradled me in his arms while I unleashed a fountain of tears. I remembered in college when I'd come home for a weekend and walk through the door and the mere smell in the air would take me back to childhood. Being close to Marty again was like walking through that door. It was like being home.

We sat like that for a while, Marty holding me in his arms and loving me more than I deserved. I didn't want to tell him what I'd feared, that the possibility existed that I might never have a child, whomever the father might be. I didn't want to need him. I didn't want him to feel sorry for me. I was doing a good enough job at that myself. But for a few moments, we let down our defenses, and I thought that maybe, just maybe, we could make this thing work.

My cell phone rang, and I looked down to see Jonas's number across the screen. I didn't take the call, but it didn't matter. My body tensed, and I pulled away.

Marty said, "I lost you again, didn't I?"

I got up, unable to answer.

If only there wasn't Jonas, Jonas, who had stolen my strength and dignity, the man who would make it impossible for love to be uncomplicated. Marty was standing before me, and I saw in his eyes what I already knew. He was right, I was gone again. And I hated myself for it.

Chapter 40

The flight back to New York was a difficult one. My mind was full of confusion and longing that clouded my better judgment. Jonas was expecting another procedure, and instead I had to tell him that I wasn't sure it could happen, that our promise to our sick child might be broken.

When I arrived at the hospital, there was a bustling I felt around me at once. You just know something important is going on when a flurry of doctors and nurses speed through the hallways and urgency fills the air. I found Jonas heading in my direction. We always met in the lobby. He seemed pale and distressed about something. My instincts took over.

"What's the matter?" I asked, knowing right away something was wrong. "Is it Michelle? Is she back in the hospital?"

He didn't answer. I don't think he physically could. Something deep within his body was choking the words from coming out.

"Come with me." He took my hand and led me to the elevator.

"Tell me, Jonas." His eyes were glazed over. The life inside them had all but vanished.

The elevator doors opened, and there they were, Michelle's parents turning the corner toward us. Mrs. Sammler was openly crying, Mr. Sammler was trying to comfort her.

It wasn't registering with me. I couldn't get a handle on what the others already knew.

Dr. Greene appeared in a doorway. He was hiding his pain behind a stoic face. He was a doctor, but nothing prepares you for the death of a child.

"I'm so sorry…" I heard him say.

Mrs. Sammler let out a groan that sounded more animal than human.

"She's gone," Dr. Greene confirmed.

I clutched on to Jonas, unable to support myself.

Mrs. Sammler was whisked away by her husband, barely able to walk. He had to physically carry her down the hallway while she flailed in his arms shouting, "No, my baby, no…" I knew I would never see her again. I wondered if I would always picture her face as it was when she was dragged through the hospital corridor. Would it haunt me for the rest of my life?

Jonas and I comforted one another, tears heavy down our faces, the finality of death taking over. He wanted to see her again, to say good-bye. I couldn't do it. I couldn't look at her beautiful face without life. Instead, I waited in the hallway as he went in the room. When he came out, I could tell he'd been crying. He said she looked peaceful, free from suffering, and then he grabbed me by the hand and we left.

We drove without speaking until we reached his apartment building. Jonas maneuvered me into the elevator and then through his doorway. He brought me to his bedroom and helped me onto the bed, covering me with a blanket and asking if I'd like anything to help me relax. I said no. I didn't need anything. I knew the pain and suffering would eventually put me to sleep and take me away from the crushing truth. I longed for the darkness and the silence that would lead the way.

He stroked my hair as I silently cried myself to sleep. There was so much lost that hope was no longer an option. When sleep finally came to me, it was a broken slumber composed of fitful dreams, and when I awoke the following afternoon, Jonas was there beside me. At first, I thought I was imagining him there, that I was still dreaming and he was a part of the dream, but unlike the times before, he was there, releasing me from the longing.

"How are you?" he asked.

I didn't know if I could answer. The question flooded me with sorrow.

"It's going to be alright," he said, and understanding my need for silence, he held me in his arms and allowed me to cry on his shoulders. I closed my eyes and wished that it were me who had died and not another child of mine. In those moments of darkness, it was starting to become clear to me. For too long I'd been unable to rely on others, as if needing someone would make them leave. Maybe Marty hadn't left. Maybe it was me who had become frightened and scared and retreated into places I didn't dare speak about. Maybe it wasn't so terrible to need someone. Crying in Jonas's arms, I wasn't ashamed anymore.

He left me there and went to his office. Life had to go on. Patients needed to be seen. I continued to dream and sleep and remember, tossing and turning, venturing into another restless slumber, one bursting with visions so much like real life, I couldn't distinguish the two. My cell phone rang. It was the doctor with my test results. I listened as she told me what I wasn't prepared to hear.

Chapter 41

The cemetery was beautiful that time of year. The leaves were bright green; the grass lush and full of flowers. I kneeled at his grave, knowing I should be at hers, but there was something I needed to do first, something I should have done a long time ago.

I had never been there before. I hadn't even known where it was. My mother had to give me directions. She was surprised, I could tell, and I think she was happy too. My fingers brushed against the letters that formed his name, and I traced the dates, the numbers that would forever represent time given and time stolen. The in between was time borrowed, reduced to a dash.

I whispered, *Bernard*, so unfamiliar to my tongue. I'd maybe said it two times before in my whole life.

And then I said good-bye.

"Good-bye, Daddy." I'd never said that before. What followed was a release of grief, the kind you keep locked up inside for years, because it seems a hell of a lot easier to tolerate than the aftermath of loss. Processing my grief is what I avoided, and now I understood why. The sadness was unbearable. I clutched at my belly, feeling the ache deep within my stomach. This was the father I'd lost, the man who was supposed to take care of me forever but couldn't. I finally let it settle in my heart, where it had been hidden my whole life. I forgave him, and I honored him at the same time.

Sitting there looking at the space he occupied, I knew I was saying good-bye to so much more than the man. The tears weren't his alone, although he started them. I cried for the things I'd held onto for too long, the stuff I should have let go of, like the game of fairy tale I knew better than to believe in. I cried for the emptiness inside of me, the soul that ached for someone to fill it up, and for the awareness that no one ever could, not when the standard was set so high. I cried for the boy who tried, the one I thought I loved. The only thing he filled me with was more longing, an emotion that tricks you into thinking it's love. And then I cried for the man who was big enough to love me when I deemed myself unworthy, proving to me that love belonged here on earth and that it was present in my life. You can't always see love, I learned, but you should always be able to trust that it's there, and now I did.

"I love you, Daddy," I said, just like I did when I was four. "And I miss you so much. I really do. I'm sorry I haven't visited. I should have… so much has happened, so much I want to tell you."

And the rabbi was right. The timing was off, but the unveiling was truly precious.

Chapter 42

"With Michelle gone, there's nothing else connecting us." Jonas winced, and I continued. "Before she died, I'd had some tests done in LA. We just wanted to be sure there was nothing physically wrong with me, preventing me from getting pregnant; and you know me, I was already thinking the worst, resigned to the fact that I wasn't ever going to have more kids. That's what I was planning to tell you when I arrived at the hospital."

"What did the doctors say?"

"That's not the point. That's not why I'm telling you this."

I looked at him. We were standing on a bridge in Central Park. It was the kind of fall day you knew you would never forget. Jonas's sweater was clinging to his body. I'd always remember the way his hands were tucked inside his pockets, like he was trying to stop something from happening.

"I've always been so good at reading signs. We should have seen it as a sign." I was thinking about the hostile environment inside my womb that wouldn't hold onto Jonas's child. There was a medical name the doctors called it, but the name I gave it seemed appropriate. "We weren't getting pregnant, and maybe it meant more than we were willing to accept. Maybe things aren't as neatly tied together as we want them to be. I should have seen this coming." Jonas was still listening. "We weren't meant to save her, and we weren't meant to be more to each other, not a second time, not when we're still recovering from the mistakes from the first time around."

When he opened his mouth, the wind picked up, and his words flew around me. "I love you, Jess. I always have. Tell me what I'm supposed to do with all that love."

I had thirsted for those words for years, and now they were left to puddle around my feet. I did not need them anymore.

"If we weren't meant to be together, why are we still in each other's lives after all these years?" he asked. "Why does it hurt so much when you're away from me?"

Our eyes met, and I was glad it was Jonas that I loved for the first time.

"I think you're confused about the way you feel," I said. "I think you *want* to feel those things again, and being here with me again reminds you of them, just as it's tricked me into thinking the same; but we're not kids anymore. What we used to feel back then won't sustain us today. That part of my life needs to be over. You want more from me now because your life is incomplete. It breaks my heart to tell you that I'm not the missing piece. I thought I might be, but I'm not."

He had never heard me speak so rationally before, not when it came to matters of the heart. He said, "You're letting me go."

"Yes."

He turned away from me, choosing to watch the ducks wading in the pond instead.

"Jonas, a part of me will always love you. I'll always care, but I can't give you more than that. You deserve to have a child, your own child, with a woman you love."

"I thought that was you."

"You should build a life together. You're free to do that now. There's nothing tying us to one another anymore."

"You don't mean all this," he said.

"There's a man who loves me back home," I began. "He gave me everything you never did, and I thanked him by walking away from our life and into your arms. I let you in first out of responsibility, then out of fear. I was angry. I was scared. You were the Band-Aid that was going to hide the gash, make it a little less painful. And then I realized something. It wasn't *you* I wanted, not *you* today, but the *you* back then. I wanted that non-complicated life I had when I was almost sixteen, because this one is sometimes too painful to deal with."

"We love each other, Jess. You can't say you don't feel it."

A part of me wanted to drown in his words, forgetting everything that was important to me while the strokes of his words brushed against me. Have you ever imagined getting exactly what you wanted, closing your eyes, making that wish, and poof, it was yours? I was this close to it that afternoon, to realizing a dream that I had built up inside of me for a lifetime. I yielded from it, giving someone else the right of way, instead.

The timelessness of his words should have bothered me, but I was soothed by them, knowing what I had known all along. He had loved me once, maybe he still did, but our chance had passed. It was time to move on.

"I know we could be happy, Jess. We've always found ways to make each other happy."

"We've also found ways to hurt each other."

He turned away as if I'd wounded him then, and I had

I was trying to say good bye to a life that once brought me so much comfort. He was making it so difficult. When you love someone, when he is instilled inside of you, beyond words, the love doesn't ever go away. Eventually, it changes shape, void of a physical presence, but the spirit lives on. Now it was weakened in the shadow of a living relationship. I sighed, knowing I was free from all the expectation, the countless suffering, and the ambiguity of childhood dreams. I would never forget Michelle, and I would never forget Jonas. They were the special gifts that came into my life and made it worthy, turning it into something meaningful rather than regretful. There was comfort in knowing that Michelle would look after my baby and that Jonas would find love again. He had a lot of it to give, just not to me.

"That's it? That's all you're going to say?"

"No," I said. "There is one more thing." I looked at him. I wasn't sure the words would come out. I watched years of my life pass in his beautiful eyes, but it didn't stop me. I said, "Good-bye, Jonas."

And a minute passed, maybe two, and then he was gone.

Chapter 43

I flew home to my family on a clear summer day. Marty was waiting for me at the door when I stepped into the house. He looked handsome and unafraid. It was like putting on glasses. My eyes were seeing things in a whole new light

"I'm glad you're back," he said. "I want to talk to you."

I said, "There's something I need to tell you too."

I followed him into the living room, where we sat across from each other just a few feet apart. I could make out his beautiful features, the lips I'd always loved to kiss, the cheek I'd rest my head upon. How could I tell him what our future held for us—no more children, a wife who was barren and infertile? Marty wanted a big family. He said that from early on. I couldn't give it to him. I didn't know how he would take it.

"You first," he said.

"When I lost Joshua, my whole world was turned upside down. You know that."

He nodded in agreement.

"I turned away from you, the only person I had ever trusted because I felt like a failure. You can't imagine the depths of my grief and my pain. I felt unlovable, unworthy of someone like you.

"And then when I found out about Michelle, she became this mission for me, this way that I could redeem myself, make my wrongs right. It didn't matter who I hurt along the way. As long as I could get that feeling of wholeness that had all but vanished when Joshua died.

"Michelle died," I said. "It happened quickly. There wasn't much warning."

"I'm sorry, Jess," he said, and I knew that he was.

"Something else happened…"

Apprehension seized Marty's face and saddened his eyes. I took his hands into mine.

"I didn't go to New York for another insemination," I said. He was watching me carefully. "I found out about Michelle, and it was a horrible couple of days, but it confirmed everything I had known to be right and true about you, about us, about Jonas."

"I don't think I'll ever be able to get pregnant, Marty. The doctor told me that there was some damage from the accident, and they did tests, and…" the words were flowing from my mouth, and as ugly as it was to say them, I wasn't afraid. I knew how strong our love was. I knew I was not the empty, loathsome person I once believed myself to be. I deserved Marty's love. I wanted Marty's love. He would still give it to me. This couldn't be the thing to tear us apart.

He didn't say anything, not one word, not even, "Are they sure?"

"Did you hear what I said?" I asked.

"Yes, but I think you're mistaken."

"That's not something even I would joke about."

"The doctor's office called the other day saying your tests came back within normal range, and they see no reason why you can't have more children. That's what I wanted to tell you."

I could barely hear him, my heart was pumping so wildly.

"They said they tried you on your cell phone in New York, but you didn't answer." My thoughts took me to Jonas's bed and reckless sleep that roused dreams and nightmares. It was a dream. The scary words weren't real. The realization made what I was about to say next more powerful.

"You asked me once if I loved Jonas, and I didn't answer because I didn't know," I said. "I know now." I got down off the chair, kneeled in front of Marty with my hands holding onto his knees, and said, "I loved him, once, a long time ago, and it meant a lot of different things to me. Holding onto his memory prevented me from ever letting go of my pain and knowing myself and allowing for pure joy." Marty's eyes were filling up with something.

"I never felt entirely worthy of you, Marty. I waited and waited for something to take you from me, even attempting to cause it myself. If I felt so bad about myself, how could someone like you want me?" He reached for my face, his fingers brushing through the strands of my hair.

"I'm here to answer your question," I said. "It's important to you. It's important to us."

"You just did," he said.

"No, I want to say it. I want to look you in the eyes and tell you." I could feel my body trembling, but it wasn't from fear. "The answer's no, I don't love him. Did you hear me? I don't love him. I love you. That's all of me. Not just a piece, not just a part, all the good and all the bad." His eyes locked onto mine. I stared into the blue and had one thing left to say, "I'm sorry, and I hope you'll forgive me because I need you, Marty, only you."

He didn't let me finish. He kissed my lips, and the promise that I had once let slip through my fingers was alive again with possibility. "You never lost me," he whispered, taking me into his arms. "I'm right here, where I've always been." We kissed again, and Marty grinned at me. "At least I can still bring you to your knees." And I smiled and he told me I was everything, and he would give me everything, and for the first time I understood.

I had found in my husband the fairy tale prince I once dreamt about as a child. He didn't ride in on a white horse, and he didn't own a stretch white limousine, but he was gallant in his own simple ways, brave in the face of adversity, and loved even when love wasn't always enough. For that, I am grateful.

Epilogue

"I was surprised when I got your phone call."

"No more than I was to make it."

"It's been a long time. How are you doing?"

"Better," I said.

"Tell me what's going on."

"Where do I begin?"

"Wherever you want."

"I wish there was more time," I said, looking at my watch, knowing we only had forty-five minutes. "I really made a mess of things—for a while."

She didn't say anything, just waited.

"I guess I should start with my dad."

She moved her glasses from her nose to the top of her head like I'd once remembered, and it didn't even bother me. Even though she'd aged, she still looked exactly the same. There was something peaceful about being around her.

"Tell me," she said. "Tell me about your dad."

First my eyes found a piece of furniture in the room and stayed there. Then they carefully made their way to her face, where they rested on her eyes, the ones that were now staring back at me.

"I miss him," I told her. "I miss him a lot."

Acknowledgements

This novel would not have been possible without the love and support of many wonderful people. These acknowledgements are in no special order, and if I have omitted anyone, I apologize in advance.

First, I would like to thank my earliest critic, my dear brother Rob Berger. He stole my diary in middle school and deemed my words worthy enough for comment.

Thank you to my grandmother, Lydia Wiesel. While in her nineties, she was able to finish the novel in one day and share her masterful critique. Lydia was a gifted writer, and I hope this finished product makes her proud.

To my first readers and staunchest supporters: Patti Weinstein, Debbie Bloomfield, Amy Berger, Jodi Hurwitz, Ricki Hollander, Marla Morningstar, Maria Marx, Randi Schwartz, Jackie Berger, Jessica Dornbusch Kavana, Dori Ornstein, Tirza Dalkoff, Pamela Fries, Wendy Kingsley, Lauren Warsing, Ariela Mars, Denise Fiske, Rachel Sapoznik, Jacqueline Sapoznik, Amy Siskind, Dori Solomon, Sandy Kapp, Lois Brandenburg, Valerie Berger, Barbara Amoils, Robin Gale, Lisa Levine, Marsha Staller Levine, and Mandy Zaron.

Tara Solomiany, for orchestrating the most memorable book club experience with Elise Scheck, Tammy Woldenberg, Tila Levi, Amy Gelb, Mimi Klimberg, Valerie Mitrani, Devorah Leah Andrusier, Tammy Attias, Cynthia Stein, and Natalie Wolf. Melissa Grosfeld, aka Dr. Gray, for her hours of psychologically stimulating conversation and fine-tuning. Stephanie Oshinsky for her introduction to Mitch and Jessica, among many other acts of kindness. Mindy Blum for our walks and talks and the many times you have told me you like my book better than the one you're currently reading.

Thank you to Jennifer Unter for your honest insights and utmost professionalism. Martine Bellen for working your editing magic and teaching me to be a better writer. Rosalind Wiseman, Elise Capron, Stephanie Norman, Brad Meltzer, Jim Grippando, Rick Yorn, Debra Borden, Jason Port, George Perez, Ina Yalof, Jennifer Joel, Matt Cooper, Shari and Harvey Schwartz, Michael Subarsky, Scott and Cindy Orlinsky, Lauren Sorof, Charlotte Tomic, Mitch Kaplan, Jessica Jonap, Kirby Kim, and Elisabeth Weed for their guidance, willingness to open doors, and valuable feedback.

Evelyn Rok Moskovitz, you have traveled this road with me for too many years to count. Your unending support and unique spirit have lifted me up and motivated me to never give up. Thank you for cherishing my hopes and dreams as if they were your own. You are my soul sister. Merle Saferstein, my friend and so much more, you are the woman with whom I hope to share many colorful, comma-filled stories. We were brought into each other's lives for a reason. I can't wait to walk beside you through the next chapter.

Judith, for being there for me when my life was turned upside down. Jill Fastenberg and Doug Cohn, for making me feel close even when you are far away. Hester Esquenazi and Lainie Ginsburg, for your creative genius. Ari Grosfeld and Ella Zaron, future novelists, don't ever give up on your passion. Jan Blanck, for being my new editor. Liz Feder, for all the times I hung up on you because I was writing, and to Eric Feder who brought Liz into my life. Joni Meiselman and Linda Blaustein, now you can finally read the book! And for all my music industry colleagues and friends, a big shout out.

Dr. David Weinstein, for sharing his infinite wisdom. Geraldine Weinstein and Justin Weinstein, for sharing David. Faye Berger, Rylee Berger, Rose Berger, Jake Berger, and Jack Berger: dream big. Alan Weinstein, Dale and Charles Gratz, Jon and Marti Berger, Kathy and Richie Lesser, and all my extended family, your love and support over the years has meant so much.

My father, Richard Berger, thank you for inspiring me to write. My siblings, Randi Berger, Rob Berger, and Ron Berger, the four of us have been through so much together. You have provided me with an infinite supply of stories with no shortage of laughter and tears. There is no greater bond than the one we share as siblings. To my mother, Ruth Berger, who is not shy about how excited she is to see this book in print. Your strength and courage moved me to take this next step. There are no mountains we cannot tackle together. My loyal and loving dog, Jessie, who spent countless hours on my lap in an uncomfortable position just to be near me when I wrote. To my beautiful sons, Jordan and Brandon, for being great nappers as infants so that I could write in perfect quiet. Watching you grow up is one of life's greatest gifts. I hope I have made you proud. And to all the Jonases in my life…thank you for allowing me to find my one true love, my real-life Marty. I love you, Bear.

Made in the USA
Charleston, SC
26 April 2012